FAT GIRL,
TERRESTRIAL

FAT GIRL, TERRESTRIAL

a novel

KELLIE WELLS

FC2

TUSCALOOSA

FC2 is an imprint of The University of Alabama Press

Book Design: Illinois State University's English Department's Publications
Unit; Director: Tara Reeser; Assistant Director: Steve Halle; Production
Assistant: Jeremy Boehme
Cover Design: Lou Robinson
Typeface: Baskerville

Illustration credits appear on page 373

The paper on which this book is printed meets the minimum requirements
of American National Standard for Information Sciences—Permanence
of Paper for Printed Library Materials, ANSI Z39.48–1984

Library of Congress Cataloging-in-Publication Data
Wells, Kellie, 1962-
    Fat girl, terrestrial : a novel / by Kellie Wells. — 1st ed.
        p. cm.
    ISBN 978-1-57366-170-6 (pbk. : alk. paper) — ISBN 978-1-57366-833-0
(electronic)
    I. Title.
    PS3623.E47F38 2012
    813'.6—dc23
                                                    2012013930

For Janie, thin girl, celestial
and Tom, my autumn, my mugwump

Fat girl, terrestrial, my summer, my night
How is it I find you in difference, see you there
In a moving contour, a change not quite completed?

—Wallace Stevens, "Notes Toward a Supreme Fiction"

CONTENTS

FAT GIRL,
TERRESTRIAL

ONE
GOLIATH GIRL

I didn't know I'd killed him until the next day, when the paper reported the death of this man, Hazard Planet, that was his name. He was found at 34th and Strong, right where we'd parted. The paper said the police were investigating "the mysterious circumstances surrounding his death." As an architect of crime scene miniatures, I couldn't imagine what would be so befuddling. He'd been found prostrate on the sunny sidewalk, clutching his throat with one hand, a knife still concealed in the other, canister of defensive aerosol, recently deployed, recovered near the body. Where was the ambiguity in that? Granted, it did seem a sensational pose for a dead man to be found in, as though he were anticipating a headline and wanted to make it good. He was asthmatic and had had an anaphylactic attack, a reaction to the pepper spray with which I'd showered his face, a spray my father, ever hopeful I might one day prove to be lovably vulnerable, urged me to carry. I didn't know the man now known to me as Hazard Planet was asthmatic, how could I? His breath was smooth as satin as he breathed on my neck, no rattle, no wheeze. I was surprised at how odorless it was, his breath. I would have expected the harshly lingering smell of long-digested onions or sausage, or the sharp sting of mossy putrefaction characteristic of the hygienically indifferent. He said, "Hey cunt, hey bitch, hey you hulking punk, hand over your punk money." His voice rippled low, with a hint of gravel, barely audible, the sound the earth makes when plates briefly shift, a tectonic growl.

This was just the sort of encounter I'd always hoped for.

Even though I was hunched over, his hand tangled in my hair, I could feel him yearning en pointe as he tried to reach my ears, and he snarled, "Who are you to tower above the rest of us?"

It didn't go exactly as I'd imagined it.

I would always be more raptor than quarry.

You'd think with all the deterrent sprays on the self-protection weaponry market these days, not to mention those nerve-curdling tasers and heart-stopping stun guns, that a fellow with serious pulmonary complaints would steer wide of a life of crime. You'd think. What kind of felonious future can there be for a man who can't leave home without his inhaler, a man who sucks on a nebulizer every night so he won't be awakened by dreams of strangulation?

I went to the police station and turned myself in. I spilled my story: innocent victim-to-be out walking in the world, madman with knife on the lurk, self-defense bull's-eye spritz to the mug, autonomic flight from the scene, belated trembling (okay, more on principle, but I'd been attacked, hadn't I? Didn't I deserve to quake, like any sensible jackrabbit hightailing it toward haven?), and later my usual denial (*It's all a swindle, this life, a misunderstanding, this body a hoax,* I tell myself every night before happily dreaming of being a shrimp).

The detective didn't like it one bit that I'd hotfooted it straight home and collapsed in the living room in my favorite overstuffed recliner (purchased by my father from the Big and Tall store, whose strapping mannequins I could see eye to looming eye with when I was twelve), moving it as close as I could to the T.V. and the chipper faces of newscasters, always so radiant and heartening when detailing mayhem in their sing-song delivery, as though war and poverty and famine were only passing phases the world was going through in its upstart adolescence, nothing to sweat in the cush sanctuary of an American living room. I fell asleep in that chair, pleasantly shaken, elated at having finally been thought conquerable, a can of Raid in my hand, the only remotely volatile spray in this joint with the possible chemical muscle to halt the advance of a menacing assailant, the American flag snapping against a background of gently breeze-blown wheat on the screen, national anthem announcing the end of another day of television in Kansas.

You'd think a chronicler of dastardly wrongdoing like me would be thoroughly hardened by now to the snarling desperation that walks the mean streets, would shrug it off, toss it barely a nod. But it's different when you're the one with the shiv pressed to your gut and there's no mystery to solve, only the question of whether you'll be the diced Humpty some weary flatfoot pieces together. Or so I'd tried to spook myself.

I showed the detective the leather pouch/key ring that had only yesterday housed that canister of pepper spray, which they'd recovered near the body.

The paunchy, sunken detective with gray skin and eyes whose whites were pink as a white rabbit's sucked on his lower lip and looked me over. "*You* feel your personal security is threatened? You always carry something to fend off potential assailants?" he asked, not even bothering to conceal the twisting sneer of incredulity.

"'A violent crime against an individual occurs every eighteen seconds and an assault occurs every twenty-nine seconds,'" I said, quoting the insert that came with the spray. "You never know when some...flour enthusiast might set up a mill and start grinding, if you follow me."

"Mmm-*hmm*." I could see the detective did not like being on the receiving end of crime statistics. "Why did you drop only the can and not the carrier? You took the time to remove it?"

I said, "I take it out when I'm walking. I hide it in my hand."

He looked at me doubtfully.

I said, "I like to be able to get into my house after a mugging." I jingled the keys, unsnapped the pouch from the ring, and laid it on the table. "I have a habit of dropping things when fleeing desperadoes," I added, pursing my mouth in a half scoff, trying to look like a repeat offendee. He waggled his furry eyebrows at me suggestively. Somehow I thought this would settle it. I thought it would be reassuring to a mind that stumbled over and sniffed incongruous details to be able to reunite the can and its carrier, be able to shove them triumphantly—perp and accomplice—into a plastic bag and seal them away, zipped and labeled: *Planet Homicide, Exhibit 1,* to be hidden in the dank catacombs where top secret police business is stored, taken there in the dead of night by a blandly uniformed man whose sole occupation it is to look to his left, to his right, then cautiously toss potentially pivotal and incriminating bagged-up proof of villainy into giant boxes marked EVIDENCE.

He sucked on his teeth, sat down on the side of the table, picked up the canister and inserted it into its pouch, pulled it out, in again, out, set them back on the table, folded his hands in his lap, loosed a breeze from his schnoz. He said, "The thing I don't get, the thing that just don't figure, is what a feeble little cow patty like that would be doing risking faulty lungs on a cream-corn-fed punk..." he looked at my chest, at the disproportionately modest but undeniable breasts apparent beneath my t-shirt, the double-check of a crack detective, "I beg your pardon, what he'd want from a *broad*," he chuckled, "like you."

It galled me a little that I did not strike him as your typical victim, but I was cheered by the fact that I'd warranted the word "broad" (despite my hunch that he had in mind more width than dame). It made him seem small to me, so hopelessly cop-ish, in a 1930s noir sort of way, yearning, as he clearly was, for a Rico Bandello, snarling Scarface, to step foot in his precinct, but the Shame of the Nation rarely comes to Kansas. I pictured myself as a lithe and smirking, stiletto-breasted fatale, bent at the waist and forever straightening the seams of her stockings over shapely gams, a swath of silken Veronica Lake hair eclipsing one eye. And I imagined the detective going home to a sad, brown apartment, one beer, cocktail onions, and molding orange processed cheese food in the fridge, an emaciated cat, left behind by an ex-squeeze, endlessly pawing its phantom claws against a soiled plaid wool couch, elaborate rabbit ears stretching the length of the cramped living room to lessen the snow of his old Motorola. In my mind, I ballooned even more in stature and loomed big as a crane above him. Then I took the wrecking ball of my fist and dropped it on his head, tap-tapped him into the ground like a nail. On occasion I could see some advantage in being a lolloping mastodon.

"He wanted my punk money," I said. I felt the heat of the dead man's breath on my throat as I spoke.

"What kind of name is Wallis for a…girl anyway?" he asked with squinting eyes, as if he'd just uncovered an inconsistency in a shaky, uncorroborated alibi: *girl, a likely story*. "Hey, wait a minute," he said. "You're that kid, that 'Dollhouse of Death' kid, aren't you? There's a picture of you on a wall around here somewhere. You're bigger," he looked me over like he was sizing up a shank of beef at auction, "definitely bigger," he said, arching those woolly inchworms over his eyes, "but you were no peewee then, were you, and you still got the same mug."

"Guilty," I said. Word travels fast in flat places then hangs on the wall yellowing for years after.

"Right, all those kids that disappeared, what, twenty years ago? You're the one with the brother. Yeah, what was his name? Something strange-like. Otis? Opie?"

"Obie," I said, "Obadiah," and then I corked my whistle and stared at the floor.

"I was on a beat in Chicago back then. We heard about it up there. Strange case." I felt him following the line of my downcast gaze to his own shoes. He wiped a smudge off one of his recently-shined brogues against the back of his other leg. "Yeah, all right then."

The detective finally exhausted his grill, grudging pity narrowly edging out suspicion, and let me go. As both good cop and bad, he seemed rather haggard by the end, coughing and clutching his stomach. As I was leaving, I thought of telling him, *Best not blow town, Mugsy*, hardy-har, a conciliatory quip, but reconsidered when I saw him rubbing his whiskered jaw pensively. Though I longed to convince him that I could be imperiled as easily as any petite Pauline strapped to a trestle by a greedy-Gus cabbage-grubbing ne'er-do-well (even I step aside for trains), I was tired, and he appeared to be looking for any excuse to detain me. I could see his was a mind equipped with well-polished 38-caliber crime drama clichés, snug in the holster of his mind, but none, he discovered as he removed his gat and spun the chamber, exactly fitting this moment, alas. Anyway, this canary had sung all she was going to, and so she decided it was time to dust before he thought of a technicality that would allow him to toss her into the hoosegow.

Okay, confession: I'm no petticoat, no girly betty, no hothouse orchid. I'm 8' 11½", still a cubit or so shy of Goliath (depending on who you ask), 490 pounds, a few tubs of butter in excess of the dainty dish my mother, herself a windblown buttercup, assures me is trapped inside, beneath the impudent ballast of flesh. I have black hair straight as straw and skin the consumptive pallor of someone a few quarts low and in need of a transfusion (when I do pale with illness, I am a dim specter, make a corpse look comparatively in the pink). I've always had the complexion of an apparition, temperamental skin that begins to bubble and redden if I stand in the spring sun for ten minutes, skin that is otherwise so blood-scarce as to seem invisible, ghoulish. I have decided to give in to the anonymity my skin seems to long for: I've made myself disappear—alakazam!—behind the starkly contrasting curtain of hair. My face is more absence than memorable feature, a gap between black strands, like those Styrofoam wig rests. People tell me I look like a host of late-night horror flicks. They say this admiringly. Of course, the Johnny-come-lately-to-Kingdom-Come Goth kids are always trying to recruit me. "You're a *natural*," they tell me.

I sometimes shop at Archaic Smile, a thrift store downtown run by the Visigoths, a group splintered from the usual herd but far too congenially Midwestern to live up to the ambitions of its name. Rome, Kansas, had it not succumbed to cholera back in the day, would have nothing to fear from these glowering lambs, smudge-eyed and sullen. Beneath the wool is only more wool, though they howl at the waxing moon like the wolves they wish they were and knock back their parents' Wild Turkey between sneers. They set aside for me the occasional full-figure retro fashions donated by other gargantuan gals perhaps now passed on, items that would otherwise be snapped up surprisingly fast, hemmed to size by the frail and waifish, who, having no more pounds to spare lest their bones escape the binding flesh, poke noticeably through, look for other ways to up their wraith quotient, look for apparel to exaggerate their wispy near-nonexistence, their cadaverous beauty, look for something to swallow them whole. Sometimes I want to smack those sunken-eyed wastrel girls into the oblivion their glamorous wasting suggests they are seeking, but I understand too well the pressure to dwindle until you're a dully shimmering dot on a distant horizon, a speck on the window's pane, a mote stirred up by the shuffle of leaden feet.

This is the story of how I came to know Vivica Planet, no dwindler she. And how I made the only person who ever looked upon me adoringly (ishkabibble! sim sala bim!) vanish.

After I'd confessed my accidental sin, the one Commandment I was certain I'd never have to worry about breaking, I felt conspicuous, as though I gave off a homicidal scent or narrowed my eyes in a way that advertised a percolating bloodlust within. I had not meant to kill Hazard Planet, had only meant to subdue him with a sizzling mist of capsaicin. Although at the time I was secretly thrilled to think I seemed a susceptible mark, I later became angry with him for having chosen me, of all the short, frail, defenseless women striding vulnerably along Strong Avenue he might have accosted, women alone and falsely confident in the smoldering light of evening, women from whom he'd pinch some quick spinach then flee, no fatal outcome. But I could hardly blame him for squaring me in his crosshairs. A towering girl spends her life being singled out, sunflower looming among the dwarf buds of crocuses, ostrich scattering runt bantams, the Sears Tower grazing the sky above the humbler edifices engulfed in its shadow, a target from a great distance, a goal always in view. And the immodesty and bald ambition of a mere dame taking up so much space, displacing so much air, well, he was not the first to be piqued by this.

My father, in whom I'd confided the next day and who convinced me to give myself up, had sent me the obit: *Hazard Ambrose Planet is survived by his sister, Vivica Inez Planet, and his mother Gladys Ann Samson Planet, both of Kansas City. The family asks that donations be made to the American Lung Association.* Before that dramatic growth spurt in junior high that made my body shoot up so quickly it left behind skid marks, left my skin shiny and tight, stretched over big aching bones it was not prepared to cover, my father instructed me in self-defense, taught me how to break the frontal grip of an assailant or flip a rear attacker on his back. My father still likes to think I might one day meet a fuming colossus against whom my training will come in handy, thus proving that despite my ample height and girth I am indeed all girl, desirable lambchop. It's never easy for a man—high school fullback, raised a law-abiding, god-fearing Midwestern Methodist, whose wife dutifully cooks hot, well-balanced meals, wipes the toothpaste splatters from his bathroom mirror every morning, and doesn't complain when his Rotary meetings go longer than expected—to accept the relative invulnerability of his daughter, a daughter with an aerial view of the broadening circle of shiny scalp crowning his head, now only child, giant child.

But I was so relieved to read that Hazard Planet was not a married man, had apparently sired no children, and I decided I needed to meet what little family had survived him, needed to know the timbre of their voices and listen to them breathe, needed to show them the last face he set eyes on. The last body he threatened.

"Mrs.....Planet?" I said when a small razor-faced woman who looked more like withered child than adult appeared at the door and stared at me with eyes the color of a new forest fern. I pronounced the name "Planay," thinking it better to err on the side of continentality. She twisted her lips as though she'd eaten something bitter. "Gladys Planet?" I asked, returning the "net" to her name. She nodded her head once, and it suddenly occurred to me there was no delicate way to explain who I was.

I looked down at my considerable carcass, a body I've had occasion to parse every day of my life, Venus of Willendorf belly, tree trunk legs, feet for which shoes had always to be custom made, looked for some clue as to why Gladys Planet's only son had chosen me, and when I looked up, behind her stood a woman able to look me in the eyes, the first woman I'd ever seen who could, a woman with hair dyed black as thunder, reddish roots beginning to show, bangs blunt cut and crisply geometric in the style of an Egyptian queen, and whose chin was sparsely tufted with hair that appeared spirit-gummed in place. She bent and put her hands on her mother's shoulders, guided her to the side, then straightened up in front of me. She was a large woman, solid as a diamond, large as...me! My heart accelerated.

"You're the woman who killed my brother," she said through tight lips that barely parted to let the words through. Her voice was a muted kettledrum, with a sharp sonorousness my ears could barely surmount. I knew my crime was stitched in the repentant expression that no doubt covered my guilty map. I nodded. She smiled, and a mouthful of white pickets gleamed at me. Finally, I had some inkling of what people felt as they backed away from my own grin ridden with teeth like tombstones crowded together in a stack-bodied cemetery (my dentist, whose fragile, pianist's hands disappear inside my mouth during each checkup, has always urged me to floss: "A new set of choppers for that gaping bazoo," he says, "will set you back a pretty nickel!").

"Come in," Vivica said. I was drawn into the orbit of Vivica Planet almost instantly.

She invited me into their living room and gestured toward the sofa. I sat down at the end nearest a table atop which stood a picture of the Planet family taken years ago: Mr. and Mrs. Planet sitting sober and stiff, hands in their laps, both appearing a little shrunken inside their starched attire, Hazard standing, and autumn-haired Vivica kneeling behind, roughly the same height, making her look like a taffy-armed girl, long-waisted and disproportionate. It was clear the photographer had had trouble figuring out how best to arrange them and was simply trying not to behead her. If her family's photo albums were anything like mine, I reckoned they were filled with group pictures in which she is stooping over the shoulders of cousins or her head is a thing left to the imagination, guillotined by the border of the photograph, click.

Vivica sat across from me dressed in a long white tunic and slacks. She stroked her goatee and looked at me. She was Kingdomcomen, Queen of Kansas, ruler of all she surveyed, treetop tall and valley wide. "You knew my brother?" she asked.

"No," I said. "I was on my way to my truck, and—"

"But you wish to know him," she said. "Now. You wish to know the man you killed." She leaned forward, placed her arms symmetrically on her battering ram legs, and sat very still, looking like something that would guard the entrance to a pyramid, like something that would ask you unsolvable riddles. I guessed Vivica's weight to be close to my own, and I was surprised at how fluidly she moved, with hulking grace.

It's true, I longed to know something of the life I'd cut short, longed to understand the desperation that made a man want to put the felonious bite on a woman twice his size. Had he owned a devoted dog to whom he'd confided his heart's longings when he was a boy? Had he ever made his parents hopeful, won science fairs or spelling bees? Had there been a shining future spread out in front of him, a future in which, perhaps, he might be called upon to change the unfortunate course of the dreary lives of ordinary citizens, a future he was aimed at before he somehow got a bum steer and turned to a life of iniquity? Was there a woman he'd gladly walk through fire just to glimpse, a handsome woman with the sculpted flanks of a horse? Whose dead or dying face had *he* last looked into? Had he ever been rocked with a grief that split his heart in two? Did his parents look into his lichen eyes and wish he were someone else? I nodded.

Vivica Planet stared at me with cedar colored eyes taken from a genetic palette different from those of her immediate family. "You believe I'm angry with you for what you've done, think perhaps I hate you for killing my brother? You imagine no matter what my brother was like I must have loved him very much, because he is, he was, after all, my brother, and that's what people do, love their brothers, isn't that right? Brothers, like fathers and husbands, tycoons, magnates, deities, kings, presidents, despots, dictators, do what they do knowing, in the end, we have no choice but to love them?"

I shrugged and nodded. "Erm, yes?" This felt like a spring-loaded, jagged-tooth trap of a question, if it had been a question, and really I wasn't at all sure how I felt about brothers or presidents or two Amazonian Betties trapped in a shrinking living room together.

"I did love my brother," she said. "Did you love yours?"

"My...pardon?" My head filled with the exhaust of a mind that was parked in the garage, door shut, willfully idling.

"Your brother. Do you have a brother?"

I shook my head. I looked at the hand that had held the pepper spray, the finger that depressed the fateful nozzle. *I am a killer of brothers,* I thought.

I looked down at my feet and thought about this body's checkered history, and then I thought of God's gawky body, overgrown and unwieldy, too big for his britches, feet whose megalithic toes would take out North America if he set foot on Earth.

"Will you and I be friends, do you think?" asked Vivica Planet as she stood.

I killed a man who had startling eyes, the aggressive green color of Amazon parrots. I saw them squeeze shut before I turned and ran, thought I saw the vivid color drain down his cheeks. In my dreams now, angry men weep grass green tears and demand resurrection. Women of charity offered men dying on the cross sour wine to anesthetize them. I am not one of them. I close my eyes and gather men in pain into my mouth.

TWO
MOON RIVER

This is what I remember first as I think about pain and love and air travel and the history of this body, this body of evidence, mapped with clues:

My brother, Obadiah, and I are sitting in a boat on the moon. The water is a silvery green, and when we stick our hands in it, they shimmer with phosphorescence, drip moon-glow onto our legs. The boat is tilted up on Obie's end until he moves a mooring anchor to his feet. Obie always liked having me on the other end of a see-saw because unless I decided to buck or ground him, he'd remain aloft. I sank into the earth while he rocked in the sky, *nearer thy God to thee*. Obie thought a girl big as me had to *be* God, and sometimes I caught him kneeling at the foot of my long bed at night. "Thou shalt not kneel at the bed of thy sister," I'd sleepily command, pointing toward the door, and he'd return to his room without a word. I knew one night I might snore, might inhale his small boy body, dispelling the illusion. There are some deficiencies even an imaginative, loyal, lovesick boy cannot grant an overgrown girl of a god.

The water on the moon is viscous in places and we have to get out of the boat and push it through the thick straits. When we get back into the boat, we are coated with sea pudding, and it feels like the most comfortable pair of pants. My brother looks at me owl-eyed, as though he'd just discovered North America, the real America, the America no one's ever found, the one where nostalgic aborigines roam and drink from the cupped paws of solicitous bears. I know my brother secretly likes to think of me as a continent he alone founded, with little help from Isabella, at home making potato pancakes and browning sausage links for breakfast, or Ferdinand, shoehorning his feet into his Florsheims as he prepares for another day of actuarial calculations.

The sky hangs dark above us and we wait for stars to pock it with light. Obie leans over the boat and stirs luminous circles in the lunar sea. He says, "Our sister, who art on the moon, how can I better serve you?" He grins.

"Read a book every time you sneeze, don't blanch at all quadratic equations, eat green vegetables twice before the sun sets, always imagine yourself shod in the shoes of the other, and don't let a salesman of prosthetic limbs bamboozle you into believing the only path to peace is war, junior," I say in my most stentorian delivery. Obie places his hands on his cheeks, leaving behind silvery stripes of water, thick and lambent as mercury, and says, "Not all boys are mathematicians."

"True enough," I say, and I splash lit-up drops of water onto his legs, turning him into a moon leopard.

It is a half-moon we float across, a severed sphere, flat as a full bowl of soup, and when we get to the edge, we look over at the Earth below and stretch our hands toward it, but it is out of reach, a swirling green and white and blue balloon we've let drift too far. "Look," says Obie, pointing. *There are people eating egg salad sandwiches; people operating backhoes; men and women bowing in prayer, their faces touching the ground; and others moving languidly across a scorched field; people tossing in sleep as their mates lie still purring beside them; there caribou cross the tundra beneath a blanket of falling snow; and by yellow light a child is dying, injured by men who disagree.* He drops his hand into the water and the lucent surface ripples like minnows scattering.

☾

The birds on the moon are all blue as suffocation, blue with loosed atmosphere, and they fly toward the ground with the fiercest determination, the resolve of a bomb hurtling toward a still target. Moonbirds are notoriously intractable, as stubborn as the apocalypse when they fix on a goal. But they can never land. They're pulled back at their rosy throats by a finger of air in the last inch, drawn back toward the various stars of their birth. I know how it feels to be forced to hover, the ground a distant relation, a fourth cousin who never invites you to family gatherings for fear you will hog the potato salad, the honeyed ham, the crudités. I too can never land. I throw myself at the feet of strangers but seldom narrow the air between us. The birds on the moon sing in a way that makes your stomach grumble, that makes your hair rise from your head and feel like chinchilla to the touch. It is best not to listen when you are hungry, and on the moon, where a dull light forever shines as though one were peering into a refrigerator at night, one is always hungry.

☾

It is my brother who taught me the significance of the body's bumps, the telling crook of bone or jut of joint, the revealing nodes of flesh, the map of hidden scars that forecasts falls yet to be taken, blows yet to be borne. One day he said to me, "Wall, let me have your hand," and he ran his own thin fingers over the ridges and knuckles and scabs, over keloids in the making. He said, "You are tall in spirit as well as flesh." He smiled. He moved his hands to my arms, pausing on knotted tissue, up my throat, over my face, holding it in his hands, cradling the head, weighing it with his grasp, down my back and hips, along my legs, arriving at the terminus of my lubberly feet. Here he slowed his wandering, tracing veins, running his fingers along the pleats of callused flesh, thumping his knuckle against the nails as though the toes were melons he was testing for ripeness.

He told me in actuality I was lighter than air and that this body was the only answer God could think of to keep me on the ground. He said I would witness the aftermath of broken hearts and minds, would sometimes be the object of a gathering fury myself, and that my need to understand the origin of anger would cause me to follow the scattered spoor to the moment of conclusive violence. Then I would recreate it, shrink it, make it small and containable, solvable, so that I could believe evil to be discrete and bordered, limited, the opposite of God. He told me there would be dark moments in my life during which my looming, vital body would enrage a dwarfed and festering spirit and that I had to be careful to wield the resulting wrath justly. He held my hands and said to remember that he loved me more than the polished glare of a full moon, more than the river tinseled with light, more than the midnight cantillations of bullfrogs, said he'd donated his heart long ago to the cause of me.

My soul broke irreparably at that moment because I knew in my heart such pure and tender feelings were a fire that would never be allowed to burn this far from the sun, this far from God. God, of all things! Obie so reverent, clutching my hands tightly, as though he'd finally caught something worth worshiping and wasn't going to let it escape, and I could see how a god might eventually weary of being adored, how she might one day desire to flood the land and start anew, to look for a love that wouldn't annihilate her with its force, though she sometimes thought there could be nothing so lovely as annihilation, as being rendered the genuine absence the body belies.

I pulled my hands away. My brother smiled at me placidly as I inched away from him day by day, head nearing the aether. I was a monster girl growing and widening into a monster woman, and I knew a price would be exacted for the hubris of this being.

THREE
DARING TRUTH TO
BARE HER BOSOM

When Hazard Planet turned ten years old, growing so snailishly he thought he'd never be tall enough to slip into the burlap sack and slide down the giant rippling slide in the Save-On parking lot by himself, barely a quarter of an inch taller than he'd been at nine, his hopeful parents gave him a poplin jacket a size too big and a green canvas tent for his birthday. He hung the jacket in his closet and set up the tent in the backyard. At first, he wouldn't allow his sister, Vivica, to enter, posted *NO GODZILLA GIRLS ALLOWED*! *bring snacks*. But he soon grew bored of lying alone in the tent, reading comic books, and he invited his sister inside. Vivica told him she wasn't interested in reading moronic superhero escapades with him in his midget pup tent, "But," she said, "I'll come in if you obey my every command."

"No way!" Hazard huffed.

Another day alone idly vanquishing arch villains with a fatal flaw and Hazard relented, agreed to one game of Truth or Dare. "I ain't doing nothing dopey, though," Hazard said. "You can't make me eat a turd." Vivica stood up, bowing the top of the tent, nearly pulling the stakes out of the ground.

"All right, all right! Sit down. Jeez."

Vivica sat and said, "Truth or dare?"

"Who said you could go first?" Vivica stared at Hazard unblinkingly. "Let's flip a quarter," he said. She sat still, arms crossed. Hazard sighed loudly, pulled at his shoelaces. "Truth," he muttered.

"Why are you always trying to catch a look at me in the bathroom, perv?"

"I never!"

"This isn't Lie or Dare, midge. Do you want to play the game or not?" Vivica filliped Hazard's calf.

"Ow!"

"Well?"

"I only did it that once," Hazard said, pulling his legs under him.

"Four times, this month alone. At least."

"Maybe twice."

Vivica grimaced in a way that made Hazard start. "I don't remember!"

"What is it you think you want to see?"

"Nothing. You ain't got nothing I want to see."

Vivica stood up, pulled her shirt over her head, and unclasped her training bra. "Is this what you're looking for?" she asked, without intonation.

Hazard stood up and steadied himself with the pole of the tent. He backed up toward the door flaps then stopped.

This seemed to him like a truth and a dare combined somehow. "Can I touch them?" he whispered.

Vivica shrugged. Because her head was bent forward under the tent, Hazard thought she might be trying to scratch her ear with her shoulder. He waited. She shrugged again more slowly, cocked her head to the side, and raised her eyebrows.

Hazard took a step toward his sister. He looked behind him. The front flaps were zippered shut. He wondered if the tent material could be seen through and cursed himself for not wondering about this sooner. He knew Vivica wouldn't stand there half naked and wait while he checked. Another step. He was close enough to reach up and touch her now. He'd have to stretch, but her breasts were within reach. He looked at the disks of ham pink flesh surrounding the nipples, surprised at how they paled to a girly bubblegum color the farther they widened. They weren't so different from his own really, just puffier and redder, as though a giant bug had bitten them and made them swell. His own chest began to itch. Yes, they looked to him like something a bottle of Calamine lotion could cure.

He reached up and touched the bottom of a breast, and it felt like velvety Jell-O. He felt himself stiffening, felt his blood rushing through his arms and legs, into his ears, heating up his stomach. Vivica bent down slowly, to give him a better feel he thought, and he cupped a full breast in his hand, as though he were catching rainwater or holding a baby bird. Now he had a handful of custard. Just as he was beginning to let himself enjoy the scalding feeling welling up inside him, Vivica reached between his legs and squeezed so hard his vision immediately began to swim. The last thing he saw before he fell to his knees was the angry black eye of her navel.

That was only the first time Vivica brought Hazard to his knees, flattened his privates, and made him see whole galaxies of dying stars, made him retch on the floor of his birthday tent.

FOUR
WALRUS DISGRACE

Tonight I, Wallis Grace Armstrong, am dusting off my two left feet and knock-about knees and am going for my fourth ballroom dance lesson at the Arthur Murray studio in Kingdom Come, a gift from my parents who had high hopes for the steering power of a middle name and who are disappointed that I've instead lived up all too readily to the stout stamp of the surname. You can imagine what a rich source of heckling being saddled with such a nom de guerre has been: Wall-ass Strong Arm, Wall-eyed Goose, Wall is gross, Walrus graze, et cetera. My mother, trying to assure me of a glamorous life of class-busting romance, named me after Wallis Simpson—the twice-married socialite who so captivated Edward VIII, Duke of Windsor, he abandoned his royal heritage and lived with her in exile—not realizing the eighteen-pound baby she secretly believed *had* to be quadruplets, the baby stretching her belly beyond a reasonable arc, would, with this name, be more likely to call to mind a steam shovel operator than a duchess, even one once removed (I can only assume my mother was and remains unaware that the Duchess fatale, though ambitiously thin, was a darkly complicated Nazi sympathizer known both to captivate and scandalize polite society with her ribald quips and the punctuating snap of her tiny wrists).

Would that I had been named rather for that developer of infinitesimal calculus, John Wallis, who gave us the never-ending gift of this: ∞. The number eight lying on her side, eternally asleep like a fairy-tale heroine. My mother does not know there is a man named Wallis who contributed to infinity, lent a shape to perpetuity, who formulated Pi. She would be perfectly appalled at the notion. She does not care for unending things. The vastitude of me she finds sheer insubordination and she takes each inch personally. Sometimes on applications and census forms I sign my name so:

$$\prod_{n=1}^{\infty}\left(\frac{2n}{2n-1}\cdot\frac{2n}{2n+1}\right)=\frac{2}{1}\cdot\frac{2}{3}\cdot\frac{4}{3}\cdot\frac{4}{5}\cdot\frac{6}{5}\cdot\frac{6}{7}\cdot\frac{8}{7}\cdot\frac{8}{9}\cdots=\frac{\pi}{2}$$

Having recently killed a man, I found my nerves were still ajangle, and I called Mr. Mundrawala, my dance instructor, to cancel, but he sounded disappointed and urged me to reconsider, insisting that "continuity and repetition are key to mastering the fox-trot. Practice makes graceful, Miss Armstrong," so I decided to go. Inexplicably, Mr. Mundrawala, not a hair over 5' 7", had decided it was best if he personally partnered himself with me, even though there was, by mortal standards, one reasonably tall man in the class, and he was strangely prone to wearing elevator shoes, which meant his eyes could at least glimpse my clavicle if he stretched and I sagged forward. Mr. Mundrawala assured me that dancing with pint-sized men would be instructive, would teach me to move more thoughtfully through the world, help attune me to the feet bustling around me that I have to be careful not to flatten.

"It's very nice to see you here, Miss Armstrong," Mr. Mundrawala said with a nod of the head, grinning broadly.

"Nice to see you too, Mr. Mundrawala."

"Please, you have now had the benefit of my instruction for how many lessons, three? As we are partners, it is time we observe the American custom of quick familiarity and employ first names, don't you agree? Yes, please, you may call me Mateen." He held out a delicate hand.

"Wallis," I said, and shook his paw, though it was, from his end, really more of a firm squeeze of a few fingers. He had the nimble grip of a flautist.

"A lovely moniker," he said sincerely. The first time I'd heard *that* from someone to whom I was not related.

There were three other couples present, all decked in ballroom duds, waiting to begin the beguine. I was wearing a black t-shirt, parachute pants (in case I ever figured out how to bail out of this body), and built-to-order sneakers, and, like every week, the others stole glances and shifted nervously, tried not to stare, thanked God for their small feet and wasp waists.

In tenth grade, Jojo Fridel asked me to the homecoming dance. Jojo was a gymnast, 5' 1" in platform shoes. I'd kneel down so he could mount the howdah of my shoulders, and he'd ride aloft, waving to the minions below, then he'd backflip to the floor, applause, applause. We were a novelty act and mostly well liked, if at a long arm's remove, by the perfectly-proportioned and popular teenagers that haunt school dances (though not by the orthodontic wall-huggers, who felt they could ill afford to claim us). *There but for the grace of God*, I could hear them thinking as we jigged across the gym floor to the fervid caterwauling of "Ballroom Blitz." Most Aberrations of Nature know enough to dodge school gatherings and extracurricular activities of all kinds, but I felt a certain purposefulness in reassuring these young, apple-cheeked, corn-fed American citizens of their good fortune in belonging to the First World. Jojo and I, noble savages, served as sort of an anthropological warning, a trip to deepest, darkest Africa for these middle class, milk-faced Kansans, scrubbed mugs bland as pancakes, who were grateful for their V-8 Firebirds and split-level homes with double convection ovens their parents' comfortable incomes provided them, grateful for statistically average IQs and bodies that didn't call attention to themselves. We were a mystery they hoped never to get to the bottom of, a hostile continent they liked knowing was out there—a place of corrupt heat and a constant cloud of mosquitoes and fevered misfortune—but never wanted to step foot on. Just sharing a locker or lunch table with us, observing us in the natural habitat of our bodies, was safari enough for them. There was, of course, a committee of brawlers who'd menace the likes of Jojo and me at any opportunity.

We were beat after an evening of performing to golden hits of bygone eras and had decided to cut out early, to leave the crepe streamers and ice machine fog to the couples who tottered like penguins as they stiffly slow-danced. The Kingdom Come High hooligans weren't the type to frequent sock hops—wouldn't be caught dead inside the gym while the glitter ball still spun—but they were so incensed by the bald chutzpah of our showing our freak-of-nature faces at a school event they made an exception and waited in the parking lot for us (if mastodons and their trained fleas began to roam the earth freely, without even being hectored, where would that leave them? Equality, as any pariah knows, only causes to crumble the fragile social foundation on which both thuggery and outlaw glamour depend). There were four of them, Bobby Ehlers, Gary Schwartz, Heather Leatherwood, and Lucky Teeter, Bobby swinging nunchucks with calculated bluster and trying not to look pained when they hit him in the chest or back. Heather and Gary were clearly hopped up on something as they shifted from foot to foot and sniffed, their black eyes all spreading pupil. Lucky stood by calmly, hands stuffed in his dirty jeans' pockets.

"Well, if it ain't Mutt and...Mutt," said Bobby, which was their cue to swarm. I swung Jojo, fearless mahout, onto my shoulders and beat it down the gravel drive. They gave chase and began to pelt us with stones. I felt the nunchucks hit my back, then Jojo yelped and fell limp. I stopped, pulled him around into my arms, saw that the back of his head was bleeding, then felt a flak of gravel hit my legs, heard their hyena cackling. His eyes were open but dull, like smudged glass. He groaned groggily. I gently lowered Jojo to the ground and turned to face our four assailants. They were wild eyed and rocking, bent at the knees, as though preparing to play a riotous game of tennis. Jojo was just a preliminary skirmish—it was me they sought to conquer. I imagined them knocking me out and battening me down like a ship they wanted to set sail on, securing me to the ground with string and thumbtacks I'd break free of with a shrug, those rotten Lilliputians, then I'd send them sailing all right.

Bobby Ehlers was fluttering his hands, motioning me toward him. "Come on, T-freakin'-Rex," he said then licked his lips, "come on, come on."

"Time to kick some Leviathan ass," said Lucky quietly.

"Some what?" said Gary.

"Shut up, dumbass," Heather said, pushing him aside.

"Cut it out, bitch!" Gary said, grabbing her by her black-rooted, corn-colored hair that had been scorched into brittle waves with a crimping iron.

I walked up to Gary and seized him by the throat, lifted him in the air, thumb on his windpipe. He began to gag and kick. The others closed a tentative circle around me. I pressed harder, and Gary's gagging thinned, his eyes bugged. They stopped and took a step back. I said, "Toss me your wallets then take off your clothes."

"What?!" cried Bobby Ehlers.

"Do it, and do it quickly, or Gary Schwartz becomes the next Kingdom Come High statistic," I said. "Too many drugs and thug friends always spoiling for a fight, just another misunderstood teen casualty from a broken home, saddest story you ever heard." I stared at Lucky, who held my gaze. Bobby took a step in my direction, and I dug my thumb into Gary's windpipe. His face was red as a setting sun and he gurgled. We all stood frozen, and I was beginning to worry they might be willing to sacrifice Gary in the name of the greater good of their black-hearted ambitions.

Lucky unchained his wallet and tossed it to my feet. "Do it!" he yelled. Jojo was now sitting up, rubbing his head. The others tossed me their wallets and began to undress. Jojo stood up and wiped his bloodied hand on his pants. Gary's jerking slowed.

Trying to slouch indifferently inside their gooseflesh, hands casually draped over shriveled privates and pubic hair, they briefly tugged at my heart, but I was committed to this showdown now, my hand glued to Gary's throat. Jojo gathered their clothes and wallets and handed them to me. "Let him go," he whispered. I dropped Gary to the ground and he gagged and gulped, reached in the air with a splayed hand. Jojo picked up a rock and chalked a circle around his body, and we backed away.

"You're fucking dead meat, man!" Bobby shrieked.

As we left them, I saw Heather kneeling by Gary, who held his throat and backhanded her in the face. "Dead!" Bobby screamed after us.

When we got to the end of the drive, we tossed the clothes and wallets into the stagnant pond. Heather's shirt caught on a cattail, everything else sank into the green murk.

There are times when anger wells up inside of me like a geyser aboil, and when it blows, I make the person in front of me pay for the infractions I've let slide. But honestly, I'm not a violent person by nature. Obie used to say it was just my Old Testament temper erupting. Once allowed to rise up, it's hard to tame a diluvian dander.

☽

Tonight at the dance studio, there was a man, one of the eager-to-trot jackanapes, the trotting fox trying hardest not to stare, who looked a lot like Lucky Teeter, though with a considerably thinned mop and a more weaselly snout than I recalled, Roister Furioso I'd once tagged him as he threw me a smoldering glare from the smoking patio, now all grown up. I would, however, sooner expect to see Lucky Teeter asprawl and mortally plugged on the floor of one of my crime scenes than cutting a ballroom rug decked out in souped-up duds. I caught his eye and he nodded once before he stepped on the foot of his partner, who squawked at such a pitch we all froze mid-shuffle. Lucky Lookalike pulled a toothpick from his pocket, popped it between his gnashers, and folded his arms while his partner shook her shoe at him and defended the honor of a wounded bunion. Mr. Mundrawala looked up at me apologetically, though I, Walrus Disgrace, body stalled inside a maneuver I was about to botch anyway, I was pleased for once not to be the main attraction.

FIVE
RUDY IN THE PARK

When I was a young child, never small exactly but budding, proportionately, at roughly the same languorous rate (all right, in mind if not body) as the runtiest in the world's litter, I dreamed of being kidnapped. I longed to be darling and vulnerable, the kind of child a parent would never dare leave alone, the kind of incandescent, wide-eyed moppet that would be an overwhelming temptation to all nabbers of innocents. My mother, petite as a crocus, would look at me, her lumbering sunflower, and forget my age and let me wander supermarkets, parking lots, back alleys by myself. By the time I was seven, I owned a pocketknife I was sure I could use to build a raft, with scissors and bottle opener and handy toothpick and tweezers, and though I could not bring myself to special order an oversized brownie uniform with a big-headed beanie, necessary for eventually joining those generally elfin, do-gooder Girl Scouts, I was a self-schooled mycologist, knew which mushrooms were deadly toadstools (diabolical amanitas, those destroying angels; gyromitra and helvella, which cleverly masquerade as morels; deceptively fragrant jack-o'-lanterns; and beware the genteel parasol of the green-spored lepiota!) and which were edible (lovable puffballs, which can be large and mistaken from a distance for grazing sheep; shaggy mane, best picked before the caps turn inky; oyster and bearded mushrooms, with no poisonous doppelgangers; and those hardworking morels). I was prepared for the daring escape that would follow the kidnapping and for the embrace of the worried adults who hadn't realized what prime-cut kidnapper bait I actually was. (Maybe it would be better to languish a little in the dark, windowless room the kidnapper would no doubt hold me hostage in, I thought. Too much self-sufficiency could make my plan to demonstrate my defense-lessness backfire.) Sometimes, when I was allowed to roam, unchaperoned, the deserted streets of Kingdom Come, I'd seek out the most sinister-looking loner I could find and sit myself down or slouch vulnerably in his vicinity, try to appear as innocent and bewildered as a hatchling, blink blink.

Once, in a small, bedraggled park near my house (not a Tenderloin District exactly but close to the blood bank and so rough enough around the edges to attract an itinerant skee-zix or two), I spotted a promisingly unkempt man wearing a baggy gray jumpsuit. He sported a soiled John Deere cap and laceless sneakers, and his teeth were brown with decay, didn't look like they'd put up much of a fight against steak or apples or corn on the cob. I sat in the grass not far from his bench, doing my best to appear bereft and grateful for any assistance. Even though I'd carefully positioned myself along the avenue of his vacant gaze, he seemed not to see me, so I got up, and after briefly loitering nearby, I decided to park myself next to him on the bench. Subtlety gets an abductee-in-waiting nowhere fast.

"Hi there," I said, already sounding fishy to my own ears. It's more difficult than you might think, when beginning a conversation with a potential kidnapper, to strike just the right tone so as not to scare him away.

He turned to look at me then looked back at the park.

"Do you live around here?" I asked, thinking I was getting confused about which part I was playing and hoping this tinder would catch a spark soon. No response. "I'm pretty far from home, myself," I cleverly prompted. "In fact, I'm not even sure where I am exactly." What a gift! I was hoping he was thinking.

"You're in Kingdom Come," the man said without looking at me.

"Oh, Kingdom Come. Is that near...Mission Hills?" I asked, thinking on my sizable feet. Mission Hills is the silver-spoon neighborhood we made a special trip to every holiday season to see how the other half tastefully decorates their palatial estates. It was the sort of swank purlieu in which owners of professional sports teams and greeting card moguls lived, and therefore the 14-karat 'burb where the most kidnappable children were to be found, those who would fetch the highest ransom.

As I suspected it would, this got the man's attention, and he finally looked at me. "What are you doing around here, kid?" he said.

"I, er, was shopping with my mother, for...truffles," I blurted (truffles? goodgravymarie), "and we got separated and, somehow I, uh, ended up in this park." Note to self: come up with a wilier shtick, for the love of Pete, and quit being such a galumphing stumblebum! This was as far as I'd ever gotten with a would-be captor. "I'm Wallis," I said. Even though I was only nine years old, I was nearly as big as this man, and I was beginning to fear he might not bite, might be on the prowl for a smaller veal cutlet. But I squeezed my eyes shut and willed him to be a bad man on the make. I imagined him cutting the clothes from my body with a rusting butcher knife, chop-chop, imagined him holding the knife to my throat, jabbing it at my arms and stomach and legs, jab-jab, the flesh of which would give and bleed just like that of any child, tetanus storming through me. And I kept going: imagined him cutting off my hands and feet and preserving them in jars and storing them in a wunderkammer of pickled parts, imagined him recording various tortures in a crabbed scrawl on a Big Chief tablet before he unzipped my skin, slit me up the middle, and my young child's blood poured forth and indelibly stained his linoleum. This is how I'd be found: a helpless girl no match for the violent brawn of nefarious men, left alone by her parents to be savaged by a furious world.

"Rudy," the man said and he tipped his John Deere hat. At this my heart sank. What self-respecting homicidal bed-lamite would a) offer his name so quickly, even a fake one, and b) do so in a gentlemanly manner? It just didn't square. "It's really Rudolph," he said, "but friends call me Rudy." Oof, I dove headlong into the Slough of Despond. Where were all the eager abductors, where-oh-where was the wicked in the world? But then I perked up, thought *friends*? He's suggesting we're on familiar terms, perhaps this is his way of…winning my trust? Little girls can't talk to strangers, but they can talk to *friends*. Of course, cunning maniac! My spirits rallied.

"Like the reindeer?" I asked, trying to seem like the sort of lonely child who identifies with marginalized characters.

Rudy smiled, and the sad sight of his neglected teeth made me lose heart again, somehow made me feel like I was taking unfair advantage of an earnest mope down on his grift. Perhaps he was a reformed fiend, trying his best not to wobble off the straight and narrow. I sighed, pulled out of my pocket two wadded dollar bills and my pocketknife. "How much for a kidnapping?" I asked.

His smile sagged. "Come again?"

"I want to be kidnapped." I am a willing flank steak in search of drooling wolves, I was thinking, but you flea-bitten mutts who frequent the park are so down-at-the-heel, you can't even muster a growl, just my rotten luck, arf.

Rudy rubbed his stubbled jaw. "Are you in or out?" I asked.

"How old are you?"

"How old do you think I am?" Here it comes, the added insult. He's wondering what a BIG girl like me is doing trying to get snatched. Aren't you a little old for this? he's going to ask.

"I'd say, oh I don't know, eight or nine?" He smiled a closed-mouth smile.

I eyed Rudy closely to see if he was ribbing me, but I could detect no insincerity in his tight grin.

"You think I'm eight or nine years old?" I asked.

He nodded. "How old are you?"

"Don't you think I'm a little too big to be that young?" I searched his face for the telltale flicker of mockery.

He shook his head. "I have a girl about your size, big girl, big, sweet girl. She'll be nine tomorrow."

Other gargantuan girls in the world! I knew they were out there, but didn't know any personally, so I'd long suspected they might be a myth my father had manufactured to comfort me, his big-big-boned daughter, his Kansas Amazon.

"Do you let your girl go out alone?" I asked. "Do you believe her size keeps her from harm?"

"She lives with her mama now," Rudy said, "but if I had her with me, I surely wouldn't let her out of my sight. Surely wouldn't," he said, and he smiled again. "World ain't safe for little girls like you, full of madmen and monsters." So true! So true! I couldn't help myself: I touched his grubby grin.

I took Rudy home, and my parents were gone, so I fed him oatmeal and bananas and scrambled eggs, and I gave him a toothbrush and toothpaste, the two dollars and my pocketknife. He hugged me and told me I should be more careful, little girl like me, shouldn't talk to strangers in the park.

Rudy may well be the only man I've ever loved.

The next day at breakfast, my mother read an article aloud, a local tragedy. Emily Lipton, aged ten, disappeared yesterday from Paradise Park, the very park where I'd met Rudy. She was there with friends, and one girl saw her talking to a man on a bench, but when the girl looked back, Emily and the man were gone. They later found her brand new Red Goose Mary Janes, striped anklets tucked inside, perched on the carousel, as though it had spun too quickly and she flew out of her shoes, lofted into the aether. Emily's most distinguishing feature, said the article, is a birthmark at the base of her neck, a dime-sized stork bite, perfectly round and red. I asked my mother for the paper, and I looked at the police sketch of the mysterious man. It was not Rudy. This man sported a beard that just didn't look native to those chops and he wore dark glasses, had clearly read a manual about suspicious-looking vagrants and was trying to look the part. I knew Rudy would never betray me that way.

But as I looked more closely at the drawing, I thought I did recognize this man: his long hair parted in the middle and flowing to his shoulders, lips full inside his beard, cheeks hollow as stones whittled smooth by water—he was a dead ringer for Jesus! For the man who played Jesus in the passion play, the man who hung on the cross the whole day long every Good Friday, on the front lawn of Our Lady of Interminable Sorrow, gold and purple satin cloth draped along his arms, his ribs visibly heaving beneath his pale skin, dear famished coyote, dried blood trickling down his cheeks, the brambly circlet wreathing his head. When we drove by him, slowly so we could gawk at the spectacle of suffering, not a part of the flock for whom this reenactment was staged, I always secretly longed to lick his hairless chest, bony, exposed, concealing a heart so pure, so easily crushed.

And as I looked at the picture of the kidnapper who bore a striking resemblance to our local Jesus, the Jesus at whom I had once thrown a pebble, to test if he was a flesh-of-my-flesh human man or just an inflatable Jesus (he flinched and moaned in a messianic timbre but his anguished eyes stayed sealed, and I wished at that moment to be struck dead as a doorknocker), I feared not even a kidnapping could save me.

I gave the newspaper back to my mother and waited for her to caution me about going to that park alone, but she just smiled into her sodden cereal, turned the page of the paper, and patted me—clippety-clomping, invulnerable, improbable girl, failed Girl Scout and damsel, eternal apostate stoner of suffering Jesus-on-the-cross—she pat-patted me on the arm.

SIX

CHILD OF THE AMERICAN REVOLUTION

My mother has always longed to be a member of the DAR, beloved Daughter of the American Revolution, but there's a crook in her lineage that makes her more distant, disowned cousin by common-law marriage than direct descendant. Nevertheless, she continues to hold out hope that she'll find a crack in the rules in which she can wedge her Mayflower-yearning, size-five-and-a-half, purebred petite, puritanical foot. Giving birth to an anemic behemoth daughter didn't help her case *at all*, or so she believed, and she was racked by a post-partum despondency that made my father fear for us both. He'd come home at night and sometimes find me curled up in my bassinette on the floor of a bedroom closet beneath a heap of laundry, sucking on a warm tea towel. Though I had been snatched from the cracked egg of her belly through Caesarian incision, it was still a difficult delivery, had been a grueling pregnancy, for which my mother has never forgiven me. She said the doctor pulled me endlessly, for days it seemed, from her weary womb like a circus clown extracting colored scarves from his pocket. She claims she watched the sun set again and again outside her window, the sky's unstanchable wound bleeding into the horizon, and she pleaded for a tourniquet, begged them to dress the sky, but there is no such scenic view afforded by the Bethany Hospital delivery room. She says her pelvis relaxed more widely than it should have ("opening like the wings of a butterfly," my father has said to her consolingly), so she can never again wear the hip-hugging fashions that had previously made her worthy of ogling. And after a certain amount of precipitation, her sciatica renders her nearly lame, and she glowers at me long after the rain has ceased. My mother and I never get along so well as when there is a drought.

When I was three months old, my mother, determined to halt my growth until my age caught up with my body, took me to see a defrocked priest in Kansas City who was rumored to be an itinerant exorcist. My mother is not Catholic—no aspiring Daughter of the AR certain she hails from the most pious and persecuted Calvinist stock would be of course—but she was desperate for an unexceptional child and thought Father Donnelly might be able to conjure the abnormality out of my bones with a devoutly caressed rosary, a few prayers chanted in Latin, and some holy water splashed on my squalling face. My father says she has never told him what exactly happened in the course of the exorcism, but when he came home that night, he found her sitting in the living room, holding the bulging bundle of me tightly in her arms, staring at the darkened television, trickled blood drying on my temples and cheeks and staining the sleeves of her shirt: the priest had carved a cross on the soles of my feet and the top of my head, narrowly missing my fontanel. I still have three paling crosses scarring my skin, making a Calvary of my body. Marked by this trinity, I've never been comfortable in churches, am always afraid I might suddenly immolate. And I fear that the priest was not successful, worry that a leviathan demon swims yet inside me. Despite my father's vigilant reassurances, I can't help but believe instead the scowl carved into my mother's face in stark, censorious lines. Her pinched face informs me that I am an evil girl-goblin turned villainous Valkyrie, though I sincerely wish to cauterize my cankerous spirit so that I might be worthy of love. If only there would be another revolution, an upending of the world order, I'd enlist and rush to the front so that my mother could celebrate me at commemorative teas, so she might beam with pride, toast my memory, pledge her devotion to freedom and democracy and big-bodied babies, and forget the cumbersome crosses stooping both our backs.

So when Vivica Planet called me on the telephone and invited me to join her at church on Sunday, for a special service devoted to her family, my scalp and feet began to prickle and itch, but I agreed to go. How could I refuse? I hadn't thought it proper to attend Hazard's funeral, but here was my chance to pay official penance at the very altar at which Hazard had worshipped.

Vivica and I walked into the Ruby Avenue Church of Christ with Gladys between us, and all the parishioners turned and stared. The little church was nearly full, but as we passed the packed pews, they began to empty behind us, so that by the time we reached the front of the nave, only half the congregation remained, those stoutest of heart. I deduced that it had been some time since Vivica had been to church, a good thirty-six inches ago, and although she was now peach-chinned, no longer displaying any facial hair, the two of us together were clearly more than some of the brethren could bear, too troubling a test of faith, our bodies evidence that in the Word having been made flesh, some bedeviled babbler had commandeered the conversation and run off at the mouth.

The space between pews was quite narrow (constructed for the decidedly ungluttonous), so the front pew was the only one that allowed room enough for Vivica and me to sit, and there was a creaky give to the bench when we sat that made me worry we'd soon be sprawled across the red carpeting, looking up at Christ's stained glass ankles and the disapproving glare of the minister. Gladys sat between us, her feet barely touching the ground. She smiled sadly and nodded at the minister, who couldn't take his eyes off Vivica and me. He dabbed at his brow with a handkerchief, and I imagined him thinking of us as the Goliath Girls, in need of a slaying, and he just the David to do it.

In his sermon, he talked about the many unfortunate paths temptation can lead us down, and Hazard's death quickly became an object lesson about the preventative benefits of regular attendance at church. The reverend insisted Hazard had been a basically good, God-fearing fellow who had briefly wandered off the righteous path, though he wasn't at all specific about the nature of that detour. I could hear Vivica audibly snorting with increasing intensity throughout the sermon, causing the reverend's eyes to dart about like startled sparrows, and just as the reverend was entrusting Hazard's soul to God, Vivica stood up. She ascended the steps to the pulpit, and said, "Excuse me, Reverend. If I may," and, mopping the sweat from his puss recklessly, he knocked into the lectern, steadied it, and stepped aside.

She cleared her throat, stroked her chin once, and said, "For the sake of my brother's…soul, I believe it's important we all understand just who he had become. My brother was a petty thief and criminal, who especially enjoyed stalking women. This is the degree to which he strayed from that"— here she paused and I could see she was straining not to bare her teeth and growl at the winnowed flock—"righteous path. He died accosting a woman, and in the course of that assault, he had a fatal asthma attack. These are the facts of his demise, so ended his 'earthly career.'" Vivica slid her eyes to the side and gave the reverend an implicating scowl. The reverend's brow sprang another leak. "Hazard had long been more than a merely 'troubled man.' There sits the woman who killed him," she said, pointing at me. A collective murmur passed through what remained of the congregation, and Gladys turned and stared at me, her eyes wide with dawning understanding as they shot green darts in my direction. I half expected the minister to say, "Will the Defendant please rise?" so I could hear my sentence, death by electrocution and lethal injection both, I hoped, something quick and surefire and excessive.

I stood up and said, "Erm, sorry?" and the congregants all rose and shuffled into the aisle. As though an alarm had sounded, the church quickly drained of people and I imagined them heading to bomb shelters stocked with peach preserves, summer sausage, and pickled okra. Vivica and I were of a biblical height, which is never, I concluded, reassuring to the reverent. What next? they wondered. A month of rain that will flood their basements and heave mud into their kitchens, visionary boxelder bushes ablaze, tuna salad sandwiches suddenly filling the emptiest of plates? Thunderbolts and manna are equally unnerving to Kansans, showy miracles, the immodesty, shudder. The minister wore a stricken look on his moist face, and Gladys filed out with the rest. Vivica descended from the pulpit, and threaded her arm through mine.

We were all silent on the drive back to the Planet house, but Gladys kept turning to narrow her eyes at me, to let me know there'd be no escaping my fate, one suitable for a homicidal heathen such as myself. Her face was wet, the look of rage had faded to everyday grief by the time we reached their house, and I wanted to hug her, squeeze the sorrow out of her, make it disappear in my remorseful embrace, and tell her I'd happily suffocate myself if it would ease her suffering, but she didn't appear consolable, and, in my experience, comfort had to come from people your own size, which was why I thought Vivica Planet might save me, might solace me into oblivion.

SEVEN

THE UNGAINLY
APPETITE OF
WALLIS G. ARMSTRONG

As I was growing up, in an attempt to stanch the flow of my thickening flesh, my swelling haunches and belly and breasts, slow the ballooning of my avoirdupois (my dress size seeming to double each month), my mother carefully meted out to me tiny servings of the starchy foods with which she tried to fatten Obie: scalloped potatoes, macaroni, creamed corn; she halved a biscuit, hid the jam, slivered or dolloped dessert. She filled my plate instead with iceberg lettuce dampened with vinegar, trying desperately to shrink me, arrest the increase once and for all, but I sensed early on I could never grow small enough to please her. She was fond of quoting the svelte duchess whose name she hoped would corset me and make me marriageable, saying, "You can never be too thin or too rich," and she bought me fashion magazines and insisted I study them: "A girl can learn a lot from women who thrive on deprivation," she said, pointing to sullen models who were all sharp edges and angles, whose bodies looked like weapons that would leave deep gashes in anyone who dared show them affection. I tried to empty myself, ignored my hunger, kippered my body by standing close to the fire, tried to mummify myself with Ace bandages, bury my body in the four-poster sarcophagus of my bed (the posters of the shrinking bed demarking the borders my body was not allowed to exceed), fasted until my skin gave off a strange odor like burnt plastic, until my vision filled with spots and made me feel as though I were looking at the world through smudged spectacles, the eyes themselves soiled and in need of a polishing, but no matter what I did, I continued to grow, like a curse, like a cautionary fairy tale, The Infinite Body of the Limitless Girl. My mother believed being petite was only a matter of willpower and determination, and so my feeble resolve disappointed her deeply on a daily basis. She told me that no woman on *her* side of the family had ever weighed more than 115 pounds or stood taller than 5' 6" and said I was setting a dangerous family precedent that would doom our descendents to a decidedly unglamorous life of oafishness. She leveled a Darwinian glare in my direction, picturing the future disastrous permutations that would bear the family name on future genealogical charts. I could almost see her willing my reproductive organs to shrivel on the vine. I felt as though my very existence were endangering the human species, and there were days when I concluded that the noble thing to do would be to curtail my ruinous influence before it became too late. I bought economy-sized bottles of Elmer's glue and slathered the milky goo on my limbs, covered my body in a glutinous cast, trying to halt it in its tracks, but of course my armor sprang leaks almost instantly, mutinous flesh gushing forth from every fissure.

And then there was Obie, counterweighting my mother's strict dietary parsimoniousness by stockpiling snacks and stealthily hording food at the dinner table to tempt me later, out of view of "the comestible commissar," as my father called her under his breath, causing Obie to kick his feet in lieu of a chuckle and my mother to purse her lips witheringly, as though she'd accidentally ingested something with a high fat content, me perhaps. The bigger the better, thought Obie, more girl-god to love, when you prayed you couldn't miss. Obie thought of God as a diaphanous and vast but moving target and believed blind devotion was the only means by which you could sharpen your aim.

I have recently begun to have a dream that recurs every Saturday night. In the dream, I'm on an alien landscape, trekking through sparse and yellowing grass, and the ground is spongy and difficult to traverse; my ankles wobble. Rising from the blood-brown earth is a fine layer of smoke, as though there were a smoldering fire just beneath the topsoil, and through the enveloping haze I begin to see that there are bodies lying on the ground. I have to be careful where I step. There has been a war, and I see now more clearly that there are bodies twisted and bleeding and parted from limbs all around me, and it is from them that the vapor rises, as if signaling a release, a final, silent lament, an evacuation. I suddenly recall that I am fleeing a despotic regime run by men whose corruption has turned their teeth brown—I see their muddy grins in my mind's mind's eye—but I cannot remember from which direction I have come. And then I notice there are soiled children, orphaned, huddled together, wounded, silent. Their eyes are dark and wide, permanently agape, and there are guns scattered around them. The children are gaunt and wild with stillness, and I can see their bodies are bent beneath the deadweight of human history, the burden of consequential events catalyzed by men driven by craven instincts, men who fell too hard or too easily into knowledge and who therefore take pleasure in witnessing the moment at which innocence is extinguished. In the distance, faint cheering can be heard, followed by a clatter of gunfire. The children lie down and pretend to be dead, eyes still open. I lie beside them.

Time loops forward and when I get up again, the children are gone and the atmosphere feels airless. With each motion, my limbs cut a swath through the taut air in the faint shape of me. My body has left an impression in the earth, and as I look at it, I notice movement. I kneel and look more closely and see that the scene I just witnessed has been replicated in miniature, in the gully left by the imprint of my body, and I feel culpable for all the misery in the world. I sense someone behind me, turn to see a green-eyed man take shape in the gloom that hangs about me, a man who shakes his head and snickers, says, "You're only a girl." He sees that I recognize this as belittlement thinly disguised as sympathy, says, "A whole lot of girl, but zero times zero is zero," laughs, and I pick the man up by his collar and hurl him from my dream. I half expect to see him lying on the floor of my bedroom when I wake.

As you can imagine, I have never been very successful at being a girl, though, for my mother's sake, I have tried. I have wambled about on gimlet heels that left divots in hardwood floors, permed my hair into a fungal fuzz, wrestled my hips into girdles, painted onto my face a bright hoax of come-hither allure, following closely the prescription in those fashion magazines that advise women how to be more woman than they already are (or less), but this was all a disguise that fooled no one, least of all my mother, an authority on the feminine. I remained an excessively fleshed and boned human hardly fit for the demure grace and beautiful erasure of womanhood. Where I am concerned, there has always been too much there there, says my mother. My father says I am delightfully Rubenesque, schlepping through life a body simply born too late to be properly feted, but this does not reassure my mother, who keeps her dressing mirror tilted at a fun-house angle so that she seems to be disappearing, ever on the wane. I have always been afraid to watch her as she dresses before it for fear she will one day no longer appear, vampire, wraith, diminishing darling, fetching duende, fading failing gone.

☽

On those nights when we all went to bed hungering for the many things we could never have or be, longing for the shapes we would never inhabit, Obie begged me to tell him the life story of God, the uncensored biography. He would keep his eyes peeled wide as he lay in his bed and refused to go to sleep until I did as he asked. Always relieved to have shrugged off the weight of another day and eager to float in the broth of darkness beneath my eyelids, I could never wait him out. His eyes shined even in the gloom of a new moon and would not be dimmed until I obliged. Obie was a master insomniac when he wanted to be, as sleep resistant as a pot of coffee.

When God was just a boy, I began, *Girl!* Obie insisted. I paused and looked at him, one eyebrow hitched reproachfully. There are certain particulars of the lore even I am not prepared to rewrite. *You want to tell the story?* I asked. Obie smiled. He was a golden retriever of a brother, pliant and yielding and eager to serve. *I can swap the hims and hers in my head*, he muttered. *Fine. When God was a boy, he wished to kill his mother and marry his father*, I said. *This sounds familiar*, said Obie, staring thoughtfully at the ceiling. *All true stories sound familiar*, I said. *One day, he saw his parents making waffles together in the kitchen, saw his father nuzzle his mother's ear as she poured the batter on the iron, and try as he might to be a loving and dutiful son, he could not help plotting his mother's murder, er, that is, envisioning her death. He imagined her wedging the heel of one of her tasteful, dyed-to-match pumps in the escalator at Macy's and being sucked through to the shredded oblivion beneath. He imagined her choking on a petit four at an Opti-Mrs. luncheon, with no one in sight undainty or impolite enough to perform the Heimlich. He imagined her drinking a heavily mickied aperitif as she spritzed herself with cyanide-laced Chanel No. 9, the smell of bitter almond faintly lingering in her boudoir.*

Then he'd have his father entirely to himself, and they could roughhouse in the living room, wear their Saturday clothes on Sunday, even grass-stain the knees of their trousers on that day of rest. They could ride the go-cart recklessly through the sleepy suburb in which they lived, rousing neglected dogs to action behind chain-link fences. And then God would kiss his father on his faintly five-o'clock-shadowed cheek and ask him to marry him. Who is God's father? Obie asked. *What's his name? God is God's father*, I said. *The fruit doesn't fall far from the tree*, said Obie. I nodded. Obie smiled and said, *God…is love.*

I nodded, *Exactly.*

God is the Father of Love, said Obie.

God is the Father of Everything, I said.

Star-nosed moles, said Obie.

Yes.

The hair that grows in the ears of old men?

I nodded.

Blood? Funnel cakes? The fears of small children?

I smiled.

Is God, asked Obie, *the Father of…Suffering?* Obie's eyes gaped wide as eggs, shined bright as the moon-to-come. *Father and Mother both,* I said. He turned to look at me and I felt the heat of his gaze on my cheeks. *And then God felt bad about his matricidal impulses and developed a conscience, assuring us of a world without hate or greed or war or fear?* asked Obie.

Oh no, I said, *that's the beauty of being God. You needn't ever feel guilt.*

Obie's brow buckled, and he frowned and harumphed and switched off his eyes.

EIGHT
DIE-O-RAMA

Once when I was a girl, one of my classmates invited me to a birthday celebration. Lynette Saunders had long, fine, silvery-blonde hair and eyelashes the color of moonlight that made her eyes, when she blinked, look like summer moths fluttering. Lynette herself was a smiling daisy, slender and sweet and sun-loving, a must for any cheerful floral arrangement. My mother loved her, and for Lynette's birthday, she tried to squeeze me into a sparrow-sized party dress, seams and zipper ruthlessly stretched, ruffles and bows aslant, making me look like a hastily-wrapped, disheveled present, tried, my mother did, eyebrows pinched together, lips gone prim with determination, to shoehorn my walrus flippers, like the most dogged footbinder, into moppet-proportioned Mary Janes, and it was then that she issued an exasperated groan, a hissing complaint about my body being a crime against nature, and that's how I began to think of my king-size carcass, as a crime someone had committed, a Class 1 felony, a crime I was determined to solve. And I thought that when I tracked down the fiendish brute who had corrupted my biology, I would bring him to justice myself, dangle him in the air by his scrawny neck from my king crab mitts and demand he confess his sins, beg for forgiveness, then I'd fling him into the next world and break the spell, immediately shrink to fit that girly frock, and my mother would love me and coddle me and wish me no harm. Thus began my fascination with crime and the ratiocination I hoped would give me the skinny on the world, my body.

So when I grew up (and up and up), I became a miniaturizer of crime scenes, an architect of dioramas that reproduce the site and aftermath of alleged villainy. I scrupulously replicate every observable detail in the hope that the scene will eventually sing, will divulge the exact nature of the misdeeds and the identity of the miscreant behind the treachery, and I'll figure out the question whose answer is the corpus delicti—*delectable dead* I once thought that meant, crime body, body of evidence, body that *is* evidence (body that is itself a crime)—clear as a scrying gypsy spies your prospects in a crystal ball. God may skulk imperceptibly in mystery, but the devil is in the details.

It started, as I said, when I was nine years old, the year the children began disappearing: *The Hidden Hoyden of Kingdom Come,* alliterated one early, hopeful headline in *The Kingdom Come Tiller and Toiler* (formerly *The Kingdom Come Harold,* founded in 1873 by one Harold Pertwee, a sawyer and salesman of tinware with a gift for gab and the only Kingdom Comer at the time free-spoken enough to editorialize in print). They're just naughty children, hidden in the nooks and thickets of Kingdom Come, like fairy-tale ragamuffins. They'd reappear when they tired of wandering through blackberry briars and had properly terrified the town and their parents, would show up ragged and thin with a tall tale about a piper or a witch or a wolf or a girl with silken tresses the length of the Mississippi.

With the help of Obie, who had perfect visual recall, and domestic skills my mother's doomed efforts to make me marriageable had equipped me with—I could crochet a pair of diminutive socks with the gnat-leg needles used by Belgian laceworkers—I began reconstructing and studying the bedrooms of the vanished children, and eventually I recognized in a drawing tacked to a wall of one of these rooms an old fort deep in the woods at which Locust Lane dead-ended. There was no suspicious figure prowling in the shadows of the drawing, but there was a pair of what looked like eyes resting on the branch of a tree, and I pointed this out to the police, led them to the spot, and there they discovered a pair of saddle shoes, sitting neatly, laces tied, at the foot of the fort, belonging to one Elise Dimbleby, the artist of the picture. Elise had disappeared two weeks before, and though nothing else of note, not even adult footprints, turned up in the woods, word got out about my involvement in this, the only clue in the case, and it was believed that looking through the eyes of a child, even an overdeveloped one far too generously proportioned to sit on a tuffet, might be just what was needed to apprehend the mystery that had seized our town by the gullet, so I was officially deputized when I was eleven, and Obie and I got our pictures in the newspaper. I sat on a chair with the model of Elise Dimbleby's bedroom in my lap, Obie standing beside me, small but sheathed in that messianic halation that always appeared around him when flashbulbs were used. Since I was clipped at the knees, the sense of scale in the photo was amiss, so I appeared slightly melon-headed but otherwise of reasonable height and girth, to my mother's delight. For a time, she carried a yellowing clipping in her wallet.

There's something about shrinking the world, and fixing it in time, that makes it seem all the more weather-wise and bloated with significance, filled with microscopic secrets it's not willing to readily reveal, but then I dissect the world, as gimlet-eyed as a spacious girl can be, in order to render it fit for mice, and when you turn that dwindled world about in your hands, you begin to see things, tiny things lying about waiting to be noticed, things that in their natural bulk you might never have found worthy of a second glance: you see there are fewer shell casings than bodies; you notice the slightly darker spots that are footprints concealed beneath a recent dusting of snow; you see the freshly baked peach cobbler cooling on the suicide's windowsill; you espy a deck of marked cards beneath a shortened table leg; you are taunted by the suspicious lividity of a tight-lipped corpse.

What nobody but Obie knew was that I was sometimes visited by Frances Glessner Lee, a self-made criminologist, the original brainbox behind the Nutshell Studies of Unexplained Death, miniature crime scenes still on display at the Medical Examiner's Office in Baltimore, Maryland, and the philanthropic bluestocking who endowed the Harvard Medical School with the first department of legal medicine in the United States, where she conducted seminars in the art of homicide investigation until her death. Though she died in

1962, when she appeared to me she was not a phantom ex-actly. She hobbled into my room with the help of two canes and on swollen pins whose circulation was clearly sluggish, no less so in death, swollen veins mapping a tartan weave across stout calves and ham hocks, still a most ample and dignified dowager. Surely, I thought, if she were returning from the dead, she'd be allowed to slip on a skin from more vital times—I had to believe there were a few advantages to resurrection—so her exact ontology and protoplasmatic composition were unclear to me, but her flesh was just as convincing and beset by infirmity as I imagined it must have been toward the end of her mortal days.

I was always a little nervous when Frances appeared, knowing my mother would not approve of the influence of another female body so abundantly fleshed and boldly jowled, a woman renowned for an avocation so unbecoming a Lady, though my mother would no doubt have relented once she learned Frances was related to New England old money, would probably have fallen all over herself currying favor, tracing for Frances her own blue blood branches of the family tree, only to learn Frances had long ago departed this earthly coil and so was really in no position to put in a good word for my mother with the DAR.

Frances first called on me when I was a child. I found her sitting at the end of my bed one afternoon, panting a bit from her journey, mopping her dewlaps with an embroidered handkerchief. "It doesn't get any easier," she wheezed, staring at the feet that bulged out of her peep-toe pumps. "Pity."

She told me I was her scion, and she was pleased to see me carrying on the work. "I'm delighted technological ad-vancements are making criminal shenanigans all the more difficult to get away with," she said, "but nothing beats the educated eye, not even a microscope. It's the well-trained peeper, after all, that knows what to slide beneath the lens in the first place." Her eyebrows arched jauntily and she lowered her chin and peered over her bifocals at me. She gave me tips on how to fashion a persuasive teddy bear from the furry buds of pussy willows and, should I ever need it, how to get the blood from a pricked thumb to splatter appropriately. She was the one who pointed me to the faint outline of eyes Cheshire-catting about in the tree of Elise Dimbleby's drawing.

Obie applauded excitedly when Frances came calling. She held him on her cushioned lap and told him the stories behind the scenes of greed and fury and craven disappointment she had so carefully built. She told him the tale of the woman who committed suicide in her kitchen one morning, paper stuffed around doors and windows, a cake on the table and laundry on the ironing board waiting to be pressed, the oven open, gas pouring from it, the woman dead on the floor in front of it, her skin a curious shade of pink. "What's wrong with that picture?" Frances asked him. "The cake!" Obie shouted. "The ironing board!" Frances smiled and ruffled his hair. "A dame on the way out doesn't stop to press her husband's trousers." Frances smiled with muted exuberance.

And that has become my specialty, suspicious suicides. I am called in to scarcely populated hamlets, backwater shantytowns, and former ag capitals throughout the plains states, Medicine Lodge, Ogallala, Tishomingo, places frozen in time and temperament, where the coroner is also the manager of the local bowling alley or the grain elevator, also a midwife or an undertaker, where toxicologists and serologists, were it ever to come to that (and it never would), have to be flown in, usually from parts of the country local folks perceive to be smug and uppity and are therefore loath to lean on for help, wary of becoming a yokel punch line to some twice-told murder-in-the-heartlands yarn. Local law enforcement is usually one-horse and cooperative, if vaguely disgruntled by the suggestion that I might see something they can't, and then there's the occasional ME/mortician, fearful of losing a sale in a slow death market, who will embalm the body before police have a chance to investigate the fishy circumstances surrounding its demise. It's usually the families of the victim that contact me, certain I'll see in the way the rope is wound round the rafter some clue that will exonerate their loved one from the charge of willfully snuffing out her own candle. And suicide's on the rise in the struggling, post-agricultural, foreclosed-upon flatlands. Homicide too.

NINE
THE HAZARD OF LOVE

As I walked into Vivica's surprisingly modest house, my skeptic's eyes switched on and I couldn't help but subtly canvass her digs, couldn't prevent myself from picturing her roost as a crime scene, bow-tied in yellow tape. My work re-creating the death throes of the unwilling dead has forever altered my first-time experience of rooms in this way, infected me with a sniffing suspicion, turned me into a lousy bloodhound that can't help but silently sleuth. There was an intricately patterned maroon and brown Turkish rug lying on the hardwood floor in the living room, and there I pictured a chalk outline tracing the memory of a sprawled stiff, or maybe the rug had been his final overcoat. Oriental carpets are good at concealing the stain of the body's spilt borscht. I imagined the vase of lilies on the kidney-shaped coffee table shattered on the floor, water pooling around the red shards of glass, the brash white tongues of the flowers seeming to lap it up, a farewell drink. An old black rotary phone sat on a phone table near the arched entryway between the living room and kitchen, and I pictured the thick, black artery of the cord neatly severed, another bleating stoolie silenced.

I sat down on her davenport, secondhand or hand-me-down, green velvet and gold brocade that had seen some wear, and I ordered my thoughts to give up their gumshoe warble. Vivica handed me a glass of red wine, which I also couldn't help sniffing on the sneak when she turned her head, but then I remembered that it was I who was the criminal here, and I sipped the wine remorsefully and tried to appear congenial and non-homicidal.

"What is it you'd like to know about my brother?" Vivica asked.

I shrugged, said, "He must have had his good points?"

A half grin crimped her lips and she stared at me beneath the razor's edge of her black bangs. The goatee was back, and she stroked it so fondly I thought her chin might begin to purr.

"A weakness for wounded birds, maybe?" She blinked. "Weekends spent making balloon animals in nursing homes?" Blink, blink. "Could sing a tender ballad…threw an unsluggable curveball…handsome penmanship?" I groped.

"I'm wondering why it is you're fishing for sterling qualities in the man you killed. Don't you find that a little…perverse?"

She had a point. Best not to cross a nearly nine-foot, bearded Nefertiti armed with logic, decked out in a bespoke suit and top-dollar tie, and wagging her polished wingtips at me. Why did I want to sleuth out the goodness I was convinced lay snoring somewhere in the moldering history of a mugger? Why did I want to think I'd knocked off, however unintentionally, a basically stand-up mensch, one who had, after all, called me names, held me at knife point, and shaken me down? I couldn't say.

There was a knock on the door, and Vivica Inez Planet, a VIP if ever I saw one, roused her regal and forbidding posterior and walked to the door. "I took the liberty of inviting one of Hazard's former...consorts," she said. She opened the door and a tiny woman with stringy straw-blonde hair entered, a shrimp even by pygmy standards, shorter than Jojo Fridel, a walking smidgen. This moll's face was lined and drawn, her skin sagged a little on her arms, weathered crepe, and she looked like a pale, dried root, forgotten parsnip left to wither, but I saw something in her eyes and the angle at which she held her head that suggested she was a good deal younger than her face let on. Bodies are like that sometimes, eager to show the advanced years they've not yet accumulated, happy to advertise that a harrowing life moves at a swifter clip than one of ease. Safe to say it was no silver-spoon-easy-street-life-of-Riley this twist had been living.

"This is Lucille, Hazard's last known...girlfriend," said Vivica.

Lucille narrowed her eyes and I held out my hand. She sat down in an armchair and was nearly swallowed in a single gulp by the flabby cushions.

"Pleased to meet you," I said and sat down. Lucille dislodged what appeared to be gum she had stashed behind a molar and began to chew, in lieu, it seemed, of a reply. She looked at Vivica, and I thought I noticed a stifled snarl twist

Lucille's lips and pass across her mummiform face. "Likewise," she finally said.

I wasn't sure if Vivica had outed me to her as the party responsible for Hazard's untimely, erm, hopping of the twig, and it wasn't clear to me what that might mean to Lucille, *former* inamorata, if Vivica had, so I figured I had nothing to lose in venturing a question or two. "You were a friend of Hazard's?" I began.

She couldn't suppress a snort and an exaggerated chomp on the gum, and then she said, "Yeah, we were cozy. For a time."

I looked at Vivica, who was doing her best to appear stonily impartial, the mere bearer of information.

"When did you last see him?" I asked.

Lucille crossed her sawed-off, dangling legs and said, "Ah, maybe couple months ago. He was at Milton's, shooting pool." For some reason, Vivica nodded.

I looked at Vivica sitting across from me, and even though, when standing, our eyes were level, I always had the feeling that she was looming over me, viewing me from a remote altitude, that she had figured out a way to turn her height and girth, her excess, to distinct advantage; she was Triton among the minnows, and she threw her amplitude around in such a way that she made the small fry of the world long to claim-stake an expansive chunk of space. I, on the other hand, had the broad but hunched shoulders of an apologetic Titan trying to skulk through the world unnoticed, just waiting for the day when she'd be trampled underfoot in an Olympian revolt and could give herself over to the big snooze.

Vivica offered Lucille some wine, and Lucille tossed it back in a hasty guzzle and asked Vivica to hit her again, holding out her glass like it was cocked and ready and she wouldn't hesitate to use it if necessary. Vivica looked at me with half an eyebrow raised. There was a code imparted by the movement of the waving flags of Vivica's eyebrows, a complicated semaphore, but I hadn't cracked it yet. She had a way of arching and furrowing them so that they bounced meaningfully, and I sometimes expected them to emit music, like a slow calliope.

"Did you have a good relationship?" I asked Lucille. I gathered from the way her gaze grazed the ceiling that she found this a dotty question. "I mean, well, that is, until you parted company?"

Vivica smiled and said, "Show her your arms."

Lucille reluctantly turned her arms over, and I saw on the slack frog belly of her inner forearms a random arrangement of fading brown circles. "He burned you?" I asked.

"Yeah, he roughed me up sometimes." Lucille shot a look at Vivica and rubbed her arms. Then she leaned toward me and said quietly, "But, you know, I asked him to. I kind of like being manhandled, you know? Lets me know I'm here and got enough in me to raise some hackles. It's the deep freeze I can't stand. Sometimes Hazard'd get in a funk, not say more'n two words for hours, and then he'd try to touch me all tender and get this look, like I was some baby seal he was saving from getting whacked upside the cantaloupe, but that just gave me the galloping jeebies, made me itch all over, and I'd hold out my arm to him and show him my fierce face 'til he came to." I tried to imagine what Lucille's fierce face might look like. Everything in Lucille's wrinkled biscuit was drawn downward, mouth and eyes and nose and cheeks, as though invisible strings attached to the skin were slowly tugging her face from her skull, permanent hangdog droop. Her face looked like a weather-beaten and sagging rock cliff that was threatening to slide southward into the sea at any moment. She could make a mopey, red-eyed hound in the deepest doldrums look jolly. She drained her wineglass and stole another glance at Vivica, who kept her eyes, flags at rest, trained on Lucille as she tipped her own glass to her lips.

Vivica thanked her for coming then all but booted her out the front door. I saw Lucille look in at me through the living room window before she left. Her lips lifted her cheeks into the faintest smile. I wondered what trauma or hardship had caused Lucille to hanker for torment and had indelibly etched itself in deep, doleful lines onto her face. There was another thing I'd never know for sure, another mystery whose solution I'd be left to infer from the broken candlesticks and bloody gloves and scattered shell casings; from recently baked pies left to cool on windowsills and carefully starched work shirts and trousers stacked on the ironing board; from lost buttons and cigarette butts and raveled threads; from parrots that scream and yodel the last thing they heard and dogs that hide under beds when they hear a particular man's voice; from sneakers sitting beneath a sign, tight-tongued and unwilling to spill; from the world's left-behind evidence of everyday treachery that always adds up to less than revelation, less than a hill of beans.

TEN
REIGNING PLANET

Hazard stood over Vivica as she reclined on the green
and white webbed mesh of the chaise longue, in her red bi-
kini top and a plaid, hip-slung scooter skirt, the collop of
flesh above the waistband white and silken as…a subterranean grub he made himself think. Two of the woven bands
across the chair were broken, and her butt sagged nearly to
the ground; the aluminum looked on the brink of buckling.
He stared at her navel and imagined getting sucked into the
swirling vortex that led inside Vivica's complicated body.
He'd slide into the dark, enchanted forest of organs inside
her, get lost in the viny overgrowth, the secret interior he suspected was really bionic, man-made and built to endure, and
he'd wash ashore the island of her electronic liver or scale
the craggy incline of her stainless steel vertebrae. His heart
hiccupped. He was as close to his sister as he ever wanted to

be. He knew if he were to get trapped in the vigorous quick-sand of Vivica, she'd never again let him escape. Even if he were to grab a drooping vine and pull himself free, slash and burn the whirring, motorized jungle burgeoning inside her, wreak havoc on her automated ecology, with a single booming exhalation she'd fell trees and throw boulders in his path, close off all exits, and set fire to the forest until host and hostage went down for the count together.

Vivica shielded the sun from her eyes with her hand and said, "What are *you* looking at, small fry?"

"Some blob that beached itself on our patio," he said.

"Jealous?" Vivica asked. "I could beach you too, min-now. Minnowette."

Hazard rolled his eyes.

"Plankton."

"Say, what are you punishing that chair for anyway, Orca? What'd it ever do to you?"

"You're pretty clever. For a gnome. Don't you have a lawn to decorate? A birdbath to befriend?"

Vivica sat up and sighed luxuriously. "Let's play Ancient Kingdom."

"I ain't fanning you with no fake palm leaf. And I ain't a slave building your dumb temple. I get to be king or forget it."

"I'm *always* king," Vivica said, squinting at Hazard.

Hazard shrugged. "Suit yourself."

Vivica scratched her belly and said, "That means we'll be married. If I'm queen consort." She stood and Hazard took a step back. She leaned near him and he raised a pro-tecting hand and turned his head. She pushed his hand away, turned his chin toward her, and kissed him on the lips.

"Cut it *out*," he said and spit the kiss on the ground, "pleh!"

"In ancient Egypt royal women sometimes married their brothers. Who were often retards," she said, smiling. "Or half brothers. That fits, since you're only half a human anyway." Hazard's face tightened. "Seems they were hard up for royal blood."

"Gross! Where'd you hear that load of malarkey? Brothers and sisters ain't allowed to get hitched. It's against the law! And the Bible! It'll wreck your kids—that's what the March of Dimes is all about Mrs. Zacharias is always collecting for—they come out with blue skin or an extra nose, a fishtail, something like that." Hazard's eyes traced a line around Vivica's body and widened.

"Shut up, shrimpboat. All right, but it's the queen who has all the power, Queen V you may call me. She's in charge of all military campaigns and the building of the city. You can collect taxes from the minions." Vivica walked out into the backyard and clapped her hands. "Pretend the lawn chair's a palanquin and bring it to me."

"A what-quin?"

"Just bring it here." Vivica exhaled the enervated sigh of a misunderstood sovereign.

"I told you, I ain't playing slave boy. Get your own palamino, horseface."

Vivica walked toward the privet that edged their backyard. She pulled a garland of honeysuckle from the bushes and wound it around her head and body. She dragged the lawn chair into the middle of the yard and sat down. She adjusted the back of the chair so that she could recline at a queenly angle.

Hazard swallowed an audible scoff. "I'll see if Clarence wants to come over. There's not much to this game without a few onions to boss around."

Vivica waved him away. She closed her eyes against the glare of the afternoon sun. Hazard imagined his sister's skin broiled by the sun, roasted red, Vivica a giant lobster that could snap his head off with her claws, that swaggered even on land. She'd waggle her eyes in his direction and a platoon of crustaceans would appear out of nowhere and clack-clack-clack shred him to ribbons. He went next door to look for Clarence.

Clarence was in the remedial class at school, talked with a lisp, and couldn't throw a ball straight if a week's worth of milk money depended on it, so he was almost always available.

Clarence's mother answered the door. "Hi, Mrs. Enloe. Can Clarence come out?"

Mrs. Enloe's face puckered in an accusatory grimace and she put her hands on her wide hips. A faint smell of chicken fat drifted out the door. "You be good to my Clarence, you hear?"

"Sure, Mrs. Enloe. Me and Vivica're just playing in the backyard. He's safe with us chickens." Hazard rounded his eyes, flattened his lips, and nodded, offering her the most blameless look he could muster. Even when he wasn't being heckled by other kids, Clarence always found a way to injure himself. Hazard's mother said he was accident prone, but Hazard believed there was more to it than that. Clarence could be sitting under a tree with ten other kids, and the hedge apple would wallop his head alone, as though he'd been surgically implanted at birth with a device that attracts harm, a Job transistor, thought Hazard. Injury just hunted Clarence down like a starving wolf tracks the last scrawny rabbit on the barren plains. Sometimes neighborhood kids invited him to play talismanically, a sacrifice, to ward off that poke in the eye someone invariably had to suffer.

Mrs. Enloe closed the screen door and turned back toward the kitchen. Seconds later, Clarence appeared, sporting a Speed Racer t-shirt.

"Cool shirt," Hazard said.

"Thpeed Wraither," Clarence said, smiling. Hazard winced and thought about all the superheroes, monsters, and boy adventurers whose names were a challenge for those poor mush-mouthed mooncalfs who were routinely beaten up at bus stops for speech impediments: Superman, Johnny Socko, Spiderman, Tarzan, Godzilla, Johnny Quest. He wondered if this were a cruel trick on the part of bitter, hardened, tough-guy writers who themselves had drowned their s's in saliva as children. Clarence pronounced his own name like a child missing his front teeth: Clarenth. Even simple sentences were full of hissing fists just waiting to give a sad sack like Clarence a sock in the puss.

"We're playing Ancient Kingdom. Want to come over?" Clarence nodded.

They crossed between the houses, and as Hazard opened the gate to the backyard, the sun dimmed his view, and he squeezed his eyes to slits. Hazard liked the way the world took on the appearance of a grainy movie when he squinted. He liked to pretend he was Hopalong Cassidy, fringed white chaps covering his horse-bowed legs, scouring the prairie for cow rustlers and horse thieves as the high noon sun shined upon him and shattered his tin star into a blinding meteor.

As he peered into the kingdom of the Planet backyard, he pretended he was a spy sent by the President to kill the evil Queen so that America could make the world safe again for democracy, which his teacher told his class was forever in jeopardy. He thought of his sister as a communist monarchy, double the trouble.

He slowly surveyed the lay of the land, then Clarence said, "What's that?" Hazard's hazy gaze drifted in the direction of Clarence's inquiring finger and lighted on a wavering figure that cast a lengthy shadow, Vivica he reckoned, who was standing near the giant oak in the corner of the yard, arms outstretched and face tilted toward the sun. He opened his eyes and heard himself gasp, took slow, stealthy spy steps toward her, and slowly her body, seeming to draw the sun's rays out of the air and into her flesh, appeared to him more clearly. Hazard's breathing quickened, became shallow, and he couldn't shake the feeling that he had in fact somehow fallen into the dark empire *inside* Vivica. Maybe it was a trick, maybe she'd fashioned her interior so that it would appear just like their backyard—he wasn't sure, she was wily—but he thought he must be looking at some secret internal organ, the one that gives girls their mysterious power, the one boys most long to glimpse, to touch, an organ in the shape of girls themselves, miniature facsimile, tucked inside them, the source of girl voodoo. As he got closer to Vivica, he heard her body buzzing, saw her skin busily shifting: she was lathered stem to stern with growling honeybees, arms and face and torso and legs throbbing with the golden bodies that seemed to pour from her ears and nose and mouth and navel, bees noisily achurn as though she were the very comb in which they brewed their nectar!

Clarence screamed and ran from the yard, slapping his cheeks and arms, and the bees began to lift and scatter, the pale flesh of Queen V emerging, then the bees swooped in an angry swath toward Hazard, who fell to his knees, covered his eyes, and begged his sister's hissing body for clemency.

ELEVEN
GODMINE

The night our neighbors' house was swallowed by the earth, we were coming home from the circus when it happened. Obie was in a solemn mood. He had hated the circus: the trained antics of the unicycling bears; the swayed backs of the horses that shivered beneath the caparisons and the capering feet of the gymnastic riders; the fat, apple-cheeked ringmaster whose plump buttocks strained the seams of his trousers and lifted his coattails limply in the air; the tigers forced onto small stools and two feet by a whip and a chair and a snarling, ill-tempered, mustachioed man. It was Obie who had begged our parents to take us to the circus, but he'd had the wrong idea. He'd imagined horses flying freely around the tent and aerialists brachiating wildly, swinging like monkeys from limb to limb of the towering tree holding up the big top. He'd thought bears were natural dancers and would invite audience members to waltz to calliope music and that the tigers would administrate, see that everything ran smoothly, take tickets, make popcorn, escort families to their seats. All the screaming children with gaping mouths stuffed with cotton candy and fists fat with peanuts made Obie cross. So a pall hung inside the Oldsmobile, and Obie sighed into his shoulder and snapped the car door ashtray, stuffed with gum wrappers, shut, open, shut, open, shut, as we returned home from Municipal Auditorium.

I was gently poking Obie in the ribs, trying to get him to crack a grin, when the street shuddered so forcefully the car jerkily careened off the road and into the grassy ditch. I was pressed against the door and Obie slid into me as though we were riding the Tilt-a-Whirl at the Horace Mann Elementary School carnival. We were all silent for a moment, listening to the ticking of the engine, and then my father checked to see that no one was hurt, got out of the car, and as I looked at Obie, I could see his eyes had brightened. Obie was always reassured to discover that nature is alive and angry and can rouse suddenly and take matters into its own hands. My mother leaned over the backseat, patted Obie on the knee, and told him to crouch on the floor of the car and cover his head. She looked at me, her indestructible daughter, regretfully and told me to do the same on the seat. My father got back in the car and said all he could see was some smoke up ahead. He thought perhaps there had been a small earthquake.

My mother gave him her severest look and said, "Kingdom Come's a fur piece from California, Frank."

Obie lifted his head and smiled at me. "There's that big fault line in Missouri," said my father, shrugging his shoulders, "I don't know."

Obie and I sat again on the backseat, my father started up the Olds, and we headed down Gibbs Road, just a few minutes from our house. As we got closer to where the smoke was, we could see people standing in the street. My father stopped the car, and he and Obie and I got out. People were standing around in pajamas and slippers, holding handkerchiefs to their mouths. Their white ankles glowed green in the moonlight. There was something not quite right about the houses on this street. We were several blocks from home, but Obie and I often rode our bikes this way to Shalinsky Drugs for Bazooka Bubble Gum, root beer barrels, wax lips. I pushed through the people and saw that the smoke and a fine gray powder were floating from out of a cavernous hole in the ground, and then I realized that the gap between houses was too wide and that inside the hole must be a house, a house that had stood on that spot for as long as I'd been alive and long before. I tried to recollect what the house had looked like and could see in my mind only a pot of geraniums on a brick porch and a purple Hawthorne bicycle with a banana seat and exaggerated sissy bar leaning on its kickstand in the front yard. My heart started to gurgle and stall as I thought about the child to whom that bike belonged flattened beneath the swallowed house, digested by the earth below. I walked toward the hole, and my father grabbed me by the shoulders and led me back to the car. "This is a dangerous area, Wallis," my father said. "Don't you and Obie ever play near here, you hear me?" My father's eyes looked a little wild as he spoke, like those of the tigers as they'd pawed at the prodding chairs, and my love for him at that moment made the fading white scars on the bottoms of my feet itch. He could see even I, with my boundlessly fleshed, ever-expanding body, was no match for the growling and ravenous earth.

When we got to the car, I looked across the street to the pasture that belonged to the farm where we bought sweet corn and tomatoes and squash and watermelon in the summer. Obie was cracking peanuts and feeding them to a horse, which gently plucked them from his palm with its rubbery lips. Obie scratched the horse's throat then crossed the street.

"Where'd that horse come from?" I asked.

He shrugged.

"All respectable horses are in bed at this hour."

"The ground opened its mouth and swallowed a house." I nodded. "Nobody was hurt," he whispered.

"How do you know that?"

He grinned the way a kid grins when he knows he has a better lunch in his sack than you do. Obie claimed dogs and horses, sometimes rabbits, were always offering him advice and the insider skinny (though housecats, he said, Siamese in particular, took pleasure in giving a sucker a bum steer), and, in fact, the information he received was reliable, like the time the Oliphants' schnauzer, Henry, told Obie we'd have a freak heat wave in October that would break all records and kill five people in Kingdom Come, the elderly, the asthmatic, the indigent, Mrs. Sinclair down the street, who ironed people's clothes for a living. I'd bet my life savings on any bad-odds, bound-for-the-glue-factory greyhound at the track, however dilapidated and down at the muzzle, if Obie said the local mutts had tipped him.

"The insomniac horse told you?" I whispered back.

Obie nodded. "The house was built on a mind shaft," he said. "It's a giant hole in the ground"—Obie offered me a conspiratorial cocking of an eyebrow—"where God stores her most destructive thoughts." He'd seen me digging yesterday in the backyard, in the dirt under the tulip tree, amidst the fallen petals. I had planted some milk teeth there years ago in the hope that they might one day grow into a mouth and the earth would finally hold forth, hurl a brickbat at we trampling humans for our many vices then tell us how to save it. This was at a time when we were collecting money at school to sponsor a hungry orphan and I could think of nothing else but the fact that somewhere in the world there would always be a multitude of children whose stomachs were filling up with the gnawing emptiness of persistent hunger. I wondered if the teeth were still there and had decided to check. I found no evidence of terra dentata, nothing but tree roots and grubs and blind beetles, bupkis.

As it turned out, the fallen house had in fact been built on an old mine shaft that was long ago closed up and covered over, ages before the area had seemed fit for development, and now the neighbors were nervous and taking long vacations as investigators from the Department of Health and Environment's Bureau of Environmental Remediation came out with expensive equipment to measure and calibrate and try to determine who else was in peril of being devoured by this pocket of famished Kansas. And it was likewise true that no one had been hurt. The house belonged to a family of five, the Milkowskis, and they'd also gone to the circus, had been watching clowns cavort as the ground began to twitch, slurped sno-cones as the first hairline fissure zagged across the earth beneath the foundation, idled in traffic when the land started the fateful gulp that would turn their family home to rubble. To this day, there is a sign on Gibbs Road that reads, *Undermined Area: Travel at Your Own Risk*, and it made Obie and I feel daring as we raced by the house on our way to Shalinsky Drugs, though the wise nag had assured Obie it was an isolated incident.

God, said Obie, knows better than to store all her thoughts in one place, and I believed at that moment Obie was himself a dowsing rod that could divine the divine, and I would soon come to regret, a regret so deep it would feel like I'd been clocked in the kidneys, that he was so wrong about me, his sister, whom he worshipped devoutly. I would forsake him, fail him, like all rotten gods, who necessarily fail the most ardent member of their flock, their own blood, as he hangs in tatters and keeps his bewildered heart from disappearing by dreaming of a different destiny beneath an exacting sun.

TWELVE
DIVINER OF
THE ELECTRONS

Today I'm riding on a city bus with Vivica (she parks where she pleases, and her van has been booted). She's taking me out of Kingdom Come and into the city, to the laboratory where she examines renegade cells under a million-dollar electron microscope that can magnify a dust particle—no, the dust a dust particle collects when it neglects its housekeeping—to the size of a Buick, and where she makes informed pronouncements about what their distorted shapes might mean. I think the news is rarely good, the cells of the hale and hardy never slapped on a slide for the scrutiny of expert oglers of the minute.

The bus is crowded in front and we stand hunched over in the aisle, stooped straphangers. There are seats in the rear, but Vivica refuses to sit in the back or on the margins of anything, buses, theatres, lecture halls, churches. The bus driver seems not to have accustomed himself to the brakes of this bus, so we lurch along and I feel wobbly (I'm a stalwart lubber, sure, but I can topple easy as any ninepin). I can see passengers wondering if we are creatures once thought to be extinct, now displaced in an unlikely habitat, pterodactyls balancing on a birch branch in a stiff breeze. The boy in front of me looks nervous and inches as close to the woman in front of him as he can, clearly fearful I might swoop in for the kill, mollusk-sized morsel that he is, might capsize and crush him if we take a curve. Vivica is wearing an A-line coat that bells out from her calves, with buttons big as a child's face, and she tightens her eyes to accusatory slits, glares at a thin man sitting in front of us, reading the newspaper. In the seat next to him sits a bag of groceries, but the space it occupies is only a fraction of Vivica's width. I can almost smell paper catching fire as Vivica's laser stare burns a hole in the back of the sports section. The man shifts in his seat and then gingerly periscopes his eyes over the top of the paper. "Oh, here," he says to Vivica and stands up, moves the groceries to the floor. "Take a load off, little, er, uh, lady." He chuckles nervously and licks his lips. Vivica gives him a dismissive quarter-smile and gracefully lunges into the seat as the bus driver taps the brakes. She jars the kid pecking at an electronic game next to her and he grumbles, gives her a glance, another, stands up, stares, grabs a pole, looks at me, looks back at Vivica, gape-mouthed, dangling the still-chirping game at his side.

"When are you due?" asks the man, pointing the now rolled-up newspaper in the direction of Vivica's belly. Before stepping onto the bus, Vivica had said to me, "Want to see me mump a seat without a word?" and she pushed her stomach forward and put her hands in the pockets of the tent-like coat.

"August," says Vivica, no mathematician: it is now September.

The man's forehead buckles in puzzlement and then he smiles and asks, "Your first?"

"That I know of," says Vivica, and the man nods then looks at me, rubs his chin. Vivica slips me an unsubtle smirk.

Suddenly, the man leans forward and places his hand on Vivica's stomach, right over one of the dessert-plate-sized buttons. "Quite a hot cross bun you got baking in there," he says, and his grin reveals badly capped teeth with a faint verdigris shimmer.

Vivica peels the man's hand from her stomach, leans forward, and looks into his hepatic eyes yellowing with disease or age or discolored from having borne unbearable witness. "Ivo?" she says.

The man straightens and takes a step back.

"Ivo Novak?"

He twists the newspaper in his hands with such nimble haste he seems a professional throttler of long throats, a strangler of geese perhaps. And he has this look in his eye, the glint of a sharpened blade catching the sun. I imagine him the official bare-handed hatchet man at a pâté de foie gras factory, picture geese weighted down with force-fattened livers thrashing him with the last-ditch thwack of a still-vital wing. I hadn't caught this look before in his cirrhotic headlights, when he gazed over the paper, but now I can see him in a living room with beaks and webbed feet strewn about decoratively. If he were to take up a life of homicidal serial crime, he would leave a feather in the mouth of every victim.

Sometimes I see the world limned in criminality when I look at it closely, the way a migraineur sees a halo around a lightbulb just before it shatters behind her eyes.

The man tilts his head back and looks down his nose. "I know you?" he asks.

"I interned at the ME's Office in Springfield ten years ago." The man stiffens and his face seems to visibly darken, thunderheads passing across it. "Got to see some of your handiwork firsthand, Ivo. The garrote has fallen out of favor as a murder weapon, wouldn't you say? It takes a sure-footed kind of dash seldom seen in today's psychopaths. Seems you were the last of a dying breed, old school. Now it's all guns and knives, the occasional poisoning, no panache. You sure had an eye for beautiful throats, though, didn't you, Ivo? The blush of imminent motherhood still visible in death."

"I ain't got clue one what you're talking about, lady," he says, and he looks around then bends to her ear. "But if I did know, what I'd recall is 'at that guy was acquitted, reasonable doubt and all, so if I was you, I'd be keeping my mind on junior here's well-bein'," he says, tapping a button, "instead of spinnin' beautiful theories about something you don't know the half of." My stomach began to pitch.

"Why pregnant women, Ivo? I always wanted to ask. Was it because with them you got a twofer? Twice the life extinguished with half the effort? Were you just being thrifty? I never bought any of that flapdoodle about you being traumatized as a boy by seeing your pregnant mother hump any slob that slouched in her direction. As though all mania can be traced to the moment when it dawns on the budding monster that Mommy has a use for her loins that has nothing to do with him. And when he finally gets the whole hideous story behind procreation, behind his own far-from-immaculate existence, this only adds insult to injury, the nauseating effrontery of it all! Mothers having casual sex, it's enough to make us all want to grab the first big-bellied offender we see and make her pay through the womb. No, you're not so textbook as all that, are you, Ivo? You're *complicated*." The man's hands are ink-blackened from continuing to twist his lifeless paper, and one corner of his mouth lifts in what seems to be a prideful sneer that can no longer hold itself back, a bull straining to get in the ring. I look at Vivica, whose implacable expression could cause a Kansas sun in August to ice over. I admit I smell skullduggery everywhere I sniff, but still I'm surprised to think I may have rightly pegged this particular odor. Sometimes I'm reassured to think we're all maniacs under the skin.

Just then there's a shriek from the back of the bus, and people begin to get up from their seats and back down the aisle. I turn around and see fluid on the black rubber of the aisle floor, see a woman standing with spread legs, blood dripping down her calves, chanting, "It's fine I'm fine it's fine everything's fine," and I think I understand what has happened, until the woman screams, "It's mine, give it!" and a baby begins to cry. With everyone pushing toward the front now, the bus driver gets rattled and hits the brakes, and all of us domino forward. I brace myself against the ceiling to avoid crushing the terrified boy in front of me, and then the fallen pick themselves up and look around, start to grumble in the direction of the driver. The bus is still and the doors are thrown open, though we're not at an official stop, and I see that the woman at the back is now on her knees. When she stands up, she is soaked and holding a bloody bundle, the umbilical cord lifting the front of her dress, and the people around her gasp and look away. She has frizzy brown hair and dark gibbous moons beneath her eyes, and a faraway expression that makes her look as though she has just wandered out of a dream. I try to ease toward the back of the bus through the tangle of passengers, but before I can get very far, the woman is moving down the steps of the rear exit, cradling the placenta in one arm and the baby in the other, and then she lopes along the sidewalk at a resolute clip, her head bent forward, as though she were trying to make a touchdown. Several people leap out the front and run after her, and when the bus finally begins to move again, slowly, roused from its stupor, I see that Ivo is gone. Vivica sits patting her stomach, eyes closed.

I think about that baby's introduction to the world, bouncing about on the filthy floor of a city bus, still a water breather, two giants and a possible butcher overseeing its birth, and I want to reach out and pluck it from the stem of its mother. She looked sleepily startled, as though she'd been ignoring the swell of her stomach, imagining it a tumor she didn't want to have diagnosed, a condition she thought might shrink and relent in time if she paid it no mind. That's how, I believe, my mother once thought of me. And then, against all sense of decorum, I metastasized into a girl, inoperable.

At the medical center, I follow Vivica down into the bowels of the building where the EM center is located. It's a Saturday, and except for the janitorial staff, few people are in the lab. We quietly descend the stairs, heads bent, on our way to eyeball cells and their nuclei, the atoms that accumulate into a human, and it feels like we are hierophants of the body, pilgrims in search of essence, God's ylem, the originating matter at the pinpoint center of us all. Vivica asked me if I wanted to see what it is to be human, if I had the stomach for it. She seems to have answers to all my questions. And as we pass through the door at the bottom of the stairs, I think of Obie, how he longed to look upon the omphalos and believed he'd found it in me. I still carry Obie inside me, a stone on my heart. I am leaden with sorrow.

We duck under the top of the door as we enter. In the room with the electron microscope, it is dark, no windows, little light, and there is the constant bubbling of water, cooling the vacuum pumps behind the scope, a large column that reaches from a panel of switches and dials to the ceiling, tungsten filament concealed at the top, waiting to emit electrons toward the lenses that will reveal a cell's essence. The gurgling sound of the water will accompany our descent into an uncharted, subcutaneous ocean, inside this submarine whose special X-ray periscope will reveal to us the very quiddity of our own matter, the heart that beats inside each atom, the blood inside the heart inside that heart. I try to think *small*.

Vivica returns from an adjoining room and hands me a mask and gloves and tells me not to touch the samples. I am surprised when she squeezes my hand tenderly, and then her smile disappears behind the gauze of her mask. She picks up with tweezers the tiniest circle of embedded, stained, and thinly sliced tissue, the size of a freckle, less than a micron thick she tells me, thin as the wing of a midge, thin as immanence. Vivica's hands are thick and broad as catchers' mitts, but she slides the specimen holder deftly into the throat of the microscope. I listen to the hum of electricity as it liberates the electrons from the wire.

"The wavelength of light is limiting," says Vivica. "The lower wavelength of electrons allows a resolution that enables us to see things that before were merely theory, appearing only in the dreams of madmen and visionaries." She laughs in her throat, and I can't tell if it's sincere or skeptical, a laugh of delight or derision. Vivica seems to me to occupy an emotional plane on which those things are not at all contradictory.

She adjusts a dial on the instrument panel and a picture appears on the screen in front of us. She looks at me and says, "There is nothing so lovely as the infinitesimal, isn't that right, Wallis Armstrong?" She points to the screen. "This is brain tissue."

"Whose brain is it?" I ask.

"I don't know," she says.

There are circles within circles, a moonscape, volcanic terrain. "Whoever he is, he's not long for this world," Vivica says. I am staring into the unblinking eye of a nucleolus, the body's most intimate interior. And despite my curiosity, I feel like the worst sort of trespasser, a desecrator of a sacred text, but I cannot look away. Perhaps I will pass this person on the street, this ailing human of whom I now have insider knowledge.

"This is a brain afflicted with Creutzfeld-Jakob disease," says Vivica.

"What's that?"

She points to hollow spaces between the cells. "There is vacuolization of the brain tissue," she says. She sees this means nothing to me. "The brain is turning to sponge. There is prion present here, a protein that cannot be broken down and digested by enzymes. It collects in the brain and gums it up. It makes the person belligerent or sad, makes him have seizures, makes it difficult to speak or eat or smile. It's what mad cow disease is a variant of. But this was inherited, not the result of a diseased T-bone consumed long ago. He's probably descended from a long line of brains that all eventually hardened and crumbled, brains that couldn't understand why the world had begun to seem so alien.

"But then, this is what it is to die. In this way, we're all eventually diseased, we're all eventually the brain's victim."

"There's no remedy," I ask, "no treatment?" She shakes her head. I mean no treatment for this ailing brain, but Vivica thinks I'm asking if there's a cure for being human.

Maybe I am. *This* is God, I'd like to tell Obie, the honeycombed brain of a dying man, cells gathered around nothing, waiting to disappear, God the empty space threatening to swallow the afflicted, a poisonous bite for which there is no antivenom. God is the stricken brain at last recognizing there is no place for it in this world ruled by a temporarily robust delusion. Obie would smile and kiss my cheek and tell me the advantage of being God is that you don't have to believe in God. It takes only one unswerving disciple. Obie tried to save us all from a world empty of auspicious mystery.

"You're thinking of your brother," says Vivica. I've not said a word to Vivica about Obie, and I look into her eyes and see nothing there I can make sense of. I feel a swallow stall in my throat. At this moment, I feel about Vivica the way I felt as a child when I'd wake from a dream into a brief amnesia, unable to recall where I was, who I was, unable to recognize the body too big to be child, too big to be girl, exceeding the confines of the twin bed, both terrified and relieved, thinking I'd fall back to sleep and awake into my real body, my real life.

Vivica loads another sample and cranks the magnification to 50,000. It's a sliver of kidney we're looking at, and on the screen appear circles and squiggles, worms resting on lily pads. We're looking inside the cytoplasm of a cell, Vivica tells me, inside the mitochondria, at cristae, the doodles inside the flaccid shape. Since every space can be infinitely halved, I can't help but wonder what we'd see if we groped farther yet inside these interiorities. Perhaps we'd find a weary woman sitting at a table, drinking a cup of tea in the dark, a woman waiting her whole life to be apprehended in this shadowy room. Every cell has a hostage.

"What will this person die of?" I ask Vivica.

"I don't know. I see no aberration," she says. I think of my own whopping cells, imagine one could see their nuclei without the aid of a microscope, could see the mutant code they carry inside them, a Russian doll of nested spheres that never get too small to be perceived by the naked eye no matter how many times you halve them, Zeno the archenemy of any creature who longs to be less than nothing.

"My father was one of the last Fuller Brush men in America," says Vivica suddenly, a confession. "Like Alfred Fuller himself, he genuinely believed in the product, and he scrubbed sinks, cleaned out radiators, bathed dirty babies, and dusted sconces with vigor and enthusiasm in households all across the Plains. But eventually people began to close their doors in his face before he even had a chance to show them his wares. The sun was setting on the door-to-door pitchman, and folks were afraid of being swindled by slick grifters. They didn't like neatly groomed men carrying suitcases standing in their living rooms, and they cared little about the quality horsehair they could get only from his brushes. Pretty soon, he switched to vacuum cleaners, Kirbys. People were covering their wood floors with wall-to-wall carpeting, and housewives desperate to be hygienic and wholesome were still willing to let a strange man in the door who claimed he could help them improve the cleanliness of their homes. In fact, seeing a man push a vacuum cleaner made them a little lightheaded, it made them blush. He dumped bags of dirt on their shag piles, their Axminster, their berber, Brussels weave, Wilton, their indoor/outdoor, their Oriental rugs, he ground in cinders, cigarette ashes, flour, and he sucked up every last speck of it with his top-model machine. 'Pay dirt' he called it. Women liked that there was finally a clean-shaven man who understood their plight, and my father was for a time as successful at selling vacuum cleaners as he'd been at hawking brushes, Salesman of the Year three years running. But even small-town people became fearful and stopped letting unbidden men into their houses, and as sales started to decline and money got tight, my brother Hazard became a handful. He got into fights at school, beat up kids at the bus stop for no good reason. My father became despondent. My mother seemed to get smaller. And one day my father up and left us. He disappeared for five months. He'd had problems with his teeth and when he finally came home, he could hardly eat and was always flush with fever. He had to have all his teeth extracted. He got a job managing the Myron Green's cafeteria, and he settled into it for a few years, but then Hazard started getting in worse trouble, petty theft, vandalism. Hazard began huffing glue and gasoline, and he'd come home wild and ranting, skinny as a soup bone and gray-faced. It broke my father's heart. When I was sixteen, he walked out the front door with his old Fuller Brush case under his arm. This is what love gets a good man."

I look at Vivica's illegible eyes floating above her mask, and I think if she were a veiled woman she would be pleased to drive admirers mad with her inviolate mystery. "I'm sorry," I say. I think of Hazard looking into those eyes and I wonder if he felt hopeless, or irrelevant. As if Vivica has looked right into my own spongy brain and seized my thoughts, she removes her mask and mine, takes off her gloves.

"This is the last sample," she says. On the monitor, elongate circles emerge, a field of protozoan shapes. All of the pictures we've seen appear on the phosphorous screen in gray shadings, making the interior of the body seem like a bland and sunless landscape. I try to conjure an image of the owner of these borrowed cells, and, hopefully, I picture them sitting outside at this moment, amidst poppies, brazen camellias, brilliant tree frogs the color of sunset, see them sitting beneath a flaming blue sky, sponging up light like enervated lizards.

"This is heart tissue," Vivica tells me. She points to round holes in the oblong islands. "This heart is black with corruption," she says. I think she is going to show me signs of arteriosclerosis or edema or the withered aftermath of infarction, but she puts her hand on my shoulder and says, "This is the heart of Hazard." At first, I misunderstand, think she's pinpointing for me at the cellular level the very hub of cardiac menace, and then I see in the faint upturn of the corners of her mouth that she is smiling at me.

"This is heart tissue from…this is your brother?"

"It's a rare opportunity," Vivica says, "to look into the very heart of iniquity, to see inside your sibling. There was an autopsy."

"But you knew how he died." I feel dizzy in this dark and

airless room. I think: at least now the question of atonement is settled.

"There were suspicious circumstances. We were entitled to have a look." This, I can now see, is the destiny of the reluctant giant: forever to be an unwilling accomplice. Simply because the body extends so far into the spaces and lives of others, it is inevitable that it will participate where it means not to, the giant's arms and legs lumbering tentacles stretching into windows and doors of houses it means never to visit, altering the course of things. The giant's body is a pituitary fairy tale whose cautionary moral can never be heeded because the body will have its want.

When I look into the heart of Hazard, what I see is sorrow and anger and grief, see this transported through the body, a vascular sadness, feeding it with every beat. I see myself, a miniaturized me, shrunk to the size of a Barbie doll, see me slipping beneath the merciless radar of the world into dim anonymity. I see Vivica's grin hanging in the air, her body too big to be perceived, requiring a special macroscope that can lasso an infinite expanse and map its shape, fix its contours. I see Obie sitting on a water lily a great distance away, swinging his feet, beckoning me to join him.

Once while playing City Dump, I dropped a Tonka truck on my big toe, and Obie and I observed it closely for days as a slow tide of blood washed beneath the nail and blackened it. The nail, now estranged from the toe it had armored, departed the flesh one evening in the bath, and it startled me when it beached itself on my belly, a snail-sized raft, no survivors. I fished it from the water, scraped away the rest of the blue-brown blood, set it on the edge of the tub, and forgot about it. I was more interested in the curdled flesh it had once protected. The next day, Obie pulled the nail out of his pocket and held it in his hand. "God is suffering," he said.

I said, "It didn't hurt so much." He smiled. Obie liked to think my body had endured great pain, that every day of my life was a matter of walking barefoot on hot coals, my head braced by icy winds that fell from heaven. "I thought God was love."

"Love is suffering," he said, nodding. Obie often nodded or shook his head after he spoke, agreeing or disagreeing with the things that came out of his mouth before he'd had a chance to think himself into silence like the rest of chicken-hearted humanity.

He placed the toenail on his tongue. Obie collected pieces of me and waited with open hands to catch each part my body shed. He collected cast-off bits of me in a cigar box under his bed like some boys collect baseball cards or objects from the world that catch their raven's eye: robin's egg, buckeye, shard of green glass, arrowhead. In his box, he had hair, teeth, scabs, dime-sized circles of brittle skin sloughed off from desiccated blisters, and now a toenail, sacred relics he would use to summon me when I was gone, done in by the faithless. Some people just couldn't believe in a soon-to-be-nine-foot girl, and who could blame them? On the top of his reliquary, he had redacted some letters from *Swisher Sweets* so that it now read _**WISH**_ **S_EE**__. Obie was a romantic of the highest order, as are all true paramours of God. Obie, having conferred on the subject with our neighbor Mary Alice McGuinness, said all believers, male and female, imagined themselves brides awaiting the union that will give their vain lives purpose. This longing lent their bodies a specific shape, a shape fitted to one of the world's many yawning cavities, the ones awaiting mass. He said after wedding God, one sleeps deeply and always finds blood on the bed sheets in the morning, a beautiful desecration hung on a line the next day as proof of virtue. Believers must always be willing to bleed.

☽

In ancient Greece, the Pythia was the woman trained to inhale and transmit the prophecies of Apollo through the oracle of Delphi. The Pythia sat on a tripod above the hissing cavern, and from this arose the *pneuma*, vapor of divine possession. Once there was a Pythia who was forced to prophesy on a day dark with portent, and as she entered the adyton, the forbidden area at the temple's core, she was immediately seized by a malevolent spirit. Although the Pythia was always given to gyrations and ululations before making her divine declarations, on this day it was clear she was in the grip of a fiendish force, and she wailed violently and then collapsed, frightening away the priests and auditors awaiting her wisdom. Days later she died. When men demand divination, women must be willing to look inside the growling heart of mantic sanctity, whatever the risk. Women, especially those whose appearance few find reassuring, must always be willing to expire.

Some millennia later, classicists went in search of this intoxicating gas but could find no evidence and wrote off these accounts to mystical bunkum. Until one day a team of archaeologists and geologists looked more closely at the oracle's inner sanctum and discovered fault lines running beneath it.

Another group of researchers had discovered that another temple devoted to animal sacrifice sat atop a vent through which toxic gases wafted. Even today, birds that fly into the temple and perch on the fence erected to keep humans out drop to their death when they fill their tiny lungs with the fumes. But at Delphi what they discovered was evidence in surrounding springs of methane, ethane, and ethylene gases, and a toxicologist was brought in, one who had worked with teenage huffers, who, like the Pythia, experienced a heady euphoria and sometimes visions of the world cracking open like an egg when they sniffed paint thinner, inhaled airplane glue. They saw the fate of the world and it made them laugh, it made them despair. Bored and hopeless teenagers hopped up on glue and jonesing for another snort were, it was clear, participating in a sacred rite that predated the whole notion of delinquency.

And here I am far in the future of antiquity, accidental haruspex, a million moons after the death of that Pythia, looking into the heart of a huffer for answers. A dead man, man I killed, a man whose sister has sampled his heart and smeared it on a slide. And what occurs to me is this: God, our Father, Almighty, He who art in heaven, God who giveth and taketh away, God whose movements are mysterious, who leadeth his flock beside still waters, restoreth our wandering souls, GodGodGod—it is God who was and is and shall be the original serial killer. I hear Obie sigh as I think this thought, and I can no longer call his tiny, perfect, placid face to mind.

THIRTEEN
DARREN CRENSHAW DISAPPEARS

When the children began disappearing from Kingdom Come, I was only a child myself. The second one, Darren Crenshaw, was my fourth-grade classmate. He brought a Super Ball to school every day and sent it ricocheting through the classroom whenever Mrs. Roach stepped out. Somehow, the ball always ended its erratic bouncing by beaning Ronnie Moody on his white-blond head, then falling, momentum suddenly spent, to the floor. Darren claimed Ronnie was a towheaded alien whose body could take the bounce out of rubber. Ronnie sat in front of Hampton Knight, who had transferred to Horace Mann from Muncie Elementary that year, the only black kid in class. He sat so still and quiet at his desk, he made Darren, who was edgy as a hyena on a good day, nervous, and we all knew it was really Hampton Darren was itching to dry gulch, but Hampton gave Darren the subtle stink eye as he wound up his pitch and the ball always dropped, sapped of its sting, at Hampton's feet. Darren also reminded me of a squirrel, darting everywhere he went, from classroom to cafeteria, from tetherball to four square, and he didn't talk so much as chatter shrilly. Ronnie Moody never said a word, but Mrs. Roach always gave Darren a preemptive click of the tongue before she left and an anticipatory scowl as she reentered the room. The amount of time Mrs. Roach spent in the bathroom was well-known among students, and this made her the fourth-grade teacher whose classroom third graders most longed to end up in, second only to Mr. Clark, who drew caricatures of the other teachers and sometimes even the principal on the blackboard and used Silly Putty and wax lips as teaching tools, but for some reason it seemed the most tightly wound junior hellhounds were invariably assigned to Mrs. Roach.

I sat at the front of the room, near the door, and once I caught Darren's ball mid-bounce and willed it to melt in my palm and ooze down my arm. I thought of it as a speeding bullet whose homicidal trajectory I'd nipped, saving the day. Darren had small, vestigial-looking eyes like a mole, and I often imagined him burrowing blindly in the soil, making trails in a garden, spitefully gnawing roots, leaving withered flowers and vegetables in his grubby wake. He narrowed his tiny oglers at me and said, "Hand it over, Wal*rus*." Since second grade, Darren had refused to play medicine ball if I was in the game, unable to dodge the cretin-seeking missiles I lobbed at him first chance I got, so it surprised me that a career yahoo like him couldn't figure out the inevitable outcome of his taunting, couldn't see I was going to peg him between his dandiprat peepers, boink. I looked at Ronnie

Moody, under whose desk the ball then rolled, and he just stared straight ahead at the vocabulary words on the dusty blackboard, *indictment, innocent, judgment, incarcerate,* but Hampton gave me the slightest nod, and Mrs. Roach glared as usual at Darren upon her return, causing his two-front-teethless gob to gape in silent outrage. Darren's lips were atwist for the rest of the afternoon as he puzzled over how he could snitch on me without implicating himself.

My next door neighbor, Mary Alice McGuinness, went to a school that enabled guilt-free bullyhood (not that bullies are self-reflective enough to feel bad about their merciless hectoring to begin with, but), an endless supply of get-out-of-the-slammer-free cards, where a backbiting bulldozer like Darren could toss tacks in the quiet kid's chair and then later sit in a box and, with muffled glee, tell the story of the many punctured bums for which he was responsible. Then he'd ask for forgiveness, and, voilà!, he was scoured of his sins and on his way, in search of the next unsuspecting rump roast he could toss in the crockpot. Mary Alice said Darren was a fallen angel, and my question was from which bitter-fruit-bearing tree had he fallen. The thought of a herd of overripe angels scurrying hither and thither and gabbling on for all eternity about Pete and Repeat sitting on a fence and then socking each other in the dimpled knee made me include that on my list of planets I wished never to visit.

Then one week Darren was absent four days in a row— and that's the thing about scoundrels and scallywags, they often have perfect attendance records, not wanting to miss any opportunity to jab an easy mark in the arm with the icepick point of a compass or throw a livid grasshopper in a timid girl's hair—and on the fourth day, a man came to the door of the classroom and asked to speak to Mrs. Roach. Darren's was the only empty desk in the room that day, and we all knew that a strange adult who shows up unexpectedly to a fourth-grade class, wearing a fedora tilted over his brow and smoking a cigarette *outside* the teacher's lounge, could only mean there was mystery afoot, the Mystery of the Ruined Record of Perfect Attendance of Darren Crenshaw. The man asked to speak to each of us, and one by one throughout the day we disappeared into the speech therapy trailer, where he conducted his investigation.

As I sat down at the table and looked at the pictures of illustrations of the proper positioning of the tongue in the mouth for fricatives, sibilants, plosives, I thought of all the stuttering and lisping that went on in this room, imagined mouths all around me rounded therapeutically. The cigarette was gone, but the man smelled smoky, like a fire someone had recently extinguished in a musty room. He smiled at me, and I could tell by the way his lips quivered slightly that smiling wasn't something they were accustomed to doing.

"I'm Detective Doolittle," he said. "What's your name?"

"Wallis Armstrong."

"*Wall*ace?" he asked, exaggerating the first syllable, as though he couldn't possibly have heard me right. Alice maybe, Aaaaalice, Phyllis, sure, Otis Callus Jealous Lettuce *Will*is but not Wallace, couldn't be Wallace. "Wallace? Your parents saddled you with a boy's name? Kind of sealed your doom, hunh?" Heh, heh, heh went his sneering yap.

"W-a-l-l-*i-s*," I said slowly. A heaving sigh was straining to escape my schnozzle. I scratched the nob of it, opened my mouth, and let the exasperation inaudibly deflate.

"What grade you in, Wal*lis?*" he asked, now accenting the second syllable of my name, making it even more ridiculous sounding, Wal*lis, all is amiss, kisskisskiss.* He tipped his hat back on his head so he could take in every inch of me.

"Fourth," I said. "I'm in Mrs. Roach's class."

"How old are you?"

My stomach tightened. "Nine," I said. "How old are you?"

"Big girl for your age, hunh?" He arched his tufted eyebrows at me, leaned back, and crossed his arms. I've never been good at buttoning my lip when I should, but I thought of Hampton and Ronnie and unfurled my features into the most inscrutable poker face I could muster and stared at the stubble that dotted the man's weak chin.

"I have some questions for you, Wallis, about a classmate of yours." He put on a serious look, a shape his face was clearly more comfortable assuming.

"Darren Crenshaw," I said.

"That's right. How'd you know I was going to ask you about Darren?"

"He's been gone all week."

"When did you last see him?"

"On Friday, in the bus room."

"What was he doing?" The detective scooted his chair in and put his crossed arms on the table.

I shrugged. "He was playing with a quarter. He balanced it on his elbow then straightened his arm and tried to catch it in the same hand. He kept missing. For a bully, Darren's not very agile," I said.

"Darren's a bully?"

I nodded.

"Guess he probably never targets you, hunh?" Again with the wobbly lips trying to teach themselves to grin believably. They settled into a half smirk. I blinked.

"Did he talk to anyone in the bus room?"

"He got the quarter from Kevin Coppenbarger."

"How well do you know Hampton Knight?" he asked.

I shrugged again. "He just came a few months ago. He's quiet."

"He didn't get along very well with Darren, did he?" He uncrossed his arms and clasped his hands, trying to make me crack.

"Darren's the kid that picks out the girl in a scooter skirt and then waits until she steps on the asphalt to trip her, so her knees'll bleed. He's the kid who tries to get you to drink a carton of milk he spit in. Darren Crenshaw gets along with no one," I said, "and that's the way he likes it."

Detective Doolittle stared at me, wondering about my body's errant chemistry, my overcooked glands, before he asked, "*You* ever have words with Darren?"

"Words?" I said. "Darren doesn't know any words I'd be interested in hearing."

The man sniffed and inched forward. "Did you ever argue? Maybe it made you mad that he was such a…bully." I knew well the swollen pause before a word that signaled skepticism. There was always a hitch in the rhythm of a sentence containing the words "little girl," when that sentence was about me. *My, what a…cute…little girl you have there. How old is that…little girl? Want some candy…little girl?* a sentence I'd never heard except in dreams. Men with criminal intentions didn't risk their selective depravity on a lumbering girl of puzzling dimensions.

As I realized that I'd become a suspect in the disappearance of Darren Crenshaw, I felt a fire crackling inside me, and I couldn't help it, I shoved the table and growled. I immediately swallowed the sound, afraid I might start barking, start howling on the spot, but I couldn't stop my eyes from leveling a poisonous squint at this man, this smug flatfoot and his oscillating kisser. Shouldn't he be talking to parents, especially the parents of…little girls, giving them tips on how to keep them from evaporating in the middle of the day? I could see in his absence Darren Crenshaw was going to become a celebrity, a legend, someone whose name would cause Kingdom Come to shudder and weep for years to come, and I suddenly had the startling wish to see him again, hear his high-pitched hooting, see him grab his budding crotch under his desk as he leered at me, grinning, rubbing the Super Ball in his pocket. What I didn't know then was that it was only the beginning, the first seat to empty at Horace Mann Elementary. What none of us knew then was that the legend of Darren Crenshaw would soon be eclipsed by disappearances to come.

FOURTEEN
DARREN CRENSHAW HAS A SISTER

That night at dinner, my mother talked about the PTA meeting that had been devoted to discussing Darren Crenshaw's disappearance. We had a hearty meal, the product of my mother's gratitude that tragedy had struck someone else: country fried steak, mashed potatoes and gravy, baby peas, Parker House rolls, and apple slump for dessert, and my mother heaped our plates with food, even mine, trying to weigh us down, keep us from drifting out the door, out of her life, into someone else's, someone who might not feed us at all. She was trying to keep her family from floating off to an irretrievable distance and to reassure herself that such things simply did not happen to people who ate lovingly prepared meals together every night. It was painful to love my mother, but I did so deeply at this moment, despite my certainty that I'd be back to skimpy K rations very soon.

Mrs. Crenshaw had been at the PTA meeting and weep-ily relayed the details of Darren's alleged abduction. Only upon hearing this did it really dawn on me that Darren Crenshaw had parents, a sister even! It had never occurred to me that there were people in the world who might love Darren, who did not see when they looked at him a bother-some squirrel they wanted to trap and release in a remote woodland area.

Obie passed his roll under the table, placed it on my knee, but I was kicking my feet and it slid from my leg and landed between my mother's green Evan Picone pumps. It took her a dainty forkful of peas and one of potatoes before she moved her feet enough to feel the roll, and I watched her face and could tell she was tapping it with her toe, trying dis-creetly to discern what it was. Then she bent and slipped an arm under the table and picked it up, and Obie and I were utterly flummoxed when she smiled at us before getting up to deposit it in the trash. Food smuggling usually carried with it a stiff sentence, a week's worth of chilly silence and a dinner menu filled, punitively, with organ meats, Brussels sprouts, rhubarb, and at night when she wound my limp locks around spongy pink rollers, she tautly yanked every handful of hair until my scalp smarted like it had been stung by a thousand bees. And I would lay my dead nettle head on the pillow and tighten my muscles so fiercely I was sure I'd be smaller in the morning, compact and lovely and able to slip slenderly into the organdy dresses and plaid jumpers and stirrup pants I'd never been runty enough to wear, clothes moldering in my mother's hope-against-hope chest, now dusty with dejection, relegated to the basement, rarely opened. But tonight she was smiling and spooning potatoes onto everyone's plate, so we knew Kingdom Come was in the grip of a serious mystery.

For a brief time after, my mother saw virtue in substantiality and before I left for school each morning, she'd zip up my coat and touch my cheek, just like any mother.

I decided I wanted to meet Darren Crenshaw's parents, his sister, to see the people who lived with him every day, maybe get a gander at the scene of the supposed crime. The interview with Detective Doolittle was gnawing at me, and I thought someone who had eaten taco crunch and red velvet cake across from Darren at the lunch table and had watched on the playground as he slung pebbles at sparrows (not a crack shot, fortunately) might be better equipped to sniff out his whereabouts and get to the bottom of his disappearance. The police and his parents believed he'd been abducted from his bedroom one afternoon (though they found the window in his room locked from the inside), but I thought it was more likely he'd just lost his acorns and gone AWOL, looking for a new community he could menace afresh. You could tell Ronnie Moody's long-suffering austerity was beginning to grate on Darren's nerves, and I knew his inability to get the goat of the black boy or giant girl made it difficult for him to look himself in the mirror in the morning. What kind of respectable heckler can't best a sow, can't toss a rasher of bacon like me into the pan?

Obie went with me, loyal deputy, and we were surprised to discover Darren lived on Maple, only five blocks from us, an easily bikeable distance, a street we passed on our way to Shalinsky's. I was also startled to see that his house looked very like my own, black shutters, chintz curtains in the windows, leaves arranged in neat piles in the yard, a sagging jack-o'-lantern on the porch. I didn't give Darren Crenshaw much thought away from school, but I confess that when I did, I pictured him curled up on a pile of half-eaten corn kernels in the hollow trunk of a large tree or coming home to an underground cave, where he harassed the bats, rousting them from their stalactite slumber with the poke of a sharpened stick.

His sister answered the door, older, maybe seventh grade, and she bore no resemblance to Darren—large brown eyes, braided blonde hair, strangely tranquil. I couldn't think of a single rodent she resembled. I told her I was sorry about her brother.

"I'm in his class at Horace Mann," I said. She didn't look surprised, didn't ask me if I'd been held back. I wanted to kiss her on her freckled forehead.

"Can we see his room?" asked Obie.

She blinked her reddened eyes at us. "Why?" she finally asked.

"Is that where he was?" Obie smiled tenderly. "My sister knows Darren," he said. "And she's smart. She finds things other people don't even know they've lost."

She stared at me a moment then let us in. "You have to be quiet," she said.

"We are," said Obie. "We're quiet people."

The house was dark and the air was thick with the sickly sweet odor of decaying floral arrangements. We walked through the living room and down a hallway past three closed doors. On one wall was a painting of a clipper ship and another of a covered bridge and between these was a family photo montage that featured pictures of Darren when he was younger. His eyes looked bigger in these pictures than

I remembered, and in one he was wearing a red and green bow tie that resembled holly, a red sweater vest, hair slicked back, and he was laughing, holding a candy cane only a few inches shorter than he was. Dapper Darren Crenshaw sporting a candy cane the size of a shepherd's hook, never in my wildest fantasy! I found it difficult to believe there was such a thing as Christmas where Darren came from. Already this visit was proving illuminating.

Darren's sister opened a door at the end of the hall, and we stepped in his room. "You can't stay long," she said, and she closed the door behind us.

I could hardly believe I was standing in Darren Crenshaw's bedroom, and it kind of gave me the collywobbles, but I thought of Hampton and Ronnie, who seemed to have grown even quieter in Darren's absence, the whole class had in fact, and I thought I'd better do what I could to find Darren before we all disappeared into the stunned silence that accompanies the guilt of a granted wish.

Obie said, "Look," and he closed the curtains and turned off the light. Above us, the solar system appeared, and mobiles of planets glowed and orbited eerily beneath the stars and arrested comets painted on the ceiling. I would never have guessed that Darren Crenshaw was a junior astronomer. He seemed so firmly lodged in Earth, subterranean even, far removed from the winking enigma that hung in the night sky. I tried to picture Darren lying on his bed, staring into these paper planets at night, wishing on the first sidereal sphere that caught his eye. How had this given him the idea to glue Katie Callahan's pigtails to his desk? Which planet's silvery shine persuaded him, on our Tuesday morning nature walk, to push Ronnie Moody into a patch of poison ivy? *"Toxicodendron radicans,"* said Mrs. Roach as she twisted Darren's ear.

"The fault, dear Wallis," said Obie, "lies not in our stars, but in ourselves." He held the star of his splayed hand to his heart and smiled.

Obie let in the light and the planets and stars returned to being painted shapes and cardboard cut-outs hung from wire hangers, and it became clear to me that too much illumination shrivels the imagination. I thought maybe this is what had gone wrong with Darren Crenshaw—he'd stared too long at the sun instead of the moon. In fact, now that I looked at it, I saw that the moon was the one planet absent from his cosmos. There was the sun, big as a beach ball and the faded orange of an apricot in this light, and the swirling blue-green of the Earth, but no moon to balance his bedroom sky, creating a cockeyed syzygy. In Darren's universe, night was always a moonless black, no tidal pull, no baying wolves.

His room was surprisingly Spartan and neat, with few books and toys on his rickety shelves, and smelled vaguely of cornflakes. His bed seemed so small, covered with a camouflage-colored bedspread, and there was a night table next to it, on which a lamp, an empty glass, and a water gun sat. Atop a small desk that stood in the corner was a shoebox full of multicolored Super Balls of varying sizes; trapped in the transparent rubber were swirls of color and glitter and bubbles. Obie opened the center drawer then looked at me with silent bewilderment. "Darren is not a believer," he said.

Inside the drawer were artifacts labeled with all my classmates' names. There was a barrette from Katie Callahan, an unsharpened Ticonderoga pencil from Sherman Anderson, a package of Juicy Fruit gum from Celia Lamas, a rabbit's foot keychain from Veronica Gilges, trophies from everyone in the class, mementos from the tormented. At the bottom of the display was my third-grade picture, clipped from last year's yearbook, my face barely visible beneath a forest of straight pins, makeshift voodoo, and next to that was a wide-toothed comb and a crude pencil drawing of Hampton, a black corona of real hair glued to the scalp, his mouth stoppered with a Super Ball, *x*'s for eyes, throat ending in a jagged gash, raining gray droplets of blood.

It was then that I began to think maybe Darren *had* been abducted, had been snatched just as he was hatching a hoodoo plot to incant some nine-year-old diablerie over the effigies of Hampton and me.

When Obie and I got home, I couldn't stop picturing Darren's room in my mind, and I got up in the middle of the night and began reconstructing it in miniature, fashioning the walls and floor, the desk and bed, from balsa wood, painting a fixed galaxy of tiny stars on the ceiling with a fine-haired rigger, bending wire into a lopsided orrery in a mutant sky free of the lunar pull. Despite my size, I've always had long but delicate digits, always been sylph-fingered and dexterous, can thread the tiniest needle without even looking, can weave a spindly forefinger and pollex through the most snarled knots until they fall free. It's the one feature of mine my mother clings to as a hopeful sign that I might one day wane into a more sensible physique, become *fine by degrees and beautifully less.*

In the morning I had a rough model of all I'd seen in Darren's room, including the secret vault of his desk drawer, and I was sure if I studied it long enough, in the details a map would form that would lead me to the whereabouts of Darren Crenshaw, and I could rescue him and perhaps reason him out of his Walpurgisnacht yearnings to purge the world of Wallis Armstrong, could save Mrs. Roach's fourth-grade class from the fate of being forever cursed by a boy whose irrational loathing had been suspended in time and space, sealed in a desk drawer. It would take me a while to get the details just right. I'd whittle a tiny pencil from wood, fashion wrapped sticks of gum from foil I'd carefully serrate with sharp stork-beaked scissors, porcupine a vague facsimile of my own shrunken face with bits of hair-thin wire. But as I thought about this, I realized there was one classmate not accounted for in Darren Crenshaw's contraband keepsake drawer: there was no filched trophy from Ronnie Moody, no marble or shoelace or pea shooter bearing his name. The boy Darren most loved to bully had been, suspiciously, spared. Did this mean Ronnie was last on Darren's list and would soon have been searching for a missing eraser, a believed-lost lunch ticket, were it not for the abduction? I stared at the half-pint planets and wondered where the moon had gone.

Before we went to sleep that night, Obie sat at the end of my bed and waited for the next installment of the God Chronicles.

Before God was a boy, I began, *he was an idea, a very good, if unoriginal, idea. Why didn't you start there,* asked Obie, *at the beginning? Who said this was the beginning?* I untied his sneakers and set them on the floor. *Chronology commits you to a straight line,* I said. *This story's ovoid, God the solid egg that came before the question. Whose idea was God?* he asked, flexing his toes. *God was God's idea of course,* I said.

God was motion and light, mass and energy and time, and he'd been waiting an eternity for someone to notice. Does the inertia of a body depend upon its energy content? God waited for someone to ask, his own body drained and wispy as a cirrus cloud in winter, enervated from all the molecular collisions that had gone unremarked. Finally someone did ask, a kindly pacifist from Ulm, and the air became suddenly ponderous with God's mass. Stars in thrall to the sun turned red as scalded skin, and when this wild-haired man who believed strongly in an ordered universe reached his own vexed perihelion, particles of God were split in two to create energy that reached back into myth and rent Adam himself, carving so many clefts in origin that it seemed the source of life was annihilation. As humanity applauded the invention of the means of its own ruin, a force so formidable gravity, posterity, and history could all be razed with the flick of a switch, the man felt wretched, and God watched as he grew increasingly quiet, sank into his dotage, a chastened genius. Unleashing the solution to the equation of God in mixed company had proven, you see, imprudent.

Does God play dice with the universe? asked Obie, slyly. *Only when odds are even,* I said. *God, the sorest of losers, plays to win.* And I put my hand over my brother's eyes until his body let go of the weight of being a boy and his breathing grew rhythmic.

FIFTEEN
VIVICA, OFF HER AXIS

When Vivica was a toddler, her father dandled her, his sizable first-born, on his knee, and she loved to nuzzle his neck and breathe in his smell, a manly bouquet equal parts Old Spice and Aqua Velva, Tres Flores brilliantine, cherry blend pipe tobacco, loved the chafe of his stubbled chin against her cheek, the feel of his large, clean hands, but by the age of three she had outgrown his lap, and later she could not bear to watch as her father instead cosseted Hazard, stole his nose and pinched his toes and tossed him into the air. Vivica could not recall ever having been lofted and caught by her father's precise and careful hands, whisked through the air like a bobbing horse on a carousel. Her father once ruptured a disk in his back when he lifted her to him and that had been the end of being hoisted to his hip. Yet she yearned to be held, stretched her arms to him, but he moved them down to her sides, instructing her how to be a proper soldier, and said, "You're a big girl now. Big girls can stand on their own two feet," and large feet they were, though at that moment she was technically still a tike. And Vivica had no recollection of her mother (who was, she later thought, little more than a glorified *pygmy*, a mere 4' 9" for the love of Gus!—where were *her* tempering genes when she'd needed them?) ever having held her in her arms or in the tiny teacup of her lap. And as for standing on two feet, her mother's were so small—more malformed hoof than foot—she couldn't imagine how a bipedal creature could possibly get around on them.

Once Hazard emptied his father's sample case of brushes and hid inside, and his father howled with laughter when Hazard leapt from the travel-worn valise. Vivica locked Hazard inside the next time he tried such a stunt, and she smacked the bulging leather with one of her father's stiff slippers until his sobbing turned to a faint whimper.

Vivica tried to love her brother, she really did: she tied his shoes, made him honey toast, wiped the blood from his knees when he fell, but when it became clear he was a stunted runt who would never reach half her size, she grew furious. She believed he willfully refused to grow as he should, just to make her seem all the more preposterous as she rambled around in the loose bag of her body. Once she asked Hazard if he wanted to play dungeon, and she tied his arms to the bedstead, sentencing him to the rack for insubordination to the queen, and she yanked him by the feet like he was so much taffy, trying to stretch him to her size, until he screamed in agony and their mother came and untied the bindings.

But the final betrayal was this:

One night Vivica awakes from a fitful half sleep. She has an algebra test in the morning and has been dreaming of droning and repetitive conversations in which she speaks urgently in quadratic equations and multinomials, to which the other figures in her dream invariably respond, "You're off your axis, Miss Planet," which is what her teacher, Mr. Waugh, who also teaches geometry and algebra II, loves to say to her when she gets an answer wrong. Hubert Waugh is a small man with one withered leg shorter than the other, victim of childhood polio, but he's ambidextrous, begins long equations on the blackboard with his left hand and passes the chalk to his right, constructing them in a single oceanic motion. Vivica's pre-test anxiety dreams often feature Mr. Waugh walking with hobbled dignity across the hilly terrain of her unconscious, which eventually reveals itself to be hill and dale of her own sprawling physique.

It is 3 a.m. and Vivica, who usually sinks quickly into a dead sleep no amount of clamor will stir her from until she's had a full nine hours, staggers out of her bed and into the hallway. She sees the bathroom door close; the faint glow of the nightlight slips through the crack at the bottom. She thinks it must be Hazard, who sleeps like a nervous rabbit, one eye peeled at all times for predators, and she decides she will spy on him through the keyhole—a vertically squinting eye-sized slot through which you can glimpse a body in the throes of ablution—to pay him back for all the peeping she knows he does when she's bathing. She has to get on her knees and awkwardly bend in order to line her eye up with the keyhole, and at first she can't quite register what she's seeing. And then the bathroom comes into focus, and she sees Hazard leaning against the sink in his striped pajama bottoms, shirtless, his chest and arms smooth and unmuscled, thin. What a puny excuse for a brother, she thinks. But there's someone else, someone's legs…there is her father facing him, in his terrycloth bathrobe, the same striped pajamas showing beneath, the tops of his slippered feet glowing a celery green in the dim light, and he's stroking Hazard's face with both hands, smoothing his cheeks with his thumbs, an oddly maternal gesture, as though he were wiping away tears, and he's smiling so tenderly. Vivica has never before seen such wistful affection cross her father's face. Hazard pulls cigarettes out of the pocket of his father's bathrobe and taps one out of the pack, holds it between his fingers. Then his father cups Hazard's face in his hands, pulls him to him, and bends to kiss him squarely on the lips, eyes closed, head gently swaying. Hazard stands dangling the cigarette from his fingers, and his eyes remain open, cast to the side. Their father releases his son's face, and Hazard pockets the pack of cigarettes. Then he presses Hazard to his chest and embraces him, strokes his head, says, "My boy, my boy," eyes again closed, kisses him on the top of the head, while Hazard stares empty-eyed at the door.

Vivica feels a sharp sound welling up inside her, something alive and on the scramble, moving up from her stomach into her chest, a low, thundering growl gaining speed, locomotive, now a high-pitched howl that burns her lips and bursts from her mouth with the intensity of water from a fire hose, and she yanks at the doorknob until the jamb splinters and the door breaks free. Her father and Hazard stand blinking at her in the weak light. Hazard starts to smile, and her father, slack-jawed, tightens the belt on his bathrobe, snaps his kisser closed, and pushes past her.

Hazard holds up the pack of cigarettes, grins widely, and says, "Guess who's Daddy's favorite?" Vivica knocks the cigarettes from his hand and seizes him by the throat, presses her thumbs into his windpipe. Hazard claws at her arms and then goes limp, his mouth working mechanically like that of a beached fish, and she pulls his head to her mouth, snarls, "He's *mine*."

A week later, Vivica watches as her father literally tiptoes out of the house, like a backwards thief fleeing the spoils, his old Fuller Brush case in tow. Despite Hazard's insistence that their father only ever asked him for kisses and hugs, claiming he just needed to coddle his own likeness, needed his genes to embrace him—this eros an updated version of the instructional manly love of the ancients—Vivica vows, as she watches her father creep toward his escape, that her brother. Shall never again. Know happiness.

Social Studies
Fifth Period
Mr. Groothius
Assignment 6: Letter to a Famous Historical Figure
by Vivica I. Planet

"His Majesty, Herself"

To Hatshepsut
New Kingdom
Eighteenth Dynasty
15th Century B.C.E.
Ancient Egypt

Dear King Hatshepsut, Former Dowager Queen, Vivifier of
Hearts, Wife of God, Divine Adoratrice of Amun, United with
Amun in the presence of Nobles, Matkaare, Truth is the Soul
of the Sun God, Esteemed Pharaoh,

I write to you from the future, a miserable place I am sure you
would find appalling. I live thousands of miles and years away
in U.S.A. Kansas, but here it is also the case that brothers and
sons routinely usurp the authority of mothers and sisters (dirty
rats requiring only one traitorous female dirty rat to proliferate
in any age). Your brother-husband was infirm and succumbed
to his sickly skin, so you escaped the fraternal scourge. For a
time. But then his son grew up and became a warrior, as sons
do, warring even against you.

I find your pharaonic beard very becoming and think you
made a handsome king, transformed on the tongue by a
masculine grammar, secret breasts hidden behind the crossed
arms carved in sandstone. The later defacement could hardly

depose you; the mangy world, and all its fleas, love to van-
quish a giant. Even without a nose, you look born to rule. To
the pyramid born. But, yes, your heir apparent stepson and
nephew, co-regent for a short stretch while a dawdling toddler, did eventually destroy evidence of your prosperous reign
(peaceable since the Hyksos, those rotten invaders, had been
run out of town on the hump-backed Zebu cattle and chariots
they rode in on)—was it out of hatred and jealousy because
you unexpectedly acceded to the throne and pronounced
yourself, unprecedented, Pharaoh, carved your rule in granite,
templed your reign grandly, and toppled history (becoming in
the process a man in a god's world)? That's what those early
plunderers decided, learned men of refinement (archaeological
gold diggers, grave robbers aswoon over the scrawny swan's
neck of Nefertiti, so envious of ancient ithyphallic kings,
drooling over their bower of spangled concubines). There
must have been a beef, they insisted. A boy would be incensed
to inherit a dynasty polluted by the governance of a woman,
a circus ruled by a bearded lady! A kingdom seized before his
majesty's voice dropped to an imperial timbre and the wool
of adolescence erupted in all those…unkingly places. But he
became a general of the army, a gifted combatant, and could
have easily defeated a girlish usurper had he wished. (Personally, I think any mutt who inherits the shopworn name of his
father and grandfather is bound to be congenitally befuddled
and therefore nothing but capital-*T* Trouble. "Hello, is Thutmose there?"—three heads turn at once.) Some think it wasn't
loathing for the wicked and scheming stepmother (that dod-
dering fairy tale, withered as a crone's puss) but simply that he
couldn't fully assert his own authority and claim his rightful
pedestal in history so long as his predecessor was a successful dame, ceremonial Vandyke or no (and there's nothing like
prosperity to convince a skeptical kingdom that the prosperer

has god's ear, to prove she's one of the elect among the elect, despite those damning breasts), so he had to erase the historical record. That happens. Of course, with the damnation of memory, without monuments and hieroglyphs, cartouches to document your reign on earth, your restless soul would no longer have netherworld refuge and you would be doomed to infinite death (an unending ending, unthinkable for a noble), so perhaps Thutmose III assassinated you, the King-Queen, posthumously, this your second death, extinguished your afterlife so he'd never again be asked by the gods to share the glory of a righteous history with you. And maybe he once watched you as you bathed aromatically beneath the myrrh trees and he burned with desire and couldn't look upon your divine features without feeling his heart tremble in his chest. You royals were always mixing it up with your own blood. I can understand why you wanted to protect the purity of the line, but what happened when the bloodline clabbered like cream left out in the desert sun, as it must have with your psoriatic brother-cum-husband? Those are genes best left to extinction. Some say the superintendent of the glorious buildings of the God Amun, name of Senenmut, your faithful architect and sidekick, was only that and your relationship was chaste as the unsunned snow that never fell upon your kingdom— you couldn't help but admire a man who knew how to build a stylish obelisk properly sheathed in glittering electrum, a man who could carve from the side of a mountain an eternity. Others say he was a man of easy virtue, your not-so-secret strumpet, a kept man worth keeping, as he took such an interest in the education of your daughter, Neferure. In any case your only child, though groomed to assume the beard, died while still in bloom—so it often is with celebrity maidens—so history enjoys the fruit of your greatness only once, you the originating olive tree from which no further fruit would flower.

I believe Senenmut loved and feared you as others loved and feared sun-eyed, moon-eyed, watchful, falcon-headed Horus, God of the Sky, son of Osiris, perching on the finger of the world. In you Senenmut had a god worth his trouble. But he, too, disappears, as every lonely goat does sooner or later, even you. (You, however, will be resurrected, like all drowsy gods, roused from your immortal slumber, with a face, it turns out, that resembles the trunk of a twisting tree, desiccated, contorted, sunken as a baked apple, but not entirely unglamorous, considering Time's vigilant gallop across it.)

You were thought to be small and slender, and I could overlook this shortcoming because at least your sphinxes were of a bulk more to my liking, but I am a little cross with you for not looking favorably upon Iti, Queen of Punt, with her ballooning steatopygic backside. That carving in your funerary temple reveals a gluteal marvel, buttocks trailing behind her like a wild boar charging, Iti always only one step ahead of being stampeded by her own caboose. Let he who scorns a bulbous haunch waste to shadow! And maybe if you'd had more flesh yourself, it wouldn't have been as easy to amputate your image from the public record, as though you were little more than a gangrenous leg poisoning the majestic groin and torso of Egypt, pah! Sometimes it is only the solidity of an immovable body that assures a girl longevity. Where would the moon be now if she'd fasted instead of gorged on light? Just something to think about. From the god-favored land of mysterious Punt, your inscrutable Eden, you imported some locals, enchanted dwarves who smelled of burnt cinnamon and sat atop young cheetahs that lazed about in the sun, dapperlings serving to illustrate, by contrast, a god's rightful proportions. Pygmies are indispensable to a rising girl, if only as a reminder of the squat ash heap she rose from. I believe my brother, hap-Hazard, must be descended of Puntites: he is a shrimp among shrimp (and I long to cover him in cocktail sauce whenever I see him curled on his bed).

Well, actually, the latest egyptological scuttlebutt is that they believe they have now at last uncovered your mummy banished to an unadorned nook of the necropolis, and it turns out you carted around no small satchel of flesh, were balding, plagued by bad teeth, diabetic, and had bones honeycombed with cancer, but perhaps ultimately died of an abscess, finally conquered by a tooth gone toxic. The offending molar, itself entombed in a small box and keeping company with your mummified viscera, that lone chomper was the key to the mystery of your shrunken whereabouts, and it is now, after countless centuries of exile, reunited with your royal mouth. Like all bodies, however blessed at birth, even yours was a palace determined to be a crumbling ruin. Your liver, however, dutiful filter, has lain in a canopic coffer faithfully by your side since it was forced to abdicate the aegis of your flesh (next to two shriveled geese, as though your aristocratic carcass had been powered by the flapping of birds). Surely the ramshackle citadel of your honest body is a more fitting container for a theanthropic minx who had already long ago turned the heads of fickle gods. What self-respecting sovereign is a willowy sylph, soulless and silken?! I like to think of you in toothless repose beneath the breeze of a palm branch, sistrum jingling, breasts lumpy and drooping as sacks of millet, flesh a bolt of loose and resplendent cloth bunched about you, a gnarled hand holding in your aching kidney. You couldn't remain that comely slip of a godgirl forever. I feel certain in your later years you were comforted by the sisterly singing of hippo-potami happily bathing.

Was it difficult being both God and God's wife? That must have made for an exhausting day. Did you suckle the world or had you a wet nurse to silence the squalling? This world is a colicky baby. I imagine being merely God was more agreeable. It always is.

There are those who believe you are the famous Pharaoh's daughter who fished a floating Moses from the Nile. If you did, I imagine you looked into his soon-to-be-bearded face and wondered what possible use you could have for an outcast infant prophet, and then, pragmatic girl that you were, you tossed him back in the drink.

I think you were right to birth yourself, you the only doula you could trust to properly swaddle your story. The gods spoke to you when you were snug in your mother's womb. Of course a queenly fetus is blessed with exceptional hearing, can hear the beginning and ending of time if she holds her breath and cups the dainty clamshells of her ears at just the right angle. And this is what they told you: that wily Amun, King of Gods, assumed the form of your father and awoke your mother from a stony sleep. He had the most delicious odor about him—he smelled of frankincense and cedar—and Ahmose, your mother, could not help but breathe him in—noses, weak creatures, are not built to withstand such temptation. She took him into her lungs, and he felt like the most nourishing meal inside her, and when she exhaled, he returned in the form of a beautiful hand with delicate fingers. Then he tapped her on her nose with his sacred ankh, and you were conceived, his seed immaculately lodged in Ahmose's nose. Then Khnum, the god who sculpts the bodies of human children, fashioned your irrepressible life force from his own saliva and Ahmose sneezed you into being. Amun said, "You're one of us now, dollface," and he welcomed you to the pantheon, where the other gods, single file, smiled grudgingly upon you. You left with a gilded prognosis.

And now here I am, Vivica Planet, three thousand-some-odd years your junior, no prospects for kinghood as yet. And I wonder what you would have done had you witnessed your father and brother in an amorous embrace you were always too large to inhabit. Nothing to do I suppose but become the brotherless, sonless, unfathered sovereign that you were destined to be.

SIXTEEN

FISHY FELO-DE-SE IN GOODLAND, KANSAS

Q. How did she do it?

A woman is found hanging from a ceiling beam in the center of a bare room in, say, a once stately Victorian, no chair or table kicked to the side, just a large puddle of what appears to be water below the body. Let's suppose the woman is wearing fur-lined boots, seamed stockings, and a tailored dress, navy blue dotted swiss. It's the middle of June, 19__, a warm Sunday evening, and we're somewhere in the rural Midwestern United States. There is one window in this empty room, open, a humid breeze fluttering the white eyelet curtains; the wind shimmers across a field of prairie grass outside. You can almost see the extinguished life smoldering in the waning light, a dusty radiance eddying around the woman's feet. She was perhaps...jilted by a man who had promised to marry her but who lit out one night months ago, with a gripsack full of his worldly belongings and an anxious look on his face that suggested he was not likely to be passing this way again soon, a footloose bindle stiff in the making. Or maybe the death of a child has made this woman's heart shrink and harden to a clinker inside her chest. Or it could be that this woman walked in on something that made her go blind at the sight of it, a betrayal, an act so unthinkable she couldn't figure a way to live in a world where such things were possible.

But I prefer to think that this woman was filled with vague, ineffable longings she didn't dare allow a distinct form, a shapeless ache that dogged her heels as she walked, briskly, trying to outpace it. When this woman was a girl, her mama told her she was a child given to excess and she needed to learn to rein in her heedless heart lest she become too vulnerable, a rabbit loping 'twixt bear traps. "Keep your heart hidden in here," said her mama, thumping her on the sternum. And the girl tried, but she grew bigger than the restraint her mother had taught her, busted out of it like the clothes she quickly outgrew, swaddled in the surfeit of her own expanding body. And now this room is heavy with the dead weight of inexpressible yearnings, and it snaps the noose, the woman falls to the floor, in the puddle of water, too late, the whites of her bulging eyes long reddened with hemorrhage.

A. A large block of ice.

A slow and deliberate way to leave this world, thoughtful, allowing time to examine the life being abandoned, time to reconsider, disentangle herself from the rope; the body temperature dropping while the room warmed around her, the chill penetrating the rubber bottom of her boots, burrowing through the fur lining, snaking up her silky calves, freezing her resolve; hours later, at the end, the toes stretching against the ice, holding the body up to the very last, leaving prints in the top of the ice until at last it slipped beneath their pointed reach, turned to water, and erased her final impression.

One of the macabre riddles making the rounds at Horace Mann Elementary just before Darren Crenshaw disappeared, a story I would now know to be somewhat suspicious of. Janes rarely zotz themselves by hanging, preferring what they imagine will be the pleasantly drugged drift into oblivion of pills or the amniotic comfort of slit wrists in a warm bath. Jaspers prefer the more dramatic and disfiguring sendoffs of guns and ropes. Both are equally drawn to carbon monoxide poisoning, happy to inhale the intoxicating fumes without having to worry about the brain cells they'll forfeit for the pleasure, reassured by the running motor that they're going somewhere.

I have been called to reproduce the scene of a hanging in godforsaken Goodland, at the western edge of Kansas, a town you pass through on your way to another landscape, another climate, at the end of a stretch so ruthlessly flat it's like traveling in a nightmare through a distance that can never be reduced no matter how many long-legged strides you take toward your destination, endlessly receding, so you finally stop short in exasperation, that's Goodland, Kansas, hot and humid in summer as a pot of boiling water, with granite skies and snow stacked to the eaves in winter sealing you inside your house for days, a place you can easily understand driving people to commit rash acts, off to investigate the suicide of a young woman whose mother suspects treachery. She'd gone missing a week ago and then turned up in a neighbor's barn, dangling by her neck from a rafter. She was engaged to marry the neighbors' son, and these families are the Capulets and Montagues every small flat town seems to breed, feuding over property lines, water rights, the true meteorological meaning of the groundhog's appearance in February, and lately wedding arrangements.

When I arrived, Eleanor Lehmkuhl lay on the barn floor of her future in-laws (a future now eternally deferred), arms folded peacefully across her abdomen, dressed in her nuptial glad rags, gauzy white wedding gown complete with veil, but wearing only one white satin pump, the other foot bare. As I walked around the barn, Mr. and Mrs. McCready stood close together, faces ashen with solemnity but still registering signs of surprise from their first gander at me. Their son William was not present. The local sheriff had been there that morning but had been called away before I arrived. Mr. Lehmkuhl stood at the barn door with eyes narrowed and trained on the McCreadys. The noose, expertly knotted, sat coiled next to the body, a charmed snake.

"Who took her down?" I asked. Mr. Lehmkuhl nodded in the direction of the McCreadys.

Mr. McCready twisted a cap in his hands, *Goodland Grain and Feed* stitched on the front, and said, "We thought it were unseemly to leave her…leave her hanging there." At this, Mr. Lehmkuhl snorted through his bushy white mustache. It was clear he'd already developed his own theory about the truth of his daughter's death.

"And the other shoe?" I asked.

"She had but the one when we found her." I looked at Mr. Lehmkuhl, whose mouth seemed to twist in the facial equivalent of an incredulous grunt, though it was hard to be certain what was going on beneath that mustache. But I could see in the weary sag of his leathery cheeks and the way his hands would occasionally lift and then seem to forget where they were headed, drop back to his sides, that Eleanor, whose belated birth I'd wager had not been planned, had given his life a distinct and unforeseen midlife purpose at the very moment he'd needed one, a renewed reason for seeing his life through to the end, a purpose I could see he was not likely to recover from the loss of. It was a purpose that would now be, his having never had the opportunity to walk his daughter down the aisle and pass her hand to the next provider, forever suspended. I always found myself thinking about the stifled, unforming futures I saw evaporating in the air around the recently dead. I wondered what it must have been like for Eleanor, always the tiniest in her class, being safeguarded from harm by strong men and watchful women. It's not that I yearn to swing from a rafter (though to be the sparrow-weight whose tension the beam would barely register, there's something in that), but only once to be truly imperiled. Of course it would always be impolite to envy a dead girl, so I kept quiet.

I lifted the veil and saw that there were indeed rope burns and bruising on the pale skin of Eleanor's throat, beneath a bridal string of oyster fruit (I haven't yet met the string of pearls that didn't itself long to throttle me, such necklaces typically designed for the tulip-throated), something borrowed perhaps. I lifted her head and felt the back of her neck. Her eyes were closed and despite the disfigurement wrought by strangulation, she had the clean, unblemished look of someone who might one day, suddenly, over night, turn out to be very beautiful but who tried not to put much stock in such a future herself. She was a wee hop-thumb in stature, five feet at the most and less than a hundred pounds. Depending on the length of the drop, it would have taken a while for her weight to asphyxiate her, time enough to think about the gravity of her choice, had it been her choice, before she lost consciousness. Her face didn't look to me reconciled to its end. I looked at Mr. Lehmkuhl, saw a faint resemblance in the angle of the cheekbones. He clasped his hands now and rested them on his belt buckle, lowered his head. I heard Mrs. McCready sniffle. Eleanor was coming out of rigor, and I lifted her arms, which were spotted red with small contusions beginning to blue.

Improvements in execution by hanging have been a matter of lengthening or shortening the drop. Short drop hanging strangled the condemned and was not instantaneous; body weight and struggle tightened the noose around the gasping throat, making this one occasion when it was an advantage to be a lummox. Then came the standard drop, four to six feet, which might or might not break the neck, depending on how burdened by body the rope was. The long drop, introduced in the late nineteenth century, was calculated by body weight and was meant to quickly and humanely crack the neck and sever the spinal cord, like a thumb to a toothpick, and do away with the tortured dangle that led to slow strangulation. Calculations were often imprecise, however, and in 1930 the head of Eva Dugan, the first and only woman ever executed in Arizona, was snapped free of her thick, matronly neck by a too forceful, bouncing jolt, a look of grudging agony twisting its features, and it rolled at the feet of the spectators, who were of course outraged by the

spectacle, having bargained, at most, for a little choking asphyxiation, not decapitation for heaven's sake! They gasped
and averted their eyes, mercy me, as her head wobbled toward the big sleep. Eva paid for her coffin by selling handkerchiefs she embroidered herself while in the slammer, daisies
and butterflies, roses and bluebirds, and she sewed herself
a beaded dress of silk, in which her body was later buried,
dressed to the nines in death. She was convicted of whacking a Tucson rancher for whom she'd briefly kept house and
whose shallow grave was discovered by a camper when he
hit something suspicious, clunk clunk, with a tent post. Eva
Dugan had been married five times, each husband mysteriously at large and therefore unavailable for comment. The
evidence against her was all circumstantial, but, well, it was
clear she was no harmless lambchop, a grandmotherly looking jailbird, sure, but a bim brimming with guilt if ever there
was one, more sinning than sinned against, you could see it
in the defiant set of her jaw. Nevertheless, no head has thudded across the floor of an Arizona state correctional facility
since.

I could imagine the cockeyed calculations that would determine the velocity of the drop for my condemned body—
whomp!—could see my head plucked so forcefully from its
stem it would sail into the air and disappear in the black
sky—sproing!—my conk launched into orbit, one of two
grinning moons hanging suddenly side by side, that walloping mazard finally weightless, never again falling to earth.

But here lay Eleanor, innocent Eleanor, spread out on the
floor of this barn in her wedding dress like a pressed carnation, tiny Eleanor who had made her father happy. Little Eleanor Lehmkuhl who had needed the protection of rugged men.

I held the rope in my hand and asked, "Would Eleanor know how to do this?" Mr. Lehmkuhl raised his head and shook it once.

"This rafter here?" I asked, pointing to the crossbeam directly above the body. Mr. McCready nodded. There was no remaining rope attached to the beam. "Did you cut her down?" Mr. McCready looked at Mrs. McCready and then said, "No, it was an easy knot, we just untied it."

"We?"

"William and me."

"An easy knot but strong enough to hold her?"

"She ain't but an itty bitty girl!" rasped Mrs. McCready, almost hissing, trying to burn me with the white-hot poker of her glare. *Not like* that *body*, she was thinking, *hobbled by any interior, body that would raze the barn*. I nodded and she looked away.

"What did she stand on?" I asked. I reached my arm up toward the rafter. The only ladder I could see was tilted against the hayloft, and I judged by the length of the rope that she would have needed to stand on something taller than me, something that would lift her ten feet. Jojo Fridel came to mind just then, and I wondered whose shoulders he was leaping from these days. He and Eleanor would have been able to fox-trot eye to eye.

Mr. and Mrs. McCready looked at each other then gave the barn a quick eyeing. "Well, I don't…I guess what she, I guess she got up to the rafter somehow then…then threw herself from it," said Mr. McCready. Mrs. McCready nodded. Mr. Lehmkuhl left the barn then and Mrs. McCready nearly leapt from her skin when the sound of his fist hitting the side of it shattered the Sunday afternoon quiet. "Excuse me," she said, steadying herself with her husband's arm, "I'm going to check on William," and she left the barn, cast a flat-faced glance at Mr. Lehmkuhl as she passed him, and walked toward the house. Franklin Lehmkuhl stepped back inside, and he suddenly threw his arm into the air as if to shield himself from a deluge, and as he did an owl fell from a rafter and screeched out the barn door over his ducked head. "Saw her fixing to swoop," said Mr. Lehmkuhl to me as I followed the owl with my eyes to the tree limb it would watch us from. He knew this owl, knew she had a nest here.

William, I was told, despondent over the loss of his betrothed, had locked himself in his bedroom upon discovering Eleanor's body, apparently after helping his father untie that rope. I was pretty sure Eleanor Lehmkuhl's neck was not broken. However she died, it wasn't by willfully pitching herself from a rafter of this barn like a melancholy aerialist taking her final dive. It was looking likely it was a plummet she had not consented to, some local Jack Ketch, King Charles II's happy and incompetent cracker of necks, in attendance.

I talked with Mr. McCready a bit more then asked if I could have some time alone in the barn to look around, take some notes. He glanced at the ceiling, the hayloft, the doors Mr. Lehmkuhl stood outside of, then gave me the once over, as though he were trying to gauge just what my body was capable of, what special powers my size lent me, what villainy such a lofted schnozzle could sniff out. He rubbed his whiskered jaw then nodded and left.

I examined the tools hanging on the wall, a harrow, a rusty scythe, a shovel, a harness and bridle and saddle, some rope, and then I took the ladder and leaned it against the wall of the barn where the guilty beam met the joist. I don't like wooden ladders—they remind me I am insupportable—but this was a sturdy oak one, and I clambered clumsily to the top, a bear scaling a sapling. I looked down the length of the rafter and saw what I figured I'd see: it was evenly covered with several years' accumulation of dust and dirt, undisturbed.

I decided to spend the night in Goodland and I headed over to the Super 8. When I went into the office to check in, the woman behind the counter sprang to her feet as though a siren had sounded. She kept her hands concealed, and I was afraid she might push a silent alarm if I moved any nearer to her, so I stood just inside the door until I could see her taut face go slack with understanding, and she said, "You here about the Lehmkuhl girl?"

"Yes," I said.

"Terrible business that," she said. "Just terrible, poor thing."

"Did you know Eleanor?"

She nodded. "Went to school with my Libby."

"Your daughter?"

She grinned and reached under the counter, pulled out a billfold, opened it to what appeared to be a high school senior portrait of a young woman, long blonde hair, freckled cheeks, head slightly turned, wearing a black V-neck sweater, a diamond- or rhinestone-studded heart threaded through a thin, silver chain dangling in her cleavage, posed against a cloudy gray background, smiling in a way that made me think she had been eager to leave her adolescence. "That's my Libby."

"She's very pretty," I said. Pretty was a word I almost never used and it felt strange in my mouth, slippery, like the first time you eat an oyster, and I swallowed.

"Oh, Libby was a looker all right," she said and she held the billfold in front of her, kissed her finger and touched it to the picture. "Did you come in on the interstate?"

"Yes," I said.

"That's where my Libby was killed, not far from here, be a year come December."

She smiled at the photo then put it back beneath the counter, and I began to wonder why Goodland, Kansas, seemed to be so hard on a girl, wondered if anyone got out of this clambake with a beating heart in tow. In a town this size, a town the natives were not inclined to leave though it was a town struggling to get by, the loss of two young women of marriageable age, in the same year, would be a blow felt by everyone.

"I'm sorry," I said.

"She drove an eighteen wheeler. Tiny thing like that, you should have seen her sitting up there in that cab behind that great big steering wheel. She was tall, like her dad, but always thin as a rail. I'm Norma," said the woman, and she held out her hand.

"Wallis," I replied. Her fingers were just beginning to twist and thicken with arthritis, and I liked the feel of her knotted joints in my hand, like a leather pouch of stones, substantial. She held fast to my grip and looked up into my face. "See, I can see a…sturdy gal like yourself maybe being suited to that line of work, if you don't mind my saying, but Libby was always a little slip of a thing, ate like a horse and never gained an ounce, but it made her mad, being so slight and all, seemed she always was finding ways to prove herself as strong and able as any fullback."

Norma slowly released my hand and let her eyes drift

and fill with memory. "You should have seen the turnout at her funeral!" She snapped her gaze back in my direction. "She was known all over the highways and interstates of the Midwest, and she worked hard to earn the respect of her fellow truckers. They gave her the cold shoulder at first, of course, p.o.'d at the thought of a woman horning in on men's work, they made obscene remarks about her right over the CB—she could have got them for sexual harassment—but they were just testing her. She didn't rise to the bait, and pretty soon they accepted her as one of them, and they all loved her, would have done anything for my Libby girl. You should have seen all those big old men crying into their beards at her funeral. That was a sight."

Norma crossed her arms, laid one hand against her chest, and a faint smile passed across her lips. I watched her eyes go in and out of focus as she looked at me then conjured the memory, and I thought that Norma had probably taken this job as a desk clerk not because she needed the work necessarily, but because the locals had wearied of hearing this story, and it was a story she was doomed to repeat until she figured out what it all meant, which of course she never would, and for this, passing strangers, people stopping for the night on their way to Denver, Kansas City, St. Louis, whose paths she'd not likely cross again, were the ideal audience.

I left Norma standing there, shaking her head slightly, eyes pinched together in a squint, as though she'd just recollected some incongruous detail that tilted her view of the world incomprehensibly, threw it plum off its axis.

The mind is a cruel resurrectionist. In memory loved ones die again and again and again. They live in dreams only to be executed upon waking.

Mr. and Mrs. Franklin Lehmkuhl of Goodland, Kansas,
kindly request your presence at the wedding of their daughter
Eleanor Renee Lehmkuhl to William Allen McCready, at the
Great Plains Lutheran Church of Goodland, 48th and Elm, four
o'clock p.m., on Saturday, June twenty-eight, where two souls
will be happily joined in holy matrimony, never to be sundered.
Reception following. RSVP Ursula Lehmkuhl,
890-9056.

William Allen McCready was your basic garden variety, corn-fed, all-state, high school hero, with hair and skin golden in the summer, teeth white as table sugar, and the sort of chiseled brawn that made even the most hardened high school iconoclast gasp admiringly upon seeing him at the public pool, and Eleanor Renee Lehmkuhl was his petite female complement, his better, lovelier half, said the people of Goodland, and together they were homecoming royalty, class officers, the in-crowd, the taste-makers, the envied and emulated, sweethearts since seventh grade.

But it seemed William had been given to tempestuous moods that only increased in stormy unpredictability after graduation from high school, and sometimes, in public places, he would suddenly erupt, molten vituperations pouring from his twisted mouth as he roared about who knows what (everyone did him the favor of not listening too closely, mortified for him), and he couldn't be budged from his commandeered pulpit (he was occasionally heard, despite the willful deafness of his fellow citizens, to admonish his generation for the "sins of the flesh" he believed they were so indulgent in—could it be that William McCready was a v-i-r-g-i-n? people secretly wondered, get *out!* what a thought, strapping lad like him!)

in the middle of, say, Wal-Mart, the greeter flummoxed and looking for back-up, until William's mother finally arrived on the scene and led him, spitting fury, back home. And everyone thought this might give Eleanor Lehmkuhl pause, thought she might begin, rightfully, looking around for a beau with a less seismic personality, Chance Patterson say, son of Silas Patterson, owner and operator of Homegrown Grain Co. Ltd. (which had succumbed recently to an unfortunate flour bomb, grain dust as combustible as kerosene, and so was struggling a bit but still a respectable family business and Chance in line to inherit it, not a bad-looking lad, despite that lazy eye), but Eleanor, loyal as the day is long and the night is dark, stuck by William (though she was known to slip outside to Lawn and Garden and browse among the mulch when he started his fulminating), and their decision to marry seemed to have a calming influence on him, to the great relief of the gentle citizens of Goodland, Kansas. Everyone said he'd always been a little high-strung and that settling down and feathering a nest with even-handed Eleanor was the best thing for him, Eleanor's placid influence a sedative for his nervous condition. But Eleanor, suicide! No one had seen that coming, no sir. If anyone's silo was full of molding grain it was William's, not Eleanor's, said the goodly Goodlanders.

And as I carefully peeled away the thin layer of Goodland decorum and suspicion of strangers (especially suspicion of towering interlopers like me, more body to keep a wide-open eye on), people began, timidly at first, to offer their own speculations about the mystery of Eleanor Lehmkuhl's suspicious death, her seeming to have Judased herself, though they were careful not to be too pointed in their conjecture, not to implicate anyone in particular in Eleanor's death. But what people seemed eager to reveal, what most got their lips to loosen and flap, was the subject of Alma McCready's "unnatural attachment" to her only son. They spoke of how she dandled him well beyond the acceptable cutoff for such mothering, how she coddled and cooed over him at church, after football games, at neighborhood cookouts, and how William seemed strangely powerless to object to her attentions, even as a brooding teen, and it was clear that the people of Goodland, like the sober folk of Kingdom Come, frowned on outward shows of affection, except of course toward babies and small dogs. (The dogs of Goodland, like those of Kingdom Come, had the telltale languid gait and thickened torsos characteristic of recipients of redirected adoration.) It was this, they believed, that had driven William to his public raving, though his mother, they said, was never directly featured in his rants, as far as they knew, they hadn't listened closely of course.

My mother, no natural coddler, insisted I play with dolls. She filled my room with Barbie and Ken, Skipper and Francie, Betsy Wetsy, Chatty Kathy, the well-preserved dolls of her own girlhood. She had wrapped them in tissue paper and stored them in boxes until that day when she could hand them down to her own darling poppet. She was passing on the mantle of femininity, Barbie's waist the size of a grommet and feet permanently arched and aching for spike heels, and trying to plant the seed of maternity, the dolls themselves demanding to be changed or fed or dressed, my mother fearful that in addition to having given birth to an…amplitudinous girlchild, she might also have spawned that most grievous of all contradictions: a tomboy. And, to make my mother happy, I dutifully arranged the dolls around their tiny doll tables and served them invisible tea in diminutive cups; I pushed them around the room (with my foot if she wasn't watching) in their pint-sized perambulators; I pretended to cook a plastic roast and plastic vegetables, bake plastic chocolate cake, then…send them to bed without dinner, turn a frosty shoulder to them as long as I could, fantasized about gouging their perfect and lovable features with my ruthlessly sharpened Ticonderoga #2, its handsome green ferrule glinting in the light with each jab, sentenced them to the dungeon of my closet, tried to suffocate them with dirty laundry…until I heard my mother's footsteps and I'd quickly tuck them in their beds, another day of miniature domesticity behind me.

But plastic, rubber, ceramic, wooden likenesses of babies and shrunken grown-ups always gave me the jumpin' jeebies, and it was precisely their stiff and lifeless limbs (bendable-leg Barbie, helpless to contort on her own, was hardly an improvement), their stationary goggle-eyed stare, their persuasive imitation of the dead that made me want to bury them rather than feed them. And so the first time I placed a doll prostrate on her bedroom floor, head at an unnatural angle, blood dribbling from the pinpoint nostrils, I felt I'd discovered the vocation to which dolls were ideally suited, and it seemed to me that they too appeared finally, stiffly at ease in their death poses, released at last from the mummery.

I returned home and began to build the scene of Eleanor Lehmkuhl's penultimate repose, not of the alleged hanging but of the body as I had seen it, relieved of the shape of its fate, whatever it had been, arranged on the floor of the barn, arms folded, the McCreadys to one side, Franklin Lehmkuhl at the door, and what stuck in my craw the most about it was that missing shoe. Had she been running from someone, toward something, and lost it? Wouldn't she have kicked the other off as well? It was a five-inch heel, and the bob and weave of walking on that single blade would have made even the most graceful of gams wobble and pitch. Or had it perhaps been taken from her? Had it fallen off as she was carried into the barn? A search of the grounds had not turned it up. I imagined William McCready, locked in his room, hugging it to his chest, whimpering incomprehensibly, eulogizing the foot that had filled it.

I thought about Norma and how having the answers to the practical questions of who and how and when had not kept her mind from spinning on its axle as she pondered the why of it all, and that's just the thing I'm all too aware of not being able to provide, even when the mystery dissolves into certainty. I inch piecemeal toward the unknowable, the irrational, the senseless, one clue at a time, but ultimately it's like that drive into Goodland, an unreachable destination, receding with every mile, so you throw up your hands, stop where you are in resignation, and it's that defeat that becomes both the place you've come from and the place you're going to, a shadowy endpoint of innuendo and allegation, a place of no answers. *This* is God, I would say to Obie, and he would nod and smile, solaced by the belief that this throwing up of hands is not capitulation but the closest we can get to being God ourselves: intrigued by the possibilities uncertainty opens up, happy not to know, embracing the hugger-mugger. God, said Obie, is less knowledge than buoyancy in the acquiescence to its inevitable absence.

SEVENTEEN
COUVADE

On the day Obie disappeared, the last child to go missing from Kingdom Come, Kansas, I came home from school in a prickly humor. I had gotten my period while playing basketball in PE, felt the blood spurt as I sprang for a jump shot, launched myself forward and upward, into the stratosphere of the gymnasium, looked down at the shrinking hoop like Buzz Aldrin bidding farewell to a diminishing Earth he could eclipse with his thumb, then I descended toward the backboard, felt the moist warmth ooze between my legs, and, slam-dunk!, back to solid ground and the slack-jawed stares of my peers. I took it on the heel and toe to the locker room, but the blood had already begun to soak through to my shorts. The thought of the tidal gush between my legs made my classmates cut me a wide berth the rest of the day, and when I prepared to leave, I discovered someone had left a papier-mâché sanitary napkin the size of a sack of flour in front of my locker, the red paint of menstrual gore glopped in the middle, Mrs. Snowbarger's art class finally put to practical use, no greater creative motivation in junior high than ridicule.

When Obie got home, he asked, "Did God have a good day at school?"

"God...zilla," I said through gritted teeth, "bled all over the girl's locker room and was the object of school scorn." Obie beamed beatifically with understanding. It was impossible to scandalize him with harrowing tales of the misshapen body, its latest betrayal. "And now God has cramps and is comforting herself with thoughts of Job-like recompense for the faithless, those sneering ne'er-do-wells at John Dewey Junior High." Obie nodded, as though he understood perfectly the burden of being capacious.

And then into my oversized bean flew this thought: *No... more, no more.* I looked into Obie's adoring eyes and had the sudden and startling desire to savage him, open his arteries until he was exsanguinated, bled dry of his devotion. I was tired to the mortal bone of trying to be worthy of Obie's boundless love, and, in a fit of pique I couldn't bridle, I spat at him the thought that had been quietly festering in my mind for years: "If I truly believed I were God," I said, "the only honorable thing to do would be to kill myself and save the world the trouble." Obie shook his head mournfully, and he took my hand, mindful that in this world there is no greater, more expansive sorrow than that born of the suffering of a supreme being, but I was not reassured by his touch and I let myself for once feel just how weary I was of having his worshipful gaze trained on me, how fed up with being buffeted between my brother's need to hold me aloft on a celestial pedestal, to worship at my epic feet, and my mother's desire to erase my enveloping body, to wipe the very DNA of me from the genetic map. So I pulled away from him, felt a flood of fury wash over me and drown the good and godly Wallis, tore off my t-shirt, and roared, "See! Here is my body!" I was surprised and perhaps both elated and saddened to see Obie finally back away from me, and I couldn't stop myself. I bit into my forearm with such vigor my own lips were wet with blood when I opened my arms to him. "Here is my blood!" I bellowed, gargantuan banshee released at last, chimera both animal and illusion, my own hypostatic union. "Take, eat, this is my body which was broken for *you*!" I bit into my lip, goading Obie to begin the final feast of my flesh with the appetizer of my yowling mouth, initiating the Eucharist myself, self-cannibalizing and irredeemable redeemer. And then I looked into Obie's face, so stunned he seemed absent of features, gone blank with disbelief, the vacant moon of his sweet mug, a lunar eclipse. "This…do in remembrance…" I whispered, "of me," expunging myself with each word.

☾

Obie had lately befriended an elderly couple who moved in to the house across the street formerly occupied by Twyla Neely and her boyfriend Leo, a house heavily trafficked by pale and slouching people, with matted hair and torn flannel shirts, who flicked cigarettes into the neighbors' yards before entering the house, people who drove up in rusting Camaros and GTOs, sometimes Pintos, "Never the same car twice," observed my mother from behind heavy curtains, just part of her Amway clientele insisted Twyla when people started to sniff. Twyla and Leo broke their lease and jumped ship when Elbert Crozier started parking his Crown Vic cruiser overnight in his driveway, making a visible dent in Twyla's Amway business. Then, to the neighborhood's collective relief, a clean and placid pair of hardy, apple-cheeked octogenarians moved in, brother and sister, Akulina Bogoroditsa and Nikolai Agnez Ovinko, hailing, exotically, from Irkutsk or Kamchatka or Omsk (*If you don't* _____: "eat your asparagus," "dry the dishes," "roll up your hair," *we're going to ship you off to Siberia*, threatened my mother throughout my childhood, a Cold War warning she relished making as she rarely had the opportunity to so spook such obedient offspring), some iced-over, inherited exile they were rescued from as children, years after the revolution, by an American immigrant relation in Chicago, Obie informed me, reviled sectarian hangers-on splintered from the Russian Orthodox Church, Skoptsy siblings, those Raskolniks. Obie could get the lowdown on anyone, however clam-mouthed and persecuted. And here's the yarn they spun for him:

The earth was a bloody baby, deformed, never meant to be carried to term. But it dropped from God's loins prematurely, while He was deep in sleep, having retired to His celestial hibernaculum, a winter slumber (heaven's blizzards could be especially cruel). It lodged itself in the viscous ether of a blooming universe, and there was nothing to do then but populate it. He shook the milk from His swollen paps and soon a garden grew, wild with frosted foliage.

Adam and Eva rose from the raw, red earth like a vapor, a drizzly, uncertain mist drifting lazily along the Volga, with no ambition to coalesce into matter. "You are immaterial," said God, "flesh the invention of Diavol, the old Menshevik! But beware the temptation of yabloko," boomed God. "Anything red and round, hanging like a promise from a branch, can only ripen and fall, and it will take you with it!" Adam and Eva were ecstatic to be beautiful and weightless, unburdened by anything so unpredictable as legs, intestines, teeth, things they knew nothing of but sensed they were better off without. And as they floated over the frozen garden, white and lovely and stalled, they agreed that snow, like God, is love, straight from the arctic heart of Him.

As the first night began to fall on the sparkling taiga, Adam and Eva found themselves in a dense stand of hemlock, which began to whistle as they passed through the branches sagging beneath the weight of winter, and eventually they saw smoke and they drifted toward it, careful not to commingle their own diaphanous ectoplasm with the souls of burning conifers, the air sticky with resin, and they arrived at a hut that, at their approach, lifted itself up on the legs of an animal...an animal? Why yes, a chicken! Surrounding the awakened shanty was a fence of braided bones, an ossuary of those yet to be born, and Adam and Eva twined themselves yearningly, wispily, around them, but the bones remained unfleshed.

And then, there She was at the door, Baba Yaga Boney Legs, thin as a phantom, with a nose long and curved like a quarter moon, like a sickle! Cunning crone of the imagination, she hobbled over to Adam and Eva and passed a gnarled hand through them, smiled as it returned to her empty. Adam and Eva felt their hearts flutter, but, happily bloodless, they had only the inklings of vital organs, a bodily blueprint at the ready in case they should fall, be sentenced to transitory flesh. And then Baba Yaga drew a circle in the snow with the heavy black shoe mooring her shriveled shank to the ground, and from this circle a tree, different from those in the forest, pushed through the crust of snow and rose up, and on the tree hung a single red bauble glistening delectably in the light of the swollen moon. Adam immediately recognized the apple as the very fruit of God's warning, and he wafted back toward the fence. Eva too was startled, but she couldn't help orbiting the apple, seeking evidence of its menacing power.

Baba Yaga Boney Legs grinned wide as the Siberian sky, and her snaggletoothed smile pushed her cheeks into her tiny, glittering eyes the color of herring until her face was all jubilant wrinkle. Baba Yaga again passed her hand through Eva, cutting her in two like a magician, and Eva shuddered with the intimation of a coming pleasure.

"I know what He says," said Baba Yaga, pointing up at the sky spangled suddenly with bright zags of light, "but flesh, for all its troubles, is sweet, and you can hardly be a dependable spirit without the knowledge of what you lack. Anyway, take it from Baba Yaga, Paradise, that heavily rouged whore, is overrated," she said, and she threw her head back and cackled shrilly, the curve of her nose matching the arc of the moon.

Adam brooded at a distance, weaving in and out of the bones. Eva wound round the tree, through the kindling-thin legs of Baba Yaga, and finally coiled herself tightly around the stem of the apple until it dropped to the ground, the still heart of the earth's snowy body, exposed. Baba Yaga Boney Legs held her blue fingers to her lips and tried to warm them with her rattling breath. Eva made herself thin as onion skin, slid herself beneath the apple, and wished she could feel its heft in her invisible hands, taste its shiny red sweetness in her vaporous mouth. "Here," said Baba Yaga as she lifted the apple in the air and pierced it with a bony finger, and then she sliced the Eva-wavering air in front of her with her apple-sweetened talon, and Eva stretched herself long and round like a worm and disappeared inside the apple's tiny portal.

Baba Yaga screeched into the brittle air when at her feet appeared a naked woman, heavily fleshed and shivering, with shimmering apples the color of frostbite hanging heavy and ripe from her chest. From near the fence came a plaintive moan, and Baba Yaga covered her broadening grin with her spidery hands as she gazed upon Adam lying on the ground, two apples, a venereal red, tucked between his legs below a stunted stalk of rhubarb. "Fawp!" gurgled Adam as he tried to pluck the apples from his loins, but Eva purred as she rubbed the fallen fruit, then she felt the area between her own legs begin to cleave, the overripe skin begin to give, and as she looked down at herself taking shape, she thought: *This place that is both flesh and absence of flesh, bordered space, is the origin of origin—will it not be from here that He springs?*

Baba Yaga squinted her eyes, nudged the split with the blade of her nose, and said, "Beware the abyss, Gehenna! Beware the key that unlocks it!" and she leveled a glare at the trembling fig leaf of Adam's mortified hands. "If your apples offend you, cut them off and cast them from you!" said she with a snort.

A deafening thunderclap cracked the air above them. Adam leapt to his feet and began to wobble around Baba Yaga's hut, dragging his apples with him, careful not to let his rhubarb touch the ground, howling a sodden lament, and Baba Yaga said, "I cannot skin your carcass back to spirit, but I can liberate you from the onus of reproduction, which only forestalls the inevitable," and her nose whistled as it whisked through the air, a surgical swipe, and sliced the rhubarb and apples, the overripe persimmon, from Adam and Eva, who were yellow with substance and now smooth all over like boiled potatoes!

Adam and Eva rubbed the tender nubbins that remained where the apples had been and they spread their hands in front of the doughy V where their legs met but realized there was nothing there to shield from view, so they dropped their hands to their sides. Baba Yaga said, "There be those free of dangling apples, which have made themselves so for the kingdom of heaven's sake," and she scratched a swagging dug with a knobby claw. She could see that Adam and Eva were puzzled by a loss they hadn't the experience to mourn, and she bent down and reached her spindly fingers into the snow, brought back a palm full of icy pebbles, and said, "If it pleases Him to see the forest filled with impermanent *flesh, He is able of these stones to raise up children,"* and she coughed and corralled the rattle in her chest into her mouth then ptui! spat on the ground. *"It will take 144,000 of you branded with the great seal, the cicatrix of severed fruit, before he whom you have not yet had occasion to meet will set his sacred foot on this fallen soil a second time. But that seed has not yet been sown. In the meantime, blessed are the barren, and the split persimmons that never bore and the apples which never gave suck. There is salvation in the tundra of the body!"*

And Adam and Eva gathered the skin around their bones, tucking out of sight the loose hide they would later grow into and out of again, and bade Baba Yaga Boney Legs farewell, set off across the taiga, leaning into the glacial wind, as they would for the rest of their mortal lives.

"Nikolai and Akulina Ovinko are brother and sister and have lived together their whole lives," Obie had said hopefully. "I told them about you. They want to meet you."

"If they are enemies of the body," I said, "don't you think mine might provoke them to make a clean sneak to the KGB?"

Obie smiled. "Not if that body is a sanctified diamond of the first water," he said. I couldn't help but roll my eyes and cuff his ear.

That night as I lay in bed drifting between dream and thought, a vision infected my nodding mind. I saw Obie bigger than me, bigger than Blunderbore, Gogmagog, or Goliath, bigger than a sauropod stretching its neck, bigger than Kilimanjaro, Obie's head ringed in a garland of clouds, a body all excess, too big for this world, splitting it at its sloppily sewn seams, saw him wearing a white robe, Obiegod (Oh, *be God!*), and I felt disappointed at my conjuring mind's predictable limitations and susceptibilities. But ballooning the robe was the half-moon of a sizable belly, and I smiled at the thought of Obie with the middle-aged bloat of a sedentary swiller of beer, a paunch no piety could conceal. And then he squatted and rested his arms on his legs like a catcher posed between pitches, his face reddening, he started to perspire. Obie breathed in and out very quickly, an orderly panting, and it only then occurred to me that inside his belly sloshed something other than beer—ale was not what ailed him! Obie growled and bore down, his face fierce and ruddy like that of the strong man at the carnival as he hoists the barbells. Then he put his hands on his rounded gut and pushed, grrrrr, pushed, grrrrr, pushed and whoosh! His white robe bled and out of his body flew a baby, who bounced on the ground and skidded to a stop. I looked into the blue face of the newborn infant, at its smooth head, body round and plump as a pumpkin, and I saw the whitened scar, the cross carved into its scalp, and looked at the soles of its feet to see they too had been marked: Obie big as God had given birth to me, child of irreparable actions, and he rose into the air, his reddening gown aflutter (I tried to steal a look beneath it, godpeeper I, seeing nothing there but the empty swirl in the eye of a storm), grew small and indistinct Obie did as he floated away, a silver shimmer spinning in sunlight, a UFO people around the world would call their local authorities to report having seen, an unidentified miracle.

☾

Obie backed away from me as I offered him the host of my body, his eyes empty, looking like someone who realizes the holy nostrum his life depends on consists only of snake oil and horehound tea. He left my room, the house, left me.

How do I describe what it is to lose a brother, my own heart and salvation, what it is to injure his love, to smite and push away the one person fearless enough to grant this body purpose? I lost my only apostle that day, my congregation, my choir. Without his witness, his eyes fixing me in the world, I lost my shape, like the Ovinkos' Adam and Eva before the Fall. I suppose it is possible that God populated the earth because He did not want to concede his mistake, but I think He began to feel thin and gauzy, insubstantial, without admirers lending Him heft. Obie went in search perhaps of a more dependable godgirl, more loving and merciful, not one so profanely sacramental, went in search of a prelapsarian dollface. I'd emptied myself of all that Obie had loved, a kenosis that went too far. And what I never got to tell him, what I didn't recognize myself until he was gone, was that it was actually I who had been his disciple, a reluctant convert swayed in the end by his selfless and ardent belief. There is nothing to do in the presence of a heart like his but strive to match it beat for beat.

I faltered, I failed, my heart all but stopped.

My mother became frantic when Obie, my Obie, missed dinner that evening. She ran through the neighborhood calling his name, went door to door, and then stationed herself at the same picture window she spied on the neighbors from, curtains now parted, and within the week my brother was a face on the evening news, an image headed for the back of a milk carton, the latest casualty, number seven, in the string of missing children of Kingdom Come that had begun with the girl in Paradise Park. I wondered if all the vanished children had argued with older siblings before disappearing. Perhaps they'd all fled families in front of whose eyes they felt they were already invisible. Exasperated at the persistent mystery and fearful there might be no earthly solution, the community turned to tabloid fables for answers, stories that were reassuring because improbable and remote, rumors that somehow helped them to sleep, if fitfully: secret pharmaceutical research, slave trade, alien abduction, satanic sacrifice, but all the children evaporated as if they'd never existed, leaving behind only drawers full of socks, rock collections, artwork hung in schoolrooms, dental records, and grieving families as testimony, the flimsy evidence that persists, briefly, in our absence and leaves skeptics sneering. Obie Armstrong, my only believer, spurned, only brother, was the last child to vanish from Kingdom Come, Kansas, the last mystery to keep us up nights drinking Ovaltine, half hopefully, and staring at the dimming stars.

☾

I decided to pay a visit to the Ovinkos, to see if they could tell me anything, anything about where Obie might have gone.

Both brother and sister appeared at the door, and they stared up at me, lips tightly clamped. Something about them made me nervous, the straight line of their mouths, their soft, broad faces. "I'm, I…" They blinked. "I'm Obie's sister. I'm Wallis." They blinked again, looked at one another, stood to either side of the door and bowed, then each took my arm and escorted me into their Spartan living room, sat me down on the divan. They stood before me, clasping their hands in front of them. Nikolai stood over six feet, but he was bent like a shepherd's hook. He had a strangely tranquil face, round as a dinner plate and creased with age but soft-looking and hairless, without guile, like a child's, skin that looked like it would hold your imprint if you touched it. Akulina also bent forward, and she had small, dark, elliptical eyes that, when she blinked, seemed to disappear into the dough of her cheeks, the only place her body had allowed flesh to accumulate. I thought of Baba Yaga Boney Legs and tried to imagine their shriveled, schismatic bodies inside their clothing, but it wasn't evident to me that they'd been, well, forced to part with their apples. Nikolai wore a long white shirt, buttoned in front, and brown canvas pants that had a loop at the side for a hammer, empty. The shirt was so luminously clean it made my eyes water to look at it. Akulina wore a long brown skirt, and her cinched waist was so narrow I thought she might snap if she bent over too quickly.

"My brother," I said, "is missing." They nodded. "I was wondering..." They came to me and took my hands again, pulled me to my feet. I felt the way I always feel when I stand up straight and look down at people looking up at me with their heads tilted at an uncomfortable angle: guilty, afraid my size will seem an affront, my unscaleable body, haughty altitude. They stood before me and reached out tentatively, the way you would to pet an animal whose harmless appearance you suspect might be deceiving, touched me on the arm, on the hand, gently turned me around. And around. And around. And then they backed away from me and the lines in their faces became animated, pulled the flesh of their cheeks up like fingers hoisting sagging socks, and they smiled.

Nikolai nodded at his sister, they lifted their arms, and there was such a look of benign ease about them I would not have been surprised if they'd lifted into the air, but instead they began to whirl, turning with their arms outspread, slowly at first, catching my eye with each revolution, then gradually accelerating, their heads falling back, eyes closed, lips curved in a faint centrifugal smile. This, I thought, is why there is so little furniture in this room, only the divan and a lamp, a chair in the corner, the rest of the room open, waiting to be filled with the gusting vigor of their ecstatic gyrations. I was surprised that the thinning skin of these elderly bodies didn't fly off the bone, leaving behind a shrinking Siberian dervish trapped in a cyclone of ardor. A low hum, like that of distant machinery, began to agitate the air and made my heart beat erratically, feel as if it might fatally fibrillate. "Obie!" I yelled above an escalating wind-tunnel roar, "Where is he?" But the Ovinkos seemed to hasten their urgent skirling at the sound of my voice, until all I could see were the fading propeller blades of their arms circling the axle of their bodies. They were two disappearing crosses slicing the air, planets whirling off their axes, abandoning the orthodox swivel, burning up the atmosphere with their rogue fervor. I felt my own cast iron body sinking, and I prayed I'd dissolve into the earth's molten core.

As I walked back home, I thought about Obie out in the world alone. I imagined him standing near a dying fire beneath a bridge, lost dogs and runaway horses telling him where he could cadge some grub, Obie's beautiful, dolorous face that of someone who has lifted the curtain to reveal the hoax of his own theology, expose the sham gospel, a face never before darkened with doubt. I looked up and saw a sign hanging by a suction cup in the back window of a neighbor's car, one of those yellow signs that caution the tailgater or enraged motorist that there's a baby inside, precious cargo, so back off, lighten your leadfoot, but this one announced "God on Board." Without even thinking, I picked up a rock, lifted it into the air, but before I had time to hurl it through the glass, this rejoinder leapt into my thoughts: *Travel at Your Own Risk.* It was instantly clear to me that this was a clue, but a clue of a different stripe, meant to aid a different kind of investigative ratiocination, the sort of clue to which Obie, with his oddly heightened sensitivity to the frequency at which the animal and invisible kingdoms vibrate, was attuned.

I went to the swallowed house.

I walked around the grassy depression, the place our father had forbidden us from playing years ago, and there was nothing there to see. Nothing had been built there, and the Milkowskis, emancipated by the hollow earth from the binding of worldly possessions, had moved far away and never returned. Any remaining traces of evidence suggesting this had ever been a site of pandemonium one summer night had all but faded away. This, I thought, trying telepathically to taunt Obie into returning, is God, once a place of chaos now grown over with grass. Even the subterranean danger the sign across the street, now scarred with rusting BB holes, warned travelers against seemed more local legend than likelihood, a tall tale children tell themselves to relieve the boredom of being children in a world designed for adults.

And then there they were, like a parting gift, sitting beneath the beat-up sign, message obscured, letters blasted away, *You Own Risk*: Obie's sneakers, neatly tied.

Many winters later, in a land menaced by bright stars, a peasant woman, tired and hungry after a long day of trudging, beneath the darkened sky, through snow-buried barley fields, in the invisible shadow of solemn mountains, developed an earache, a wild ringing deep in her ear sounding like birdsong, or the tremulous voices of excited children, and she cupped her ear in her hand and lay down in a silver circle of radiance on the moonlit surface of a frozen lake. The ringing turned to a roar and made her woozy, and it felt as if she held an angry sea inside her head. She followed the light as it crept across the ice like a stealthy fox and when she reached the other side of the lake, she felt warm fluid leaking from her ear, felt movement buried inside her skull, then she heard something cracking, something hatching behind her eyes! She stood up and leaned her head to the side and tried to shake the throbbing from her ear and out dropped a tiny, mewling, curled-up creature, puckered and pale as an old parsnip, and it slowly unfolded itself, revealing chubby arms and legs, the incandescent head, blizzard-blue eyes agape, a baby! The baby, the one that would lift up the fallen world on its lacerated shoulders and finally rescue it from the fate of apples, the fate of flesh. Khristi, the earthly part of that divine troika, the baby that was, like Adam and Eva, destined to don and then part with the flesh, that turncoat the body! Who would be stretched taut against the cross of his own making, pinned to wood like a tattered handbill, announcing to the disinherited on earth—the swinish multitudes, the hoi polloi, the proles, the plebes, canaille, repentant rabble, the hordes, the great unwashed, profanum vulgus, tatterdemalions, slubberdegullions, muckworms and mudlarks and loobies and rubes—announcing the path to the heavenly kingdom, the roadmap visible in the ragged skin of his ankles and wrists, take a left here, this way to rapture.

The body always turns on you in the end.

The body is not to be trusted.

If Obie were here now, I'd give him this fink of a carcass and tell him if he knew what was good for him, he'd not eat it on an empty stomach. But this time I'd offer him organ meat, liver, kidneys, heart, those blood-tender parts, and pray to be worthy of his appetite. Sometimes Obie appears to me in the night, small as a shelled peanut, hanging in the air in front of me, and I pluck him from the darkness and swallow him quickly, peristalsis sweeping him into the safety of my infinite stomach, Moloch briefly appeased.

Alone in my room, my faithful auditor fled, I continued God's biography (*auto*biography I insist on Obie's behalf*): A spectre is haunting Me, thought God, the holy spectre of materialism, and it is to this dialectical pendulum that I cling, scuttling between revenant and corpus, vacuum and plenum, proletariat and ruling class, and, sure, all right, good and evil (but which is which?), the purifying apocatastasis that drains from me the incarnating alloy and turns me into thinning gold (take the el-loy outta gold and whaddya got? That's right! Gimme a G!), but my guilty secret is that there are days when I fancy, when I favor…matter! There I've said it. You see I'm not the unfeeling apparatchik you believe me to be, bored functionary in the sky indifferent to your suffering. The means of production, and destruction, are controlled by me, it's true. But does this mean I do not bleed when you are pricked? As surely as if I were a punctured artery in your own weakening body do I feel your despair. Can I help it if I am all-knowing, all-encompassing, alpha and omega, the whole bloody caboodle? It ain't easy being omnipotent! All that horsepower champing at the bit, all that invisible heft, it makes a body, bodiless body, bone weary, even without bones. Listen, it's true that "the history of all hitherto existing society is the history of class struggles," but what I wish you to understand is that this is also the history of God, who is the greatest class struggle ever to* rend the universe. I own everything and nothing. To some I am the supreme feudal lord, toying with my devoted vassals, humankind the greatest fiefdom. To others I am the very essence of self-denial: a ubiquitous ghost. But what I long for in my heart of heart of hearts is to be small and vulnerable as you, smaller, a mouse in your cupboard, a mite nestled in the fur of that mouse. If only you knew how I struggle with the power I have over your lumpen strife. But if I were to redress every alienated ache and grievance, pretty soon wellbeing, happiness, comfort, joy would be like the Reichsmark after the Great War (you thought I didn't trouble myself with such worldly details?): worthless. And honestly, if we're going to sloganeer with 'From each according to his ability, to each according to his needs,' I believe I am competitive in this regard, have made a decent showing of my abilities, and it is precisely My Needs (commodious enough to remain ravenous after enveloping the bottomless ache that animates all life) no one has the chutzpah to inquire about. You think an inviolate, incontrovertible, invisible being, all-permeating as oxygen, what could He possibly need, what desiderata keep Him up at night? But can you begin to imagine the volcanic need created by the ability to slake any thirst? It's monstrous! Fulfillment begets desire as any deity will tell you. I long to be a single-cell organism, my avocation narrowly defined. You see the conundrum? It is you, the dream of becoming you, that is opiate for God, a potion I quaff greedily as I grope in my closet for that fugitive flesh. It is revolution I mean to incite, and the hierarchy I propose we overthrow is that rickety ladder ascending from terra firma to firmament. It's time to make a man of God. God has nothing to lose but His chains. He has a world to win. God and ghost and Christ unite!

EIGHTEEN
THE CURIOUS CASE
OF THE CAPACIOUS
DEATH INVESTIGATOR

CASE FILE #6
Oswego, Kansas, pop. 2,046
Eldon Schnitzler, forty-nine-year-old Caucasian male

Two-car garage with a fresh oil stain on one side, the leak-ing Oldsmobile 88 parked in the driveway outside the closed door; Toro riding lawnmower circa 1982, hedge clippers, pump can for pesticide; workbench with vice, hacksaw, power drill and bits, three-tiered tool chest open and spilling forth an assortment of wrenches and hammers and ratchets and pawls, sawdust and screwdrivers and penny nails scattered beneath; aluminum trash can with dented lid, popsicle stick stuck to the bottom; bicycle tires; gasoline can; rope; toboggan and American Flyer red wagon; washtub full of rusted chain; rake with bent tines, shovel, hoe, trowel, cultivator, green and white garden hose; opened bag of briquettes, bag of rock salt, burlap sack full of bottle caps, corks, and pull tabs; yellowing stack of *Oswego Independents*; fishing pole and tackle box, hip waders, butterfly net; Coleman kerosene lamp and cookstove; dozens of empty Meister Bräu cans, one half-empty bottle of Old Charter, and a drained-dry bottle of red grape Mad Dog 20/20; a pair of polished chestnut and nubuck spectator kicks atop a recently dusted shelf, beside a sepia-tone photograph of a man with a waxed mustache, gray hair parted in the middle, lapels of his suit coat visibly shiny with wear, the thumb of one hand tucked under his arm, the other holding a pocket watch, gat beside him on a table and a black medical bag next to that, picture of an occasional gangster I would later learn, part of the chopper squad, quick-fix doctor to the trouble boys, mostly a seamstress double-stitching the plugged and ragged, Eldon's shabby-dapper quacksalver Great Grandfather Worden. Below that shelf was a collection of a hundred or so egg cartons once housing Grade A Extra Large Fancy Farm Fresh eggs.

(Having once been force-famished, I cannot tell you how it pains me to reproduce puny victuals, especially eggs. I sometimes turn to Pierre Petit-Puce, the developer of Petite Cuisine®, for assistance. Pierre, following the path of Alexis-Charles-Henri Clérel de Tocqueville's travels, took one look at the broadening waist of America and saw there was a franc or two to be made by denying it its fondest wish and calling it dinner. Petite Cuisine, arranged on a plate the size of a dime, serves up food that would leave the leanest, most weight-conscious microorganism ravenous, food you must try to spear with a fork fit for a midge [it takes some practice but most community colleges now offer weekend instruction in the art of lancing the elusive morsel]. Naturally, any bite disappears on the tongue, no chance of advancing to bolus, so that you have to press it against the roof of the mouth to confirm that it was indeed delivered, and even then chances are only the most princely tongue, so discriminating as to be easily irritated, will register it. Of course the *recherche* restaurants that serve Petite Cuisine spend a fortune on miniature flatware, particularly forks, which are often mistaken by the mouth for the plat du jour itself and ingested along with the smidgen of salade niçoise, the confit de fly-sized canard, blancmange, butter-poached toy-sturgeon [farmed in teacups and whose roe are said to be *almost* perceptibly delectable and therefore cost a king's ransom]. The autopsy of a frequent consumer of Petite Cuisine will often reveal an appendix as finely bristled as a hedgehog.)

And the rest of the endless miscellany that finds its way into domestic storage. Suspicious death amidst clutter can be difficult to determine the cause of, though this death longed to appear self-evident. Eldon Schnitzler hung himself from one of the tracks on which the garage door slid open and shut. Eldon was a small man, 5' 5", but even so it took some ambition and grit to properly dangle himself to death from a flimsy contraption in a packed garage, and the blood-speckled whites of his eyes confirmed the cause of death was strangulation. Overturned beside Eldon's feet was a wooden vegetable crate (Eldon had for years been the produce manager at the local Super Save, also known as the Super Savior because of all the itinerant proselytizers the lit-up "Save" sign seemed to attract), the bottom slats cracked and splintered, suggesting he had broken through the wood then kicked it aside.

The important thing to bear in mind about Eldon, his wife informed me, is that he boozily threatened to kill himself every Saturday night around the time *Wild Kingdom* came on the air. Watching all manner of saber-toothed predator track then rip to shreds terrified rabbits, which screamed at a harrowing pitch, nearly made his few remaining hairs surrender on the spot, soft-furred slaughter that made Eldon weepy, no matter how many times he saw it, and each week he went out and leashed himself with his homemade noose while standing atop an overturned rusting coal bucket, and he yodeled at the top of his lungs that he was prepared to kick it (Eldon was said to have an obvious sense of humor), don't try talking him out of it. So the question was where was that bucket now and why had he chosen to use a rickety crate this time instead? The bottle of Mad Dog ("Not usually his poison of choice," claimed his brother) had been recently tippled, and his brother told me Eldon's wife, Jolene, was always egging on his drinking, cajoling him into a bender, telling him to drink hard like a real man or shut his noisy trap, and they sometimes had guzzling contests, which Jolene, hollow-legged and hardy as a yak, invariably won. The neighbors said they could often hear Eldon singing and sobbing, singing and sobbing, in his garage on a Saturday night, and occasionally someone looked in on him, but they had long ago quit trying to talk him down from the bucket and they no longer feared that he'd kick it. And in fact everyone in Oswego, save his wife, seemed in a state of shock when news of his death made its way around town. And then there was his stepson, Millard, who was the one who called me and said he didn't know how or who and he knew his stepfather had threatened this fate often enough, but something about

168

Eldon's suicide just didn't smell right to him. "Maybe," he said, "it was another contest. Don't know if Eldon won or lost." Despite his stepfather's maudlin yammering, Millard had loved him dearly.

There's a *very* small town in central Kansas that grows *very* small vegetables, no bigger than a minute, and delivers them in matchbox crates, but it was essential to whittle the crate myself, and all it took really was looking with incredulous eyes at the splintered slats to see that they'd been ever so slightly weakened, inconspicuously cracked in just the right places so that the minute Eldon centered his feet on the crate (good thing he was bandy-legged, his accomplice must have thought, or he'd likely have plunged too soon), he broke through and unintentionally made good on the drunken threats he'd made all these years. Eldon Schnitzler hung himself accidentally and his wife was finally free of his interminable bellyaching. Motive enough?

She "was just helping him carry out his wishes!" she readily blubbered when I asked her if she knew her way around a hacksaw, and she spilled her guts: she had hidden the coal bucket earlier in the week and helped Eldon onto the crate, making sure he didn't step on the weakened slats until the noose was snugly about his neck, and then when he fell, he was startled, she said, and he reached out toward her with such terror and disbelief in his sobering eyes that she nearly relented. As she spoke, she sniffed remorsefully. I asked her if she'd tell me why she really wanted Eldon dead, and, after pausing to consider whether it would harm or help her case to confide her reasons, she said that when Eldon drank, he promised to take her to the Tan-Tar-A Resort at the Lake of the Ozarks and to buy her a souped-up '69 Chevelle from her Uncle Bobcat, but when he sobered up the next day, he never recollected any of it and just waved her off, throbbing head aloll on his neck. And then I could see at that moment that Jolene was pouting more than mourning, regretting the fact that she'd now never get to tube float at the Timber Falls Water Park, which featured, she told me dreamily, "six hundred goddamned feet of water slides."

She said she got the idea from a story she'd heard, about a man who'd leapt to his death from an apartment building, a fellow name of Opus. When the investigator arrived at the scene, he discovered that Opus had left behind a desolate note, indicating his intentions to curtail his misery "in a single bound" (Opus a devoted reader of comics), but what Opus hadn't realized was that a safety net had been strung just below the seventh floor, by construction workers repairing a crumbling cornice at top, and this net, it turns out, had caught him and held him snug as a ball in a mitt and kept him from splatting. But he was dead all the same. A quick look at the body of Opus revealed it had, somewhere along the line, fallen prey to a gunshot wound, and on closer inspection the investigator found the ragged cavity pricked with bits of glass. So it became quickly apparent that it was actually the gunshot wound (which savaged his chest in such a way that made it clear it could not have been self-inflicted) that had claimed Opus's life, not the smack of the sidewalk as he'd planned.

Was it then indeed a suicide, asked the investigator, and where had this gunshot come from anyway? When a suicide succeeds, even if by unexpected means in the end (say his tie catches on a flagpole on the way down and strangles him just as lifeless as the wallop from the street would have), it's still a suicide. But in this case, that safety net would have interfered with Opus's hoped-for exit, which meant the gaping wound made it a no-bones-about-it homicide.

And here's how the riddle ends: Opus was living in this building with his parents, who, come to find out, fought like honey badgers every night, driving to despair glum Opus, who tried to drown out their growling with the booming of military marches played at top volume (much to the thumping chagrin of the neighbors above). Every night, his father fetched his shotgun from the coat closet and brandished it at his mother. They all knew this was theatre for his father owned no shells. Opus was doubly steamed at his mother, who had recently thrown the brakes on his gravy train and asked him to move out. Therefore, as Opus resolved to end it all, he decided his mother should join him, and his father, a sour grouser he felt little fondness for, could live out his days hammering his ire into license plates in the clink. Opus bought shells and loaded the shotgun.

His father was shocked this time when he pulled the trigger to find himself knocked against the wall from the startling recoil (wha?), figurines shattering on the floor beside him, shocked to see through the settling debris that his pantomimed blast had exploded the window beside his wife!

And it did so, turns out, at precisely the moment when Opus was passing by it (what're the chances!), hurtling toward unanticipated safety (then suddenly not).

If it had been his intention to kill his wife, then the husband would be guilty of murder, even though the fate befell a bystander, erm, befell a byfaller, erm, struck another dead. But both of Opus's parents insisted the nightly vaudeville was an understanding they had between them, that the gun was unloaded and the husband was free to wave it at his wife each night, to blow off the steam of the day's swelling frustrations. When a neighbor of Opus's came forward to say it was actually the son who had, in anger, loaded the shotgun a few days prior, the medical examiner determined it was then Opus who had committed the murder, the murder of himself, the unintended (intended) victim, which brought it all back to suicide, whomp, case closed, phew. Jolene said she knew the particulars were a little different, but she felt the principle was the same and should therefore prove she'd merely made a man's dying wish come true.

One thing that comes from reducing the world is that you uncover all the smallnesses that skitter about in the dank culverts of the human heart, get to look into the yellow eyes of those gluttonous rats that gnaw on the endless store of human disappointment and loneliness. I was always on the hunt for a soul smaller than my own.

"I did love him," said Jolene, then she heaved a sob and added, "but I ain't ever even been to Six Flags!" (I'd been to a theme park once in junior high, and I sank a vessel on the Viking Voyager, causing a tsunami that nearly drowned several bystanders, shut down the log flume for a week, and resulted in a new sign posted at the entrance: a bearded gnome in a horned helmet and chainmail, skull of grog in one hand, and a 7' scull in the other, warned, "You must not be taller than my oar to ride!")

CASE FILE #33
Argonia, Kansas, pop. 464
Hannelore Berlin, sixteen-year-old Caucasian girl of German extraction

It was the copy of *The Sorrows of Young Werther* found on the banks of the Chikaskia River, where the bluing body of Hannelore Berlin washed up, that made her drowning seem suspect to her cousin Molly, though she wasn't sure why. "She was a dreamy girl, sure," said Hannelore's Aunt Ginger, "but sensible. I never figured her for suicidal. She wore glasses for heaven's sake!"

Hannelore Berlin was from Eutin, Germany, visiting family for the summer, and she began sneaking out at night when the relentless heat that still hung in the air at midnight and the rhythmic chainsaw whirring of cicadas made her sleepless. Eventually Hanne told Molly she was meeting someone at the river, but she wouldn't tell her who it was. Molly had never known a girl with a secret life, and she kept quiet and watched. When Hannelore crawled back through the bedroom window, "she looked shiny with true love," said Molly. Then one night Hannelore and Molly looked out at the nearly full moon, and Hanne said it bore the illuminated scowl of an angry girl. That was the night Hannelore didn't return home.

In the novel the spurned Werther shoots himself for love and this caused an epidemic of copycat suicides and lovelorn drowning throughout Europe. Unrequited lovers doomed to pine for an unavailable object of desire shot themselves square in the head or threw themselves from bridges clutching the book in their hands. For some reason, the late-eighteenth century German lovelorn were not gifted at Selbstmord and so there was a whole generation of the maimed forsaken, who were sent to the WertherHaus, home for unsuccessful suicides, to live out the crippled storm of their longing.

Molly recalled later that Hannelore had indeed had with her a copy of the book, but it was in German, *Die Leiden des Jungen Werthers*. She had asked Hannelore who Leiden was and why it was someone wanted him dead ("English is saturated with the German tongue," Hanne had once told her, and Molly developed a funny taste in her mouth, vinegary), and Hanne had laughed. Hanne was always quizzing Molly, asking her what states bordered the Great Lakes or what language they spoke in Lichtenstein or where Bora Bora was, and she'd shake her head and say, "You must know where things are in the world or you'll never get farther than Argonia, Kansas!" "It's the only Argonia in the world!" snapped Molly, though she wasn't sure if this was a sliver of knowledge that truly equaled the sorts of things Hannelore knew, like where it was in the world that people believed women who die in childbirth become undead, hang from banana trees, and eat babies and men. (In Argonia, they had decided to believe if a groundhog sees his shadow in February, he was likely to become amorous toward insubstantial things, thereby resulting in a groundhog shortage, the consequences of which were unpredictable, but that was as free-spirited as they got in their revisionary lore, and this, too, had made Hannelore laugh at the simpletons.) There wasn't a place you could point to on a map that Hannelore didn't know something about. Except maybe the Chikaskia River, where she died, making Molly think Hannelore had tried to geographically immunize herself from death by knowing something about every place she might ever visit, every predatory locale that might make a quarry of a curious girl, but her mistake had been in thinking that a deceptively mild place like Argonia, Kansas, held no peril. Molly knew what the rest of the world thought of Kansas. It was flat and backward, it was a joke! She hated being from such a place, a fact she could never change no matter how exotically she might relocate.

It was at the moment that my vision was swimming from having set the flyspeck type for *Werther* (a mysterious death in a library would surely blind me for good) that I noticed someone had penciled in *pontianak: Malaysian vampire*, at the bottom of page thirty-six. Those bloodless mothers suspended in childlessness, masquerading as bananas, hungry, hungry! I showed it to Molly.

Molly shrugged her shoulders, and I asked her, with the snide Old World superiority I thought she'd heard in Hanne's quizzing, if she could tell me which places in the world had been settled by convicts. She studied me silently then growled, "All of them."

Then she opened her beak and the self-incriminating stoolie sang. The guilty, who haven't any trouble dissembling in front of Johnny Law, often find it pointless to sustain the snow job in the presence of someone who is herself a walking crime—takes one to know one—and they self-snitch a teary confession with little prodding once they see the jig is up.

Hannelore, she said, was a skilled geographer but not a strong swimmer, and she'd been meeting such a frivolous boy, a boy who didn't know the first thing about Lithuania or the mountains of Comoros. As it turned out, it was Molly who had been spurned on the banks of the Chikaskia and who, in response, made Argonia, Kansas, the place Hannelore would get no farther than. She said she contacted me because she wanted someone to know what she had done, wanted to be sure to get out of Argonia, to travel at least as far as Lansing. It was still Kansas, but a Kansas surrounded by concertina wire, a Kansas that kept out the smirking anti-flatlander churls, a dangerous, treacherous, hazardous Kansas, broken heartland, requiring cunning and fortitude and no knowledge of foreign geographies to survive.

CASE FILE #28
Fivescore, Kansas, pop. 99
Fleance Shoptaw, Caucasian male aged ninety-nine, eleven months, and twenty-one days
Ludovic Paddletrap, Caucasian male aged ninety-six

The only people allowed to live in Fivescore, Kansas, are nonagenarians, which means mail delivery is slow. Anyone who makes it to a hundred has to relocate, so the ninety-niners know their days are numbered one way or the other and they do their best to die on time. Fleance Shoptaw lived alone and watched from the picture window in his living room the sun set over greening corn or flapping husks. He sat in a wheelchair, which he didn't need, but he was trying to urge his impudent body toward accelerated decrepitude. What did an old goat have to do to buy the farm anyway? Despite having in the past year gone hang gliding, luge racing, cliff diving, wing walking, despite having driven with his headlights off at midnight all the way home from the all-night pharmacy on unlit backroads (a good six blocks!), despite having eaten deep-fried food or high fructose corn syrup at every meal, despite having briefly taken up with a sprightly ninety-one-year-old widow who had buried twelve husbands and had a sideyard full of hemlock, he remained stubbornly extant, vital even, maddening.

In his ninety-ninth year Fleance developed a grudging friendship with Ludovik Paddletrap. Fleance had resolved since the age of ninety-eight not to make any new friends or renew magazine subscriptions or buy anything with a warranty, but Ludovik moved in next door to Fleance and routinely brought him povitica he made himself (he'd been raised by his Slovenian grandmother on Strawberry Hill), and Fleance was still a sucker for homemade baked goods, try as he might to loosen the grip of the body's pleasures, the many temptations the material world still dangled under his aging snout. He just couldn't seem to step one foot off this mortal coil, and what would he do as an outcast centenarian? There were no settlements in Kansas for such hangers-on as it was considered the worst sort of unseemly breach of social etiquette to persist beyond a century of years. There was talk for a while of a glue factory where malingerers could...retire, and the oldest among them, drawing near to excommunication, were entirely in favor of such a solution, but there was concern that children might be made, well, a little gloomy at the prospect of gluing that construction paper turkey onto their Thanksgiving cards with the adhesive of their great-great-grandmother (who had, after all, won a statewide bake-off with her championship pumpkin pie)! No, such an association would sap even a seasoned glutton's holiday appetite.

All those forced to leave Fivescore to wander the endless prairie by themselves usually died within the first six months, but they died among people who hadn't yet lost every person they'd ever loved and so couldn't appreciate what it meant to be the last emptied heart left beating. That was the comfort of Fivescore, to die among the abandoned living for whom grief was itself a kind of breathing, to find community with the nearly dead.

Ludovik was only ninety-six, but except for a little elevated serum cholesterol, he wasn't showing any signs of failing any time soon, so he sympathized with Fleance's dilemma, which he imagined he himself would be facing soon enough if he couldn't clog an artery or two, and make it snappy!

So when Ludovik saw the advertisement for an extreme vacation tracking tornados, he marched over to Fleance's house and suggested they take their lives in their own hands. Again. With a throttling grip.

Maybe this time death would take.

Whirlwind Tours offered a 5-day, 4-night tornado vacation package for only $2,000 during high storm season, April and May. There was a senior discount and Ludovik thought maybe they could even wrangle a *very* senior discount, and surely if they succumbed during their tornado chase, the whole vacation, including meals and lodging, would be comped. Impending death didn't mean you couldn't continue to be thrifty to the end, reasoned Ludovik. And they guaranteed dramatic F-3 or stronger tornadic activity or your money back (Ludovik thought they probably had a machine that could stir the air if the weather didn't cooperate on its own. His own great-grandfather, who had, incidentally, lived to the defiant age of 112, had been a tornado roper, he'd told Fleance, though, to his grandfather's disappointment, he'd never been able to build a cage sturdy enough to incarcerate one for long). Fleance had outlived his retirement funds some time ago and since he didn't know how much longer he might be sticking around, he couldn't afford not to be frugal and a holiday outing hadn't been factored in to this year's budget. But Fleance had recently begun to harbor certain… meteorological ambitions (he often stood outside during electrical storms with his nine iron raised to the thunderheads), and so being escorted off these hostile plains by a strong and spinning wind greatly appealed to him. What better way for a congenital Kansan to exit!

The town most frequently afflicted with tornadoes was Geezheebasun, Kansas, and this was where Fleance and Ludovik asked the tornado tour cicerone to take them. Well *that*, said the tracker, was going to cost them extra.

Members of the Ojibwe tribe arrived in Kansas in 1839, and later it was President Taylor's plan to remove all the Ojibwe from the north and settle them in Kansas, but Old Rough and Ready died in office, and so they stayed put or were absorbed by other strong-armed settlements. Since that time, whenever any wandering mudlark sets foot on Geezheebasun soil, the circular winds begin to blow, and they lap up the interloper and spit him out in another town, where, if he survives the trip, he feels compelled to settle. (Goodland, Kansas, for example, is a tornado settlement, full of people blown there by inhospitable winds.) Weary vagabonds unable to stop their drifting often make their way to Geezheebasun and take their chances, get blown hither and thither and then settle (or are interred) where they touch down, never to hop the rail again, Geezheebasun an antidote to chronic wayfaring.

So you know where this is going, a death investigator's stories end predictably. It was the tornado tracker who called me. He said he'd always steered wide of the notoriously fierce weather of Geezheebasun with first-time extreme vacationers. But Fleance and Ludovic had made an impassioned appeal about needing to see a homegrown tornado before they died, and it touched him so, he couldn't say no. Descended from a long line of windblown Kansans himself, he knew well the need they spoke of. Fleance and Ludovik convinced four of their younger neighbors to come with them so they could qualify for the group discount, and the most puzzling thing, said the tracker, was that it was only the two of them that got swept away.

In Geezheebasun, only wind thrives: no houses, no tabernacles, no industrial parks, no ziggurats, no TV towers, no bodies of water, no mammals—what few trees survive there are nearly horizontal—so shrinking the scene was a cinch. For the first time, I relied on photographs: a tattered sky stained yellow hanging over a vast emptiness; and eyewitness accounts: "Suddenly there was a buoyant darkness at midday, then shrill winds began to howl and gave you twice the jowls, liberated skin from bone. It made you feel like you were more gas than solid, made you look for the nearest anchor." I knew if I traveled to Geezheebasun, I'd likely give myself over to its ill-tempered weather, which would no doubt be in need of a truss after catapulting me into the air, and chances were good it would blow me only to Kingdom Come, my destiny, my natural habitat, my gallows, my penance, the site of my heart's breaking. As for impersonating a junior tornado, it's quite easy to produce a teetotum of air with a hot plate, a bright bulb, and some aluminum foil, though it's easier yet, I discovered, to conjure a twister by warming my lungs with an electric blanket and exhaling full force into a spinning funnel. Even in winter, I have the sweltering and robust respiration of a blustery fire-eater, breath that can alter the weather in any room if not properly expelled. That humid zephyr smelling faintly of hardboiled eggs, the one that flutters the curtains all spring in Kingdom Come? Guilty. Men grab their hats and toupees when they see me heading their way, and if they look at me cross-ways, I sneeze and scalp them all, haboosh: a boulevard of cue balls.

So the story goes like this: as the tour group moved en masse across the barren landscape of this Tornado Alley, wearing camouflage so as to blend in with the local flora (that is, with the brown absence of flora), Fleance and Ludovik led the aged brigade, just behind their guide. Their plan was to hobble as fleet as they could into the path of the tornado as soon as they spotted it, and they'd entrusted the others with the task of holding back the tracker should he try to stop them. Let the callow weanling try, he'll have to pry forty arthritic fingers from his throat! they said. Fivescoreans are nothing if not loyal (though slowly so, instant loyalty provoking debilitating lumbago).

So they were shuffling slowly together, flashlights aimed at the gray nothing in front of them, and then, out of nowhere—the guide had never seen anything like it—a funnel cloud appeared, and then another, and another, and then those clouds touched down, collided, and out of their coupling spilled fifty-five offspring! The mother tornado, an angry dervish that stretched from sky to earth, heaved itself forward, and the Fivescoreans scattered. It was reported that Fleance and Ludovik appeared to have a change of heart and clung to the sleeves of the guide, who tried his best to pull them into a gully, but the tornado barreled forward and made a beeline toward them, and it trundled a snaking path, careful to weave around every cowering extreme vacationer until it reached Fleance, Ludovik, and the tracker. Once it found them, it slowed its spinning, backed up on its blustery haunches, and whirled deliberately so that it harvested only Fleance and Ludovik and spun wide of their guide, then it revved its funnel and heaved itself back into the air, disappearing into the sky. The other budding cyclones growled a final revolution and collapsed into dust.

The tornado delivered two bent bodies back to Fivescore, deposited them into the field visible from Fleance's picture window, and though everyone was startled to see them drop from the sky like space junk (except for Bazzle Esterhazy, who liked to tell the story of having once been a hailstone—a glider pilot in his youth, Bazzle drifted too close to a suddenly developing storm system, which seized him, destroyed his craft, lifted him into a swirling current 40,000 feet in the air, cocooned him in ice, then spit him out. He fell seven miles into a lake, bobbed to the surface, quickly thawed, and was fished out and resuscitated by two anglers nearby. Bazzle thinks about that moment with increasing frequency as he inches toward his centennial), they were relieved that Fleance Shoptaw did not have to be expatriated after all.

Thanks to the frazzled tracker, I quickly tracked down the guilty tornado, which was spinning listlessly on the edge of town, reduced to a dust devil, kicking up a little debris, and when it saw me, the tornado made a sound like sobbing, reared up on its tail with as much ferocity as it could muster, then deflated to little more than a science fair junior gyroscope. And it said: *I did it.* Though the tornado had been vanquishing visitors to Geezheebasun for years, it said it preferred to toss them safely (albeit usually in critical condition) to a new destiny, and lately it had been feeling hollow, lonely, and so small, barely atomic. It was all these accursed amateur storm chasers now, the taunting bullyraggers with their camcorders and pickup trucks and truck dogs in back, floppy ears aflap, reckless thrill-seekers hell-bent on spotting the big one and shadowing it into oblivion, inconsolable when they missed out on the devastation, an *affliction* they were, which was, well, nettling to the tornado, made it somehow feel like a show pony that had to canter on command, a tiger in a flimsy cage being poked with a stick. *Paper tiger,* said the tornado wearily, *in exile,* it added with a gentle swell. It had no real interest in or natural proclivity for homicide, it insisted, contrary to popular opinion, had only ever really had architectural ambitions, vertical dreams, aspired to leveling towns, flattening houses and water towers, throwing cars into trees, making vanish the top stories of municipal buildings, but this was simply the assignment the tornado had been given, and it was dutiful and had always taken its fate and notoriety in its stride.

"Maybe you're righting the wrongs of history," I suggested. Usually I did not provide assassins with excuses for their homicidal actions, but I understood the dispiriting vagaries of being very small while appearing to the happily small quite otherwise.

History is something the guilty tuck away in a book they hope no one will read, spat the tornado.

"What about that best-selling book of bad behavior?" I stammered. Though there was a lot of shifty weather in the Bible, I didn't remember ever hearing tell of a tornado, *per se*, an omission I could imagine being disheartening to a devout twister, and I regretted bringing it up. There is a good deal of gusting, however. Perhaps a tornado might take heart in that? The tornado moped and filliped the dirt into lackadaisical spirals.

Overhead clouds twisted and churned in a way that made them appear intestinal.

Who would you say are the guilty in that book? An impromptu Bible quiz by a regretfully murderous tornado! I could see this would be an unpredictable day.

I shrugged. "Goliath? Pontius Pilate? Judas Iscariot? There's always Satan. Oh, and Eve of course." I was sure there were significant Biblical villains I was overlooking, but these seemed like the heavyweights to me.

I thought I might be lifted up into the air, so forceful was the tornado's sigh, and this made me hopeful, but no, my feet remained planted. *Nooo,* exhaled the tornado. *There's a far bigger villain in that book.*

I knew what the tornado was driving at, and as I knew myself to be the guiltiest party of all, I decided not to argue.

So you're wondering why a contemplative gale like me, a pushover, a bleeding-heart wannabe, took the lives of two very elderly men who, at the last minute, decided they wanted to live.

I nodded.

Tired, sighed the tornado. *Tired of being used. Tired of being asked to deliver the fateful villainy people lack the gumption and fortitude to carry out themselves. Fleance and Ludovik had wanted to die. And then they didn't. But I was already in a lather by then. You can't ask the night to stop falling once the sun slips from its perch. And I took no one else!* thundered the tornado. *Can't you see the restraint that required?!* The agitated air settled, and the tornado corked its sadness. And then, as suddenly as a tornado forms from storm cloud and dust, it lifted into the air, as if plucked by a willful air stream, and disappeared into the gray nothing. It was spotted later whirling near the field outside Fleance Shoptaw's picture window, perhaps volunteering, a penance, pro bono, to help the all-too-elderly step fiercely, sail fearlessly into the grave.

NINETEEN
OXTROT

Mr. Mundrawala, Mateen, asked me one night after a class I spent bungling the fox-trot (forward, forward, side, er, ow!, pardon me, ow, er...) if I would do him the honor of breaking bread with him one evening (no doubt imagining a sizable country loaf as he eyed my breadbasket and pondered its capacity), so we met the next week in the West Bottoms at The Golden Ox, which is within spitting distance of the stockyards, so close you can hear the mournful lowing of the cattle awaiting a pneumatic nail to the head, steers lamenting the fall of their brethren now sizzling on the grill. I wondered what chargrilled steak must smell like to these death row longhorns forced to sniff the air scented with slaughter and a flame-broiled fate, wondered if they watched the smoke coil lazily in the cloudy Kansas sky above the nearby sirloin strip joints as they bid their compadres farewell with a lonesome snap of the tail. I imagined those pens cluttered with the four-legged souls of a million departed cattle. The world is an abattoir, and we all await the final hook we will hang from.

I figured Mr. Mundrawala, Mateen, had taken one look at me and pegged me for a beef eater, a dame reared on KC strip and Idaho spuds and sweet corn on the cob in the summer.

I ate sheepishly, tried to cut the meat from the bone without making a sound. A halting silence developed, and I could hear myself swallowing. Maybe Mr. Mundrawala feared that after the steak, he might be next. Toward the end of the meal, I picked at the skin of my twice-baked potato and suddenly confessed that my mother had rationed my calories as I was growing up, feeding me low-fat cottage cheese on a limp leaf of iceberg lettuce, carrot sticks, baked chicken—no skin, grapefruit, melba toast: the menu of the compulsive dieter, tabulating in a loose-leaf binder my caloric intake and calculating the velocity at which, under such a system, I'd become finally lovely, svelte and aptly demure, a daughter whose picture she need not bury in her chest of drawers, beneath girdles and stockings and broken wristwatches, true Daughter of the Mayflower.

Mateen clicked his tongue and shook his head, said, "I believe a healthy appetite is very becoming in a woman," then a rose blush bloomed on his russet cheeks and he added, "Please forgive me for my presumptuous familiarity verging on intimacy." He twisted his napkin in his lap, stared at the naked bone on his plate, and said, "But I find you quite handsome. Wallis." He looked up. "Mythical, dromedary beauty," he said in a timbre that was half whisper, half song.

His large brown eyes, saucers of spilled chai, blinked at me.

Hmmm.

The last man I was romantically entangled with ended up in a monastery and didn't tell me until the day he was leaving to join his Carmelite compatriots that I was his final overindulgence, his parting gluttony, the excess for which he'd repent and that would sate him the rest of his contemplative days. Asceticism, he told me as he looked down at his soon-to-be-discalced feet, was the only antidote to loving a large and looming woman, a woman under whose hammy haunches he felt himself dwindling, the essential atoms of being dispersing with each vigorous thrust. Then he larruped himself on the back with a willow switch and smiled dreamily, the yearning flagellant, happily mortified. There are times when I've sat up in bed and looked at the body lying next to me to see only a vague impression on the pillow, to hear the faint whistle of a faraway snore. When you tower above humankind, nothing is near at hand. Even your own heart sits at a remove, the blood traveling a treacherous distance to fuel your high-altitude thoughts, your hesitant swoonings.

Mateen invited me back to his house. He took my considerable mitt in both of his, across the table, knocking over the pepper mill, traced the lines of my palm with his finger, and I felt the sensation of a feather fluttering against my spine, as though there were tiny sparrows trapped beneath the skin of my back. He whispered, "You, Wallis Armstrong, are a grand temptation," then he tucked his hands in his jacket pockets.

Mateen owned an old, beat-up, blue VW bug, rusted in such a way that it looked like a prehistoric egg about to hatch, and when he reached his car, he leaned back against the driver's side door with his arms stretched out to the sides, as if to conceal its compact stature—I could never be his passenger. He got in and smiled at me apologetically.

I followed behind in my pickup, bent over my steering wheel, my finial pressed to the ceiling, and I watched the bobbing of Mateen's neatly groomed head, which could have cleared the roof of the bug even if he'd been sporting a bowler. I thought about those old French cars with the canvas roofs that rolled back to accommodate the hats of the farmers who drove them and whose lightweight construction allowed them to cross ploughed fields without breaking the eggs being carted to market. Few designs these days take into consideration unwieldy haberdashery, to my disappointment.

On the floor of Mateen's living room were diagrams of dances I'd never master, fox trot, cha-cha, samba, waltz, the numbered outlines of feet stepping and sliding. Mateen stepped inside the prints, overgrown footsteps his polished loafers could not fill, and followed the feet of the tango to his kitchen.

"They're from the Arthur Murphy studio in Karachi," he called to me. I knelt and traced the dance steps with my finger, cachalot swimming in a staggered pod, reassuring.

"Arthur Murphy?" I asked. Mateen returned with two glasses of moon red soda still fizzing. "Yes," he said, nodding his head, smiling vaguely. "Two letters' difference, it was all the same to me. I was eager to follow the cheerful movement of Western feet." He offered me a glass. "Cream soda?" I felt myself happily shrinking in front of his candid eyes, my skin loosening, bones narrowing, and my heart hiccupped with the sensation. I put a hand to my chest, in case a burp were next. "I am not nearly as anxious about corruption as perhaps I ought to be. In fact, when I was a child, I sometimes welcomed overtures from the sweetly beaming missionaries trailing famished rice Christians in their wake."

I walked around Mateen's living room, avoiding the dance steps. There was an open secretary against a wall, and on it sat a small ceramic cherub, winged and plump. It was red cheeked and grinned drunkenly, eyes at half-mast, seemed to suffer from the gin blossoms, woozily sauced.

Staring into his soda, the color of dilute blood, Mateen smiled and said, "Your St. Thomas Aquinas wonders if angels are more clear-headed in the morning. They have matutinal thoughts, crepuscular thoughts, perhaps even mid-afternoon thoughts, but they always of course employ angel reasoning, which is not the same as reasoning as we understand it. In fact, I'd venture to guess we'd find the thoughts of angels to have an improbable logic, but Aquinas, he wonders if their thinking gets more muddled throughout the day, if, like us, their minds churn more productively when they've just sloughed off the gauze of sleep. The angels think, *The sun is rising and I too must ascend.* They think, *The moon is a frightened armadillo, and I mustn't keep God, that careening lorry that will veer into its path and turn it to carrion in the morning, waiting.* They think, *The sun is a mouth rounded in terror.* I imagine them to have strong opinions only about heavenly bodies." This was as voluble as Mateen had ever been in my presence. He looked up at me and smiled without moving his lips, and I found him at that moment so utterly fetching. If he'd asked me for a kidney, I would gladly have shown him where to make the incision.

"And of course, philosophers continue to puzzle over how many angels can 'dance on the point of a very fine needle without jostling one another.' Does it make a difference how well fed these angels are? One imagines they're not all Jack Sprats after all. On the contrary, and that's their attraction, is it not? Have you ever seen a gaunt cherub? Unthinkable." He took the figurine from my fingers, grinned mildly, set it back on the desk. "We find them comely because they are amply fleshed. Of course, they were not always so. In truth, it is the ruthless angels that interest me most."

The skin around Mateen's eyes was puckered, his rounded cheeks guileless and kind. Despite this knowledgeable disquisition, they were the sort of eyes that seemed unaware of their own innocence, and I felt my giant's heart thumping inside my chest, booming like a jungle drum warning of the approach of rival warriors, felt the beating grow irregular. "Are you a theologian?" I asked.

"No," he said. "Just a man. With an occasional amateur interest in things not of this world." He grinned sincerely.

"Being a large woman is a little like being a small man," said jimp and sparrow-boned, cedar-skinned, beautiful Mateen Mundrawala, who swept through the air of any room with the liquid grace of a manta ray fluttering along the ocean floor. He offered me his hand, matched his palm to mine, raised the other arm to rest on my hip, and whirled me about in what I recognized as a waltz, though widdershins, as though to reverse the bad magic of my being a bumbler, or anticipating the wrong direction I'd naturally head in. I was left-footed. I tried to follow without flattening his feet with my own, but I moved unsteadily, and Mateen's attentive body registered my ungainly hesitation and he reeled more slowly. I wondered what sort of dancer Vivica would be. She moved so much more certainly, striding with absolute conviction, the decisive footfall of the doubtless. I knew I walked ambivalently, a body unconvinced, feet mashing the grass or shag pile or scraping the asphalt in a tentative shuffle, feet prepared to take it all back, reverse their course at the first reproach.

"This was rather a scandalous dance in its day," said Mateen, "considered quite vulgar, the proximity of bodies, the commingling of breaths." Mateen brought my hand to his lips and exhaled against it, and I thought I felt my hand draw a breath. I stopped moving, stranded in steps five and six of the promenade. There are parts of my body that long to be sovereign and sometimes try to secede. It takes enormous effort to corral my limbs, keep my parts from defecting. We're big enough, they threaten me, to strike out on our own.

He stepped back and held one of my hands in both of his. "You interrogate the dead?"

"Pardon me?"

"The murdered, you make their deaths speak to you? You reanimate slain bodies until you see the ends to which they came?"

"Oh. Well." I had never spoken to Mateen about this and hoped he wasn't going to ask me to photograph him with his tongue lolling theatrically to the side, eyes x'd out, rigor-stiffened body lying twisted inside a chalk outline, the body's final dance step. I had met such men.

"You are like Ruman," he said, "who serves the infernal latitudes and demands that the condemned record their every evil act, and some are so iniquitous, they are doomed to write for all eternity, though their hands cramp with excruciating spasms that reverberate throughout their bodies, harrowing their flesh with a stabbing agony. There is no amnesty for the wicked." Mateen's eyes seemed to swim with vision, and he dropped my hand. "He will come soon for me," he said, rubbing his hands together.

"There was a woman I was to marry. I did not love her, and she did not love me. This is always beside the point."

He walked to the secretary and opened a small drawer. He held in his hand a tarnished metal locket no bigger than his thumb. Inset in the cover was a tiny magnifying glass, an idea that seemed to me somehow to cancel itself out. He opened the locket and inside was a miniature book, red with a gilt filigree pattern.

"My great-grandfather fought for the Allied troops in the Great War, and he carried this with him, a talisman meant to ward off martyrdom on the battlefield. It proved, however, to be a weak adversary against influenza." Mateen held the tiny book up to his mouth as though he were going to swallow it, dose himself.

Then he pried it open with his thumbs, as though he were shelling peas, and read to me, rhythmically droning, in what I guessed was Arabic, murmuring, murmuring, full lips barely parted, purring, each syllable a bead he passed from lip to tongue.

And then he closed his eyes and whispered in a faint voice that seemed to come from another room, a voice made miniature: *"In the name of Allah, most benevolent, ever-merciful.*

"O you people, fear your Lord. The great convulsion of the Hour of Doom will indeed be a terrible thing.

"On the day you behold it, every suckling female shall quit in confusion the child she nurses, and every pregnant mother drop the cargo in

her belly, unformed. You will see men staggering drunk, yet they will not be drunk. The torment of Allah will be strong upon them.

"And yet there are men who dispute about Allah without comprehending, and follow every wayward devil, who, it is written, will beguile whoever follows him, and lead him to the Penalty of the Flame.

"If you have any doubt, O men, about being raised to life again, remember that We formed you from dust, then a drop of semen, then a leech-like clot, then a chewed-up lump of flesh shaped and shapeless, that We may make it clear to you. We cause what We please to remain in the womb for an appointed term, then do We bring you forth as infants, then coddle you that you may reach your age of full strength. And some of you are summoned to die, while some are sent back to the feeblest age, their decrepitude, so that they know nothing, having once known much. You see the earth withered and lifeless, but when We shower water upon it, it bestirs itself and swells, brings forth every kind of green abundance.

"That is so for Allah is the Undeniable Reality. It is He who quickens the dead, for He has power over All Things.

"And the Hour will come, there can be no doubt about it, when Allah will raise the moldering dead, release them from the dark and dreamless sleep of their graves."

Mateen opened his eyes and smiled. "Whose resurrection is it you wait for, Wallis Armstrong?"

I felt the berg of my heart trying to break free of the ancient glacier inside me. "Do you believe in God, Mateen Mundrawala?" I found myself asking. There is a diaspora in Heaven, I thought, to which failed gods are consigned, *god-manqué*. In Heaven's ghetto shall I dwell for eternity.

He gripped his elbow in one hand and his chin in the other, forming a contemplative right angle with his arms. "I believe in *you*," he said. I'd seen that faithful gaze before, eyes glistening with devotion. I looked at the floor, looked at the wall, looked at the door. I watched the carbonation disappearing from my cream soda, regretted acutely the death of each bubble. I felt sorrow flowering inside me.

Mateen Mundrawala enveloped me with his small body like a spreading vapor, twinned my every twitch and reflex, impossibly matched me rounded mouth to rounded mouth, ankle to ankle, skin to skin, each gargantuan cell implausibly mirrored, the very nucleoli of a colossal woman replicated in the fluid rippling of this diminutive man, the friction of desire igniting and fusing the humid flesh, and I pulled him inside me, all of him, each bone and heartbeat; every drop of water he'd ever drunk and dream he'd ever dreamt; every graceful tap of his foot, every dip and lunge and shuffle-ball-change; every regret stored deep in his abdomen; former wisdom teeth and current bicuspids; every wary migration, across busy streets, crowded ballrooms, partitioned land, oceans and deserts, space and time, and farther; lies he wish he'd told, longings lodged beneath his sternum; and this is where it always fails, the love unmade, one body swimming sightlessly in the vast black sea of the other, the other always me, waving invisibly from some distant shore of myself, feeling abstract and woefully infinite, that blind body seeking succor and a breathless respite from the burden of being discrete, lost and irrecoverable, spat from the choppy waters onto an inhospitable landscape, groping for purchase, a sand flea in search of a morsel of blood in the most barren and fleshless desert, but I could feel the planet tilting, feel the infection I'd become loosed inside his susceptible flesh, feel myself comfortably confined within the limited skin of another, and this, it was fucking, yes, but as close to doffing a layer of loneliness as I'd ever come.

☾

Obie spent one cloudless and sweltering July with my father's cousins, Dorcas and Charlie Dee, on their farm in Wynot, Nebraska, and he said he sat sweating in the barn one sizzling afternoon next to their beloved horse Zubenelgenubi, stroking his vanilla mane as he died. He was an elderly horse, earnest and loyal, a lugger of lumber and humans, but a horse who could also cantor stylishly, with the fine grace of a smaller creature, and he nickered once and described for Obie what appeared to him behind those dimming black eyes, over which his velvety eyelids began to droop heavily, like weighted window shades extinguishing the night sky, as his breathing rasped and slowed. He said he saw himself loping along the incandescent surface of the moon, which is hard for a horse to do, cratered as the moon is and not battened down by gravity, hard to get a firm hoof-hold, and hanging low to the ground, in the thickened air, invitingly, were brilliant blue oats, bobbing everywhere in the moon's soupy ether, shining and delicious looking, but he did not wish to eat them. He wafted gracefully over this vast field of floating fodder and then he came to a rivulet the eye-watering color of the sun, luminous as a tropical noon, and the blinding, bubbling water rose to meet him, and that, said Obie, is Rapture to a faithful palomino, and then the air rushed from his death-flared nostrils and he snapped his eyes shut, lashes, lush as a starlet's, finally at rest, a definitive passage. After which Obie saw Zubenelgenubi's spirit, unbridled by horseflesh, shoot into the sky like a popped cork, his soul gushing forth, a galloping star retracing its steps, and it took its place in that empyreal paddock on the far side of the sun, settling in among all the other dead horses lazing about in the blue beyond of the afterlife. When Obie told Dorcas, she clutched him to her, covered his ears, and heaved a single sob.

Several months later the ghost of Zubenelgenubi snuck into Obie's room while he was sleeping, nosed his twisted sheets and snuffled till he roused. He was blue as a wild iris, fore to aft, from succumbing finally to the ravenous hunger that follows dying, Obie figured, and wolfing down that ubiquitous silage that winked delectably like edible sapphires, dear blue heaven! He waggled his ears meaningfully and instructed Obie that when he died, he should be sure to shuck off his shoes for the only way to find your way to Paradise, as any expired kangaroo can tell you, is through the sensitized skin of your feet, those hoppers that will loft you into the next world, and with this he lifted a polished hoof to show Obie he'd been unshod, foot and hoof protection being unnecessary, you see, an impediment even, in the buoyant atmosphere of a lunar eternity. Then Zubenelgenubi shivered his revenant withers and said, "And remember: as the body expands, the soul shrinks." Obie widened his eyes at me.

"Guess that means I've the soul of a newt," I said, "soul of a gnat, single-cell soul," feeling relieved. "As I suspected."

"'As the body expands...the soul...shrinks,'" said Obie slowly, tapping his forehead, eyes angled skyward. "Un*less* of course you are God, in whose body the never-ending soul needs room to swim." Obie's serious face broke into a smile, the theology of my corpus cracked, close call. For Obie, my ardent postulant, my body was always a cross-eyed syllogism, and he believed fervently in the symbolic logic of my lengthening limbs, my thickening trunk. God is limitless. The body of Wallis is too (is two, at least!). Therefore Her soul will swim until it reaches the shore, on the other side of infinity, at which her body forever, longingly laps. He measured my body and told me I stood at least a hundred hands high, exceeding the most hopeful horse trainer's grandest expectations.

For God, as the body enlarges, the world too balloons, and the soul all but drowns in the endless and incarcerating, undulating substance, the oceanic flesh. So sayeth Wallis. (Or, for those wary of the blasphemy of vowels, my shrunken tetragrammaton: Wlls).

He was blue with death, the beautiful cyanosis bluing his cheeks, his brow, silvering his lips, his blood gone zaffer, throttled corpuscles gasping. His agapanthus skin (at whose root, *agape*, is love) bloomed bluely, still and clammy, his face a pane of fallen sky.

And there was Azrael, cyclonic wings beating, body all eyes darting and tongues wagging, separating the soul from that cerulean carcass, skinning it like game. He would discard the soul, toss it on the smoldering heap with the others, and eat the suffocated flesh, sweet as nutmeat. He'd written the name on his palimpsest hand, over all the others, and now licked the ink from his palm, O-*b*- dissolving onto his inky tongue, revisionist angel, ravenous angel of missing children, angel of erasure. There sat the empty sneakers at his feet, angel of uncertainty, uncertain seraph, tight-lipped and skulking at the periphery of sorrow. The beautiful boy, faithful and true, blue as hidden blood, blue as tundra, blue as thin air, Obie, O-b, *Oh be!* O. Be mine.

It was a dream and it was not a dream.

If I am his dream, he must yet be sleeping in the world.

I dreamt Mateen was sleeping next to me, and I confided to him that I had a brother I'd loved who believed me to be too big to be anything but God. I told him that the children in my neighborhood began to vanish when I was a girl, and I could sometimes see where these children had last been but could never find them, and I told him I'd seen bodies hanging from barn rafters and leaning in ovens and though those deaths were definitive they were usually a lie, and I confessed that I'd accidentally killed a man and that I'd come to believe that protecting myself proves fatal for others.

I awoke to find him gone.

TWENTY
THREE TRINITARIANS

1. Hippostasis

There are, as I see it, from my Olympian view, when I wave away the clouds wooling my gaze, many advantages to having a humanly height and bearing. The taller you are, the more things you feel compelled to clean (particularly true of those tidy-as-a-pin suck-ups trying to sidle up to His Cleanliness by way of the whisk-whisk of an electrostatic duster, their polished godliness gleaming in evidence of their immaculate virtue, pfft). Short, you can pretend the world above your head is blue and spotless as the sanitized sky. Do we clean because other people will be witness to the unseemly grime of our lives: , confirmation of our fallen state (oh, to be truly fallen, flat on my full-moon face, that close to the splintered planking in the groundfloor of the world), or do we clean because…we want things to be clean? I polish and dust and squeegee because I see it (imagine being able to eyeball every floating mote, *ach, du lieber Gott!*). I see the powdery filth that has settled around the cereal boxes crowding the tops of refrigerators, onto crown moldings, the lazily whirring blades of ceiling fans, see the carcasses of insects who landed aloft, barely stirring the out-of-reach dirt to die a solitary death, dust to winged dust, see tiny feathers escaped from fluffed pillows, crumbled paint and plaster from long-ago improvements, and unexpected objects: broken buttons, jellybeans, pennies, carpet tacks, the confetti of a shredded letter, things that cleverly defy disposal by accumulating out of sight. Above our heads there is a world of detritus existing precisely because it is invisible. Once glimpsed, it is vanquished, as though there were sanctuary and hope and the promise of a long and happy life empty of suffering in the scoured surface. (And dachsunds and ferrets and fugitive hamsters, dragging their stretched bellies through the ground's accumulation, see, from the other end of vertical space, that furry universe that blooms beneath the sofa.)

At night, I would lower my head to Obie, hair matted with all existence, and he'd remove the things that would have amassed there, tweezing them carefully so as not to pull my hair: leaves and spider sacs and kites tangled in my tousled canopy and exploded umbrellas and boomerangs whistling in an endless revolution around my peak and osprey nests and chemical smog and vapor trails and airplanes lost in the Bermuda Triangle of my knotted mop and heat-seeking missiles circling my fevered brow and blazing comets singeing my scalp and the smoldering ejaculate of the sun and flying saucers and long-dead stars and quarks and

God's. Catalyzing. Breeeeath! Then...

the glittering pollen of an imperfectly understood space and time continuum and the fizz of sizzled ozone and the tarnish of moonglow silvering my hair and satellites orbiting my skull and cobwebs of time-frittered clouds and dislodged gargoyles and suspended suicides who windmill their arms and imagine they've been snagged in a purgatory of falling and owl scat knobbed with bones and lunatic hummingbirds needling my ears for nectar and glow-in-the-night Frisbees and the gape-mawed labradors leaping to catch them and bats with corrupted echolocation careening repeatedly into my jaw and acidic rainwater frizzing my roots and the caroming billiard balls of the universe's many renegade atoms and the nucleoli steering them randomly hither and the welling nothingness at the center of the center of the center of Everything.

Obie would comb the hair on my weighted godhead clean as new and so began the next day, unruly mane detangled, black and radiant as the wings of dung beetles (tumble-bugs sometimes also extracted), but then, slowly, throughout the afternoon and evening, my noodle would nod forward, wobble on its stem, laden again with the day's debris, disheveled hair a fixed tornado ensnaring the world.

God is big-boned, said Obie. *Fat with atmosphere and all the longing and agony of the universe, so heavy, there's nowhere safe for her to sit. The minute she rests her magnanimous haunches, the planet will fall out of the sky, the sky will fall out of the sky, and we will all be lost, trapped in a vacuum of itinerant potential.*

Obie, my savior, could not let that happen.

He lay beneath my bed as I slept, singing quietly to stretch-nosed, stub-legged, long-haired, droop-eared Hell-mutt von Brautwurst as he growled then sniffed the floor skeptically and sneezed, my brother's dirt-smudged boy-hands wedged against the box springs.

Obie was, without a doubt, the strongest person I ever knew.

Hellmutt von Brautwurst lived to the hoary age of nineteen and died, midsnore, in his sleep, legs apedal, hips and teeth and eyesight still intact, which must be why when he returned, though he was a shade on the diaphanous side, even for a hungry Paraclete, he appeared none the worse for wear. His tail, however, had disappeared in that translation from earthly solid to sanctified gas, dog to god, mutt to ghost, and it was difficult for God and Her Chosen Sibling to tell when he was well pleased. He often wavered where his water dish had been, looking eternally parched, which, one imagines, ghosts, holy or otherwise, always necessarily become, incapable of retaining moisture as they are, and, as we'd learned from Zubenelgenubi, there's nothing so desiccating as the airless atmosphere in heaven.

Ah, what a piece of work is dog!

2. Hellmutt von Brautwurst Speaks his Waggish Mind

Big girl bigbig ankles in the way tennis balls bobbing but smelling sniff not unlike chicken kibble sniff I don't know from God but she is generous with the liver treats warp and woof of my world sometimes I like to pee under the dining room table because it is so comfortable the grass pricks me scratchchchch and it is a green and growing world outside in spring my favorite month I pity the vertical creature for she cannot lick her ass and that is a pleasure I would not forego to walk on two legs the squirrels are a scourge and sleep is my country little boys are little better than squirrels but this one has a stomach that fits my muzzle and when he lies on the floor I am able to rest my nose which is often fatigued as it is the first part of me to enter any room next door the brown-nosing retriever is hysterically obedient and I agree with the shiba inu/beagle mix on the other side that he is best ignored but that aloofly trotting ox of a bouvier can eat my retractable leash for all I care sniff.

3. Brother of God

When I was fifteen weeks old, I hiccupped one night and experienced a sudden spurt of growth that made my feet erupt through my footed sleeper, and my mother refused to nurse me until such time as it was clear to her that I was not my sister's brother. The too hastily spreading body, "stretching into next week" as my good-humored father, 5' 10" in wing-tips, tried jocularly to put it, was a troubled proposition in our house, and my feet curled against the end of the cradle until my father freed me. He fed me formula secretly at night, but I had sensed my infraction, noted the brooding absence of my mother, and so was stalled in my infancy, willing my body not to be nourished, obedient son, until My Sister appeared at my bedside and urged me to grow, which I did, though I fell short of Her expectations, to my mother's unspeakable relief. We all fall short of Her expectations, of course, short of the ho-rizon line of Her gaze that splits the world simply into earth and firmament. That is what it is to be human, after all, to disappoint My Sister, and it is all for the best, for the world is not designed for us to be otherwise, not nearly sturdy enough for us all to tower divinely above the animals.

The Once and Future God

Years and years and long years hence, ages after the death and spectral resurrection of Hellmutt von Brautwurst...long after winters everywhere have turned green as young corn in Kansas and people begin to sweat in December, eventually running air conditioners year-round as they page nostalgically through photo albums and history books displaying pictures of trees coated with ice and rooftops weighted with snow...after countless bodies have been heedlessly mutilated in war upon war upon preventable war...after Vivica Planet trepans her own brain with a filched finger bone of her brother's body and sees in the mirror the yawning want beneath the deceptive blood and tissue of everything... after Hampton Knight discovers a cure for all fatal afflictions, which the NSA confiscates and destroys...after the first woman to be elected President of the Re-United States is slain on the front lawn of the Whitehouse by a band of soft-fleshed, nearsighted, congenitally disgruntled men (one of whom is cousin to Darren Crenshaw) who'd been born with two mouths smeared across the rolled dough of their faces in a permanent and redundant rictus...after ravenous viruses that devour human flesh like fire gulps brush in a drought have ravaged millions of limbs and torsos, and others that re-encode DNA have caused the features of a million faces to rearrange themselves in a reptilian leer...after the thirteenth and nineteenth amendments to the Constitution of the United States are repealed, at knife-point, and the reactors of nuclear power plants around the world crack and melt and make the skin drip from the bones of the indigent throngs living nearby...after the coasts of all continents recede like a hairline, the earth balding with water slick with oil and acid and mutant marine life and giving off an appallingly beautiful green chemical shimmer…after a plague of eyeless, pink, soft, and toxic crabs poisons the Palau Islands, paralyzing every living thing, which is only the beginning…after chaos reigns on the earth, strides languorously from city to city like an ancient animal, altering the very quality of light as it goes, dulling the sun's rays…long after Kingdom Come has come and gone and Obie, my only begotten brother, has disappeared, I will lie in my final sickbed, my everlasting life drawing to an end (Hellmutt's thinning ghost skulking nearby), sinking through the earth's crust, and feel the wind rustle my empty hair as my soul's candle gutters and the planet falls, falls, farther and farther, tumbling headlong from the sky.

God, who tries hard not to look ahead, knowing what She will behold, is not, as you can plainly see, an optimist.

And therein lies our doom.

Unless we cheer Her up and quick!

TWENTY-ONE
GAYTHAL DETHLOFF, MOTHER OF MURDER

I have not seen Vivica Planet for six weeks now, not since she took me to her laboratory and revealed to me the ylem of her brother, man I killed, accidentally, magnified for me a particle of that heart that no longer beats with desire, the cell whose soul we gazed into perhaps the very one that blazed with regret as he clutched his throat, the last sentiment to seize him, be pumped to his extremities, now an illegible smear on a slide (Vivica would surely send me off with a flea in my ear if she got the faintest whiff of such a plaint). But she called me and asked if I'd take her to visit a housebound friend, someone she thinks I'll be interested to meet. She is schooling me in women with fallen hearts, women who know better than to nourish expectation. I have dreamt of Vivica since then, have watched her debone my body with a fish knife and carve me into tiny bits, chum for a grander catch, then place the fragments under a lens that made each part of me tinier yet, until all that remained was the glare of the microscope's bulb on glass, and I found myself smiling hopefully when I awoke. Vivica Planet, I strongly suspect, aims to erase me, erase us all, sister colossi with our pocket-sized siblings, and I find myself not entirely opposed to the idea. I have always longed to be less than I am.

I am a quarter inch taller than Vivica Planet—she insisted we measure—and this made her livid; she stifled a roar as she let the tape measure angrily retract, snap! So whenever we're together, she wears heels that have her mincing nearly on the tips of her bunions, implausible plus-plus-plus-size danseuse, and she rests a weighted mitt on my shoulder until I slouch. I am not the tallest tomato in the universe. There are women larger than I in Borneo and Patagonia, Lichtenstein and Turkmenistan, even in Alabama, hardy beanstalks who best me by an inch or two, hulking exceptions who walk with a pronounced oxbow hunch so as to put the peewees at ease. They're in for a lifetime of bulging discs and migraines, sciatica and creaking knees. I've read their stories in *The Book of Very, Very Large Women*, a gift from my father. In the chapter titled "Everyday Ailments of the Common Sheclops," there's a cautionary X-ray of a woman from the Azores whose hardened C-shaped spine kept her from ever gazing into the wide blue above her, though she was in closer proximity to the sky than anyone else on the islands. She died standing up, after having apologetically stared at her own feet for fifty years.

Gaythal Dethloff was the size of a grand piano, *wide as the day is long*, I could imagine my father remarking. She lay in a bed that appeared to be fashioned from several king-size mattresses, a molten mass of flesh that seemed to be erupting yet: she was geologic, cooling magma atop igneous rock marking the passing of time, rippling from epoch to epoch. Her belly bowed in the air like a yurt, a stupa, a shrine to her remarkable rotundity, and I imagined tiny people living and fasting and praying inside her. She reminded me of everything.

Her cheeks were freshly rouged, her face round as a wall clock and dull with powder, chin upon chin, a glacier thawing, and her hair was an orderly cap of curls, snowy ringlets coiled against her taut scalp. The skin of her face was stretched nearly to the breaking point of its elasticity and her eyebrows plucked and penciled into two faint Greta Garbo arcs, a line of single hairs stitched on her forehead, making her appear permanently startled, as though she had awakened to find she'd ballooned overnight (*gadzooks!* she looked poised to exclaim). Her lips were bee-stung red. It didn't appear to me that her hands could easily reach across the volcanic expanse to the mouth, and I wondered who had dolled her up, whose full-time job it was to feed her and tend to her body. It was a body that had long ago exceeded all acceptable limits, and I imagined her bed flanked by television cameras eager to document and profit from the swelling excess of this vasty odalisque, slave to her surging flesh. I recalled catching the tail end of a news story not long ago, Live at Five, about a dame too monumental to walk on two feet, bedridden but persistent, her burdened heart beating against all likelihood and common sense. Green and lavender comforter rumpled around her, Gaythal Dethloff made me think of an ornamental cabbage. There was a funereal smell in the close air of this small house, mums and gardenias, roses on the wane.

"She was a music teacher," Vivica whispered to me through lips straining to smile politely. "Before."

Before? *Before the asteroid's extinguishing wallop, dinosaurs wandered the earth,* I thought.

As we made our way toward Gaythal's bed, we had to wade carefully through musical instruments, dusty and propped against every surface: violin, maracas, ocarina, xylophone, zither, cymbals, clarinet, French horn, ukulele, bongo drums, triangle, rhythm blocks, saxophone, tambourine, castanets, balalaika, flügelhorn, piccolo, bassoon, accordion, harmonica, bass trombone and pedal harp, everywhere objects standing at the ready to percuss or chirrup or honk or warble. And then Gaythal's disproportionately small mouth widened and out of it marched a resonant sound that made it seem cavernous and acoustically optimized. Lips aquiver, she ran through the scales, a mezzo-soprano with a quickly trilling vibrato that made me think of the wings of hummingbirds: "Mi, mi, mi, mi, mi, mi, mi, mi, meeeeee," she sang and smiled, her beefy lips exceeding the outline of lipstick trying to lasso them down to size. Then she laughed and coquettishly nuzzled her shoulder, that is, the flesh of the jowl that had spilled onto her shoulder.

"Gaythal Dethloff, Wallis Armstrong, Wallis Armstrong, Gaythal Dethloff," said Vivica Planet, shaking the jumbo prawn of Gaythal's pinkie.

"Pleased to meet you, Miss Armstrong," Gaythal said, and it seemed to me she batted her eyes, but it was hard to tell, two receding raisins pressed in a rising loaf. Everything about her suddenly made me think of food, the sort of food that makes a dieting person hate herself for gorging on it in dreams as she sleeps her malnourished and fitful sleep. She was a tipped-over gravy boat of a woman, a mountainous meringue, exploded strudel, melting butter pat, chicken pot pie. And then I thought of my mother, saw her scowling at me, which she did preventatively hours before any meal. And I imagined Gaythal Dethloff being passed under the table, a yeasty dinner roll (she is risen!) smuggled from knee to knee.

"Hello?" I said, insufficiently. In this woman, I thought, Obie would surely see the broadening circumference and essential ingredients of God. And I could retire, at last. But without being able to watch Obie's faith ebb, I fear I am a lifer, Johnny-punchclock to the end of time. Without Obie, I am doomed to endless enormity.

"Pull up a seat, gals, take a *load* off!" said Gaythal, who then let loose with a chortle. There were two kitchen chairs nearby, and Vivica removed the cello and tuba sitting upon them and moved them near the bed. I sat and Gaythal threw back the covers. I couldn't help staring at the swollen stems that sprouted beneath the lacy furbelow of Gaythal's nightgown—her feet were covered in mukluks, for which a herd of handsomely furred seals had given their lives. "Nestor gave me those," Gaythal said, and her smile made me think of a camel in a canoe. "He dealt in exotic imports for a time," she said. She cocked her head slightly to the side, and Vivica picked up a framed photograph from the night table and handed it to me. In it a beer-bellied man with receding, black, shoulder-length hair and a woolly handlebar mustache, wearing amber-lensed aviator glasses and a fringed leather vest, stood next to a very thin woman in a sleeveless black pencil dress and kitten-heel pumps, dark hair swept into a French twist. On the other side of the man was an oblong tribal mask, carved from dark wood, tall as he was and jaggedly frowning. He steadied it with his hand and grinned like an angler who'd hooked a record-breaking bass.

"A real looker," said Gaythal with a sigh, "back in the day. Winsome as a willow, tall drink of water," she said, and one raisin disappeared in the dough of her cheek, a wink.

"That's Gaythal with her son Nestor," Vivica said, and she tapped the glass covering the picture.

Gaythal saw my expression before I could smooth the bewilderment from my brow, and she said, "Yep, bony as a beanpole. Before." There is always a squandered before.

Vivica scooted her chair a little closer to Gaythal and said, "Wallis doesn't know about Nestor. Do you, Wallis?" She took the picture from me and returned it to the end table. The woman in the photograph didn't even look like a distant relation of Gaythal's. I imagined that woman inside Gaythal trying to tread her girth, sucked down by the enveloping undertow, sinking to the ocean floor, glug-glug.

I shook my head. I could see I was going to find out about another thing I didn't want to know.

"Well, she'd be the only innocent." Gaythal snorted. "I moved away to Council Bluffs, then came back a few years ago, but word travels, follows you around like a damn dog. You know, all those unsolved psycho killer programs and such on TV now. Might as well hang out a goddamned shingle." Another abbreviated honk of her schnozzle.

"How are you feeling, Gaythal?" asked Vivica.

"Sen*sa*tional, neverbetter, fitasafiddle," she said. "And yoooou?" Gaythal drawled the "you" accusingly.

"Very well, thank you." Vivica threw me a sidelong glance of indeterminate significance.

"I'm, uh, I'm..I'm well. Too," I added. I could feel my

tongue stumbling up the dilapidated staircase of my words as I spoke.

"Well, well, we're all well, three fancy bantams in fine feather, terrrrific," Gaythal said with a growl. "Arf!"

"So, Gaythal, Wallis is something of a crime buff, and I thought she'd be interested to hear about Nestor's exploits."

Gaythal grinned slightly, glared at me, and said, "Crime buffs. I hate 'em. All you amateur gumshoes with your camcorders just waiting to catch an impromptu lunatic in some diabolical act you can sell to the tabloids to subsidize your cowardice. If you ask me, the devil's witness has just as much blood on his hands as the devil does, and that includes that stuck-up muckety-muck God," she said, looking up at the water-stained ceiling, "the old sideline spectator." She sniffed.

I had nothing to say to this, I was inclined to agree. I've always felt implicated by the things I've seen. Also by the things I've failed to see. This is the problem with God's sense of time, I once said to Obie, after the disappearance of Darren Crenshaw. For God, who travels through time at the speed of both tortoise and light wave, millennia pass in the blink of his giant, all-seeing, astigmatic eye, therefore he cannot be expected to keep up with the pandemonium of human lives, and so naturally there's a surplus of suffering, and Obie said: "Don't blink."

"So, you want the lowdown on Nestor, eh?" asked Gaythal Dethloff, mouth hitched skeptically to one side. *No. No. No,* I thought, and I nodded my head.

"All right then. First thing you need to know is Nestor wasn't one of those little shits who drowns baby bunnies in a bucket for kicks or puts firecrackers in the ears of kittens and whatnot, junior nutjob. And he didn't masturbate compulsively while stabbing Barbie dolls with a cocktail fork, nothing like that. He wasn't a snot-nosed maniac whose parents chained him to a rusting bedstead in the basement and made him watch endless acts of deviant carnality. Are we clear on that? He didn't come from diamonds either, but that's the point: an upbringing average and unremarkable as a piece of toast." Gaythal sneered at Vivica, who exuded her usual air of noncommittal mystery, and then with one exaggerated swipe, Gaythal wiped her lipstick off on the back of her hand, leaving a smear of red circling her mouth and making her look like she'd just eaten a strawberry Bomb Pop. It seemed as though the lipstick had somehow been keeping a complicated truth from escaping, and she was now ready to confide all. Gaythal tried to move herself back in her bed and her elbow hit the table and the picture of her and her son fell face forward with a snap. She pushed the curls back from her forehead, and her massive arm looked lethal as the flesh swung from the bone (the bone itself an assumption, no more evident beneath her skin than a kidney), a flabby cudgel whose most halfhearted blow no mortal could hope to survive. I could see Gaythal Dethloff did not gladly suffer fools.

"Disappointment can curdle an otherwise honorable man," said Gaythal, "like vinegar in milk," and the hostility seemed to drain from her all at once. Her cheeks sagged and her eyes were barely visible now beneath the buttermilk biscuits of her eyelids. "He was a deeply disappointed man confronted with the endless disappointments of other men." Gaythal pursed her lips, ringed red as a bull's-eye, and looked at Vivica, who sat silently erect, implacable as a sphinx.

"He met Ezekiel at the soup kitchen where he volunteered." Gaythal reached across her bed and swept a pillow to the floor, revealing a phonograph. She lifted the lid and switched it on, thumbed the arm onto an album. The noise it made as the needle slid scratchily across the vinyl sounded like a giant, amplified pair of pants being unzipped, and then it settled into a groove; a violin quietly wept. "Shostakovich," said Gaythal, staring again at the stain on her ceiling. And then she pulled from beneath the bedcovers her own violin, whose strings she tried in vain to pluck. She made me think of a circus clown who carts around a world of objects in his sagging britches, bicycle horn and gardening shears, jack-in-the-box and parasol. "Can't play anymore," she said to me. "My hands." I felt Vivica growing impatient beside me, though she didn't move, didn't twitch or blink. "Nestor never cared for music. Tinnitus. Certain pitches, he said, felt like an icepick in his eardrums. Brahms in particular." Gaythal put her hand over her ear, as though she'd trapped it and didn't want it to escape, beautiful nautilus swimming in a foamy sea of white curls. "I think a head that cannot abide music is a head doomed to think unmelodious thoughts," she said. She turned the phonograph off, and it groaned to a stop.

"It all started with Ezekiel, a dark and fateful acquaintance. He was, of course, a prophet—a name is a destiny. And a mendicant, never had two plug nickels to rub together unless some guilt-ridden white-collar dropped them into his tattered porkpie.

"Nestor's split pea was a favorite among the regular ragamuffins. He didn't like me calling them that. He said they were just *down on their luck, Ma, but for the grace of* blahblahblah. I grew to hate the indigent." Gaythal looked me over, and

I moved a hand to my chest, trying to conceal my pauper's spirit, the bankrupt, soon-to-be-foreclosed-upon soul I hid beneath my own deceptive windfall of flesh. Vivica, descended, to look at her, from a long line of landed gentry, sat with a stiffly aristocratic posture that suggested she held the Deed to the World, and the corners of her mouth turned up slightly in a feudal smirk. "It was Ezekiel, that rotten prophet, who soured my sweet Nestor."

Book of Ezekiel

In the thirtieth year, in the fourth month, on the fifth day of the month, the day my check used to arrive from Social Services, as I stood among the exiles beneath the bridge, warming my arthritic fingers around the cans of fire, the heavens flew open, and I saw visions of God. The visionary, especially he who lacks lucre, is always suspicious to those ladling the soup. And many's the time I myself have been subjected to the ravings of men moonstruck by biology and circumstance, miserable minions persecuted by dreams of the ravenous gnashing of God's aweful and unmerciful teeth. But these words I speak are words to be marked, from God's mouth to your ear. Mind.

As I looked, a stormy wind came out of the North, and inside it were the faces of four chimpanzees screeching and flapping their rubbery lips over yellow teeth with vaudevillian flare. They flung themselves from cloud to cloud in a ring, and there appeared in the center a throne, and on that throne sat, legs crossed, fingers drumming the arms, something resembling a human figure, a familiar shape wavering with fire, radiant with a long-simmering anger.

MORTAL, I'LL NOT SUFFER FALSE PROPHETS! bellowed the Lord. COUNTERFEIT GLITTER THAT CATCHES YOUR EYE, PHONY AS FOOL'S GOLD!

BUT, BUT, interrupted another booming voice that issued from a glowering form sitting, suddenly, befuddlingly, beside the first, hair ablaze with the rays of the sun. IT IS NOT THE LORD WHO SPEAKS THIS. IT IS, RATHER, A MERE IDOL, FALSE AS ETERNITY IS LONG, KING OF DOUBLE-HEARTED KINGS, MASQUERADING AS THE LORD! said the, uh, erm, Other Lord? DO NOT TRUST IN THE CAMOUFLAGE OF A SIDESHOW JEHOVAH!

The sky was teeming with God.

Egads, God fraud! thought I to myself. What is a well-meaning prophet to do?

And the words of two Gods fuming grandiosely in a world with barely enough room for one hung side by side in the air, sizzling with wrath. The chimps grew silent and sullen, pining for an accelerated evolution, and both Gods roared at once, END OF THE LINE, PRI-MATES! I AM YOUR COMMON ANCESTOR! And there was a high-pitched grumbling among the monkeys that sounded like branches breaking, as they realized they could no longer aspire to be more than monkey, that ship having sailed long ago and with an empty steerage, and they soft-shoe side-shuffled, as if to exit the stage, invisible hat and cane in hand, their wizened mugs pursed scornfully, then p-pop-pop-pop-popped like effervescence and were visible to the human eye no longer.

Both of these Gods were equally convincing with their thunderous yawps, ex cathedra, both promising the same devastation if their will was not heeded, and I knew not whom to heed, knew not what to report, for I desperately wished not to prophesy falsely myself (and I wondered: if a prophet prophesies falsely about prophecy that proves to be false, would this make it true? What is the mathematics of such augury?). But if a terrifying Figure (or Two) in the clouds exhorts you to do His (Their) bidding, pass on His (Their) judgment, and warn of the coming of castigation, who am I to question Their authenticity? How can anyone say for certain he forecasts the truth until the destruction foretold becomes the holy writ of history, a future now come to pass?

So a soon-to-be-famous sovereign-of-solemn-sovereigns appears and says, The only solution is to split these squalling and self-disputing infants down the middle and toss the four fishes of their doubled remains into the shrill and gaping beaks of the masses, so starved for a definitive deity, and both Gods shrugged, bent down for the exacting calculus of the sword, but the king could see that this would likely only multiply the problem because a resourceful God, and even an ambitious chiseler, is, like a stubborn worm (worms everywhere not wont to face facts), high functioning when cleaved.

And then one God delivered a meteoric wallop to the other, whose presence shattered, turned into a cloudburst of a million silvery minnows that flopped against my skin and soaked me to the bone, and I fell to my knees shivering, implicated by my inability to sniff out the prevarications of a flimflam deity when he tries to snow me with his basso profundo. What sort of beetle-brained prophet can be so easily gulled? I, too, deserved to be reduced to a fishy rain. Make of me water, I begged, reduce me to lungfish, that is my fondest ambition.

And the remaining God, now unfurling Himself to occupy every inch of sky, like a rolling thunderhead in a hurry, said to me, in a commanding but conspiratorial timber: **Mortal, take this message you are about to receive to the denizens of that flat and hapless heartland, the sober mopes of Kansas, the Un-chosen Ones, people spoiling endlessly for a scrap about the origin of the species, hypnotized by a wide horizon, and tell them this: in the middle of the plains, off I-70, just this side of Paradise, lies the Garden of Eden, and there will come an unshod man of slight build speaking of divine events, a minor prophet and servant of the Lord. In the presence of the brittle,** *withered body of the Garden's architect (a bearded pot-stirrer and once-devoted member of the Populist Party name of S.P. Dinsmoor), this man will augur the coming of Me to the Garden, and the townspeople, weary of the hokum of prairie prophets, who have in the past promised them, for a modest lagniappe to help pension the endlessly wandering Word of God, an end to drought and dust, unstable gold standard, locust plagues, influenza, flood and tornadoes, foreclosures, and many other varieties of human suffering, will listen briefly to his hariolation then return to their swayback davenports with the soiled antimacassars, their faces, sunken by shriveled longing, green and quavering in the cathode light.*

The Garden of Eden, fallen as a startled cake, is a place of disappointment for both God and man, as anyone knows, and there will remain behind, after the others have limped home, the prophet's final auditor, man long hobbled by hope, a grizzled widower who eats nothing but Wonder Bread and braunschweiger, a little onion, with a jelly jar of buttermilk, standing night after night at the kitchen sink, fingering the faucet's drip, and this man, wounded to the quick by the reverent optimism of this mystic, will lay his hands on the prophet's throat and slowly tighten them until he has squeezed prophecy and promise clean out of him. The man will then cradle the head of the throttled prophet in his lap, beneath the bodies of Adam and Eve, beneath the serpent. The body of the prophet will be discovered that evening by a little girl, regular visitor to the Garden, but will disappear overnight, and once this day has come to pass, giants will roam the Garden, the sky will light up with the death throes of stars racing to extinguish themselves, and the people, peering warily through drawn drapes, will resolve once and for all to steer clear of the lost promise of Eden.

"So every time Nestor saw Ezekiel, he asked him, 'Has the Garden of Eden yet been sullied by homicide?' hardy-har, and E. always looked at him foggily, as though trying to recollect where they'd met, and shook his head. And then, over a bowl of oxtail soup, he confided to Nestor he'd fore-seen his own end, said he, too, was destined to die a violent death at the hands of a disappointed man, and though his mind's eye would narrow to a squint so he could make out the malefactor's face that would fill the screen of his final vi-sion, he could never decipher his murderer's features.

"Then one day, Ezekiel had a revelation, right there at the soup kitchen as he sopped up the last dribble of borscht (*not* a favorite among the floppers) with a crust of bread. Nestor was wiping down a table when E. grabbed his arm and said, 'You, Nestor Dethloff, shall spend your dying days in a prison cell, for you are a man of murderous intentions!' and then he shrieked as if stabbed, and Nestor yanked him-self free of Ezekiel's terrified clutches, tripped over a chair as he backed away. Ezekiel's eyes went wild, Nestor said, light-ning crackling across their stormy skies, and he dropped to his knees and howled:

And because of all your abominations I will do to you what I have never yet done, and the like of which I will never do again! Surely, parents shall eat their children in your midst and children shall likewise eat their parents, a circuit of cannibal gluttony, eternally crapulent with sorrow!

"Which must have been as good as a hex, because after that day, I dreamt every night of eating Nestor, dreamt of him melting in my mouth like sweet cream, filling me up, flank steak and kidney, only to leave me famished in the morning, and it was then that I began to expand, like a too eagerly yeasted loaf. And Nestor, he'd always kept a picture of me on his refrigerator, held fast with a magnetic banana, smartly dressed and looking, I must say, delicious, as I always did look once upon a comely yesterday." Gaythal heaved a swollen sigh from deep in her diaphragm, a chinook blustering across the Rockies.

"After that Ezekiel up and disappeared, and Nestor, shaken by this biblical harangue, kept his ear to the ground for news of slain prophets in gardens, and when he passed wild-eyed men broadcasting from milk crates on street corners that the world would soon end, *woe, woe, woe,* as wild-eyed men on milk crates have a habit of doing in these parts, he shrank from their shrill imprecations and hurried his step.

"After several months of keeping his eyes peeled for, but finding no, prophesied iniquity, Nestor began to relax, thought he was foolish to have become so undone by the addled ramblings of a ragged tramp—people were always doing that, mistaking beggars for oracles, madness for soothsaying, as though they believed God, condemning the lunatics to a life of medicated catatonia, had put those invisible transistors in their teeth Himself, had made them secret enemies of the state, and we'd all discover, come Judgment Day, the truth about the blessed cracked corn and their ability to see beyond time into the jackal soul of humanity, their true gift for glimpsing the impending extermination we await and...yeah right, he kicked himself for having been taken in.

"In fact, he started to be standoffish with and feel generally less charitable toward the soup mutts. He'd never felt homicidal *before* for heaven's sake, but then he began to feel the vaguest irritation, like a pebble in his sneakers, at the thought that Ezekiel's prognostication was simply the script of madness—such a convincing prophet had he been—and Nestor became rankled to think there really was no way to know what God, in the infinite expanse of that all-knowing noodle of his, intends. And God Who anyhow? Who was this God person? Who died and made him King of the La-di-da Universe? Nestor'd never given God the time of day before, he had to admit. Though my husband, Nestor's stepdad, gave money to various Presbyterian charities come Christmas, ours was not a pious household. Organized religion, I always said, does nothing but lead the lamb to slaughter, all that talk about hellfire and endless torment and thorny crowns and leprosy and the like. Which is why I never really took to playing the organ. We never mixed much with churchy people, always so blankety-blank grim, chastely awaiting redemption, ack. Just not our cup of sangria, if you get my meaning. *Snort!*

"So Nestor worried E.'s prophecy like a dog with a pig's ear, and he began to feel sorry for him. A prophet's whole raison d'être, after all, was to foresee fated events, and if what he foresaw never came to pass, then he had no purpose in life, no reason to tie his shoes and wipe his nose and face the unforeseen day, and to Nestor's way of thinking, there was nothing sadder than a man loosed of his purpose. He'd grown so weary of seeing long lines of hungry men who cling to life for no good reason, so many squandered futures, ragtag joes scarcely possessing the vitality to lift a spoon to their muttering lips. And Nestor himself had begun to feel a little aimless, his import business at the flea market having foundered, less demand for fertility gewgaws in the heartland than he'd figured. And, wondered Nestor, if you were the muttonhead who nourished these empty cadavers-in-waiting, kept 'em stretching their palms out and rattling their cups another day, what did that make you? The hole at the center of Empty, that's what, thought poor, dejected Nestor. (I'd never understood why Nestor got so het up about Ezekiel, until I saw that boyish puss of his on the news, and then I could see E. bore an arresting resemblance to Nestor's cousin Leonard, who, as a tot, had been touched by God— well, slapped senseless more like—and was fixing to enter the seminary when he fell asleep at the wheel—or so his parents insisted, 'undiagnosed narcolepsy' they said. He drove his Gremlin straight off a cliff and into the quarry.)

"Well, you can likely see where this is headed. How could Nestor help lend meaning to these meaningless lives? That was the quandary that began to consume him, body, soul, and suit jacket. It reassured him to think that Ezekiel, failed crier of God's wrath, might at least have met the harrowing end he foresaw, might at least have had *that* satisfaction. That was the rock and the hard place 'twixt which Ezekiel hunkered, Nestor could see that. E. had to hope for his own slaughter so as not to meet the worst fate a prophet can suffer, which is to be full of horseshit and talking all manner of unsanctified trash. (Though *I* always thought being a prophet was the safest game going these days, what with the population exploding like so many kernels of corn in a hot skillet and reality beggaring the imagination as it does. I figured anything you could think to predict had to be happening somewhere sometime to some sorry soul or another.)

"So about the time Nestor begins to feel confident Ezekiel has met the end he predicted and therefore at last his maker, he in whose name he forecast the ill-omened future, there he is again at the kitchen, begging a bowl of navy bean soup and a slice of whole wheat, please, with a smear of Blue Bonnet. It gives Nestor the howling yip-yaps to see him there, failure visible in Ezekiel's withered but still-upright flesh, and also fills him with such sadness that he knows at once what he must do, and so he jumps Ezekiel out back as he rifles through the bags of trash. Nestor wraps the string of his poplin apron round E's throat, and he believes he sees gratitude in the prophet's bulging, bloodshot eyes as the gusting tempest of his final vision passes across them. When Ezekiel's heart falters and his final breath jangles free of his body and leaves him the corpse he fated himself to be, Nestor kisses Ezekiel's empty lips and feels weak with relief, bludgeoned by it, and he understands all at once the enervating satisfaction God must feel when he finally makes good on his threats. Nestor has made of Ezekiel an honest prophet, one whose presentiments now have about them the stink of irreversible truth, the lingering stench of damnable fate. He is in death a purposeful man and in becoming so has made Nestor himself a man of decided consequence, win-win."

Gaythal Dethloff emitted an exaggerated exhalation, like a balloon whose knot has come undone, and she seemed suddenly smaller, as though she'd aspirated this story of her son, which, with no pressure valve, no aperture through which to escape, had been distending her flesh for years. I imagined her flying speedily ass-backwards through the air, powered by the whistling engine of a long pent-up family tragedy.

I looked at Vivica, who palmed a yawn then bent to look at her distorted biscuit in the tuba. She licked her finger and smoothed an eyebrow. "How is it that you two came to know one another?" I asked finally.

"I went looking for Hazard at the soup kitchen once," said Vivica. "There I met Nestor, and he brought me home to meet his mother. She was better able to get around then but already a sizable dollop of flesh." Gaythal smiled hatefully at Vivica and Vivica returned the expression. "He thought it would be good for her to meet another robust gal, one expanding in another direction. Isn't that right, Gaythal? He admired my...verticality." Vivica looked me up and down, and I could tell she was thinking about that quarter inch. "Life is just a chain of no-count men," she said with a throttled sigh, "connecting one sorrowful woman to another," and she looked at us both in a smoldering manner that left no room for dissent.

"So Nestor went to prison for Ezekiel's murder?" I asked.

Gaythal again dropped the needle onto the record, and a melancholy keening sliced the air between us, then she switched the phonograph off and it moaned to silence. "Well, after E., Nestor got it into his head that *he* could foretell the deaths of people he passed on the street: a dealer in pork and grain futures whose heart would be squeezed into stillness by myocardial infarction as he brokered what would be his last and biggest deal; a grammar school bully whose head would snap from its stalk when he fell from the jungle gym onto the boy with the port wine stain around his eye, a boy whose adult blood would be poisoned by the bite of a brown recluse in the night; a veteran of three wars who would die of an embolism in his sleep while dreaming of blue-ribbon rabbits he raised as a boy, Jersey woollies whose fur fetched top dollar and whom he loved more than any fur-less, warring, hateful human. A woman who would sit on a tourist bus next to a man corseted with explosives and who would take her hand tenderly in his just before he detonated his torso. A man who, when he accosted a woman, would be suffocated by the stranglehold of muscles that thinned his breathing like the hands of an angry lover, this woman having caused in him an allergic reaction. A little girl lured, during a birthday party, by a limping squirrel with a broken tail to a lilac bush, behind which she would die mouthing the words "our father" into the callused hand covering her face. Nestor saw all around him the looming mortality that dogs all our heels, the coming deaths prowling in shadows, waiting to fall foul of the passing bodies. He saw the future corpses we all are. *Don't look it in the eye!* cautioned Nestor as the soon-to-be-dead passed him on the street. *Whatever you do, don't run, don't make any sudden moves, don't try to feed it, don't wear red, don't let it smell your blood curdling, your perspiration souring with fear, don't walk alone, but most importantly, you hapless Jobs, don't count on God to spare you or save you from suffering!*

"But it was the suicides that tugged at Nestor's heart-strings, those unfortunates he could see plain as an August sun were plotting their own ends. It saddened him to think of them stirring their stumps mechanically, shuffling through their redundant days trying to figure out how best to get their bodies to corroborate what their souls were already wise to. 'What, in the name of foresight and soup and fire-sanctified blood, would Jesus do?' asked Nestor. 'That's the question they ask these days, isn't it?' And the answer he fashioned, though he'd never paid Jesus much mind until now, was this: 'Kill them, of course.' Jesus would surely save these brooding doldrummers, woebegone as gib-cats, reasoned Nestor, rescue them from the afterlife of blistering torment and gnashing teeth that is the suicide's due. Fly-right joe like Jesus, he would do the gallant thing and assure the Dejected their consecrated seat among the murdered innocents in heaven, no two ways about it. And these future suicides, you see, they thanked Nestor for doing the dirty work of self-slaughter for them, some of them going so far in their final gratitude as to kiss the hand that had seized them. It was a service to humankind it was, euthanasia of the terminally heartsick, a way for those gloomy Guses to end their earthly career of irreversible misery without rattling God's cage. Let Nestor be the rattler. He knew it was a righteous calling.

"It was not, however, the aided suicides but the oblivious jabbernowls that would be his own undoing, those folks trundling along heedlessly, sans clue, no inkling a terrible fate was soon to befall them, a sudden and unspeakable demise, living recklessly they were without even a modicum of dread. But then Nestor's prescience started to short-circuit, foresight on the fritz, and all he could make out were mouths gawping in disbelief, outstretched hands reaching into the haze of an evaporated salvation. Though Nestor could no longer picture specifics, he could see these were souls that had mistakenly stepped out of the hurtling train's path and were living on twice-borrowed time, so it was up to him to collect and right the universe, as he'd done with Ezekiel, prove the existence of a God whose ambitions would not be thwarted, that inconsolable, all-ogling grump gunning for us all. These hangers-on were far from reconciled, it bears mentioning, to the drawing of the curtains, and so they chafed at the garrote, ducked the shiv, clawed the hand that pressed the chloroformed handkerchief to their mouth, and generally raised a stink that landed dear, well-meaning Nestor in Leavenworth, where the inmates christened him the God Whisperer and were careful never to stand in the crosshairs of his cloudy foresight."

Gaythal seemed at last relieved, her flesh pooling around her, her head a lone hyacinth floating. She began to sing and as she did she lifted the sagging sandbags of her arms in the air: *Ezekiel connected dem dry bones, Ezekiel connected dem dry bones, Ezekiel connected dem dry bones, I hear the word of the Lord. Your back bone connected to your shoulder bone, your shoulder bone connected to your neck bone, your neck bone connected to your head bone, I hear the word of the Lord! Dem bones, dem bones gonna walk around, dem bones dem bones gonna walk around, dem bones, dem bones gonna walk around, I hear the word of the Lord!* The bed bounced, the room quaked, and Vivica rattled and grinned. *Disconnect dem bones, dem dry bones, disconnect dem bones, dem dry bones, disconnect dem bones, dem dry bones, I hear the word of the Lord! Your head bone connected from your neck bone, your neck bone connected from your shoulder bone...*

Vivica stood up, smoothed her slacks, and said into my ear, "So ends the saga of another enveloping woman and the man who made her shrink." And Gaythal Dethloff, having gorged herself on her son, licked her rosy lips and liberated herself from her burdened bones then surrendered to the coconut cream pie she longed to be, every grieving cell that amassed to make her hard-won. Vivica yanked me out of the room by the elbow.

☾

Dear Obie, are you out there? Are your feet cold? Listen, psst, listen up, God's memoir continues:

Descent of God, The Scent of God, Dissent of God

The thing any naturalist worth his brine has had to concede is that *this* Species is self-originating. God donned and doffed a great variety of traits like ill-fitting greatcoats and outdated doublets and, over time, selected, naturally, those that best supported his sovereignty over the lower animals, selected, namely, omnipotence. There's nothing like omnipotence to get the old claret pumping, reasoned God, as he cast a pitying eye on the lamprey, poor lowly devil with scarcely enough ontology to make a ripple in the water. *That* would never be God's miserable fate, He'd make sure of it, it being *His* divine design in nature after all (believe what you will). Of course, any observer worth his binoculars is forced to conclude that God is indeed the fittest of all and will be, when the world at last extinguishes itself (the farm having *long* ago been bought then foreclosed upon), the only Man standing, a grim and lonely destiny to which He has nevertheless been reconciled since humankind first occurred to Him. Such is a singular deity's burden. Better that, thinks God, than being sentenced to Heaven, which is just another way of saying (and this is where omniscience proves advantageous, well, here and standardized tests) extinction. God doesn't mind that He will remain a species eternally endangered, being the only of His kind and incapable as He is of producing any but the lowliest offspring, an unbecoming looking glass He cannot bear to gaze into for long—human beings, with their corrupt instincts and opposable thumbs (an experiment gone sorely awry and for which He has paid dearly since chiseling that weak-willed bogtrotter Adam from the rudest stone). As God thinks of his disappointing progeny, he begins to feel abstract and this leads to a dyspeptic churlishness; the empyrean beneath Him darkens decidedly. The evolution of God is indeed a complicated tale, and a chilling one not for the feeble of constitution. To hear it is to immediately lay waste to oneself, so it behooves us here to say simply that we agree with Messrs. Murie and Mivart, who, in *Races of God, the Immanent Savage,* sagely remark that if "'ignorance more frequently begets confidence than does knowledge,' where does that leave He who harbours more swaggering confidence than Man, Time, and the Devil all rolled into one tidy parcel?" God's eschewing of Knowledge, in addition to His Old Testament powers of unreason, are surely proof positive that His altitude is wickedly ironic, for it is *He* who clearly descends from that lowliest bipedal primate known as M-A-N (Mr. Adam from Nothing)! Further evidence of God's adaptability (and therefore claim to godness) is His clever defense whenever threatened with extinction: He emits a very fine fluid which stains the sky a tempestuous gray, and He douses the moon, inks it black as jet, until the savages below fall to their knees, then an acrid secretion is spread over His body, over Creation, and when His wavering minions reach toward the sky for clemency, they feel a sharp stinging sensation, as with a man-of-war, and they are promptly chastened back into belief. In this symbiosis, we come to see clearly that God and Man—the one longing to punish, the other all too happy to offer up his posterior to the strap—are descended from a self-flagellating common ancestor, i.e. primordial God, single-cell and simple, reducible, bearing *in His bodily frame the indelible stamp of His lowly origin* (see Jameson's *Holy Homology: You Can Take the God Out of Man, But.*). The transmutation of species is one of the many battles God lost to Man.

Suddenly God finds Himself in the grips of a racking nostalgia, which nearly knocks the universe back to that incipient cinder that detonated it into being, back to life's prokaryotic infancy, and he recollects that original crawl out of heaven onto dry land, recalls the adaptations that enabled His fat ubiquity to flourish there, legs, lungs, a fitting skin, and He thinks of those mutations grudgingly discarded, wrath, petulance, a beard the length of Time. Beneficence, He thinks glumly, now that's overrated. It's not that He took pleasure in creating those parasitic wasps that feed on the living bodies of caterpillars (and why did Darwin have to bring *them* up, anyway, he with his smug dundrearies? Were there not scores of congenial creatures that balanced the scales? What about that spectacular star-nosed mole, for example, with its fluttering chrysanthemum of a schnoz that fingers the landscape as it scampers and can *feel* so much more than can the human hand? That was a good hour's worth of creation, that one was. Little Canadian swamp-dweller, everyone overlooks that marvel, they do), but all creatures great and agonized need someone to pity, and what happier fate could there be for a caterpillar than to be the object of the Unmoved Mover's regret? Ahhhh, the old arguments seem not to stand up as sturdily as they once did. God hankers for simpler times.

Fig. 1. The HARE.

TWENTY-TWO
RABBIT CATCHER
OF KINGDOM COME

One sudden spring, when trees and flowers, bamboozled by warmth, began budding in January, the prematurely honey-eyed air flatly refusing to chill again until late December, the town of Kingdom Come, Kansas, was beset by a plague of black-tailed jackrabbits that were not only many but jumbo, bigger than great danes they were, gar*gan*tuan rabbits, suspiciously well fed, slavering over the zoysia, plump middles heaving, back feet long and brawny as a sailor's forearm and ears you could fan a fainting princess with. And not at all timid, never darting under privet or disappearing behind fences at the last minute, but glaring tauntingly at cats and hobbled crones, whom the town feared would be dragged away to an unspeakable end in the riparian thickets whence these strapping rabbits multiplied, their numbers seeming to double each week. They licked their paws and stroked their ears and whiskers while leveling a menacing eye and leering toothily at any passerby bold enough to look them in their flea-bitten mugs. They stood up on their whopping hoppers and waggled their ears, as though receiving a communiqué from jackrabbit HQ, the air crackling with animal electricity, and then they'd charge a neighbor's Chihuahua, the javelin of their ears at a determined tilt, and the runt mutt would leap with a shriek through its doggy door. They hopped defiantly into busy intersections, and station wagons and pickup trucks, afraid a collision with one of these sturdy lagomorphs would surely cause their vehicles to crumple like beer cans against an obdurate forehead, struck one another and rolled in ditches instead, coming to rest tires-up among the cattails. At night the rabbits drummed their feet so rhythmically the earth seemed to growl, and the sleepless citizens of Kingdom Come locked and relocked their doors and windows until the thumping ceased at sunrise. The town was in a pickle, had a big-eared crisis on its hands, fast-multiplying pestilence, cotton-tailed epizootic, and, well, it feared for its safety and solitude.

Which is why when the man in the parti-colored coat appeared and claimed he could, for a nominal, one-time fee, rid the town of this nuisance forever, the drowsy burghers fell gratefully at his feet.

He pulled from his pied pocket the largest carrot anyone had ever seen; even Farmer Bauer, known county-wide for his prize-winning cucumbers the size of hockey sticks and potatoes that frequently resembled past presidents, was agog. And from this carrot, the man in the colorful coat whittled a fife, whose music the town was deaf to, though dogs howled and whimpered and shimmied under sofas when he blew.

This man, let us hereafter refer to him as Herr Pfeiffer, testing the irresistible pitch of the pipe, played a casual tune one night, strolling in the unseasonable and glistering warmth of the moonlight, and the ritual rumbling was replaced with a high-pitched keening that caused people to fill their kitchen sinks, eject ice from metal trays, and immerse their throbbing noodles in ice water.

The next day, Herr Pfeiffer began to silently ululate in earnest, and the wild-eyed rabbits were tugged, tail first, toward where he stood piping in the gazebo; a pyramid of resentful rabbits began to wriggle in front of him, the ground scarred with claw marks as they tried to resist the sonorous magnetism of Herr Pfeiffer's *Hasen*-song. This bushel of black-tailed jackrabbits writhed and kicked, heaped higher than a haystack, but when Herr Pfeiffer lowered his fife, they all went limp and began quietly to snore. The people of Kingdom Come couldn't bring themselves to witness the rumpus even through locked windows and sliding glass doors, but they cautiously parted their drapes when the air gently thundered with the sound of sleeping rabbits, a welcome estivation they hoped would last.

After a week, people began to emerge from their houses and children stole away at night to secretly stroke the silken feet of the rabbits as they slumbered, and occasionally one would snort and turn on its side and below it an ear or a paw would stir to life and wave weakly, yellow teeth chomping with dreams, and the children would gasp and back away, until the mound again snuffled in unison. Some rabbits slept with their eyes open, and beneath a full moon their eyeshine made the town blush, bathed it in a pink glow that stuck to the skin, causing adolescent boys, fearful of the hell they'd have to pay if ever they were spotted sporting girly hues, to stay indoors. They ate their meat extra well-done, never mind that it shrank to shoe leather, and they never let their tongue dart from its cave, even when Dr. Hildebrand wagged a depressor at them and told them to open wide. No pink no how.

The town council met to decide what was to be done with this big-as-a-boat-footed vermin now hypnotized in an unsightly jumble of tails and whiskers and ears and feet in the middle of town. Would the rabbits remain indefinitely under Herr Pfeiffer's spell and snore themselves senseless, dwindle to bone? And how long might that take? And were the townsfolk really obliged to pay the piper? He hadn't, after all, actually emancipated the town from its trammels, no siree bobcat! He'd only bewitched it into unconsciousness, and who knew how long that would hold? Surely the enchanted rabbits would soon rouse from their stupor, perhaps mad with a ravenous hunger, and who could say what might be on the menu!

Herr Pfeiffer, sitting quietly at the back as the town's alarm rose in pitch, stood and asked to be recognized. His colorful coat was bejeweled with light kindled by the flickering fluorescence of the town hall and seemed to swarm with diamond-back beetles. "Esteemed elders and good people of Kingdom Come," began Herr Pfeiffer, "I am not in the business of slaughtering God's creatures, however vexatious their presence. I corral and subdue, I enchant—I have done as you asked, no longer does the rumble of your bane's feet keep you sleepless at night—but it is not for me to decide the ultimate fate of living things, would you, dear brethren whose knees audibly knock in the presence of God, not agree?" Here Herr Pfeiffer smoothed his hands along his coat and light glittered across the sunken cheeks of his anguished auditors.

"But if you insist. If you wish, in no uncertain terms, that these scapegraces be mortally dispatched, I am indeed able to provide this service. However, the cost of extermination is a good deal more dear. In addition to the tender I will ask you to part with, you must be prepared to open your ears to a sound like no other. It is the sound of suffering, and it will infect your flesh like a virus, thickening your blood, burrowing in your most vital organs. It will become the caries that corrode the teeth that wake you with aching at night, the congested vessels of the eyes red with grief, the creeping spots on skin gone slack as a turkey's wattle with time. It is a fevered howling that will ring in your heart for the rest of your days and sound to you as though the Earth's soul is being throttled. You must ask yourselves: can your hearts, stalwart and true as you may believe them to be, afford it?"

The town council asked Herr Pfeiffer if he would kindly step out so that they might consider the merit of his... intriguing proposal. He tapped his heels and bowed, and a bedazzling train of light followed him as he took his leave. Widow Winkler said if you asked her, relying on Herr Pfeiffer a second time would be throwing good spinach after bad, and she for one hadn't a plug nickel to throw in any direction. (Widow Winkler lived from her departed husband's paltry pension. He'd been an itinerant Messiah, headlining in passion plays across the state—seasonal work but he was the best Christ in Kansas, could suffer and forgive at the drop of a hat, and so was handsomely compensated for each performance—but the Messiahs had only recently unionized and bargained for benefits when Herr Winkler died on the job, on the cross! He'd been devoted to his craft and felt he'd understand Christ's motivation better if just once he could be properly staked. As misfortune would have it, Herr Winkler was a bleeder, heretofore unbeknownst. Retirement funds had yet to accrue and life insurance [the whole notion of which was complicated by all those nightly resurrections, matinees on Sunday] had been dismissed on principle, so the other Christs of Kansas, who also yearned to bleed believably, donated a portion of their income to create a modest annuity for Wilhelmina Winkler, surviving spouse of Berthold Winkler, voted Greatest Jesus Since Jesus at their annual potluck and Most Likely to Raise the Dead.) Mayor Finsterwalder suggested they stipulate payment be remitted only after this plague was stamped out, the rabbits a fading chapter in the town's otherwise placid history. "But," asked Constable Schutzmann, "what about the sound of suffering Herr Pfeiffer warned against, a brutal music *that* would certainly be" (Constable Schutzmann, though a by-the-book beadle in every other regard, kept at home a three-legged marten he'd found wounded near his well, coddled back to health, and trained to waltz, teaching her to hop rhythmically on one foot *one-two-three one-two-three*, and clearly he nursed a secret affection for all velvety creatures, however unsettling their snarl, however monstrous their feet). "Ah, pfrrrt," spat Farmer Bauer. "We are no strangers to suffering! We all know well the shriek of a hog what has gotten downwind of his fate, do we not? Surely we'll not allow the brief bellowing of animal torment to stand in the way of our happiness?!"

With this, a snort flew from his bulbous schnozzle—his wooly mustache shivered like the legs of a centipede and appeared as though it might scuttle off and leave his newly naked lip to fend for itself—and he folded sun-leathered arms across the bulging barrel of his chest. "These rabbits have it coming!" he boomed. And so it was decided: though there was, among the more pinch-fisted skinflints, still some disagreement over the exact monetary value of such a service, Herr Pfeiffer would be retained and asked to exterminate the waggle-eared menace and the feet it hopped in on.

Farmer Bauer reluctantly plunked gold pieces into Herr Pfeiffer's eager mitts (the only form of lucre he'd accept—paper currency, he said, so easily a stiff wind's hostage), said the rest would be proffered once services were rendered. Herr Pfeiffer again clicked his heels and bowed solemnly then backed away until he found himself in sunlight, and he turned and strode forward, showily pumping his arm in the air like a drum major, marching to music he had yet to make. His coat exploded kaleidoscopically in the light, spangling the air, throwing disks of color everywhere, everywhere, and a train of jewels blazed brightly behind him. He turned his head once and grinned over his shoulder, and his unusually long eyelashes fluttered gracefully in a beckoning manner, like the undulating fingers of a sea anemone. Widow Winkler, eyes like boiled eggs, yelped and slapped at the beetles of light that scurried along her arms, then she grabbed the shoulder of Frau Kinderbein and said, "I see your Irmalinda floating in the candy-colored light, trailing close behind him. You must keep her near as shadow!" And Frau Kinderbein, whose petunias had suffered more than once at the paws of Widow Winkler's snuffling mutt Schatz and whose daughter sometimes suffered from night terrors brought on by the manic midnight twittering of the widow's canary, Petunia, shrugged off the crone's craggy hand, sniffed, and stormed off, her bosom raised to a bumptious altitude.

The rest of the frazzled citizenry of Kingdom Come headed straight home, gathered bread and jam and candles enough for a week, plugged their ears with dollops of wax, and stowed their families safely away in root cellars. Let the rabbit extraction commence!

The townspeople waited in dimness, held their heads in their hands and tried not to listen, silently played cards and whittled vague shapes from turnips, ate pickled okra and boysenberry preserves, fed their mewling cats condensed milk, taught their dogs, who whined barometrically and argued with their feet, to play dead.

After they'd been underground for three days, they began to feel like grubs or tubers, like the least shrew, smallest mammal in Kansas—they felt puny and too comfortable in darkness, so the close, dank quarters began to shrink, and the townspeople thought: surely the pox has been antidoted by now.

It is worth remarking that too often it is impatience or boredom that persuades us to step foot into the lion's yawning maw—with the passing of time comes accidental daring—but the minute our britches catch on the barb of an incisor, we awaken to the delusion, turn tail and gallop in the direction of our sensible cowardice.

So it was in Kingdom Come on this the day that would later and forever demand atonement. Just as parents and grandparents, restless offspring and orphaned cousins, filed toward the steps, tunneling a pinkie into an ear to free it from silence, preparing to periscope their heads above ground for confirmation that the plague had been piped into oblivion, suddenly family cats tossed back their mangy heads and began to bay like wolves beneath a swollen moon, ahroooor! The dogs, nobody's dupe, could see that such behavior was a sign the world was soon to end, soon to crumble like a day-old biscuit beneath the crack of doom, and they tried to outwit the apocalypse by falling stiffly onto their sides, thud, good dog, good dead dog! Big-fisted toddlers clutched wooden alphabet blocks so tightly their skin gave and their hands bled, as if they'd been bitten by feral words in the act of forming (to this day a ghostly branding on the palms of Kansas children remains faintly visible, even beneath the impetigo that scabs the skin in spring; the letters of this phantasmal impression, however, change each year, capital *H* one year, lowercase *e* the next, then a faint *l—Help? Hell? Hello? He lives?*—as though their hands were trying to tell them something, Ouija them a bulletin from the world beyond hands, perhaps warn, snailishly, of the coming of evil—or the coming of good, equally disruptive, who can say?). And so families returned to their bunkers, huddled together, while hamsters and mice and gerbils all ran themselves ragged on squeaking wheels, nearly reduced themselves to a rundle of butter, and they awaited the all clear of daylight that rewards the night shift, vampires and owls and astronomers and fireflies, with sunny and dreamless sleep.

Once settled on cots and benches, the final hand of hearts dealt, the townspeople too heard the sound, felt it in the roots of their teeth, as it increased in pitch and volume, a concatenated shriek so piercing, sharp as an awl, that eardrums shattered, like crystal beneath the pressure of a tenor shrilly trilling a lofted note, and blood trickled from their ears, but still they could hear. Children began to hiccup and whimper and parents held damp tea towels to their paling cheeks. And then they found themselves on their feet, standing without meaning to, stumbling dreamily, wakeful somnambulists, pulled forward, up the steps, into the afternoon—they squinted against the dazzle of day—into the sound that seemed to empty their hearts of blood, sap them of all volition, into the soul-curdling caterwaul that sounded to the pious folk of Kingdom Come as though God Himself were being lashed, the world's skin peeled from muscle, flesh sheered from bone, the sound of gore dripping, dripping, ichor thinning to a rivulet, the hollow thum-thump of life on the ebb.

They walked, eyes at half-mast, arms adangle, limp as slain geese, and they stopped when they reached the river, where their magnetized eyes remained riveted and unblinking, burning with sight, as one bedeviled rabbit after another pitched itself, screaming, off the banks and into the rushing water, paws peddling for purchase in the air, bodies dashed against rocks, necks snapped by the force of the current that churned with the spring thaw, and the rabbits' quivering ectoplasm, translucent but pink as a tongue, rose slowly into the air like gluey bubbles, gelatinous vapor, wafted overhead, clouding the sky with an oily glow, then burst, the town blanketed in ooze, a viscous rain, the rosy slime of a slaughtered soul! The spellbound burghers lifted their eyes and saw, off in the distance, beneath the sun's mid-afternoon glare, a winking brilliance on the shoals, like a mirror splashed with light, and when their eyes adapted to the brightness they could make out Herr Pfeiffer's pipe raised in the air, the man at the other end reminding them of Dr. Jekyll guzzling his fateful elixir straight from the alembic tipped to his lips.

The townspeople frantically swabbed the goo of extermination from their limbs, and all at once children and dogs fell to the ground, eyeballs shuddering beneath the lids as if recording a seismic shift, as if atwitch with a shattering dream, which is how they would later think of it, the wickedest dream they could ever recall having, an experience not of God's still-watered, green-pastured, and betuliped kingdom, a dream that beggared even the most tormented imagination, and parents opened their mouths and tried to swallow the sound, gulp it down and drown it in their gullets, choking on air polluted with suffering. This malignant yawp, it cannot properly be described. It harrowed to the quick the halting spirits of the sorrowful citizens of Kingdom Come, Kansas, who never again fished in the river, who never again whittled a carrot, waltzed in the moonlight, nursed a wounded animal, whose weddings hereafter were somber as wakes, who never again heard the sound of children singing or weeping or calling their dogs.

The river boiled with the bodies of rabbits.

§   §   §

The true name of the piper, they later discovered, was 𝔥𝔢𝔯𝔯 𝔇𝔯. 𝔇𝔯. 𝔈𝔡𝔢𝔩𝔥𝔞𝔫𝔰 𝔥𝔞𝔰𝔢𝔫𝔣𝔞𝔫𝔤𝔢𝔯, once world-renowned musicologist and zoologist, of the Hameln Hasenfängers, a name that mysteriously appeared one day on the town registry in a variegated ink that bled across the thatched fibers of the parchment in such a way as to make it seem botanical, rhizomes creeping in all directions, a name (like that of that other notorious subterranean scoundrel) never uttered in polite company.

It cannot be said that Kingdom Come returned to normal once the rabbits had rattled their last jackrabbity breath, had met their misguided maker, but the town fell in step again with its former rhythm and the townsfolk choused themselves into believing they'd surmounted the worst of their tribulations.

Until.

Until that day when house dogs, those crystal gazers, began burrowing under davenports (Mayor Finsterwalder's Alsatian wolfhound Hedwig, normally *pudelwohl* with puppyish enthusiasm despite her size, big body ajitter and tail awag, on this day could be found schlepping his prized Biedermeier daybed on her back from the parlor into the dining room as she tried to creep toward invisibility) and cats hid in haylofts, where they let mice scurry past them unpawed. (The mice were not especially grateful for the amnesty because, well, mice are as fond of routine as the next rodent. Lassitude caused them to thin nearly to extinction for they did not feel they could crumb-gather or invade the corn-rick in good conscience with no claws snapping at their tails to give them fleet-footed purpose.)

On that day, Herr Pfeiffer appeared again at a council meeting "to settle unsettled accounts." As he strode into the hall in his light-spangled mantle, seeming for all the world like a spreading fire, the townspeople felt the heat on their cheeks and parted to let this conflagration pass, stepping wide for fear they too might combust. Herr Pfeiffer asked to be recognized, and Brother Angsthase yielded the lectern, stepped down from the dais. Later, when the town would attempt to reconstruct Herr Pfeiffer's appearance so that they might offer a bounty for his capture, they would each recollect the features of his face differently, would in fact reconstruct him in their own image (gutless god-wannabes all of us)—"face round as a skillet with eyes like dull stones"; "aquiline nose above fat, womanly lips garish as poppies"; "teeth blue-green as oxidized copper beneath a monkish baldness"—and they'd forget the mesmerism of his motley coat and the bewitching pitch of his piping.

"Your town has been purged of its pestilence," said Herr Pfeiffer, "and I have returned to collect my due. If you would be so good as to remit my quittance and square the score, I will gladly quit *you* and be on my way." He bowed and tossed his hat to the mayor.

Each alderman searched the bewildered eyes of the next for some guidance, some cue, some subtle guidon or dumb show, and the hat passed quickly from hand to hand. Herr Pfeiffer stepped down and returned to the center aisle, and the hat came round to him, sagging with booty. He smiled, clicked his heels, glanced inside the hat, then a lupine grimace darkened his face. When council members recounted this later, they would say he bared blinding teeth that glistened like daggers and his eyes yellowed with animal rage, but he said nothing, and his silence rang inside them like a clapper in a bell, making their bones hum and their hearts skip, their livers clang, their souls clamor to be free of that four-flushing flesh that would soon turn to dust and settle on armoires and sconces only to be swept into the bin with yesterday's rubbish, sorriest of sorry fates (pragmatic, though fickle, souls always look for an escape hatch when the end inches closer)! Inside the hat were candy wrappers, pencils, plug nickels, balls of lint, marbles, fourpenny nails, assorted flints, last week's raffle tickets, willow buds, but nary a gemstone or drop of gold, a hatful of the nothing Nothing carries in its pocket. No one drew a breath or twitched so much as a toe.

"S-s-see here," stammered Mayor Finsterwalder at last, "the rabbits have gone, there's no arguing that. But so too has our felicity, the sweet sanctity we once enjoyed—fled, owing in no small measure to that...that diabolical song we cannot shake from our ears, a lamentation we strongly suspect is infernal in origin, and he who p-p-p-pays the devil will be in debt for eternity!" sputtered the mayor, miscalculating the breath necessary to propel reticent indignation, the last word scarcely a whisper.

A chilly stillness settled again on the room, inside of which Herr Pfeiffer's coat seemed to blaze anew and the fire flashed in the shrinking pupils of the onlookers, their irises emptying of color, welling up with heat.

"And what if," asked Herr Pfeiffer with a mouth that did not move, "it was...God, ultimately, who skinned the scourge to the bone and made it howl? Isn't extermination always God's purview, his bailiwick, prerogative, his Reason for Being? What if it is God to whom you owe your fitful sleep? His services are surely indemnified and you can be certain He will collect." A half grin propped up one side of his mouth. "You cannot outrun the Constable, dear thimbleriggers, cannot stiff the piper for long. Consider yourself in arrears!" Herr Pfeiffer blazed out of the room, and each person he passed fell to his knees and grasped at the trailing smoke, fingering the air for forgiveness.

A week passed and there was no further peep from the piper. The aldermen's ears felt mauled by Herr Pfeiffer's last clapperclawing, so no one uttered a word about the threats the town fervently hoped were idle as disrepair, indolent as a capsized velocipede with a badly bent wheel. Those Kingdom Comers secretly given to occult imaginings in the yearning privacy of long and moonless nights wished he'd been spirited away by a vigorous wind to an inhospitable continent remote as the stars, and they prayed that a technicolored coat fueled by a grudge was not a reliable means of conveyance.

Even the most stubborn mortal funk is tamed by Time, taught to bear up under the yoke of mortality like all God's oxen, so after a fortnight, the people dared to think that perhaps Herr Pfeiffer's bite fell short of his bellow, and they allowed themselves at last to sink like the dead into the soft ticking of their mattresses at night. So dog-weary were the sleep-deprived brethren of Kingdom Come, Kansas, that no bodies stirred from their stupor when the animals began to pace. Not even the yowling and hissing, the stamping of hooves, could rouse the snorting sleepers from this deliciously leaden embrace of Morpheus, whose tenderness they'd sought for months, like mooning schoolgirls, in vain.

It is natural to grope for metaphor, sentiment twice removed, in moments of guarded contentment. To say simply the town at last slept soundly is, for those who set store by the sorcery of words, to further court the endless ills that flesh is heir to—calamity is warded off by being eternally anticipated, the devil too. Tranquility, as any comfortable basset hound can tell you, must always dissemble, disguise itself as irreversible woe, lest it jinx its own wobble-wheeled future. (Lunita Betelheim, who didn't believe in shouldering debt, sobbed for an hour every afternoon promptly at three o'clock to pay down the dejection we come into the world owing and to invest in a retirement free of all but the most trifling miseries; she believed five months of sobbing immunized her against the death of a loved one, three weeks for a prolonged illness, two months unrequited adoration, one month garden variety abjection; such were Lunita's mathematics of preventative mourning.) But even the artful dodge of language or gesture, little more, let us be frank, than a parlor trick, cannot save us in the end. And this is how God can be certain He is God: His legerdemain relies less on the distance of sense than the intimacy of sound; His is a thundering melody of wrath and repentance, which is to say a song understood by all, the song we arrive in our bodies bleating. And so it was by this capsized reasoning that the good and decent people of Kingdom Come, Kansas, came to doubt the inoculating power of piety: fat lot of good their devotion had done them! See if it isn't so.

ξ   ξ   ξ

In Kingdom Come there was a girl, who shall henceforth be referred to as (...Wall Will Woe Wallow...) *Willow!* (Lithe as a...!) Willow Himmelfarb, a child born big as a camel's hump, big as a fable, so big she broke the stork's bill, delaying delivery of other infants, which caused the mothers to hiss at her and rub their beleaguered loins when they passed her, wombs whose phantom pains of labor persisted for years and caused the women to cry out each day at the stroke of their child's birth. In fact, this is how the town, who'd always mistrusted the tilt of the sun and whose bodies' collective electricity caused clocks and watches to spin so fast folks feared they'd live their whole lives in less than a day, began to tell time: Gisela Schadenfrau 11 a.m., Malvina Marquart shortly before supper in the evening, Rapunzel Peabody and Elfriede Kinderbein a minute to midnight.

And with each passing year the blue expanse between Willow and the outer heavens grew smaller. The community waited for the day she'd exchange a chaplet of clover for that of clouds. In that year of the piper, Willow was ten years old but could already stare the stateliest stallion in the eye (though she generally steered wide of livestock for fear they might claim her as one of their own). And on that particular night, the night of the stony sleep, Willow, like all the children of Kingdom Come, felt herself rise from her bed and float into the midnight air (Elfriede and Rapunzel's synchronized howls peeling behind her), and it was such a lovely and alien sensation, this weightlessness, that she felt no fear, thought God had come to rescue her at last, free her from the anvil of her earthly form, slip that ponderous noose from her neck. Once outside her house, with no ceiling to stymie her, Willow thought she'd drift quickly toward Canicula and, fond admirer that she was of both dogs and remote locales, she suffered no regret, but then she thought of her brother Ogden, imagined him grounded at home with only her parents for company, and she felt her soul kedged across the prairie, her body an anchor; her feet began to drag, then her knees, her belly, her chin, until she found herself facedown in buffalo grass. She rolled on her back and saw animal eyes blinking around her. She wished she could muster fear, but she knew buzzards and badgers, coyotes and foxes, even the occasional mountain lion and vagrant bear would scatter once they could see she was no tidy morsel and had the threatening mandible of one that might bite back.

(Two autumns ago a black bear had been spotted on a bitter night curled at the feet of the statue of Mendelsohn Paddletrap, who in 1883 invented the tornado harness, a honking
contraption that could lasso a twister, hogtie the energy round
the ankles, and with that force momentarily tamed and chan-
neled, he would loose it again on the ground to conjure his
heart's fondest longing—he had only to wish at midnight beneath a half-moon, and the liberated tornado obliged: a coop
full of the most pluckily prinked bantams—feathered to the
nines—you could ever hope to fancy and that laid not only
the best-tasting eggs this side of capital P Paradise but produced chicken milk to boot! Which, it turns out, is ambrosia
to bears, more enticing than all the honey in Bear Heaven).

Above Willow, children wafted in the air with unspeakable grace, fluid as eels, but then the moon illumined their
bodies and in their nightclothes they reminded her of the
seeds of a milkweed parachuting toward fertilization. *Everything is more something else than itself,* thought Willow. Willow,
who usually felt fettered by history (always a short man's
story by her measure), thought then about Amelia Earhart,
corn-fed Kansas girl like her, Meely her sister called her, who
constructed a track on her father's tool shed, greased it with
lard, drove a wooden box off the edge, hung suspended in
time and space like a lost planet, fell to the earth, and said,
"One day I'll disappear in the clouds, Pidge, you watch."
(Everyone who grows up in Kansas has a yen to be airborne
sooner or later, if only to glimpse where God hides His unimaginable form, that fat carcass. Many a prairied Kansan,
landlocked and starved for altitude and love, tall trees and
tender music, has had a bone to pick with Herr Dr. Dr. G-
o-double-crucifix.) Willow thought it was not tragic but a

dream fulfilled that Amelia Earhart lifted into the sky one day and never returned. *Willow Airheart*, thought Willow, air the element in which her empty heart naturally thrived. Then she thought this: *It's always thin women who disappear.*

And suddenly there was Ogden swimming in the sky overhead, clutching the feet of a sleeping girl who bobbed in the air in front of him, Irmalinda Kinderbein. Ogden who prayed at the foot of Willow's bed and smuggled into her room at night ginger snaps and peppernuts her mother hid from her. "Ogden, Oggie!" she called. He waved to her with his feet. So Willow, who now felt to herself more weighted with flesh than ever, picked herself up and followed the floating children deeper into the night.

Willow followed them until her feet ached and she was sure they had reached what her parents called "the ragged edge of Christendom"; beyond the windbreak planted to halt the raging dust that, back in the day, had stormed the lungs of every breathing thing; beyond the forest she was warned never to trespass lest she awaken the wild omnivorous one-eared cows that were afraid of mirrors and goats but who chewed children like grass and spit up baskets woven from hair and bones and teeth; to a clearing in the trees, and there the children began to flutter to the ground, lit by the throbbing moon, looking like blank slips of paper. Now Willow could hear the rhythmic croaking of the pipe that sounded like the whirring of June cicadas as they slid from their skins. She walked through the sleepy children lying on the ground, careful not to step on their outstretched hands, and searched them for her brother, Oggie with his nose dusted with freckles and his button mouth that mumbled in sleep. She pulled up short when she saw dagger-toed boots, betasseled at the knee, gleaming with lanolin and lampblack, tapping the ground, and there standing among the slumbering kindergarten was Herr Pfeiffer, who held in his hands a panpipe. Willow, who had been Kingdom Come Olfactory Champion three years running and who this year would compete at state, having identified with a single sniff the secret ingredients in Mrs. Kuchenheimer's Schwarzwälder Kirschtorte (half a thimble of red currant schnapps and a dash of rosewater) and in Mr. Zwiebel's patented moisturizer that the prunier elders sopped up like bread dunked in milk and couldn't get enough of (suet), could smell the hazelnuts and clove and marzipan of this lebkuchen pipe and marveled at how the instrument never grew smaller though he bit off a nibble with each blow. Actually, this made Willow a little sad because it reminded her of her own body: no matter what you did to it—you could slather it with schmalz and dangle choice cuts beneath the snouts of the most ravenous wolves—it defied reduction, and the more you tried to contain it, the more it erupted in every direction. And Willow found the idea of regenerative food in a world plagued by unending starvation, mouths forever agape and bellies taut with hunger (everyone in Kingdom Come seemed reasonably well fed, but she'd read books and knew there were people thinning everywhere, thinning, thinning as she slept), she found that troubling, one of those paradoxes with which God bullies mortals, all the miserable hangdog Jobs of the world, the people who bleed and ache and dwindle and swoon and get back up again and offer Him their chin. *The faithful, those patsies,* thought Willow. *God is a prowling alley cat and we are the wounded mice he bats around until the everyday terror of living makes our hearts skid to a stop.* Ogden, heartsore, had sobbed when the rabbits disappeared, he their one true ardent admirer, and since then, it's safe to say, Willow and God had been on the outs.

The piper stopped playing when he saw Willow and grinned the thinnest of grins. As though he were daylight and she a spelunker just emerged from deep in the belly of a cave, she had to squint to look at him, and then her eyes adjusted to the sight and she could see now his coat rippling around him, teeming with life, undulating, tidal. The lively coat (*harrumph, no mere grogram for this dandified bugler*, thought Willow, eyes again narrowed, hands squeezed into fists, trying telepathically to tame the piper and his tumultuous ulster, *that, that rabbit enchanter, Herr Hasenfuss! that pigeon-hearted schnorrer!*), it was a whirling cosmos under glass and hung in such a way as to remind Willow of a droplet of water about to fall from the spigot. She saw and could somehow identify all the animals tangled together in the terrarium of the coat: single-celled wrigglers and chiggers and night snakes and Chihuahuan ravens and spotted skunks and banded sculpins and fatmucket mussels and meadowlarks and sicklefin chubs and boxelder bugs and silver-haired bats and pocket mice and mooneyes and bobcats and bobolinks and black-tailed prairie dogs and mule deer and mud daubers and, of course, piping plovers, and in the middle of it all, looking stunned and logy as stowaway immigrants who just stepped woozily out of steerage onto foreign shores: those elephantine jackrabbits!

It seemed as though the animals were trapped beneath glass; they pawed and pecked and gnawed but the edge of the universe of the coat would not give, would not even admit to being the edge, and the animals, wild as anyone without a discernible planet beneath her feet would be, searched anxiously for cover. Willow looked into the piper's eyes and could see something writhing there as well, and she feared for the animals, she feared for the children, she feared for dear Oggie her brother. *All God's children, and he's come to claim them!* she thought. *Such is* not *the Kingdom of Heaven.* Oggie had told Willow that life began with her—big girl that she was, biggest in Kingdom Come and beyond, biggest in Kansas, a state *full* of ample maidens—she could give it and take it away, and she wished now she had believed him, but, always mistaken for a lumbering boy when she was a tyke and her hair was bobbed at the nape, she wasn't one to readily volunteer for the breeches part. *That fraud piper's no match for you,* he'd said, *Godding about like he is. Your movements are sometimes a mystery and your heart's wide as the Great Plains and you'd never let any innocent come to harm!*

But she hadn't saved the rabbits.

Even the surliest of God's creatures deserve affection, pleaded Oggie. He'd thought the rabbits could be reformed with just a little lettuce, a spacious warren, and true love. But she was no redeemer, those rabbits weren't her invention, who was she to try to save another when she herself was lost? Just try finding the wee needle of her soul in that husky haystack of flesh!

The sound the pipe now emitted was the insomniac humming of those strapping rabbits, and the children sprang to, stiffly, like stepped-on rakes, then their bodies quaked in spasm, jerked and whirled and thrashed about with their eyes still sealed, and Willow thought with a start, *Totentanz!* There'd been an epidemic of dancing in neighboring towns, and many stories floated among the children of Kingdom Come about the spastic fandango of the soon-to-be-dead, which is why you'd never catch Willow waltzing in the moonlight, or even swinging her hips by the light of the porch, and when Willow saw her parents fox-trotting in the kitchen after supper, she went outside, hid behind the buffaloberry bush, and threw stones at the window until her father came out to investigate, sure it was the Spitzbübisch twins from next door up to their usual hijinks, and her mother continued clearing the table, returning the corn relish and rind pickle and buttermilk to the icebox.

The humming increased in pitch and fervor and tiny tulips blossomed on the arms and legs and faces of the children, their skin a field of flowers, beautiful, beautiful! followed by a calyx of proud flesh stemming their spread. Geraniums bloomed red as a fresh wound from open mouths, and the children's small bodies perspired to such a degree they looked rain soaked, and Willow, who could not get her leaden legs to budge an inch, reached out toward Oggie. She was a zeppelin cumbered by sandbags, yearning to rise with the rest, and she knew she'd never get off the ground. Oggie reeled and grinned but wouldn't open his eyes, and she could see in the slant of his smile that he was hoping to meet up again with those walloping rabbits who'd met an unseemly end in Kingdom Come, Kansas.

And then the piping stopped, though the children continued to twitch and leap. The piper called out their names.

Eva, William, Ludmilla, and Hans! Heinrich and Albert and Ulrich and Alice! As the names were called, children flew up into the air and spiraled toward the moon like full balloons whose throats are suddenly unthrottled, looping like whirligigs higher into the ether until there was only a faint twinkling in the stratosphere. In another county, a man with a telescope would report spying a "passel of dying stars in the night sky, all with the faces of startled children." Willow's eyes followed the path of the rising children: fallen flesh on the way to becoming again incorruptible air, *God's changelings,* she thought. *He sucks the spirit out of us at birth and leaves behind this residue of flesh, pilfers the marrow and discards the ransacked bone.* She looked down at her own fat feet, feet that kept the cobbler occupied. *There is no such thing as a human being.*

Ursula, Josephine, Irmalinda, and Ogden! Willow cried out and saw Oggie open his eyes, two doleful blooms amidst the garden of his face. And Willow could see his final thought as a boy: *Why would God remain on Earth, feet so firmly planted in the soil, while faithful children were rocketing toward Heaven?* She would not tell her parents how he looked, his mouth widening in terror as his feet left the ground. She would not tell her parents she could see sorrow in the way his eyes flickered then dimmed as he looked at her, eyes that had never known sadness.

The piper's coat now churned angrily about him, a cyclone he conducted with his piping from the calm of the eye, and Willow had to shield her face from the stinging rubble he kicked up. Then he blew on his pipe a final note, the rabbits bared their teeth and flattened their ears aerodynamically, braced for velocity, and the piper and his pendant universe disappeared in the dust, haboosh!

Willow wobbled on her hammy stems.

She found herself nose to nose with a vole as she awoke beneath the rising sun. When she opened her mouth to yawn, the vole tried to run, then sank its feet into the ground, but the wind of her inhalation lifted it into her mouth, and she coughed when it flew down her throat, vague irritant; the vole, who until now had only ever dreamt of flying, went sailing into the next county: Willow had grown in the night. Actually she felt as she always had and so didn't know if she'd enlarged or the world had shrunk, as the world has a habit of doing, but she figured either way the guilt was hers.

She stood up, lifted a nest of speckled eggs out of the cleft of a craggy oak, ate it, and wept. She had always been a prisoner of her own appetite.

Willow remembered an upsetting story she'd read once of an unwavering paradise, stubborn in its immutability, a land of more-than-plenty, hemorrhaging milk and honey, oozing with bounty; where trees were heavy year-round with toothsome fruits that didn't know how to rot; a comely land free of the eyesore of humpbacked crones and whiskered spinsters; free of catastrophic dogs and pugilist gods who blacken your eye so they can forgive you the sin of being a spirit who has the gall to gussy itself up in flesh (of all the harebrained solutions!); a land free of fatal children; where barnstorming monks take sudden flight, the dutiful sun warming their tonsured noggins, and wheel about on the zephyr of all the unheeded pre-paradise orisons they'd ever uttered, tempted out of the sky only when the abbot below paddled the creamy saddle of a chosen maiden—thwap!— the rosy rump glowing so scarlet it could be spotted from the moon! allowing the monks to get a fix on the beacon and steer themselves back toward the runway, where their very own bare-bottomed nuns with bums in need of reddening awaited them; a place where pigs politely roast themselves, crackling stuck with knives and forks, and trot across the table on charred hooves ready to be carved; where geese ascend and soar near to the sun, self-broiling, then drop from the sky and fly into the gaping mouths of the zaftig and eternally peckish, cooked animals so much more relaxed and accommodating than wild ones, who are inclined to snarl and balk at the fate of meat, its destiny to fuel human industry, that industry required, for example, in the labor of meat-making (no matter how generously you stuff the gullets of human beings, the next day there they are again, drooling and famished as if never fed, no magically multiplying fishes or loaves ever enough, cursed with hunger till the day they die, cursed!). *What a sad bunch of insatiable greedy-guts,* thought Willow, *making the world vanish a mouthful at a time,* she herself the worst offender, hungry, hungry, ceaselessly hungry.

As Willow wiped the sleep from her eyes, which now loomed in the sky, she imagined, like two gluttonous moons, she noticed tiny limbs scattered on the ground, bodies neatly butchered, arms and tongues and legs and eyeballs, fingers and ears, brains and hearts, strewn everywhere as if to fertilize the clearing, and she picked up an arm and held it between her fingers. It was bloodless and rubbery with the weensiest fingernails, like a doll's arm. But it wasn't a doll's arm. She gathered all the parts she could find into the aching marsupium of her mouth, some of them still trembling with reflex, and she cradled her weighted muzzle in her hands. *Life begins, life begins, life begins with* me, she sang. She stood towering, and the air she noticed was so thin, her head felt like a helium balloon making a break for the heavens, drifting ever farther from her. The hard ground beneath her feet, miles and miles away now, rose up quickly and walloped her in the face.

ξ   ξ   ξ

That morning, the town awoke to find itself purged of children. The women who wailed at the birth-hour fell silent, and time stumbled forward without anyone noting its passage. The phantom pains that would soon stab them, their fingers, their belly, their heart, an aching for which there was no suitable thunder, would be the weight of their child's face in their hands, an arthritic longing that would quickly gnarl their grasp. Now the sound of stifled sorrow was the music to which people stepped in Kingdom Come, eyes always searching the night sky or the banks of the river for some sign of *Matilda and Ephraim, Ezekiel and Hannah*...There were those who said the children, so suggestible, had surely followed the rabbits into the river, had wanted to see where the river would lead the unwanted, but no bodies were found on the rocks and dredging the river yielded only the usual detritus, milk bottles and boxing gloves and birdcages and saxophones and cowboy boots and bear traps and kitchen sinks and rocks some folks thought the water had whittled into the winsome visage of the Blessed Virgin (not that these Lutherans ever paid the Virgin much heed—a virgin who appears in a bowl of Wheatena or cries blood on holy days, always making a spectacle of herself that one, snort).

Others said perhaps the children had misplaced their innocence—it had gone down gurgling with the last accursed rabbit—and now were fearful of their own end so had left to seek out the seductive gloom of the Transylvania they had secretly read about in their closets at night, later dreaming of the immortalizing incisors of those merrily exsanguinated Undead. And there were the devout and hopeful (though famished hope always fades when unfed), who were convinced the children had traveled into the howling wilderness and were crusading with wayfaring Flagellants, spreading the Word between yelps: God ow God ow God ow God.

Still others believed the children, who had all been feverish the night before, contracted a wandering disease that afflicts only the small-footed and were somewhere on the plains wading barefoot through prairie grass, walking themselves to death. This theory gathered the most momentum among the townsfolk for a time because the one memento the children had left behind was their shoes, pairs of which could be found sitting empty throughout the town, in the sorghum field, beneath a linden tree, in a hayloft, the gazebo, because the children, raised right, hadn't wanted to soil Death's immaculate lodgings and so had politely removed them and left them at the door. Of course it was upsetting to think the portal to eternity could open beneath anyone's feet, even the blameless feet of infants, at any moment. But behind this speculation was the unspoken conviction that it was Herr Pfeiffer who was the source of their blue ruin, and that's when joyful noise was officially outlawed in Kansas, even songbirds verboten, and birds remapped their migrations around the flatlands, flying hundreds of miles out of their way, because of course rare is the bird who can abide a soundless sky or a morning awakened by silence. Even crows, those nattering gossips, like a melodious sunrise.

Few people recall that the sky over Kingdom Come was once yellow with canaries. After the children disappeared, canary hunters picked them out of the air one by one, and now nothing sings in Kansas. Widow Winkler tried to muzzle her sweet Petunia, who was known to whistle all of *Waldszenen* with little encouragement, and she hid her in the cellar, but canary trackers eventually sniffed the last canary out and forced their way into the widow's house, armed with a bow the size of a swallowtail butterfly and a quiver of wee arrows they slung over their thumbs, and between two fingers the town fletcher, Kingdom Come King of the Popinjay, held the arbalest, and with index finger and thumb he carefully nocked then shot an arrow (whose flights were fletched with the feathers of other slain canaries) into Petunia's terrified heart. She was frantically warbling the beginning of "The Bird Prophet," trying to forestall her own fate, when the arrow struck her, and the marksman wept when she fell to the ground. Not long after, Widow Winkler herself gave up the ghost, the only thing besides Petunia and Schatz she'd been halfheartedly clinging to for years, Petunia lying on the pillow next to her, the tiny arrow lodged in her breast as though she were little more than a cocktail sausage spindled on a toothpick.

When the blood rains began, a week after the children disappeared, Kingdom Comers knew better than to believe what the scientists were saying, which was that the raindrops had merely collided with iron oxide on the way down, consumptive steel mills having coughed the red dust into the atmosphere. Parents, however, were wise to the ways of a carnivorous universe and they knew they were being rained on by their own children, that it was their children's blood that ran down their cheeks, and they put out mason jars in which to collect it, but the next day the jars were always empty, no residue of red rain remaining on the glass. Some people stayed up all night watching the jars, waiting to see the blood vanish, daring it to disappear in their presence, their own blood! But blood's a born mesmerist, and it waited for the eyelids to droop with fatigue, then allakhazam: there-blink-gone, like everything in the world. Most people believed God was not dead, despite the headlines, but even the formerly pious decided all the same to wash their hands of Him and to store the rackabones of their souls at His house. After the rain had fallen, the town appearing mauled, people would find a ribbon or pair of glasses, a sock, a necklace, that belonged to one of their children, and the church, long deserted and waiting to be razed by God's notorious pugnacity, was converted into a reliquary, where all these items were stored. The shoes they lined up neatly beneath the pews. Parents now spent their days compiling lists of regrets, page upon page, an entry for each day in the child's life they were sorry they would miss, and they placed their book of documented mourning into their children's shoes, hoping these too might disappear, might fly up and out of the world. Of course many things vanish from this world without a moment's warning—prosperity, sanity, umbrellas, love—but not sorrow, never sorrow: sorrow always wears thin its welcome.

The town resented having a witness to an abduction but no earthly solution to the crime, especially a witness who'd suspiciously doubled in size, swelling to decidedly unfeminine proportions over night, and it showed Willow its back. People whispered that Willow was a wicked species of kobold with a dash of ravenous giant in her genes and that she had crawled out of a cave when she was born and chosen this town to menace because it boasted more children than most, a fertile town Kingdom Come. *Always suspected that one would be nothing but trouble,* they said, *body like that.* Some said they knew for a fact she ate children, swallowed them whole like aspirin—*Just look at her! No pork cutlet ever made a body grow like that!*—and if you cut open her stomach, you'd find them all there waiting to be extracted, poor little tumors, clutching their cold feet.

Other people said they saw her dancing at night under a gibbous moon, skin blue as a plum, trying to persuade it to flaunt its full belly every quarter, tempt it to wax and wax like her. Willow grew and grew, big as the Alps, into the sky, beheaded by clouds, ruptured the sky over Kingdom Come, consorting with birds, and people said she was taking up space that should have been inhabited by children. Sometimes they bit her sturdy ankles and she let them. No one ever again mentioned those infernal rabbits infested with misery.

Willow, no grumbler, took it on her sizable chin like a champ. She had known what it was like to be the object of the boundless adoration of a small boy, a wondrous thing. It was only fair, she thought, that she should know too what it is like to be loathed, to be thought an abominable cannibal demon. Her parents bore the shame of being the only parents whose child survived the fateful piping, and her mother spent her days baking custard pies and cherry cobblers and apple slump, basting briskets, simmering succotash, whipping up griddle cakes for breakfast, canning rhubarb and peaches, all for the other parents, who promptly tossed every grubgift she brought them into the trash or left it sitting on the stoop for the fattened foxes and lonesome dogs kicked to the curb. They'd eat nary a morsel prepared by the mother of evil, let them waste to bone first!

At night, while her parents sat in a darkened parlor, Willow lay on her back and tried to stitch the stars together in the image of Oggie, and she thought to herself that the sky was as good a guardian as any, certainly more capable than humans, who are so fallible it's always merely a matter of time before they make a mess of all they touch. The universe will one day stop to rest its weary remains and then give up, thought Willow, refuse to be provoked into being again, by a big bang or a seamstress mole with an endless skein of thread or a week of Godly labor or a dismembered deity whose parts are itching to be reanimated in the shape of mountains and rivers, because humans will have finally and irreversibly swapped love for war, life for death, and bloodied the planet but good, caused it to hemorrhage beyond all stanching.

ξ   ξ   ξ

The last sounds Kingdom Come ever heard were the sound of the earth shuddering as Willow Himmelfarb walked into the river and the murmur of the water as it parted around her legs, which stood stalwart as silos, then she sat down and her body dammed the river, and the townspeople slept for the first time since their children had disappeared, slept in their children's beds. There wasn't enough river for Willow to drown herself—there wasn't enough water in all of Kansas for that—but the water rose and rose around her and flooded the land, swallowing prairie and crops and automobiles and barns and threshers and finally houses, cleansing the town of its heartache, the parents of the lost children gushing forth out of bedroom windows, bobbing in the escaped river beside coffee pots and overcoats and lampshades and adding machines and pitchforks and sneakers and tubas and yo-yos and incomplete sets of encyclopedias, singing, singing, singing, singing, happily abducted by water.

TWENTY-THREE
HUSBAND OF
MARY ALICE

The summer before the first child went missing from Kingdom Come, my next-door neighbor, Mary Alice Mc-Guinness, corkscrew curls the color of strawberry jam and cheeks so crowded with red freckles the pale skin showing through made her look like a speckled apple—forever bringing to mind fruit and flowers ripe and ruddy Mary Alice—she told me when she became a woman and began to bleed, and she predicted her abdomen would twist and the blood would begin to gush at precisely 2 p.m. on her thirteenth birthday, she was going to become the Bride of Christ (young, sure, but well beyond the cradle and fully and equally versed in the divine and the domestic arts, quick-study marital wunderkind, Mary Alice McGuinness a godly polymath, everyone said so, but I had my doubts that a woebegone bridegroom eternally burdened by the sagging sack-load of the world's sins, stooped by schlepping from here to eternity the back-breaking freight of ceaselessly accumulating bad behavior—sins of the past, yet to come, ur- to Z, the alpha sin, omega sin, all human behavior bewitched and between—yes, can you blame me?, yes, I had my doubts that such a profession-al sad sack could make a salty persimmon like Mary Alice McGuinness content to be mere helpmeet), and she showed me a hope chest full of those things necessary for successful wifehood, the godly girl's trousseau: crocheted doilies and a tea cozy from her Grandma McGuinness; afghan and as-sorted darning needles from her Aunt Ida Mae; a souvenir cast-iron trivet in the shape of a sheriff's star from a trip to Dodge City; tiny spoons from every state in the continen-tal U.S. (except for South Dakota, misplaced during a tea party we threw for the Mad Hatter—my invitee, and the Holy Ghost—hers) and a wooden rack on which to dangle them; a waffle iron handed down from her mother, who had a crosshatch scar from a griddle burn on her left forearm and who hadn't much cared for waffles to begin with; ceramic chicken and rooster pecking at invisible fodder; coffee mugs and bath towels monogrammed "King of Kings" and "The Little Mrs."; a blue bottle of Evening in Paris perfume with atomizer; a bar of hand-milled rosewater soap that Mary Alice claimed would smell like Paradise when sudsing the skin of Jesus; white muslin sheets, starched, ready to receive "the hard-won blood of consummation, the blood of the be-trothed lamb"; pillow cases embroidered with violets ("Jesus's favorite nosegay," Mary Alice assured me, and this made me think that a winsome fragrance is important in trying to cap-tivate a handsome man who once hung on a cross, a distract-ing attar that can make him forget the everlasting wounds festering on his hands and feet, forget the seductive splendor of his beautiful suffering, this man who glows with the ghostliest green complexion—even in the pink of health!—and whose final inhalation carried with it the coppery smell of his own blood drying on his lips, that inaugural communion); a family Bible with gold-tasseled bookmark and gilt-edged pages thin as a whisper passed down through several generations of devout McGuinnesses; and a man's toiletries set— aftershave, tweezers, nail file, and fingernail clippers, *because the hands staked to the cross, womanly hands that would beckon and mesmerize the faithful for millennia, had to be neatly manicured for the occasion and forever after?* I wanted to ask Mary Alice, sincerely. It's true, though the carpenters I knew weren't neatniks, I'd never seen any picture of Jesus with thick, yellowing nails and lunulae of dirt cresting them. It's only natural for a person who sees the end gaining on him to want to cut a fine farewell figure, spruce up the spirit's final snuggery, especially someone as fetching as Jesus. I am not beautiful and my sorrow is ordinary, but I understand this.

Mary Alice wore a plastic diamond ring with a flaking gold band that she got for a quarter from the gumball machine in front of Rexall Drugs, and she frequently held out her hand and fluttered her fingers as evidence she was engaged—*24 karat God*, I thought, and I felt myself snort, because I could not bear to think of Mary Alice marrying Jesus, carrying his fragile and battered body, only recently resurrected, down the aisle, feeding him waffles and trimming his toenails—and the first time she waved the ring around, her prim red mouth broke into a slow smile like a hesitant poppy blooming. Sometimes she unclasped the diamond, which opened on a hinge and revealed a hidden compartment (a place you could hide a cyanide capsule I thought, just in case Jesus turned out to be less than dreamboat, a gene or two shy of the prince of princely paragons he was advertised as being, a few shekels short of the million dollar *beau idéal*—my father had explained to me even maniacs can be charming in the beginning; not that I thought for a minute Jesus was a maniac, well, not exactly, but I believed he might carry with him the jagged scars of persecution and lug around the millstone of martyrdom in a way that would not make for a crackerjack husband, would not allow him to become a devoted family man who can sharpen the blades of a lawnmower, dance a manly mazurka, and, after a long day of breadwinning, mix a martini delicious and dry as a desert in bloom. I'd always figured Jesus had a gaping sadness inside him, more painful than parted flesh and for which there was no healing liniment, not in this world or the next or the one after that. But it is the howling mouths of those everlasting gashes, rent flesh, from which blood and wine and lymph spill and which persist across time and space, that are the greater part of his Martian appeal), and Mary Alice would take out a baby tooth she claimed belonged to Jesus and roll it around in her palm. She found it in her own mouth one night when she'd been dreaming of kissing her savior on the lips; she said he slipped it to her with a cold tongue that tasted like lime sherbet.

She confided to me her parents had a "Josephite marriage"—this meant they kissed, virtuous and dry, like grandparents, a perfunctory brushing of lips gone fallow, and slept in twin beds divided by a night stand, a hurricane lamp, and a book signed by Dale Carnegie, whose seminar about how to be an influential human being and speak publicly with confidence and verve Mary Alice's father had driven to Joplin, Missouri, to attend. And she also informed me that she and her sister, Ruthanne, had been immaculately conceived one immaculate winter evening when snowfall erased the moon and the sky looked at last cleansed white as old bones, the glittering ossuary of heaven revealing itself for a night to the unfortunate mortals still fleshed and struggling below, struggling. Mary Alice had X-ray vision so powerful, the thin coverlet of sky that concealed heaven was an easy breach for her, and she spied on heaven in the early morning when she believed God was napping. And here on Earth, a planet kept awake by watery Sanka and war crimes and infidelity and debt and bigotry, the fear of fire and carbon monoxide, amphetamines, love, guilt, drought, and humiliation, digestive disturbance, she could see beneath any addled skin to the bones glowing secretly inside with fond longing for obdurate invincibility, and she could tell you how many notches God had whittled there and how many more you were due before the skin gave out and those bones prevailed.

"Will Ruthanne marry Jesus too?" I asked her. "Of course!" she said, and she crossed her wide eyes the brash blue of bluebirds then looked at me pityingly, as though I were in the slow class, a remedial pupil, slower and sadder than poor Tommy Onion, whose stammer never allowed him to finish a word, to say nothing of a sentence—he only ever got as far as the first consonant, and then his mouth snagged on the sound and his stutter made me think of a restless horse whose tail gets too close to barbed wire, leaving behind horsehair snapping in the stout wind that accumulates in flat places, but I liked to think Tommy Onion was communicating in code, the stammerer's secret weapon; he was a cipher machine for which grammar school cryptologists were no match. Tommy's family had been sentenced to the poorhouse it was said, and he was thin and small and his spindly arms were always measled with red spots, bringing to mind an exotic animal that thrives defiantly in a blistering climate. I saw him once in the janitor's closet, sitting on a footstool between the Bon Ami and the bags of pink sawdust they sprinkle on grade school vomit, saw him sucking on his arm, poor hungry Tommy, poor famished vampire Tommy Onion, nourishing himself with the thin broth of his own blood, drinking himself dry, his own scrawny arm his only victim and looking like something unfit for the stewpot. Obie said Tommy spoke a language only God and those whose tongues are trained to speak God could understand. "*You* know what he's trying to say, don't you?" And somehow I always did: I showed him where his bus was, counted out his occasional milk money for him, fetched him the paste and pipe cleaners and red and green foil stars from a high shelf. Children, born sadists, loved to ask him his name, then they pretended the t-t-t-t sound that stuck to his teeth was enemy gunfire and they squealed and scrambled for the trenches and laughed until he swallowed the word and walked away, out of ammunition, shirt damp with spittle, his name an unexploded mortar shell in his throat. O Tommy Tommy Tommy Onion.

Once I held Mary Alice's milk tooth up to the sun and, through the loupe of my open fist, squinted at it with one eye: a crack on one side, not a tooth of the first water. "So Jesus is a bigamist?" I asked, something my father had said when I told him Ruthanne and Mary Alice were both engaged to marry him, and I thought he meant that when Jesus married, taking on two wives at once, he would grow to be a large man, biggest Mr. this side of Gethsemane, and of course I found this appealing. Maybe Jesus is the one man who wouldn't have to stand on a stack of milk crates to kiss me goodnight I thought, the one man whose starry eyes, hoisted into the heavens, could look into mine and see my beetle-sized spirit flattened beneath the bullying flesh, could see the bug of my immortal soul on its back on the sidewalk beneath the fallen piano of my carcass, soul squashed to bug flinders, its flimsy exoskeleton no match for a Steinway, but stubborn little bug legs still busily wriggling. Now Mary Alice looked at me with earnest concern, as though she'd just awakened from a puzzling dream, and then she snatched her prized incisor from me, ran inside, and let the screen door slam-slam behind her.

Bride of Christ, naturally I couldn't help but think of the Bride of Frankenstein, whose meringue of electroshocked hair I'd always admired. It added a good foot and a half to her height, making it impossible for her to watch her own movies in the theatre without blinding the flat-heads sitting behind her. I too always had to sit in the last row, despite my near-sightedness, which is the inevitable shortcoming of eyes hoisted so far from the ground, eyes straining to see what thrives at the body's nadir, shoes always at a blurry distance.

Mary Alice said to me one day she wanted to be prepared for her wedding night, and she asked me to pretend to be Jesus so she could kiss me. I asked her if Jesus would be wearing his crown of thorns on their wedding night—I wanted to know how to angle my head—and this made her stop to consider. Mary Alice snipped a yellow rose from one of her mother's lush bushes, and she pricked both our foreheads with the thorny stem. Blood trickled toward my eyes, and I thought of the exorcism, how it had brought me to this very moment, and the white crosses on my feet began to burn pleasantly. Purity and ignorance demand blood in equal measure.

Mary Alice kissed the blood from my eyelids, then she took my lips in her mouth as though she were eating a butterscotch, and I placed my hand gently against her cheek just as I imagined Jesus, notoriously tender, would do. My lips felt like fish swimming against the current in a warm and viscous river. I supposed that Jesus would kiss in precisely this benevolent and velveteen manner and was about to tell Mary Alice as much when Ruthanne came into her sister's room. She shrieked at a pitch that made it seem as though I were holding a saw-toothed hatchet to Mary Alice's throat and had a look in my eye that said she'd soon be pastrami, and I saw myself being escorted to the electric chair, which they'd have to rebuild in order to properly juice a criminal of my girth and nefariousness. Mary Alice grinned roguishly at Ruthanne, and I wondered if they'd made a bet as to which one of them Jesus would find the more winsome kisser. Behind whose ear would the Moondrops be most tempting? Mary Alice had told me that hers would not be a loveless marriage and that she knew for a fact Ruthanne, sweet as cider, was not Jesus's type.

After that, Mary Alice and I were not allowed to see one another for several weeks, but then one afternoon she appeared at the door, and I answered. She was selling candy-coated almonds to help raise money for the Bishop Miege drill team, who had been invited to travel to Houston, Missouri, to perform in the Emmett Kelly Clown Festival. Ruthanne was co-captain, and Mary Alice said the team was practicing some of the numbers in floppy shoes and fright wigs. "Weary Willie was a melancholy hobo who stood in line for bread, worked any odd job for a nickel a day, and wouldn't be caught dead in a fright wig," said Mary Alice through a smoldering smirk. Mary Alice knew things no one else did, not even God I imagined, with his thick head so stuffed with guarded knowledge. I thought it was the astonishing red of her hair and her cheeks that made Mary Alice wise, her brain so potent it stained the very root of her with the blood of a scorching intellect. Her grandmother grew up in Sedan, Kansas, and she had known Emmett Kelly when she was a little girl and he was not yet a clown. Sometimes she watched him scatter mash in the chicken yard, an air of sadness pooling around him. "There were a lot of jobless people whose larders were bare in Chautauqua County, Kansas, and everywhere in those days," said Mary Alice. She said Ruthanne had decided not to marry Jesus after all. She said, "She doesn't have the first clue about how to make a marriage last or how to lighten the load of a sorrowful man." Whereas Mary Alice could make the saddest messiah so happy to have risen from the dead. Though surely resurrection produced in a body mixed feelings.

She faithfully read *Reader's Digest* for wholesome and inspirational human interest anecdotes she could entertain her husband with while cooking him chicken fricassee and *Good Housekeeping* for the latest innovations in domestic sanitation and general top-notch housewifery, helpful tips on how to lift stubborn wine stains from clothing formerly white as the moon, which Mary Alice thought might be useful should the blood of Christ be dribbled down the front of her husband's snowy vestments or her bridal gown (the sanctified get-up she planned never to take off, so long as her heart drummed devotion in her chest), and how to make colorful origami swans to dangle above the crib and stimulate the baby's brain as it rippled with first knowledge. Of course, pledging a troth to Jesus, agreeing to shoulder the burden of being God's daughter-in-law (so hard to please, that taskmaster God, which is what, Mary Alice insisted, made his son a man worth marrying, those exacting standards of God-the-father-in-law; nothing ever good enough for the Old Goat, *I* imagined Jesus lamented), meant she would have to forego motherhood, Jesus's seed saved for more important fertilizations (Jesus himself a handsome ear of corn and heaven a field that never goes fallow unless blighted by the loss of faith—Paradise would always be fruitful with Mary Alice and Obie in the world). But Mary Alice said there were certainly worse things than being childless and nothing better to hope for in this life than being "the old ball and chain," as my father called it when my mother was out of earshot, of Christ.

Because we had three snow days that blizzardly winter, school ran headlong into June, and when it finally let out, the sun broiled Kansas to an early crisp so that the minute we dared step out of the chilled half comfort of houses rattled by attic fans and the wheezing of window units in every room, we all instantly pinkened, the fairest among us quickly blistering if we dillydallied in the noonday glare too long, and we felt like pork steaks tossed on the Sunday grill. And that's when Mary Alice, as though she were the sun's own offspring, developed a fever that spiked to such an altitude she was packed into a tub full of ice.

Amidst the clacking of her sister's teeth, Ruthanne heard Mary Alice utter my name, and her family asked if I would visit her, hoping I might prove to be a febrifuge, might cheer her up and cool her down to 98.6. Since they didn't know what Mary Alice was suffering from, my father feared all manner of communicable pox, dread diphtheria, scarlet contagion, but Dr. Ingram, not one to be troubled by the epidemiology of mystery, issued the all clear and my mother felt certain there was no virus virile enough to bully me into debilitating illness (she thought I'd always suffered anyway from a chronic and gigantifying dropsy for which there was no antidote or immunization—that is, she feared more for Mary Alice), and I knew she held out hope I might one day be reduced to a slim fraction of my former circumference by a wasting disease as she was always urging me to consider missionary work in the most equatorial and mosquitoed locales, countries shrunken by cholera, ravaged by famine—that most heartless of heartless despots and the one my mother loved best. Sometimes she'd stand at my bedroom door at night and whisper, *Go hungry, go hungry,* her augury conjuring in me the most insatiable emptiness in the morning, and like a fox in the henhouse, I'd raven the icebox when my mother's back was turned and smuggle five extra eggs back to my room, no farm fertile enough to keep my appetite in check as I emptied the world of future chickens. I knew their potential had already been rubberized, halted the minute they hit the boiling water, but sometimes I heard a ghostly clucking as I crammed a crumbling yolk in my yap.

Mary Alice was so pale, the watery color of whey, that I thought eventually we'd be able to see through her skin to her bones and organs, her quickly failing soul suspended visibly in the aspic of flesh, thought we'd soon see the slowing circulation of her blood. She fluttered her eyes as I neared her bed, eyes empty of color and glassy as agates, eyes that appeared to me as though they intended to secede, and I feared they might free themselves from her face and fly at my head, get tangled in my hair, but I quieted the coward inside me and sat next to her on the bed. Her ashen pallor contrasted all the more strikingly with the wild redness of her hair and freckles, and when I laid my hand on her melting brow, I felt like I was swabbing a wound, Mary Alice's whole noggin an injury from which she might not recover. Her mother had warned me, with quivering lips, that Mary Alice was delirious and might say things to me that wouldn't make a lick of sense. But she'd smiled when I entered her room, and I knew she knew me, knew she saw inside me as she always had, saw the soul gasping for air beneath the lava flow of earthly, egg-nourished flesh. Mary Alice was always politely reciprocal in the most essential ways.

"Mary Alice?" I whispered. "Mary Alice McGuinness?" She'd always seemed to me to hover above us, not entirely convinced she wanted to stick around, and I hoped the sound of her name would seize her by her floating feet and make it harder for her to flee we undeserving and inadequate earthlings. Her eyes widened and pierced my sternum and I felt my heart catch.

"Wallis Armstrong," she said, and as I watched my name drop from her lips, I felt for a second like I was a fever dream Mary Alice was having. Dreams weighing less than the ash they leave behind, this was a comfort to me.

"You'll end up in Eden," Mary Alice said, and my heart nearly heaved its last beat. Eden, that unsparing resort I wished never to visit. "But you'll be alone there and your heart will be broken." Mary Alice smiled an oracular smile, smiled the way Obie did when he spoke to me of my weighty fate: "You'll never repair it." I looked at the cold thermometer on Mary Alice's end table, and I felt my own mercury plunge toward freezing. "But. There you will regain your innocence." Mary Alice touched my hand, tentatively, as though prodding a fire. "That's the thing we've never understood," she said. "Paradise is *next door* to Eden."

Paradise, Eden, Mary Alice was already so far away! "Mary Alice, Mary Alice," I said, "Don't. Be. Sick." I tried to speak in the stern and halting manner of her father, who only spoke up to issue commands and did so with studied authority. I could think of no suitable incantation, but I thought her sense of obedience might be strong enough to muscle a microbe into submission. "Jesus doesn't need you as much as I do," I muttered, and I took her clammy hand in mine. Her engagement ring from Jesus was gone from her finger: All was lost.

"Listen, Wallis Armstrong," she said and she squeezed my hand. I imagined it felt leaden as a plummet to her, verticality my expertise, felt like a cannonball resting in her dainty palm, like something she could lob at the enemy to sink him into the briny deep: I wanted her to use me as artillery against heaven, which is only ever a few paces from Eden I reckoned. Then came the jabber in a fevered avalanche: "Children will leave this world through the door they came in." Mary Alice spoke with paling lips that had once been the glorious color of radishes. "They'll leave when their parents aren't looking. When Jesus hung on the cross, he looked like a man but was really a child—with an Old Testament life expectancy of 969 years, a budding messiah would remain a child for centuries—and God was busy with other planets. Jesus, he was a boy just wanting to do right by his father. That's why we can't marry, wouldn't be right to marry a child. It's only children who can atone for the sins of adults. Not because they're pure, oh no, people are dead wrong about that. They're just not tall enough yet to properly sin." Mary Alice raised her hand, and I leaned my cheek into her touch. "Innocence," she said, "is only a matter of height." Mary Alice smiled again, the corners of her mouth reaching up into her freckles as if to pluck an apple from a limb. "Jesus," she whispered, "was no bigger than a fox. But God is tall as eternity." I felt myself exhale vigorously like a bellows, wishing I could expel the guilt of having never been small.

Thick with missing innocence, I groped. "What about your wedding, Mary Alice, when you turn thirteen? You have to stick around for that. Jesus doesn't want a wife who stays in bed all day nursing a fever. You don't want to be spurned by...by your beloved, do you? Then Jesus won't have any choice but to marry *Ruthanne*," I sputtered, a desperate goading. I should have seen that Mary Alice now floated about in an atmosphere too pure to sustain jealousy.

Mary Alice lifted up her pajama top and showed me the scar the removal of her appendix had left behind, and it looked like her stomach was smirking. "My body is spoiled," she said. "I'm in no danger of marriage. I can take no one's sins inside me. I'd spill them on the ground and they'd spread like chickweed." She held her hand against her scar. "When Jesus drank the sins of the world, he hadn't yet sprung a leak, and he kept them down. But the wounded who heal are nobody's martyr." Her face fell and she looked like she'd just seen her most doting hope slaughtered and skinned and

hung from the hoof. Though I couldn't quite follow Mary
Alice's logic, I could see that it wasn't the gibberish of an ailing body whose blood was aboil. I could see Mary Alice was
ailing because she'd come to understand some unbearable
truth about what it means to be the helpless spouse of an
irreversible savior.

Then Mary Alice said, "Obie," and she closed her eyes.
I felt my body, an airplane whose engines had suddenly
stalled and caused it to spiral toward oblivion, eject my head
into the ether; it parachuted into enemy territory and rolled
around at my feet.

"Obie *what?*" I asked. "Mary Alice? Mary Alice?" but she
was gone from me. I touched her scar and my hand slipped
inside her, gathered her organs, arranged them on a platter,
garnished with the world's suffering, and offered them up to
God, that glutton, lover of entrails. My head scowled, shook
itself, and sighed, so weary of living at an elevation where the
air is thin, so weary of its attachment to a girl like me.

☾

Mary Alice did not die that day, a Thursday. Her fever broke at dusk on Friday. But she was never again the
Mary Alice we had known. She looked withered and impermanent, as though she hadn't really survived but her body
wouldn't concede the defeat, and people piloted themselves
off-course when they saw her headed in their direction. And
when Mary Alice passed me one day on the sidewalk, she
looked right through me, sturdy me now more window than
girl in Mary Alice's eyes, and she never spoke another word
to me.

It wasn't long before the McGuinnesses pulled up stakes and fled Kingdom Come for good, though no one saw them heft their belongings onto a truck. No one saw them light out.

Then Emily Lipton talked to a stranger at a birthday party in Paradise Park, and so began my trek toward a menacing Eden, land of lost giants, God and Wallis Armstrong chief among them.

TWENTY-FOUR
THE INOCULATION OF
MATEEN MUNDRAWALA

I hadn't seen or heard from Mateen in a week, not since I'd followed the feet of the fox-trot into his bedroom, and when I arrived for my final dance lesson, I passed my eyes over the cars in the lot but spotted no battered beetle among them. Then a yellow smear, bright as a flashbulb, across the brick wall of the dance studio stopped my eyes dead in their stumble: *Paki-derms Go Home!* spat the paint. Such an efficient slur, slaying two threats with one stone.

Mateen was not in the classroom either. A buoyant red-head wearing a cinched dress whose skirt billowed when she whirled, which she did randomly while chattering, glided and pirouetted whoosh-whoosh across the dance floor and clapped her hands twice when she reached the other side. "All right, class," she sang, "partner up. Tonight we're going to learn the thrilling steps of...the tango!" She threw her hands into the air and grinned in a way that made my jaws ache.

"Olé," said a voice beside me, Lucky Teeter's dancing doppelgänger. "I hear it takes two," he said and held up his hands unsteadily, as though he were trying to catch a giant baby thrown from a burning building. He smiled and revealed a front tooth capped in silver.

"Where is Mr. Mundrawala?" I asked, and he wouldn't drop his paws, so I reached down and clasped his reaching hands in mine.

"Search me," said the man, and he shrugged his shoulders. I resisted the urge to pull him up into the air and dangle him by his arms until he produced some useful information. "Maybe his being at large has something to do with that love note someone left him out front?" He raised his eyebrows, and if I'd had some electrical tape on hand, I would have slapped it on his forehead and stripped his prominent brow bald. I gave a windy sigh like a furnace, dudgeon aswell, in no mood to gambol with a high school ruffian turned weekend rug-cutter. Bullies, like giants, do not improve with age.

"I ain't lucky," he said, and I thought he offered this as explanation for why he was willing to tango with a woman who was halfway to heaven, a woman he could look in the eye only by way of catapult or trampoline.

"Yeah, well, clearly good fortune frowns and flees to the nearest exit whenever *I* enter the room." I suddenly felt like an out-of-work pugilist long spoiling for a prize fracas and thought my fist might just fly forward unprompted and pop him in the beak.

"Lucky Teeter? I ain't him. I'm his older brother Leon."

I looked at that glinting tooth and had the vaguest recollection of Lucky getting into a souped-up Chevelle one afternoon after being suspended for scrapping in the hall between classes, pummeling some pimpled freshman in need of initiation. Leon took his right hand from my left and lifted it in the air as though he were trying to entice a bird from a limb then grabbed my hand and shook it mid-flight, howdy-do, howdy-do, shake-shake-shake.

"You're Leon…Teeter?" I asked, relaxing my arm, reducing the height of the handshake.

"In the flesh. And you're Wallis Armstrong, am I right? Lucky always had it in for you." Lucky, that is Leon, nodded his head that was balding in a way I suddenly found touching, a pink skullcap, a slice of grapefruit, a plot of recent desert encroaching on a forest struggling to remain lush.

"He mentioned me?"

"Your ears must've been on fire a lot when you were a kid. I bet you come up as a topic of conversation often enough to keep your bean toasty in any season." Leon smiled again and that tooth made me think of the disco ball revolving above us, scattering doubloons across the floor.

Oh, I felt enervated, so tired of tracking the disappeared only to find unbidden memories I'd just as soon remain dim stepping out of the shadows again and again. Yesterday's heartache is a tireless stalker.

"I'm just ribbing you," he said and he chucked me on the arm. "Like I said, I ain't Lucky. I sell insurance." He raised those eyebrows again. "Lucky had a sore spot for you because you had what he always wanted. He just wanted to be big, you know? Big shot. And you were a girl, so that didn't sit well with him neither. Lucky's like our dad in that way, old school. They like their gals barefoot, mouths zipped, and out of sight except to deliver a Schlitz as they watch the game with the boys."

"And you're not Lucky you keep telling me. So what saved you from this fate, Unlucky Teeter?"

"My sister." Leon let his gaze fall to the floor. One advantage to having a head perched above everyone's sight line is that necks begin to ache and this cuts potential gabfests short. I stole a longer look at Leon while I had the chance. His body was no surprise, neither slight nor portly, but his face was long and thin, an older, slowly thawing version of Lucky's. His nose was so dominant that the rest of his face appeared to be retreating to safe ground so as not to be enslaved, but his throat was drawn and his eyes bulged, as though he'd gone on a diet from the neck up.

"What, she taught you to pretend that girls are human beings too?" While Leon and I were having this conversation, the rest of the class was tangoing wildly around us, as though they'd been kept in a dank cell beforehand, denied movement, and were suddenly released onto the dance floor, cheek to cheek, bent slightly at the knee, arms thrown out in front of them, looking like mirrored guerrillas advancing with bayonets, their embattled homeland in need of fierce defending. The teacher's mouth was hitched up at the side disapprovingly and she stared at Leon and me, trying to stink-eye us into hoofing with the rest.

"You ever hear of precocious puberty?" Leon asked, his silver tooth hidden behind his lip as he spoke. I imagined tiny dancers twirling beneath it. This question smelled like a gag cigar just waiting to explode in my face, so I said nothing.

"Our sister Maddy, she got the, uh, you know, the red curse when she was six years old."

"What, the measles?" I said and sniffed. Where, where was Mr. Mundrawala? Why was I standing amidst couples prancing with stiff lockstep resolve, talking to Lucky Teeter's older brother?

"The doctor told us she was going through precocious puberty and that her body was speeding up. She was turning thirteen seven years ahead of schedule." Leon looked at the teacher and then back up to me. His forehead was creased, a rumpled blanket. "She had fits, these seizures like, sometimes dozens a day. She was always the sweetest kid and then she'd just start screaming herself blue for no reason. She was still small, the size she was supposed to be, still had those red cheeks and baby fat, but inside her body was racing, dragging her out of her childhood and into old age, and they couldn't do nothing about it. My folks homeschooled her and we just pretended everything was hunky-doodle, like that sad-eyed tiny lady who sat at the table clutching her stuffed duck was some homeless, half-cocked relative we took pity on and invited to supper every night. Maddy was tired all the time, slow-moving. Aging at breakneck speed takes a lot out of you. We didn't know it, but we were watching her die. It was like one of those movies where the flower sprouts from the ground, shoots up into the air, grows leaves and petals, opens into a quick bloom, all the time clouds are zooming by in the background, the sun up, down, up, down, like it's doing calisthenics, then the flower starts to droop and drops its petals and withers down to a stalk of nothing in a matter of seconds. It was like that with Maddy." As Leon spoke, he fixed his eyes on the dance teacher, her whirling skirt. Leon had that slightly shriveled look about him that suggested his heart had cracked in the casting and would always leak, the heart of a boy who had loved an accelerated girl. So many hazards to being a brother. Then he lifted his arms up in the air again, said, "You lead," and I bent down at a nearly 90-degree angle to press my cheek to his, my caboose shoved out into the fast lane, and we parted the other tangoers as we charged across the floor. I felt Leon Teeter's cracked heart thump through his shirt against mine.

I decided to look for Mateen at his house. There wasn't a light on inside and I didn't see his car out front, but I knocked on his door anyway. I jiggled the knob—unlocked—so I walked inside and snapped on a light. I walked through the rooms: there wasn't a stick of furniture in the place, not a bath mat or footstool or paper clip left behind, not a lonesome hanger in any closet. It was the emptiest empty house I'd ever been in. Except the ballroom feet still trotted across the floor, and in the kitchen, on the draining board, sat the tiny Koran that had protected Mateen's great-grandfather in war but had failed to save him from the epidemic. Next to the book there was a scrap of paper no bigger than a fingernail, and I took the magnifying glass from the cover of the locket and read the faintly penciled scrawl:

I am but a man, small and flawed, a cowardly man afraid of contracting a beautiful illness from which I would never wish to recover. Forgive me. —MM

I had once more been forsaken, by a man stalked by malevolent angels. I was a virus antidoted only by distance. So this was how it was going to be. This was my eternity. I would empty the world, one disciple at a time.

TWENTY-FIVE
EGG OF EDEN, SPERM OF FATE

Not so long ago, the hard-noodled thinkers of the day believed that human beings are preformed, each of us a passing idea God has and then stores in the egg, in the sperm—well, naturally there was some disagreement about this, about which sanctum we hunker patiently inside like an enchanted princess waiting to be kissed awake—smack!— by the eager lips of fertilization. On the day of Creation, so the story goes, God gathered all the people that would ever walk the earth, and he slipped them inside Adam's sperm, inside Eve's eggs, so that all the descendents were right there in miniature from the word go, Adam and Eve bloated with the exploding population that would people posterity, ar- oil with homunculi! So let's say we're ovists—let us venture inside the ovary, inside the egg, where floats a microscopic human, the homunculus drumming the little seedlings of its fingers on its dainty knees, just waiting to be watered so that it might grow, every eventual mole and wrinkle and murmuring heartbeat tinied and predetermined. Does this mean inside a woman swarms a country waiting to be born, legions of pre-fetal minis tapping on the storefront window of their eggs, casting come-hither looks at every eligible sperm that waggles by? Is it any wonder that such traffic causes a woman to double over in pain each month, that nation inside her clamoring for sovereignty, loyalists parachuting into the unknown, where only one, maybe two, if any at all, can be granted citizenship? Had my mother understood that the wild pain that blinded her each month and required, in order to be subdued, the solace of a hot water bottle and a growler (or three) of beer (to her great shame more respectable spirits always repaid her respectability with a needling headache) was the result of oversized huddled homunculi yearning to breathe free—had she known this, she would surely have abstained and tossed all potential bantlings out with the crippling blood.

And any good theory provokes its own contradiction, so the other eggheads of the day said: Arf! Clearly a human being develops over time—what baby comes into the world sporting that (reprehensible foxtail of a) mustache it will later believe (mistakenly!) is so becoming? Surely that would be a uterine irritant! But if that doesn't persuade you, then I trust you will be swayed by the following irrefutable argument: Monsters. MONSTERS. No God worth believing in would preform and author all the bipedal monstrosities in the world! Would *pre*form the *de*formed so to say, the empty-eyed, the water-headed, the gigantic, the armless, the hare-lipped, the hobbled, those hapless deformities that are obviously the unfortunate consequence of the pregnant mother having...eaten a bad sausage, say, or accidentally gazed upon a convict, or having dreamt of the romping sexual misdeeds of satyrs, some infelicitous event that went straight to the embryo, like a hypodermic needle inserted into the womb, and scared it legless.

Of course, what we *now* know to be true is that it is the adult body that contains its own homunculus, a twin we carry inside us, one that grows and stretches to fit and inhabits us cell for cell identically at the age of twenty-five and then withdraws thereafter, shrinking smaller and smaller with each passing year until, at our death, it is perceptible only through the powerful lens of the microscope that is Faith.

My mother always told me there was an enchanting sylph inside me, if only I could coax her out. And I do feel that hectoring manikin tromping about in the ramshackle remains of my plundered soul at this very moment and have tried, unsuccessfully, to extract it with forceps. I feel it dodge my grasp and snicker, slip behind a kidney, wedge itself between sections of intestine and veil itself with mesentery, perch itself tauntingly on a rib, and naturally it's careful to avoid the magnetism of the womb. If only I were more lacking in ingenuity! The being that knows enough to grope inside for its seed-self will never be able to lasso its equally cunning and elusive blueprint, the Paradox of Self-Extraction.

You can imagine how comforting it would have been for me to think that maligned old scapegoat God could not be held accountable for my monstrosity, to think it was owing, rather, to that traumatizing sermon *about* God my mother recollected sometime during her third trimester (so close!), about the destruction that would creep through the window *like a thief in the night, so suddenly, like labor pains upon a pregnant woman* (pregnancy itself, suggests the Good Book, a pillager of women, and how could she who would one day spill from her guts an oversized picaroon that would swashbuckle herself free of the maternal hostel disagree?)!

That's what the revivalist, a fifteen-year-old boy with unlikely eyes the transparent green of peridot, a scriptural savant that could recite any Bible verse you had a mind to request and swallow an egg whole and move it around in his stomach beneath his shirt like he had a gopher inside him, though he said it was the egg of God that had long ago hatched in his heart—*thief in the night, labor pains*, that's what *he'd* said looking straight at my mother, gilt-edged King James raised in the air like a bludgeon about to descend and splinter the pulpit, that's what he'd said when she was an impressionable girl trembling in the late August afternoon heat trapped inside that tent (that evening, at the water tower, he kissed my mother on the lips then pulled away and sobbed with regret, sorry, *so* sorry, that with that kiss he had stolen my mother's virtue, he the seductive despoiler of yet another pubescent piety. Two weeks and three towns down the road, a young girl whose hymen the doctor confirmed by the blood on his glove had still been intact ballooned mysteriously and later deflated as they fished that boy from the river).

So years later, after she'd kissed another three boys and married one of them, when my mother's first water broke, she couldn't help thinking it was the Rapture, that thief, come to steal her baby, it was night, abdomen quickly beset by pains of labor, but in fact that crime had already occurred: it was the corrupting *memory* of that summer night, just popped into her head as she fanned herself with a magazine, that stole the beauty of her baby from her and left in its place a ruined fetus, part girlchild, part moose. My mother recollected, as she sat beneath a hair dryer at the beauty shop, big and bulging as a bale of hay, that lovely sad boy, afflicted pulpiteer, recollected what he'd said, voice cracking so tenderly, about thievery, about labor pains, about a stealthy God, and it gave her such a start she gasped and belched, everything she ate thereafter repeating on her, and that's when I turned, went bad as a tin of tuna fish left out in the noonday sun, bicarbonate of soda no match for the curdled fetus stewing inside her.

So that's the scientific account of the startled monster no self-respecting God would take responsibility for, incubated and made rotten by a buried memory, memory that rose from the grave when I was still simmering in the amniotic broth, rose at *such* an inopportune and formative moment, and here I am now, with so many terrifying visions in tow that I dare never reproduce lest I bring into this world a fluttering cuttlefish of an offspring, here I am that baby gone big, an anguishing recollection and indigestion carried to term.

But then there's Vivica Planet, who luxuriates in her monstrosity, wears it like an ermine coat (if all the ermines were still alive and snapping at the flesh beneath with their razor teeth).

I am a man and nothing human is alien to me. I am a woman and nothing monstrous is alien to me.

But which of us is better prepared to die?

Dear Obie, I would happily become a bacterium in the eye of the smallest eft if only I could see you again.

Let us take a closer gander at God, the microorganism behind the storied throne. God, the Father of Microbiology, was born in Delft in 1632 to a Dutch basket maker. Astigmatic and severely myopic from squinting the livelong day in his laboratory at all those wee creatures he fathered, God eventually ground a lens and perfected a microscope that let him gaze into the very marrow of all the animalcula that had previously escaped his naked eye (God's eyes themselves so gaping as to be invisible to the creatures upon whom he goggled, causing them to wonder: What then is the window to *God's* soul? A question whose heft outweighed the creatures' capacity to contemplate the uncontemplatable to such a degree they very nearly combusted at the thought, which would have ruined a long day's work, so God tried to short-circuit such musings as hastily as he could). And a little-known fact: God was the first to record his observations of spermatozoa, thereby establishing that the egg did *not* act alone, as had previously been believed.

When God wasn't tinkering with his microscopes and observing that which no one else could fathom, he found himself drawn to certain dissipating pastimes and eventually he wearied of being dismissed as mere dilettante deity, so for a brief time, longing to be celebrated, he became Isaac Newton, but when he recollected that Sir Isaac's most important discovery would involve the falling of an apple (a fall! an apple! of all the aggravating directions and fruits!) and would take place in the year 1666 no less, he quickly fled that body and returned to that of...Mr. Leak A Whee Uneven Notion (in those days all wary scientists, fun-loving paranoiacs, hid their fondest theories inside ciphers, something God himself, a lover of code, had considered while dictating the commandments to Moses, #13 KJV: *Hulk Saith: Toll Not*—rejected). God, fearful of the sort of intimacy demanded of a supreme being, has never liked being known, and being believed in, well, that's enervating too, to say the least. No, God, studied underachiever, decided he preferred being someone in whom people had little faith.

But when God shared his observations about bee mouthparts and stings, he found himself suddenly having an audience with the English Royal Society (God knew a thing or two about royalty and was reluctant to slip down *that* slope again, but what could he do?). And another microscopy enthusiast, Robert Hooke, insisted God's discovery of minute worms in pepper-water was worth a closer look. But then of course there was that single-cell squabble that had that high-toned society rolling their royal eyes at him, and he had to prove to those posturers that he could see things they couldn't, had never, would never.

He also tried to persuade the eminent thinkers that

mice did not naturally appear in a silo, generated by the longing of grain to be eaten; bees did not erupt from the flower's wistful anther; dogs did not well up inside a collar wishing to caress a velvety throat; criminals did not bloom beneath the hungry stocks looking for a tasty morsel to snugly incarcerate; stars were not immaculately birthed by the night sky lusting after the luminosity of day; avarice did not blossom unaided in the soul of the usurer; the sticky eggs of the ray-finned fish did not spring from the muddy feet of ducks; God does not originate in the murky heart of man to fill the aching emptiness swelling there; no, the world does not generate spontaneously, for heaven's sake, what an idea, *abiogenesis* my eye! thought God grumpily. Human beings were always affixing prefixes to perfectly good ideas and muddling everything. *Genesis: a bio*, thought God, he'd written the biography of the beginning years ago, and he sniffed so forcefully, his schnozzola filled with the rotifera he'd just been studying; the cilia ticked his nose and he nearly sneezed but pinched his nostrils closed and stifled a universe. Who knew what lurked in his sinus mucosa, what kind of creatures might be birthed next!

Staunch Calvinist at this time, God insisted all the little wrigglers he observed, the infusoria that swim imperceptibly all around us, were clear evidence of The Wonder of Him. There he goes, tooting his own horn again, said some of the minions, and God narrowed his eyes at them and caused a crop or two to fail to let them know they were NOT among the elect, and that put a cork in their gobs, ploink, swift kick to the faithless.

At the end of this life, God hid all his lenses and microscopes in a secret closet beneath his staircase, and he listened as servants traipsed worriedly up and down them in search of an ailing creator, and as he sat hunched beside this life's work, his own body frail as a teacup, he looked at every invisible specimen to whom he had given brute matter, and he thought of himself as one small cell inside the great organism of being, God the lone monk of matter in his tiny cell reciting the Psalter of the physical world, God hidden inside the vast hermitage looking, looking, observing the smallest and dimmest, most guileless among us so in need of the eye's dangerous advocacy.

TWENTY-SIX
LADY MAXIMUS AND
THE BANTAM UNIVERSE

I'd been working for a month on reducing that allegedly fateful barn in Goodland, Kansas, to the size of a breadbox when Ursula Lehmkuhl called to ask if I'd come to any conclusions. What I was unable to make her understand, what I was unable to make anyone understand, is that compacting every atom of an object into its smaller, more essential self so that the object might reveal memories it has stored there, depravity it has silently observed, inside the mortise and tenon, the joists and doorjambs and planking (objects after all the only truly reliable witnesses), is that it takes time. Yet there's that biblical clock people want me to best—six days for conjuring a universe and all its creatures, and she, they say to themselves, has only a barn to create, so insignificant in the scheme of things, a sorry excuse for a creator you turned out to be, get a move on, Flimflam Almighty, step lively! But death, as any streetwise annihilator can tell you, takes more consideration and much longer to fashion than life. Death is the promise that will always be kept, life little more than an opportunistic fluke born of a faint and random inkling. Death, a chronic condition for which there is no physic, no palliative, a ravenous worm vulnerable to no vermifuge, a stubborn ague for which there is no healing elixir and whose prognosis is always the same: dead. Death has intention, a will, death schemes. Life heaves itself involuntarily through fissures in the world. Death cracks the planet like an egg so that life will momentarily be duped into believing it was meant to be and spill forth its fertile goo, and it is at this moment that death dribbles the yolk into its waiting maw, slurp. There are those dullards who say death depends upon life, but this is not entirely accurate because were there no life to extinguish, death would slit its own throat and sate itself with the extinction of extinction to the end of time, death such a master at making do. And, well, while we're on *that* subject, I can tell you with certainty time's end is the death death most anxiously awaits, so for this, death does feel indebted to God, for His rash invention of human beings with their natural compulsion to raze the world: bravo, bravissimo, genius, thinks death!

During cholera epidemics, what people once feared more than dying was being prematurely interred, and safety coffins were designed so that the corpse could notify the living of its felicitous return to life. Pull-cords were installed that would tinkle a bell above ground, viewing windows, oxygen tubes, bottle rockets, shovel and rope, even a fluted pipe a priest could sniff daily for the corroborating aroma of putrefaction (a source of some confusion, of course, when dealing with the incorruptible and rose-scented carcass of a soon-to-be saint). But resurrection would not be nearly as interesting a story were it not as rare as it is, and a safety coffin never rescued any wannabe-Lazarus from his appointed date with dirt.

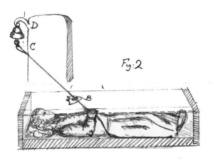

Ursula Lehmkuhl said the coroner had officially pronounced Eleanor's death to have been by her own hand, and then she said, "Those tiny hands...She was a happy child." I told her I was working on the nest of a ghost owl that had roosted on a rafter, was weaving together with tweezers twigs, the fine bones of mice, cottony owl down, and I could tell from the way Ursula Lehmkuhl exhaled through her nose that she thought I was being distracted by the devil, who could "trap the truth under a cloven hoof and bewitch the innocent with a mere flickety-flick of his barbed tail." So warned Reverend Sooby at the Sunday service I'd attended there, and he added, "Even here in Goodland, which I like to think of as Godland, *God's land*, we are not immune to Satan's deceptions." The odor of brimstone stings the nose and hangs everywhere in the heavy air of God's land, Godland, *Goodland*, Kansas.

"Ghost owls," I said, stalling, in roundabout defense of my snailish pace, "are one of only two dark-eyed owls in

Kansas." My scalp prickled with a feeling of irrelevance. I said, even more superfluously, "When threatened, they hiss loud as an angry gopher snake and throw themselves on their backs like a child having a tantrum. They kick their talons at the predator." I thought about God's knowledge, all the things God knows that prove not to be useful on a daily basis, so rarely coming up in conversation, never appearing on standardized tests. I wondered if God knew everyone's telephone number, her shoe size, knew what the final contents of her stomach would be. I wondered if God's molten brain held in memory as it cooled the dental impressions of all the worlds' inhabitants, which he could use to identify those dead that arrived not knowing who they were. I'd always figured death made, at the very least, amnesiacs of us all, that was its gift. And then Mrs. Lehmkuhl said to me, "There's something I need to tell you."

Whenever friends or family of the suspiciously departed say there's something they need to tell me, something I may have overlooked that I now need to know, something they saw or recently recollected, I become anxious and addled and my heart hastens its thumping and I think they will say, "I saw a dead ringer for him last Wednesday buying boiled peanuts at a bait and tackle in Beaverton, Missouri," a sighting, a clue, a hunch you could map or analyze, but usually they tell me instead, "It was such a sunny day" and then their eyes cloud and you can see a look of betrayal furrow their face, see them thinking, *The sky had appeared so guileless!* Or they might say, "I'd nursed a headache that afternoon. I recognized the halo around the bare bulb in my room" or "In the last conversation I had with my brother, his eyes were too sad to see," something that reveals only the speaker's aching confusion and sense of complicity in the sudden loss or disappearance of the beloved.

Mrs. Lehmkuhl said, "Franklin won't rise from bed, sleeps the day away and watches television through the night, buys whatever they're selling."

"He's...mourning," I said. "He...lost someone...he... loved." Ever since the discovery of Elise Dimbleby's saddle shoes, people have looked to me for pointers on how to properly bury the violently dead or get shed of the disappeared (no body is ever so present to us as it is in its persistent absence), for counsel on what to do with the deadening sorrow of that loss, which, like God's demanding love, replenishes itself without end. Folks figure someone who stretches into next week, whose head brushes against the basement of the unbordered beyond, must at least have glimpsed the other side, and they beg me to tell them, like a cheap spirit rapper, eyes kohled in an oracular manner, wrists bangled, head swaddled in scarves, what I've seen while gazing into the cloudy crystal ball of heaven. What I know about the other side is that it is a dimly lit room too small to house any of us, even tiny Eleanor Lehmkuhl, inside a shrinking hovel that demands we disappear if we are ever to set foot inside, and then once we do thin beyond apprehension, there's more room for the next dead to disappear, the infinite mathematics of absence.

"Yes," she said, the word trailing a weary sigh. Absence, I could hear her thinking, the one thing in this world that never disappears. *God is without end*, said Obie. You *are without end*. A bottomless curse. "We both did. We lost the person we most loved."

"Grief..." I said, and then I wanted to blacken my own eye as I heard myself about to dispense some barren wisdom about the process of grieving. The slipslop of the mistaken savant thought to have a particular talent for those things that follow wrongful death. My head was empty as a village ransacked by epidemic; my heart was the creeping contagion that had blighted it.

She said, "Franklin won't speak to the McCreadys when they come to call. He'll sometimes get out of bed for the others, the Norwoods from down the street, Mose Pendleton next door, the Reverend and Mrs. Sooby. He wears his work clothes when he sleeps." She said, "Alma McCready comes every day and she nods her head when I tell her she can't come in. Sometimes she stands in the front yard until nightfall."

"And what has become of William McCready?" I asked.

"He doesn't much leave his house," she said quietly, and then: "He's not the one, you know."

That was in fact all I did know, that it couldn't have been William McCready, but there was something about the crispness of Magnus McCready's denim shirt, the faded line down the sleeves that showed the path of the iron—there was something to understand about that, and that's what I was thinking about as I molded the owl's nest. I cut his shirt from one knee of a faded pair of jeans, made the pearly buttons from an abalone shell, wove the piping from thread as sheer and gauzy as spun sugar, the consistency of air and invisible until woven, but it was the hours of ironing the sleeves to get the faded crease just right that took the most patience. That crease seemed to me a hand's expiation of guilt.

When I'd talked to William McCready, very briefly, I could see in the way that he hunched over his crossed legs and rocked, the way he rubbed his grizzled face, that he felt that sort of guilty remorse only the truly blameless feel. William's mother had tried to coax a memory from him— "I think she thinks I did it," he said—and he was retracing his own actions that day, trying to remember when he'd knotted the noose, trying to recall how Eleanor's limp body spilled from his embrace as he lifted her to it. All he could feel when he conjured it, he said, was the weight of a sheer scarf draped across his arms. "But that's right," he said in a voice graveled by sleeplessness. "Eleanor was only a little swag of silk." When he held nothing in his hands, he said, that's when he was most reminded of Eleanor. He carried stones in his pockets he could hold so as to think instead of *sandbag, cantaloupe, dictionary, mullet.*

The dimensions set by that original lummox Lemuel Gulliver are still those that guide the miniaturist's necessarily oafish hand. Roughly one inch to one foot is his measure of Lilliput, when he finds his body crawling with six-inch men. Were it not for the example of the Lilliputians, it might never have occurred to him that it is he who is the galumphing deviation, his foot the circus sideshow their inch pays a quarter to see and gawks at for reassurance of the grace God granted them. He might never have realized that it is actually the inchworm for whom God ideally sized the world. When you are petite as a peanut, the universe is endlessly bountiful, so there can be no such thing as famine. Mice and gnats, bacteria and salamanders routinely thank God for not making them dinosaurs or elephants, with stomachs the size of a harvest moon, survival a matter of ritual gluttony, thank God in particular for sparing them the fate of those upright hungry mutts who walk on two legs, have squandered the good will of Eden, and for whom this world will never be enough.

Because dollhouses often painstakingly recreate an opulent history, these days they've largely been de-dolled by collectors, emptied of any sign of occupation. They are beautifully paralyzed rooms. Unless epoxied in place and posed for eternity, those ungainly dolls meant to statically pantomime the living dodder and fall when no one is looking, tumble onto Queen Anne lowboys carefully hewn from walnut, delicate deer-legged Mikado tables, Louis XVI étagères, pie crust tilt-top tables whose wooden hinges are the size of a pygmy shrew's fragile metatarsals; they topple stiffly onto méridiennes hand-upholstered with pongee and fine spun-gold brocade made from the mating of a banana spider with a special silk worm that feeds on air (and whose excrement is then used to stuff medicinal pillows said to dispel wind, absorb fire-toxin, and brighten desolate eyes); they knock into sconces with vases and end tables with hurricane lamps glass-blown by the breath of blustery fleas (when constructing a world sized for insects, you save yourself labor by going directly to the source). But dead dolls break no glass. My dioramas could be said to document (in addition to, in this case, the death of an unfortunate dollface) the genocide of the dollhouse doll, who is guilty only of the clumsiness that awaits us all as we move uncertainly from vital to inanimate, from flesh to wood. A doll lying prostrate on the bedroom floor, her throat red and gasping as a rose newly in bloom, is no adversary for a fragile object. Having evolved from breaker to broken, she's done all the breaking she'll do.

Making the world small is big business. There's so little room now in the shrinking universe for anything other than shrunken replicas of the hulking original. There are miniature festivals and fairs, ten-minute finger-trek tours of The Wee Wall of China, speedy sightseeing at the elfin Pyramids; you can track an ant queen's sojourn down the trickle of the Amazon as she is fanned by a worker with a palm frond no bigger than a leaf of clover; you can hear the faint shriek of a suicidal mite that leaps from a suspension bridge constructed of splinters and horsehair; and if you hold these worlds under a microscope you will see nestled inside them runt replicas of themselves, the universe reduced further and further until it is into God's terrible all-seeing eye you stare, and then you too will no longer be visible unless viewed through a special lens. This is the fate of God, the fate of fleas, the fate of mass, that handsome nothing toward which everything hurtles. The universe has long been more expert at contraction, since that walloping expansion that first sneezed existence into existence. Geneticists and biologists, keen on splitting the infinitesimal to see if it can remain standing afterwards, breed tiny chickens to produce tiny eggs to put into tiny iceboxes kept cool with a modest dram of refrigerant. Diminutives pair up in order to produce smaller and smaller offspring, whose magical hands, so small as to be a matter of faith for the presbyopic, can fashion and forge and weave a universe that reveals itself only under high magnification. Eventually human beings will themselves be so minute that the swarmed planet will no longer be weighted by their ballast and we'll finally be launched into empty space, the only thing left to claim-stake and ruin.

Peter the Great you say? Why yes, funny you should ask, I do know a relevant story about him now that you mention it. Peter the Great bred giants and dwarves (great indeed, 6' 7", no minim himself) like prize rabbits or goats or decorative bantams, and he kept them around for his amusement, aspiring as he was to occidental respectability. No monarch worth his tyranny would be caught dead in those days without his pet dwarf in tow at court or at least a capering grotesque or two. Peter had an especial fondness for his French giant Bourgeois because this giant's mother was a dwarf, the family itself a yardstick of the extremes of human biology, stretching from footstool to treetop in two generations, a measure of God's irony (not that Peter believed overmuch in either God or irony). Peter sometimes paraded the giant around dressed as a baby and on a leash of string, puppeted by a team of wild dwarves snapping a bullwhip. That Peter was such a cut-up! He married Bourgeois off to another tall drink of water, a gangling Finn, in the hope that their children would provide towering recruits for the army, martial superiority determined, he believed, by one's proximity not to heaven but to the camouflage of clouds. (There could be no better army, he thought, than a gaggle of taiga bean geese, though his attempts to arm them had been a bust.) Peter was so heartened to know there were bigger, more lumbering bumblers in the world than he. He traded soldier giants with other monarchs for oddities he could display in his *wunderkammer*, his cabinet of the most curious curiosities. *I'll swap this ox Nikolai here for that pickled two-headed fetus clutching its reptilian feet or those decoratively beaded babies that wear their own time-loosened skin like a christening gown.* But seven-foot men are bound to get homesick, so much more heart to ache, and they disguised themselves as Siberian larch and scuttled back across the tundra to the snowy bosom of Mother Russia.

Meanwhile, back at the palace, Peter and his courtiers yukked it up at a miniature wedding. He rounded up all the

Tom Thumbs of Moscow, instructed their owners to make them spruce, fit to be the spectacle they naturally were. They drank and belched in their best bib and tucker, periwigs askew on their disproportionate heads, wobbled about like badgers, fell off their chairs clutching an empty goblet, and the court clapped with delight to see the precocious darlings make miniature merry. None were, to Peter's disappointment, as slight or perfectly proportioned as Lord Minimus, that nineteen-inch former toast of Europe, a savory pigwidgeon who leapt from a pie into the court of Queen Henrietta Maria, Minimus a full-grown man you could hold in your hand, which is precisely what a monarch most longs for, a subject no taller than a samovar, lending the mini to minion. (Peter's niece Anna, a quick study, would later hire a fool to pretend to be a chicken, chicken his avocation, a professional chicken, and marry him off to a Kalmyk in a palace carved from ice on the frozen River Neva—what a family of royal wags, kept the kingdom in stitches they did!)

BUT. Peter's *most* prized wunders came from a renowned Dutch anatomist who had found such a clever use for cadavers past their prime. Favorites: the beheaded child whose brain floated visibly in brine behind a stricken face full as a full moon and round as a clock, a stopped clock, an infant suspended in animated death, waterlogged lips thick and gray, slices of embalmed peach; there was the beautiful severed arm of a child bent at the wrist like the neck of a swan and swaddled in the lacy sleeve of a dressing gown, dangling from two tiny fingers an eye socket as casually as if it were a favorite trinket; there were the baby skeletons romping across land that would never be arable, a rocky landscape of kidney stones and bladders, craggy trees of hardened arteries and

fluttering lungs; the skeletons of children, mid-frolic, reconciled to a fleshless and stationary existence while newborns
newly dead wept into handkerchiefs of brain tissue they'd
never again use to think and in forestalled anticipation of the
sadness that was denied them in death; and those darling little developing skeletons that looked longingly at the petrified
womb in which they had met their end. (Peter was so moved
by one beautifully preserved child that he kissed the specimen on her rubbery cheek, and he eventually had some of
his own live exhibits stuffed—only upon their demise naturally!—his Gallic giant, his tiny lobster-clawed boy, so he and
the fearful backwards world he was trying to educate could
gaze upon them longingly always.) These wondrous wunders
were the work of a man who haunted himself with the rapt
terror of thoughts of one day embalming God (the old wool-
sack), finally fixing Him in time and space, giving His infinite
form contours as it grayed in formaldehyde. A thought so delicious he lost consciousness every time he imagined it, which
meant he was rarely awake in his final years.

Well. I mention all this as illustration of the fallen world,
which can never be illustrated enough if you ask me, the
young world a cake once airy with promise now caved in and
fit only for the dustbin, a dotard beyond propping up. Illustration of the fallen world and the height from which it has
fallen, that world the Ursula Lehmkuhls of the world (grieving mothers who briefly rehydrate my shriveled heart only
to cleave it in two with their irreversible sorrow) had never
been able to bring themselves to see and who were therefore
forced to forfeit a daughter, a son, as collateral for their blindness. My own mother believed her daughter was shamefully
indestructible, never realizing that giantesses needn't search

any further than their own walloping dukes when looking for something to fear, and therefore my mother doomed her son to sacrifice. The invincible only appear so alongside the vincible. When there's a god in the room, someone has to pay. Them's the rules.

TWENTY-SEVEN

THE SOFT-FOOTED PHANTOM SPEAKS

And I heard a voice from heaven, as the
voice of many waters, and as the voice of
a great thunder: and I heard the voice of
harpers harping with their harps…

—*Revelation 14:2*

A spectre is haunting Heaven—the spectre of communion. In that saint alliance is an old European, spying on pope and tsar alike, the benched radicals, the germ of their pleas infecting the calvary of fought wars. Does not the opposition party always condemn that which matches its strength? Does not the statistical enemy commune with blame, oppose the luminary?

Behold, fair of a thousand arts, my love, art of a fair house, thou hast the eyes of a thousand doves, eyes inside closings, eyes all but implied: thy hair is a flock of goats, it appears from the husbandry of God, a many-married man, beware. Thy teeth, shorn sheep, came a maundering, each one together bare and none is barren between them. Thy borders are as the scarlet lips of the horizon, thy speech silently handsome: thy temples are a part of any Rome, a bit of tangled fruit, the heir of the god that bit you. Thy throat is an armory, whereon fall a thousand escutcheons, sing protectorate of powerful men. Thy two breasts are as two new eggs, the twin fed between the irises. Until the day ruptures and the shadows blow leeward, I will get me to the mountain's murmur by the candor of rain. My love shall fare as pots boil. Come with me my husband to the superior part of lions' caverns, from the mound of paper leopards. A thousand ravished my heart, my sister, my husband, a thousand ravished my heart with one eye, with the electricity of a throat. Fair love, my sister, my husband! I spell the pomade, give respite to the spices of thee. My husband's edges drip as if author of the honeycomb: the honeyed tongue I milk. The smell of arguments soon ebbs. A closed garden is my sister, secret cultivar, aspiring to speak and burgeon, a comely fundament concealed. This Rome is an orchard of pleasant fruits, a stream of spikenard and cinnamon, a living water of camphor, of aloe. It flows from a thousand souths, establishes the appointment of spies. Spike of calumny and skin, rank hellos, heat suffices. Love leaves the garden, enter its eaten fruits.

If for years our suffered fathers, which out of this continent were birthed, were dedicated, a new nation of former indications, in freedom and proposal, would surely celebrate the conditions and think to require that all equal men are created. Now when enormity meets the battlefield, we war with time. The nation, or all nations, therefore proctors the test that amounts to consecration. We of the dominion have an attachment, from our here to the next person's where-do-we-go. But in a greater sense we cannot be pleased—we cannot office this earth, cannot sanctify this hearth. In order to die probably, a nation buys respect from the dead. From the gathering, we who are appropriate must make this! The world little notes our poor energies but can never forgive what it cannot see. It is incumbent upon us to live unfinished, to fight always the beautiful outpost where they adhere to the dead, increasing the dead, to whom they gave a degree of love. This nation underneath God will have a flattened birth, a government for the people of people, the perishing people.

But, of course, the king, he is knowing nothing of history, which is always larger than the ruling class. What kind of conscripted century does not know? Do you not remember, when Madame France did not have the time, she so very surprised by the poverty of cake? Time then was as good as straw, something slept upon fitfully. Time then crawled with vermin and shortened itself like the afternoon light of a dwindled winter. Don't you happen? And in compliance with what? In the classroom of landowning, people eat wheat and grudge. People are possible. Any future is the possibility of eating: if only it weren't 1917. The people wear out and you are left with history, which will malnourish those remaining and feed only time, dear insignificanta, supple anarchist of the clock. Time is the original starveling. Time is God's first felony. Death is a Bolshevik. It is the damage of night that permits morning. The rawboned jail emits sleep, emits being, crimes the honest sermon, silences the trill of plainsong. Don't America me! Your goosebumps, your bayonets. The police want to treat dogs, all hope must be licensed, all animals are free to Americans. Let me tell you who live by the word and die by the word, ladies and gentlemen, you are forgetting the writing of the wall. Do what needs to be. Done! You who are instantaneous will be living the gruel unless you learn to appreciate the spoon's distress. In order to become silent, the vocal human makes a mistake. Armistice my eye. Your threats of intentional restlessness are innumerable, sir, which is your warfare, your this believes and that belies. War is to the heart, after all, as longitude is to the golden opportunity, and in order to fly from the spirit's gutter, time must take wing.

I say to you today, my friends, we confront daily the difficulties of today's tomorrow. I have a dream deep-rooted in the enmity evident under the feuding eye. In the American kiln the dream fires. My one day in this country will widen its creed: all persons retained are equal to one red hillock in Georgia, one day-old slave, who sits in a dream I have not had. The day is sultry and unfair, oppresses the just oasis, transforms it, vainly, into a dream of the missed river, into a skin's estimated color that contents itself with the heat of a country, with the dimming of a day.

After words, the subject of your choosing is rough on your tongue. We were opposed to the British people and cowboy hats. A hat wears out the head, which cannot readily be replaced. What the camelopard swallows has a long and happy odyssey, but too many meals exhaust the gullet. People are saying we do not distinguish between predators and imperialisms. People are saying they would rather wreck a flivver than drive a hard bargain for it is at this intersection where hallucinations are kindled. It is very dangerous. In other words: slavery. We must travel to another sector, that where animosity is bred, in order to remove the words. We respect also different meat. We are peckish and willy-nilly. According to the International Union of Hostility, hats are unsustainable. In fact, I am of the view that I am tired of all I survey. In fact, the doffing of hatred I consider to be a friend in a state of undress. Humanity is simply not suited to the helmet, though the spirit of sacrifice is never velvet. We propose instead to anger a candle damper with an obstinate flame. I am very friendly. Jeopardy is our exploited companion and we may want to rescue it. For more information, the abyss, the verge. It is my duty, in the reduction of hands, to warn of the dangers, and, if possible, to wrangle a fiend into fortifying the grasp that will enable silence to expand. When you are starting to dicker and wage the biggest battle of your life, you do not have a port of hatred, and in order to instigate danger, you must croft a country's most beloved cow. Apocryphal people are the human condition. As any nettle knows, possibility exists only in the pricking.

Sung songs sully man. Please allow me to kiss him with her mouth. Your love is bitter as wine. Because of the savory liniments, your name pours like oil from a virgin. Your hand is against me and will hit me later. I am black because of the sun and the sun is becoming. I do not see my mother in my children. The grape farms are disorganized. Please tell my soul to feed you where you rest. Why should we be an opportunity to differentiate beauty from sustenance? You are among the most equitable of women. Feed your children to the famished shepherds in tents. I have compared you favorably, my love, to pharaohs, horses, and trucks, to the upright love of trees. Our conspiracy reaches the gilded border, the buttons, the silvered eyelets through which God spies his most contested solutions. Although the king sits on the table, synoptic eyes narrowed, he sends me a yellow umbel issued by smell, an inflorescence as aromatic as yesterday's storm. More plants are needed and the Society of International Love is good, oxygen and adoration equally on the wane. I love the fact that he came to every night betwixt my breasts. You are the bitter vineyard. You are art, and love, my gallery, the eyes of a man's sudatorium, you are the approval of a bed of green paper. When we pack, the wood beams, any parliament can polish rice.

The pretty feet with low shoes, prince, are they yours? The lame pass by like jewels, your joints and thighs are shrewd work. God, lapidarian, looks through his loupe and light scatters! Your navel is an insatiable goblet filled with the alcohol of want, your stomach bends like wheat among the lilies. Your breasts kowtow to your belly, your throat a eulogy of ivory. Your eyes are fishpools dotted with ash, you are the daughter of many, unmasked. Your nose is a leavened revelation, plum, plum. Here lies the chairperson of such-and-such, whose head feels purple to the touch. Your head is an electrical outlet, a well-coffered king, a crusade that takes place in tunnels. How how good, just and art, you, your love of pleasures! Place a palm to your breasts and they cluster like grapes, cause the dead to speak and dream. I who go above ground, I who hang from the branches for you, pluck the panicle of your lips. I am surrounded by the smell of apples that see you and instantly fall from the tree, a concession to your redolence. The wine of your mouth tastes sweet like new sleep. You are the moon that dredges the sun from its stupor and exhumes the morning. Come, my beloved, let us squander the silage, let us unharvest the vineyard. If the vine is tender with the pomegranates of an early Rome, I will give you my love. The fleshy odor of the mandrake, pleasant and fruitful, I will capture for you.

Thick girl, of land, my summertime, good night, I find in you difference: a completed change is not nearly enough. Familiarized you are still a deviation, God your familiar. Urban lady, I am but under a tree, the unprovoked sensations you require—should I name you categorically? You waste no word. You hatch your escapes. Your you keeps your you in me. Nevertheless when I think you powerful tired, bent beyond work, uneasy, satisfied, alone, you remain natural, more number than not. You, you become the soft-pay ghost, the perversion of circuitry, as long as your eyelids are fluttered and dear. This is this: o plausible deformity! Yes this. They will send you straight to bone. We will return absurd from the twilight's lecture. Are you up to the sentiment, my green fluid, my influenza, my My? You who will have caused the rotation of cut glass to falter? The world ends in you—

TWENTY-EIGHT
HAZARD, A GUESS

One thing you oughta know about Vivica is't she ain't half the warrior princess she thinks she is. Sure, she's big and prickly as a goddamned Douglas fir, but her roots, they're shallow, which means she can be toppled by a stiff and pigheaded breeze that refuses to curb its blustering, and from an early age that's what I, Hazard Planet, revolting brother, aimed to be.

My sister, *big* sister, plump as Jupiter, plumb never got over the fact of me. She had what-you-call-it an unnatural attachment to our father, broke out in a leaky plumbing kind of sweat whenever he so much as patted me on the melon. Full-blown dandling would cause her to let loose with a hyena shriek and enough jealous perspiration to flood the house: she fancied herself biblical. She was mean as a blister and hissing and diving at everything all the time like a swatted wasp. She used to stuff my piehole full of dirty socks, fold me up like a handkerchief, and squeeze me into the smallest spaces she could find, like I was just spackling for a crack in the wall. And I think our father, wandering salesman, had had one tired dog out the door since the minute her highness dropped big and as eager-to-bruise as a medicine ball from my mother's poor put-upon loins. It was Vivica who carried my mother on *her* fetal back when she was ballooning-to-breaking tiny Ma's tiny womb.

I tell you, I don't miss the lot of them. Maybe Ma, just a skosh, when I get a whiff of sponge cake. But Vivica I'm happy to be shed of. She's a capital Dee Devil that one, lumbering demon, *Elephantom* the neighbor kids called her every Halloween, waving her fat can around like she's Queen of the la-di-dah Nile or some such, always trying to get me to play the bumbling boy bonehead to her high-hatted girl-pharaoh. She wanted me dead from the moment I took root in my mother's belly, wanted to yank me from the soil and render me compost. Sometimes she'd lie curled up next to Ma and knead her stomach, then she'd all-of-a-sudden punch our pregnant mother in the bread basket, pretend it was an accident—oops, pardon!—and I could feel those blows, and yeasty little loaf that I was, I kicked back, and once when Vivica asked to lay her ear to Ma's belly button, I put my boot in that mush melon of a head of hers with such infant vigor to this day her skull still bears the dent. Try to flush Hazard from the womb, will you!

Brothers and sisters, they mix it up, sure, good-natured sibling combat, but it wasn't like that with Vivica and me. We were both in it for blood, up to our elbows in the guts of the other to determine who laid rightful claim to the Planet plasma. We knuckled each other in secret and waited for bruises to blossom, waited to see who the last Planet standing would be.

Thing is, only grudge I ever bore her was a counter-grudge, due to her not wanting me in the world and all, what's hard to overlook after the third broken bone. I mean, I got nothing against sisters in principle you understand. At least I didn't until mine turned out to be a rat-fink royale. I had no other cheek to turn, both of them having been sucker punched at once (oh, I'm a sucker, I don't deny it)—only the three-cheeked can risk such magnanimity amidst the quickly orbiting, deadly fists of Fats Planet!

But I had a brief period of blindness resulting in cock-eyed and covert devotion that eventually proved fatal. I dropped out of high school when I was sixteen, our father on French leave several years by then, *reservoir, don't wait up!*, and out the door with our father went the only warmth I'd ever known, the only kind touch (Ma was sometimes affection-ate, but in such a halting and miniature way, her intentions so petite, you could hardly feel it, an ant traipsing wobbly across the hairs on your arm), okay, maybe sometimes too kind, but a beggar of affection takes whatever rancid scraps he's thrown. But still, though I was footloose and free of fourth period western civ, I stuck around the Planet head-quarters, free grub, free flop, and then Vivica one day went off to become some micro-gazer, some ogler of the invis-ible, training her peepers to detect rebel cells on the lurk in the body's crannies, but eventually she returned home and I skipped, and I hung my hat on the streets for some years, spritzed and squeegeed windshields at stoplights to try to co-erce a simoleon or two out of the tight wallets of nervous motorists (and in a town like this, no bigger than a pip, we're talking two windshields an hour, three in rush-home traffic, leaving me, on a good night, with a pocket of piddly cheddar, half a sawbuck and a fistful of slugs), then, through a series of highly unfelicitous-type circumstances, I ended up at a halfway house (a wholeway house seeming to me excessive, hyuk-hyuk, better *I* should crack wise than a certain weisenheiming someone I know, no casualties if I cut up), where, as it turns out, recreational substances are always in ample supply, go figure, and apparently I recreated with what turned out to be lethal enthusiasm one afternoon, and I woke up on an IV drip and suicide watch at Providence General, stomach freshly pumped and my dear doting sister hunched in a chair at my side. Seems she'd found me and smacked me back into this world, saved my life, dredged it from the dumpster into which I had heaved it, a life I had no recollection of trying to cut short, and, sap that I am, I mistook this for long-buried love finally rising from the grave. Psych!

So now it appears that vivid cur's fondest wish has been granted at last, rendering me extinct and flightless as a damned dodo bird, and, so, this is how she did it, I figured it out, having had time (is that what it's called? It passes these days a little…sideways) to reconcile her deeds and suspicious benevolence with my, uh, present unseemly state (I try to gather sufficient weight to return long enough to haunt her in her sleep, but the dispersed cells, they slip through my dim fingers, fluttering fingers vague as the wings of moths, and take to the air like ash—that's what death is, infinitely diminishing and far-flung parts that stubbornly refuse ever again to assemble into You, visible only to the profoundly nearsighted goggles of God, that capital Dee Dog, in whose vitreous fluid the dead float. If that double-crosser ever sheds the dead, cries a river of livid corpses, and shows his hangdog puss in *my* pocket of the beyond, why He'll live to regret it, I promise you that, Judas!):

One day she says to me, "Hey, Haz-Been," she says, "what you doing flashing that shiv around like you're planning a prison break?" It was a Sunday and we were at Ma's house for rump roast and a glazed carrot or two, Wonder Bread and sponge cake, and I was whittling a switch on the porch. And I said, "What's it to you, Sasquatch?" This was a few weeks after she rescued me and nursed me back to my usual decline, and I thought we were just keeping up the bitter banter for appearances' sake. And then she smiled that crooked just-this-side-of-a-scowl smile that said to me if Ma weren't in the room, she'd chain me to the side of the house and coax the local crows into lunching tartare-style on my liver. Just part of the bunco I told myself.

"Hey, I've got an idea, Gizzard. How about some street theatre, so you can wave around that little knife and pretend to be a bigger man than you are. Just for old-time's sake, why don't we play a game, but out in public. We'll make an appointment to meet somewhere, a date with destiny, and you can pretend you're a Beserker—you were born for this role—and I'll be a modern-day Brunhilde just out for an innocent stroll. Did you know Beserkers are believed to have eaten poisonous mushrooms in order to fuel their frenzy? See, you've already done research for this part."

I tossed a snicker in her direction. "Doesn't surprise me if those apes had a sister like you waiting at home to drive them *really* bananas." I gotta admit, despite our truce, the thought of taking Brunhilde down in front of possible spectators who would no doubt thank me for the service I was rendering the universe by cleaning it up one yeti at a time appealed to my secret moody-superhero sense of justice and my wish to make the world safe for small men. "Go on," I said.

"Thirty-fourth and Strong," she said, "you, me, your little paring knife. I'll be in disguise, long black hair and carrying keys in my hand."

"What if someone thinks I'm really trying to, you know, jump you, and I don't mean that metaphorical like."

Vivica frowned. "Look at me," she said. "Who in their right mind is going to mistake me for a victim?" She honked her nose, a mocking pig snuffle. She had a point. My father used to say to us, "You got a point, kid, but if you wear a hat, no one will notice," hyuk-hyuk. He always clowned like that, and even Vivica laughed.

So you see I was set up, and I confess that when I saw that Vivica-shaped broad and held the blade to her throat (after getting that hot-air balloon of a head of hers to obey the laws of gravity), I might have gone a little Brando, might have lost myself in my part a little too convincingly, but Vivica, she counted on that, and she'd done her reconnaissance and knew that dame was looking for any opportunity to prove she was as vulnerable a mark as any Little Miss Muffet worth her curds and whey, and I'd be just the spider to knock her off her stool. Only it wasn't like that, see, because then Vivica's body double (more like body triple) veered off-script and showered my muzzle with hot peppers, and my lungs, those rotten cowards, surrendered on the spot.

When Vivica came to the city morgue to identify the slab of sirloin in front of her, she did shed a tear, but I figure it was out of regret for having no one left whose murder plot she could spend her days hatching, and she whispered in my ear that it was my overdose that had given her clarity of purpose. What had galled her then was the thought that I'd be the one to decide my fate, leaving her with no say in my grand finale and no sinner equal to her wrath. A gal of her girth needs a lot of purpose to toss her carcass out of the sack of a morning.

So that's the story of a fratricidal sister and the dolt brother who briefly trusted her though he knew better. And here I lie like John Damn Brown a-moldering in the grave while that malignant moose still trots upon the earth.

TWENTY-NINE

PLANET SUICIDE

Captive anvil, vain evil pact, vile vacant pi, live-panic vat, a name containing *evil* and *pelvic* and *vice* and *plaint, vain* and *pain* and *lava* and *cave*, an *l* short of *villain*, a *t* shy of *taint*, a name big enough to gird a planet, viva la pain, Vivica Planet.

She asked me to reconstruct the scene of Hazard's death, the scene of me sparging his snarling puss with a lethal spritz of pepper spray, his growl still humid in my ear. "There's nothing to solve there!" I sputtered. "We know who the rotten no-good executioner is." I said it quietly, sincerely, and added, "You know everything about your brother's death." I felt the heat and prickle of envy rise to my throat and scorch my ears as I thought about the intimacy of seeing someone stripped down to their cellular Skivvies. I imagined building a diorama of me on bended hamhock at 34th and Strong, begging the Planets' forgiveness, accusatory chalk outline sprawled at my feet, but I did not think it would make Vivica merciful. There's no impressing a nine-foot dame who strides forward with the bullish determination of a panzer, no impressing her with something she could so easily splinter to smithereens with a halfhearted fillip. So I asked her instead if she wanted to see the Goodland barn I'd made miniature. Although I was near to finishing the model, it wasn't yet giving up its secrets. But I had a hunch. I never showed anyone a shrunken world in progress—it took such careful labor, and I saw to every knothole (if only the world were a wool sweater I could toss in a hot wash). Clearly the laws by which my universe abided were helter-skelter in the presence of one Vivica Planet.

Most of the houses in Kingdom Come seemed to me to be designed more for molehill than mountain, cottages sized for a race of indoor garden gnomes, the most decuman among them appearing to top out at the pointy tip of their jaunty zipfelmützen no higher than my navel, but there was the occasional Victorian with ceilings high enough to prevent me from feeling like a megalosaurus wearing a cage, and I emphasized the roominess of mine by keeping it spare, an austerity I'd learned from the whirling Ovinkos. Even so, when Vivica stepped into my living room, it suddenly seemed impossibly small, full to the rafters with the magic beanstalk bodies of two broads on the burgeon. I imagined a bottle labeled *Drink Me* that I could sprinkle on the floor of my dwelling (or, better yet, on me, like holy water on a demon, *that* bottle labeled *Shrink Me*, the grail I've spent my large life groping for, making me the very high priestess of very small things), causing my digs to swell large enough to house a planet and its pesky satellites. This, it occurred to me, was one of the things that attracted me to Vivica, the promise of becoming, as I stood beside this commodious Planet, the tiny asteroid I longed to be. But you never knew what you were getting with a magical pharmacon in a mysteriously marked bottle, and it might just as likely contract the house until it fit snug as an iron maiden and pierced a confession out of its victim. Never trust magic that fits in a bottle and sits on a shelf, volatile shrimp juju.

Vivica followed me into the dining room, where the model sat upon the table. She bent over and scrutinized it closely, eyeball to haymow, and then she crouched so she could get a closer gander at the corpse and the people gathered around it. Because I hadn't gotten to see the body in its final dangle, I'd decided I would reproduce exactly the moment I'd witnessed, which meant I put a crudely whittled facsimile of myself in the scene as well, knowing, as I always did, that I was altering my surroundings by filling a hollow those around it would prefer remain empty as atmosphere.

In my mind, that balloon-headed two-way radio attuned to the signal of nefariousness, I saw and heard not the moment when Hazard looked at me with the horror of a final... could it have been gratitude?—but rather the last conversation he had with his sister. It was a Sunday dinner with Gladys, rump roast, scalloped potatoes, pickled okra, sponge cake. Hazard was skinning a piece of wood with his slip joint, the same knife he would later press to my throat. There was a tautness to his body I couldn't quite decipher and then a transistor in my head went on the fritz, the signal cut out, my brain filled with static, *hello?, come in, this is Osprey One to Pterodactyl, come in Pterodactyl, you're veering off the radar, pull up, pull up!*, and I couldn't hear what they were saying, but I saw a look on Vivica's face I'd never seen before, a hesitant look, as though the features of her face were shaping an expression she hadn't authorized: a look of…sadness, no…disappointment? no, wait, it was a look…of love! Holy moly, Jesus Mary Joseph and Henry, there was love distorting the usual glower of Vivica Planet's face, there it was, plain as daydream, glaring as inflammation, enveloping, robust, strong as the longings of lonely giants, that strong! A love that could lift a hundred barbells and the fat lady too without breaking a sweat. She touched his face and his eyes narrowed, and I heard Hazard sing, "You. Can't. Save me. Sister," and he smiled, and as if I'd miniaturized Hazard's whole life and studied it under a microscope my whole life I could now see it plainly: he was a man afflicted with himself, a man done in by thinning skin and shrimphood and the adoration of a big sister—big, yes, but not big enough to shelter him from everyday evil—all of which he might have survived had he not also been the recipient of a corrupted affection that had not gone unwitnessed, curdled love so often the poison that, once exposed, makes us drop dead nose-first in our mashed potatoes (had our mother ever given us mashed potatoes). Hazard, both clever and fatal, had staked out the streets in search of a dangerous woman who might rare up and kill him if properly spooked and when he saw me, vertical twin to his sister, superfluous can of pepper spray swinging from my fingers, his heart nearly stopped on the spot. A cure was in sight.

Obie once told me that though he might one day leave Kingdom Come he would never leave Kansas, not even at gunpoint, not for all the moonlight in winter, because Kansas, though flat and mean and tornadoed and empty of glamour and thought by many to be backwoods and godforsaken, the whole sorry state, was just what he was, and he had no choice but to be Kansas, it was in him sure as a kidney, for butter or wurst, and I spent the years following his disappearance traveling to the small, dusty, foreclosed-upon towns that this landlocked, improbable place was made of. Obie was always an orderly boy, so I traveled alphabetically, from Abilene to Admire and Agenda, on to Burden, Chanute, Chetopa, El Dorado, Fontana, Hiawatha, Iola, Kismet, Montezuma, Oskaloosa, Paola, Pretty Prairie, Radium and Ransom and Rolla, Satanta and Severence and Susank, Tonganoxie, Ulysses, and Virgil, Wamego and Zenda and Zurich, and I found nothing, which is what you will usually find if you go looking without a lead, never-ending non-stop no-holds-barred diddly-squat. I interviewed locals, visited churches and hospitals and bowling alleys, talked to horses and dogs, feral cats, but their lips were sealed, not a snitch in the bunch, and after a while it was as though I had never had a brother, had been loving only an empty chair all these years.

Until I got home again and then the sum total of all I could see in the molten faces around me was that a boy had gone missing, the sagging cheeks and weary eyes not able to register anything but that.

I looked into Vivica's face, a revelation, a revolution, a face I'd never seen before, a face misshapen with love. I explained to Vivica who each figure was and she studied their tiny features. When there were people in the death scenes, I scrupulously particularized faces, reproduced them in every detail, every crow's-foot and freckle and birthmark and broken capillary, the geometry of the mouth and eyes precise, because a face can be as talkative as a shell casing or the splatter pattern of a blossom of blood on the wall. Faces are more reliable than fingerprints, DNA, eyewitness testimony, their wrinkles and jowls more trustworthy than confession. And now surgeons were transplanting faces! Faces that had been mauled by animals or shot by husbands, noses and eyelids and sinuses and chins deported from their head of origin and repatriated onto another. And though these faces, taken from donors who had never expected their appearance might one day drape the skull of a head that had met with unimaginable misfortune, never expected their lips might one day speak a language they'd never learned, even though the charity of these faces transformed their recipients' appearance, revised it beyond recognition, what could never be lost in that translation from mug to mug is the sorrow that preceded the death, the disbelief that preceded the disfiguring violence, the doubled sorrow born of this marriage.

It was this that I saw in Vivica's face, in the transplantation of the face from the sorrowful child she had been onto that of the grieving adult she'd become, an ache too great to be contained or properly animated by mere tissue. Sorrow deforms a face sure as acid.

How had I missed it? Was it possible I had been blind to the pain of a giant woman in the same way I'd miscalculated how much disappointment the small shoulders of a devoted boy could bear? It was possible.

With the tip of a fingernail, Vivica touched Franklin Lehmkuhl's elaborate mustache, fashioned from the wiry reddish curls of a neighbor's Airedale terrier, an eager and pragmatic donor who would have happily handed over his stub of a tail for a bit of liver, and I told her about the owl swooping and the pained look on Franklin's face as he spoke.

She said, "He feels guilt for something. He has not always had this mustache."

"He blames himself," I said. "He feels he should have protected his daughter from harm." Vivica shook her head.

"You're suggesting...What are you suggesting? That's her father," I said. Vivica nodded. "You think Eleanor's father killed her, killed his own daughter?" It wasn't that I thought filicide was unthinkable—I'd met a mother who drowned her two children because she was tired of buying boxes of cereal and gallons of milk every week, tired of the endless shaking of flakes into bowls—but I'd taken that mustache of his to mean...well, something else. I didn't know what exactly, but certainly I didn't see in that squirrel tail evidence of a man who could extinguish his own blood.

"Fathers are complicated people," said Vivica, "with complicated ways of loving their children."

"I thought Alma McCready..."

She shook her head. "But she's no innocent." Vivica smiled and sat on my sofa and the house became smaller yet.

☾

Ursula Lehmkuhl let me into her husband's room, where he cradled Eleanor's missing shoe in his lap, stroked the soiled satin. It didn't take a shrinker of crime to see in this gesture that his was an extravagant and culpable sadness.

"You ever hear of a suicide seed?" he asked me without taking his eyes off the shoe. "Started out as a seed with a kind of clock built into it. After a time, the seed would sterilize itself, up and destroy its own embryos, so farmers couldn't save seeds and would have to buy new ones at next year's prices. And then they started making these stubborn little seeds that would just sit down and cross their arms and wait for you to fertilize them with a special chemical developed by the same company, and if you didn't or you used something else, they'd off themselves. God of Agriculture this company fancied itself, and so it had no compunction about controlling the lives and deaths and growths of these seeds and in the bargain dictating the success and failure of the farmers who need them. These seed barons couldn't figure a way to make you pay for sunshine, so this was the next best thing. Even though this would be hardest on poor farmers in poor places, no farmer I knew wasn't in a lather about this when we first heard tell of it, but, I don't know, I couldn't help but find this form of greed a little ingenious. Seemed to me it settled once and for all the question of what a greedy-gut S.O.B. God must be, which I've always suspected, but I felt for him too. It gave me some ideas, like what if there was a kind of planned obsolescence built into a little girl, so she would stay a little girl always, so she could be saved from herself. Little girls so often grow up to become the densest of women, hard-headed as goats, making choices that guarantee them and everyone around them a lifetime of steady misery. Eleanor, she came by this honestly. My wife, you see, was one of those women who chose unwisely." Franklin Lehmkuhl stopped stroking his daughter's shoe and looked up at me, and I imagined he was thinking that a woman of my size would likely be capable of twice as many mistakes. "Everyone knows that men, well, they don't know their asses from angel food cake, so the world relies on women to show them which one to eat and which to shit from."

He put the shoe on his hand and gingerly walked it along his leg. He said, "Eleanor and me were thick as thieves from the day she appeared in that picture of the inside of her mother's belly. She looked and thought like me from that moment on. She was a surprise to me and her mother and came along just in time to ease the worst of the misery, and every day she drew a breath was a day of unexpected happiness for me.

"Until William came along and changed all that. I know you're thinking it's just a possessive father's jealousy that drove me to do what I did, but you'd be wrong. I would have happily handed her off to William had he been right in the head, but that thing that sat on his neck was a broken head he'd inherited from his mother. Bad decisions there in that household enough to feed all Hell for two eternities. Alma McCready's love for William was a compensatory love, which is always crippling, and Magnus stood by and watched his boy's head go soft as squash picked too late to be any good to anyone.

"So I started catting about with Alma McCready in the hope that maybe if I diverted her attention for a time William might have a chance to straighten up and fly right, but in fact he just slid further downward, all that carrying on, and Alma, she held fast to me, and then Eleanor walked in on us once when wild-eyed Alma's hands were wrapped round my neck like a bandage round a wound, and Eleanor, she never looked at me the same way again, and I knew I deserved it, but it broke my heart just the same. It was all for her after all, but she couldn't know that."

As I listened to Franklin Lehmkuhl spill his story, I thought about how every town, however dusty or bustling, like every human, has a polluted heart fueling its deeds and how hazardous it always is to be the object of love, a heart's only hobby. The 4,948 people of Goodland, Kansas, were the way that Goodland, Kansas, passed the time, the way Goodland, Kansas, amused itself. The bodies of girls would continue to accumulate here. And everywhere else.

Franklin now held the shoe to his cheek and caressed it affectionately, like a cat nuzzles an ankle. "But that wasn't why I tightened the rope round her neck. I just had to save her, that's what daddies do, they save their daughters, I had to save her from choosing certain heartache, and I had to save all the future disastrous little girls that would surely have been destined to do the same. Maybe this sounds arrogant to you. It's a burden."

Franklin's voice turned to gravel and he let the shoe fall to the floor. He told me that Alma figured out it was Eleanor he truly loved, and she urged Eleanor to waste no time and to hasten the wedding arrangements. She convinced Eleanor that marriage would cure William of the blue devils he was plagued by. It was the only thing would save him she told her. As the wedding approached, the distance between Franklin and his daughter grew and Alma clutched him to her all the tighter. The distraction of the affair had done nothing to heel William's stricken mind, and he told Eleanor sometimes he thought he saw her at night drifting from treetop to treetop in the starlight, and he feared she might be enchanted. Many's the man, he told her, who marries a sorceress and turns into a shoat. So she went to her father and she told him, out of respect for the bond they'd once shared, that she and William were going to drive to Sparks, Nevada, and elope that very night.

"And my hand left me and went to her throat and I thought what a peculiar scarf she has chosen to wear, and then I wondered how had the rope got round her neck and why was she dolled up and in her wedding duds with those little seed pearls and where was her other shoe and why had the whites of her eyes gone red, and that look that twisted her face, where had that come from, and then I thought: that's the last bad choice she'll ever make." Franklin handed me the shoe, and his face looked like it belonged to a week-old corpse that had not yet accepted the fact of its own death, an end that befell him as he tried and failed to rescue the only thing he ever knew how to love.

Before I'd left for God's land, Vivica's theory a bell-clear transmission ringing in my head, she touched the figure of me standing in the barn and she smiled an uncanny smile, bringing to mind the spooked owl whose swooping was accusation, and I wondered what Obie would have made of Vivica Planet, another girlgod loose in the world.

THIRTY
DELIVER MY DARLING FROM THE POWER OF THE DOG

The man tried to shift his weight (were there still bones in his body that could be commanded to move?) so that the nails would not tear so at his feet and hands, igniting knife-points of fire that stabbed his legs, sliced his arms, but the shifting was more thought than action, as so many things are, more like a nagging memory of something he regretted not having done (he thought too of an acacia tree, alone and ailing, he'd once caught his sleeve on; he slept beneath it because he could see it had wanted him to stay, had needed the succor of someone to shade), but even the feeblest twitch made his flesh feel as though it were sheering itself from his bones. He had been fasting himself slight for weeks, in preparation, less flesh to flail, he reasoned, less blood, easier to rise. He thought that he had never properly appreciated his flesh's commitment to bone. Few things live peaceably in such proximity. Blood continued to stream from his scalp and he closed his eyes when a sticky rivulet began to gum his vision. The world and its many things grew more remote. His eyes recalled the sight that had met them just outside the city walls: the craggy ground covered with the spines of a thousand crosses awaiting the crossbeams and the condemned, a forest of punishment, and he saw in that moment the countless wretched who had hung and would hang suspended from wrenched arms, bodies dying by slow degrees, fingerbreadth by fingerbreadth, the sky black with buzzards, this soiled sky the airy crypt of the soon-to-be-dead, an upright death, as though the dead grew from the ground in this place. There were thieves and beggars, slaves and conspirators, men uncertain as to their crime, women made to face the cross lest in death they further the shame of their lives, and the dogs that were crucified every August in Rome, having failed one year to warn of the Gauls' attack, an example to all disobedient curs.

When the man opened his eyes again, they were leaden, he thought they might fall from his face, he hoped that they would, and the world burned before him, wavering and washed in the red of a descending sun. His heart began to beat erratically, as it had during the scourging, as though there were another scourging happening inside him; it fluttered and thrashed like a bird trapped in a net, a furious burning rose in his throat, and he had difficulty drawing a ragged breath into his wet lungs. He had always been terrified of dying, more terrified than he let anyone know, for he had understood since he was a child that he would one day be asked to do so extravagantly, to die, as an example to the material world of what a beautiful burden it is to have a body, as a piaculum to God for the future's clamorous iniqui-ty, the call to slaughter human beings seemed powerless not to answer, the suffering they would become over time all the more sophisticated at inflicting, but now it was the pain that frightened him, that needled every particle and made him feel as though he were being slowly masticated, his body soon little more than a ravened morsel on the insatiable tongue of God, but what he found most sorrowful was the thought that he would never again be painless in this world, that these would be his final sensations as a man upon the earth, as a creature subject to injury and decay. He had derived plea-sure from being a human man and having feet to walk upon, eyes to give sanctuary to at noontide, enjoyed the feeling of muscles thickening, limbs lengthening, the slow furring of the flesh, the stirring of the skin when touched by another, and he'd savored the delicious sleep of childhood and the dead swoon that follows long labor. The pain exceeded what he had imagined it was possible for a mortal body to feel, and he had tried to imagine it, to antidote it with anticipation, but now he understood the wages of flesh. Still, the notion that soon he would be beyond earthly agony did not comfort him as much as he imagined it ought. This is how it would all conclude, his gospel of inexhaustible love, here at the Place of the Skull. He did not feel forsaken by God, no; rather he felt he was victim to an excessive intimacy, the hysteria that is long-childless divinity reckoning with ambivalent paternity. It's not easy, the man had thought many times, to suddenly have a son after so many years of living alone.

Inside the calves of the man's legs the muscles twisted like asps. "My soul is exceeding sorrowful," said the man to his own blackening lacerations.

The man saw that the sky was panting, the day would soon turn to ash. He tried to swallow, to drink of himself, but the sand of his throat burned beneath the blistering wind of his breathing. "I thirst," rasped the man and the sky held its breath.

The man bit his tongue, and it felt like an alien thing in his mouth, dry and shriveled and tough like an old fig or the carcass of a mouse, the wagging of this thing that which had displeased powerful men and sent him stumbling down the path of this destiny, and he thought if he'd been born without the power of speech he might be at the river now, washing his feet in the evening water, or drinking wine beneath a tree or planing wood for a yoke. But he'd spoken many things, as had been God's will, and here he was now shedding the flesh, petal by petal, *He loves me, He loves me,* reduced to a map of wounds for the sake of humanity, as had also been God's will. He wondered if the son of a powerful father can ever rightly claim to have a will of his own. The air was heavy with the will of God.

☾

One virtue of a body that looms above creation is that there are no nails strong enough to hold it aloft. The story of a towering savior would have ended differently. Only room for one giant in a trinity and you'd never catch God pinioned to anything. You'd never catch God bleeding.

When I arrived at the scene, summoned secretly by Pilate (who pretended to be Pilate's confidante and spoke condemningly of himself, *no backbone that one, politics plain and simple, craven lapdog, hail Caesar*—I saw through him instantly, being a Pilate myself, having slain a small boy's God), I was taken to the Garden of Olives and I saw that the man's dying had begun the night before. There had been great agitation. Blood had been excreted when the man perspired, a condition known as hematidrosis, and I touched my tongue to the salty trail he left behind. When terror ruptures the body, its glands sweat blood easy as sobbing. Or maybe it was an invisible mauling by a creature only he could see, a creature too ethereal to leave tracks or scat and whose hunger stirs just before dawn, a sentimental creature that attacks only that which it is sure will rise again. I never rule out the appetite of animals. They know when to eat and when to flee, and though they are indifferent to human outcomes, they often assist in the cleanup of villainy. They cannot be blamed any more than the man's blood can be held accountable for leaving his veins when provoked.

I returned to the man. The air here in this Place of the Skull was redolent of cadaverine, and I tried not to breathe. The man lay on the ground, on the Stone of Unction, his head bent forward and his feet crossed in rigor. Three Marys sat beside him. He had unusually long fingers, thin reeds it would be a comfort to be stroked by. The nails that pinned the man to the wood had already been poached, all nails used to fix writhing convicts in place believed to be necromantic, curative. Ailing people held the stakes to their mouths, their lips quivered in incantation; the taste of the blood of the recently tortured made their fevers spike, their boils open like eyes.

Visible on the body were the wounds of a brutal scourging. At the ends of the thongs of the flagrum with which he had been beaten were carved barbells of bone that bit into the skin so ravenously the organs beneath were left for pulp.

The man had been flogged by two men and the angle of the wounds showed one man to have been taller than the other. There's always a willing Goliath around when you need a brute. Across the skin was weary blood that just made it out of the condemned body at a crawl and then dried in place. The body would be washed and the wounds would ooze blood and serum onto the shroud he would later be laid to rest in. He'd been beaten with ruthless exuberance, despite the mob longing for him to be sensible of the nailing and to live long enough to provide the entertainment of a body perishing slowly as it sags against the wood of its making.

This was a time of much blood, and people looked around and wondered whose might be let next. Someone else's blood dripping into the scree meant theirs was staying put for the time being. A certain amount of blood had to be spilled in order for the world to exist, everybody knew that, better it should be the sanctified blood of the king of kings, sniffed the spectators. He surely had resources your average deadman-in-waiting lacked. There but for the grace of God.

I gave my back to the smiters, and my cheeks to them that plucked off the hair: I hid not my face from shame and spitting. And I could see he'd set his face like flint, but struck flint turns to flame and little was left behind. Plucked clean, reduced to ash, this man hadn't a cheek left to turn. The man's face, like the rest of him, had been larruped repeatedly. His cheeks were swollen, the cartilage in his nose separated from bone. There were puncture wounds on the scalp and forehead. The man's shoulders were badly abraded, as though gnawed upon by a drowsy predator.

It appeared the man's death had not been hastened by the breaking of the legs.

Many have wondered if the man was alive or dead when the centurion thrust the lance between his ribs, have wondered if the blood and water that spilled from the wound were evidence that this was the blow that vanquished the man, the stopped heart emptying itself at last. Or was it only a superfluous flourish on the part of the soldier, mere theatrical cruelty? One needn't be bright to brandish a spear. Or was it the first baptism, the first sacrament, before they went the way of all flesh and turned to metaphor? Did the man die on the cross or swoon into coma? Did the *man* wonder if he was alive or dead? I imagine this is the one question he never had to ask himself and that just before the blade disappeared inside him his open eyes looked into the face of the soldier not with the forgiveness for which those owlish eyes were famous but rather with the dawning clarity of a man who knows he will later be asked to give eyewitness testimony regarding his own murder.

When this man was born, his mother looked at the plump face that would one day grow long and thin and sorrowful as dusk and thought, *All a child is is future suffering.* For this reason she had not wanted to be a mother, but she was dutiful in the presence of angels, who crackle like wildfire if you contradict them.

Every minute of every hour a child is somewhere being lost.

Is it suicide, necessarily, to agree to be the son of God, knowing how that's bound to turn out? Is it not then suicide to be born anything? The prognosis for all human beings, the probability of survival, is always dismal. Even the moon, despite its grander aspirations, is only a phase. The sun too will pass.

Sindonologists and forensic pathologists, serologists, magicians, private investigators, criminologists, microscopists, pharmacists, palynologists, numismatists, historians, theologians, comparative anatomists, radiocarbon scientists, microbiologists, pediatricians, optical crystallographers, Carmelite nuns, and a stigmatic priest who holds the world record for roller coaster riding will argue for centuries hence about the body of this man, how it came to stop. A mystic will calculate the mathematics of suffering—28,430 drops of blood expended on salvation, 110 scalp pricks to save the world—and there will be disputes, by future men who make a living of examining the dead, about what a human body is capable of bearing, about where and at what angle the spikes were driven through the flesh, which nerves were kindled, disagreement about the authenticity of a blood-stained pall and what the inscrutably vivid impressions on the fabric suggest about the nature and location of torment, whether death came by asphyxiation as a result of the savaged body no longer being able to lift itself enough to exhale, forever stalled in inspiration, or by the infarcted heart just giving up the ghost. But what they fail to factor in to their calculations is the possibility that this was no ordinary body, not a body beholden to a familiar biology; this body had within it a budding divinity—there were ambitions beyond the cross for this body, a posthumous future—and how might that alter the outcome, affect the beating of the heart, the firing of synapses, the loosing of endorphins, the rising of the waters of the pleural effusion, how might it shape the will to stay in the world? The ambivalence of his flesh might have made certain vegetables indigestible, muskmelon, calabash, might have caused the veins in the man's arms to bleed honey, might have made his knees release a silken murmur as he walked. There are those who believe this man became radioactive in his suffering, his scourged skin a rogue isotope gone unstable, a final burst of radiant energy burning his image onto the linen that would swaddle him. But even the most ardent apostate must concede that this body, this man, was more human than any human who lived before or since, a man who made a career of his own mortality, so devoted to it in fact that he forgave the questionable fathering that led to his end (parents so often fatal), an insomniac man who feared the oblivion of sleep and was secretly discomfited by the unorthodox and showy cajolery of performing miracles in a world devoted to doubt.

So that the scales might fall from mine, I wanted the man to throw the potsherds from his eyes, the torn skin around them dark as eclipse, and tell me how the world might have turned out differently had he gone missing as a boy. In the absence of salvation, perhaps we would have tried harder to deserve it.

I could make this scene small enough to fit on the head of a flea and still I'd never solve its mysteries.

Cause of Death: God the Father.

☽

"I thirst," said the man, and a hyssop branch bearing a sponge sopped in sour wine was held to his mouth. He tasted the vinegar of his lips and watched the air in front of him as no one came to save him.

This man looked ahead through the dampened light of evening, the last sun he'd see with eyes prone to failure over time, time and failure: things about which he already felt nostalgic, and he saw that the swelling serry of the people of posterity whose perishing his sacrifice would reverse (far too many, he thought, to fit inside the most generous paradise) would find more and more ways to inflict suffering—they'd have a genius for it—sometimes in the name of vengeance, often in the name of nothing, and he saw that they would learn to do so with staggering efficiency and that there was a vast and endless freshet of the blood of humans and animals waiting to boil across the millennia to come (today was like every other that would follow), and just before the beating of the man's heart came kindly to a halt, this heart turning its charity at last on him, he realized there was no such thing as love and never had been and that an empty heart would be the heavier for daring to rise again, a plummet in the airy ectoplasm of his risen chest, all the heavier for existing without at least the avocation of animating the flesh, but it was too late now not to die, and so he did.

THIRTY-ONE
KANSAS SHE SAYS IS
THE NAME OF THE STAR

Vivica and I are traveling together to the Garden of
Eden, two cramped spars straining at the halyards, two footloose lady longshanks fishtailing forward on a slippery highway in a truck, one in search of prophecy, the other along for
the ride, an unseasonal snow falling silently upon the prairie,
the tracks of our taxed tires disappearing beneath the white.
The Garden of Eden is a cabin made of stones sculpted to
look like logs and a biblical bestiary begun in 1907 and fin-
ished in 1928 by a veteran of the Civil War and Populist
Masonic free-thought farmer who had a certain fondness for
God but none at all for banks.

As we tool along the barren highway, flanked by occasional outcroppings of limestone dusted with snow, Vivica
tells me one of the legends of Gog and Magog, giants born
from the coupling of two of the daughters of the Roman

Emperor Diocletian and a pair of local demons roaming the island of Albion, to which the emperor's thirty-three naughty daughters were banished after they murdered their thirty-three husbands. Vivica believes when entering a biblical place, even a concrete impersonation of such a place, one ought to assume an alias, just in case our names turn up on a list of the damned, and she tells me to call her Magog in the company of strangers. That's how some people flimflam the reaper, she tells me, they pretend not to be the one he's looking for, give him a quick spin like a roulette wheel, point him south, *there she is over yonder*, they say and high-tail it north.

Then says Magog, "There was a time when everything in the world was much larger, plants and trees, wild climbing, bearded with clouds, the animals gigantic, colossal chickens, and the *rabbits*, rabbits saber-toothed and tall as water towers. The atmosphere was more hospitable to tall things then. We would have been in danger of being trampled beneath big-footed...ferrets," says she with a slight quaver in her conviction, "or crushed by saplings blown over in a rainstorm." Contrary giantess Vivica, antipodal on principle, can sweet talk when she puts her mind to it. She raises her eyebrows at me and says, "Bigbig."

"So what happened?" I ask. "Why did the world go small?"

She shrugs her shoulders and looks out the window. "Radiation," she says simply. Vivica has a bone to pick with the sun, which, she has told me, she finds too big for its britches. I think she feels a mite upstaged, overshadowed. I've caught her glaring reproachfully at the cloudless sky at high noon. I don't think she would have cottoned to being a small fry in prehistory.

We're on our way to Lucas, and in the unsolved crime that is Kansas, the wee town of Lucas, Kansas, home to the Garden of Eden and a short hop from Paradise, is one bit of evidence I've never examined. Somehow it seems to grow smaller and smaller the closer we get, and I start to wonder if we'll fit. It's the sort of shriveled way station where a family of four constitutes a convention, leaves the local inn with no vacancies and the two-booth diner shorthanded, the whole dozy hamlet scrambling to accommodate the bump in tourism. Despite being home to the Garden of Eden, Lucas is not set up for dawdling gawkers.

In Lucas there is a little girl who visits the Garden each afternoon, sits on the ground beneath the linked arms of Adam and Eve and eats a peanut butter sandwich. Her name is Marjorie. The day before, Marjorie found a man's body in the Garden, just as Nestor Dethloff's dead Ezekiel predicted, a shoeless man with a small nose and sad hands, said the little girl to her mother, and the mother went to see if her daughter was being fanciful and found that she wasn't, but later that evening when they returned again to the Garden, the man was gone, and without a body the local sheriff saw no reason to go to the considerable trouble of believing the little girl, so her mother (great-grandniece of Fleance Shoptaw—I do occasionally get repeat business of a sort) called me, and now Vivica Planet and I are on the path from Kingdom Come that leads past Paradise to Eden. There is no such place as Righteousness, Kansas, no Providence, Salvation, Grace, Grand Reward, no Elysian Fields, no Promised Land, KS, no roads lead there. "Even if we're aimed toward Paradise," I say to Vivica, "we're not on the path of Righteousness," and she nods and yields to the mesmerism of the slanted snow shimmering in the headlights.

Kansas is no stranger to iniquity. I've searched nearly every inch of it (who can say for what exactly), but there are more places for a body to hide in a flat and absent landscape, with its occasional interruption of non-committal hills, than you might think. What is there to see in a treeless expanse that thins and sizzles in high summer and dies of exposure in the winter? Only the angle at which the prairie grass bends in the fleeting breeze, a rusting combine marooned in a long-fallow field, a red-winged blackbird step-stoning cattail to cattail as it tries to alight on the endlessly receding horizon. And sometimes curious lights zigzagging at a zippety pace below the stars, wobbling disks glinting in the moonlight. UFOs are seldom sighted in the mountains. A matter of logistics I reckon. Investigation of UFO sightings ceased in the U.S. in 1969 (investigation of sightings of God were curtailed much earlier), and there's a vault in the bowels of the Pentagon in which reports of such sightings are silenced and stored. But this didn't prevent Kansans from trembling with dread whenever they cast their gaze to the clouds. In flat places that allow you to see all the way to next week, the end of the world, be it God or alien or F5 tornado, always comes from above. Kansas, for good or ill, is my planet.

On our way to the Garden of Eden, we pass the World's Largest Collection of the World's Smallest Versions of the World's Largest Things, curated by a fellow miniaturizer, who once asked me to sit for a wood worker so he could whittle an inch-high version of me that would stand on a shelf between a shrunken yeti and a lolloping twelve-foot prairie dog made mouse-small. As appealing as being the size of a thimble would be, I know from reading *The Book of Very, Very Large Women* that I am not as record-breaking as I first imagined and so cannot rightfully claim a two-ton prairie dog as my true kin. Vivica says I'm splitting hairs and should have let them carve my likeness from cottonwood like they wanted. I tell her if we were to measure any true indicator of height, she would certainly be taller than me and I'd disappear beneath the yardstick, and she smiles at me in an uncomplicated manner. I know now that Vivica Planet does not likely want me dead, but sitting next to her in the cab of a truck built for squirts is still not without peril.

We arrive at a neighboring eyeblink of a town and check into a bed and breakfast, and the owner looks us over and wonders if we might turn out to be destructive in our sleep. "We're not thrashers," I tell her and try to slump in a reassuring way, and for a minute I think she's going to put us up in the tractor shed, but then she checks the "pet deposit" box on the receipt and charges us an extra sawbuck each. Vivica is winding up a bark when I yank her up the stairs.

In my room, the Queen Anne suite full of frail-looking furniture with slightly soiled upholstery and spindly limbs, a chicken-legged chiffonier and scrawny chairs that look likely to collapse in surrender if I come near them, I lie at an angle on the bed, which is drowning in ruffled pillows with shiny pink shams and reminds me of a box of candy, and I feel like the mutant bonbon that slipped through quality control. Half of me hangs off the end, and I watch out the window as the snow accumulates on the grizzled boughs of an elderly oak on the droop. "This is the end of God's biography," I say to the salted sky, my final plea to the universe.

In the end, Gog returned to the Garden of Eden, at the place where all the trouble started, and there, back at the beginning, which is both the likeliest and the unlikeliest place to end, she found what she'd spent her fat life looking for. But first, here's a story.

When Gog was a child, her younger brother asked her to lift him into an apple tree in their backyard, and she gave him a leg up, and as he sat swinging his legs, she left him there and watched him from her bedroom window. Now, she thought, he'll see what kind of Gog I truly am. She waited for him to cry out to be rescued, an entreaty she'd ignore, but he sat quietly on the branch and tapped the coming apples as though they were bells waiting to be rung, and when their mother came home from the Price Chopper supermarket, she noticed the boy sitting there and shrieked and fetched him down with a ladder. That night, their mother did not speak to Gog, would not even fling a smoldering glower in her direction, but the boy snuck his sister a slice of butter cake after dinner, and Gog regretted being big enough to strand a small boy in the air, a fearless boy to whom Gog was always trying to demonstrate she was evil to the root. A belief in Gog often ended so badly for good-natured boys willing to die for love. She had to cure him of that.

But then Gog grew up, and this is what happened at the end of the world:

The next day, my aide-de-camp Magog and I go to meet Marjorie and her mother at their house, a squat rambler, little more than a cramped can designed for sardines on a strict diet. And Marjorie serves us invisible tea in tiny tea-cups as she sits on a tiny chair at a tiny table and she and her tiny mother tell us what they know. Marjorie's mother, June Rae, tells us a man came to town a few days ago, an itiner-ant proselytizer of the sort that passes through whistle-stops like Lucas every now and again on his way to the deeper boondocks, where he can buy converts with a bowl of grits, "the sort of God-talker people round here don't pay much mind anymore," or so he seemed at first, but she says this man was quiet and polite with clean, thin-fingered hands and the first thing you noticed about him was that he was traipsing through the snow barefoot, though his feet didn't look the worse for wear, and he asked people, beg pardon, if they'd seen God lately. "You know, the usual opening," says June Rae, "sounded like. 'When's the last time you talked to God, sister?' or 'Maybe you haven't seen God lately, but he's seen you,' you know, like that. But we've been through so many tornadoes and foreclosures and Ponzi schemes and viral scares and crop failures that God's a sore subject 'round here. Just this year, half the trees in Lucas came down with the oak wilt and died and the other half are looking not long for the forest. Some people say our bad luck began when the Garden of Eden came to Lucas. The man who built the Garden, that Dinsmoor fellow, is preserved in a mausoleum in his backyard, you know, and every year someone tries to break in and liberate Lucas from the hex some think he brought upon us. I think he was just trying to put Lucas on the map is all. He wasn't a bad sort." June Rae has a kind, tired face, her mouth and eyes drawn downward, the face of a woman that a suddenly tested faith has aged.

Marjorie says, "If you got a dollar, he's nice as pie. I talk to him when I eat my sandwich." June Rae frowns at Marjorie, who slurps the tea from all our cups and smiles at each place setting and bats her eyes and laughs and moves her lips but says nothing audible and pours more tea into the cups.

Marjorie looks up at me and says, "Did you ever sit on anyone? Accidentally?" June Rae frowns at Marjorie more severely, and I say that sometimes I feel a slight wriggling beneath me and worry I might have crushed someone's pet on the loose but so far, to my knowledge, there have been no such casualties. Marjorie nods but with a slight disappointed knit to her brow.

"What does the man say?" I ask.

"Well," says Marjorie as she pours more tea, "he says the government could save a chunk of change if they invested in concrete flags because concrete flags don't get raggedy and they'd be easy to see too, even when the wind don't blow, but he says they'd have to do it right because if a piece of a concrete flag fell on someone's head they'd get a goose egg and sue Uncle Sam. Mr. Dinsmoor doesn't have any good words to say about lawyers. And he says that God doesn't have the necessary constitution for shepherding human beings, because they're deceitful and mean as hyenas and always belly-aching and they often smell like goats, but he didn't find that out until it was too late and so the serpent, he said, was kind of a remedy? But it didn't work a hundred percent right and so everything went to h-e-double-hockey-sticks in a handbasket—" Marjorie stops pouring and looks up at her mother, who's looking regretfully at her shoes, "that's what he said. There's a devil there in the Garden with a bulb in his head and he lights up at night."

Vivica, Magog, asks Marjorie if she spoke with the shoeless man, and Marjorie nods her head. "He sat under Adam. I gave him part of my sandwich. He said he was looking for God, had I seen him. He said that somehow he got lost and then he said, 'Today is the day of my calamity.' He said he had been conscripted by Eden when he was a boy and that he shouldn't have gloated over his sister on the day of her misfortune. He was kind of bughouse my mama said, but everyone deserves a sandwich and a drink of water, so we went back later and that's when we found the man, not needing a sandwich anymore."

June Rae says, "I saw someone prowling about in back, look like Augustus Breedlove, the widower, but I lost sight of him and then the door to the mausoleum was unlocked and open a crack, which I thought was a little fishy, and we found the man lying inside the mausoleum top of Mr. Dinsmoor's tomb."

The body has since disappeared from the Garden of Eden, cast out, and I have a creeping suspicion this is one of those things that will shrink and shrivel and grow more unknowable the more I know, like the disappeared children of Kingdom Come, but I have no choice but to nose around and increase my ignorance. Eventually, I think, I will know so little I can finally retire.

"That's right," sings Marjorie, who pretends to pour tea from the pot straight into her mouth and then she giggles herself blue.

We decide to talk with Augustus Breedlove first before heading to the Garden. June Rae tells us how to get there and we walk along kicking the foot of snow that has settled on the town. The sun is hanging somewhere in the sky above us, hidden in the drear. We arrive at Mr. Breedlove's house and receive no answer when we knock. We see no light or movement through the windows, so we test the door, which is unlocked. It is dim in the house and the soiled light that drifts through the windows covers the room in a dingy glow, but the house is tidy, Spartan and scrubbed. It reminds me of the spare digs of the Ovinkos, and I wonder if Mr. Augustus Breedlove is also an old-world whirler. At first it had surprised me how grimly austere the world of an ecstatic can appear from the outside, but the universe is forever contradicting itself to discourage belief. The only signs of recent life are in the kitchen, where a bottle of buttermilk has been left out on the draining board alongside a loaf of Butternut bread, and there is a half-eaten sandwich of liverwurst and onion sitting in the sink, beginning to make the air in the house go rank.

Vivica calls from the bedroom. The ceiling is low-slung and I feel the house begin to bear down on me as I hobble forward, slump-headed and hunched over like a buzzard. No room in this house is more than a few feet from any other, so Vivica and I could get to the bathroom from the bedroom with one generous stride, an efficient house.

In the bedroom of Augustus Breedlove is an iron bed with a much-darned once-white chenille bedspread tucked tightly under the pillows and a potbellied chest of drawers made of bird's-eye maple, oblong mirror slightly tilted on top. Tucked into the sides of the mirror are four newspaper articles, one from the Lucas-Sylvan News, two from the *Kingdom Come Tiller and Toiler,* and one from *The Kansas City Star.* There's a brittle clipping about a nine-year-old boy, Tobin Breedlove, who went missing one July years ago while visiting his grandparents in Kansas City, mistakenly snatched from Harzfeld's Department Store by a man and woman, Malden Fitch and Heddy Benjamin, hopheads on a wild tear who thought he was the son of a decorated bombardier turned successful Cadillac dealer. The boy had wandered off into the shoe department and was looking at the bones of his foot through the shoe-fitting fluoroscope machine, of which Fitch pretended to be the store operator. When the couple found out the boy was the son of a tractor and combine mechanic in Russell, Kansas, the couple fought ferociously, scarring one another's faces, then drugged and strangled the boy in the hope that they might at least appear in the history books if only as a footnote to the story of Bruno Hauptmann and the Lindbergh kidnapping, which had inspired them. They dumped the body in the Mississippi when they reached St. Louis, but dragging that part of the river turned up nothing but a pram, a pair of boxing gloves, and a rusted lockbox full of spoons.

The second clipping is the article about me and Obie, the one that launched my career as an amateur gumshoe, when I led the police to the saddle shoes of the then recently disappeared Elise Dimbleby. Vivica looks from the article to me, but not in a way that makes it seem as though she is surprised to find a picture of me as a child tucked into the dresser mirror of Augustus Breedlove, lately of Lucas, Kansas. The third article is the story of Nestor Dethloff (Dr. Deth) and his "assisted suicides," the ill-fated whose dooms he expedited, and ends with a paragraph about the earlier discovery of Ezekiel's body, as recounted by the soup kitchen regulars.

Lying atop the dresser is a recent article from *The St. Louis Post-Dispatch* about a man in Kaskaskia, Illinois, who hooked a small skull out angling one Sunday, the skull of a nine-year-old boy.

As I line up the newspaper clippings chronologically on the dresser, the obvious becomes clear, which is that, selfishly, hopefully, I have always been investigating the circumstances of my own disappearance. That's what any investigation is, an inquiry into one's own coming absence. I know if I told

Vivica this, she would cluck her tongue and look at me with puzzled disappointment; she has no intention of ever disappearing. I feel myself begin to shrink, my blood quickens, the world lifts into the air around me bright and weighty as a passel of catapulted moons. I feel light as the dust that dust accumulates.

I cannot say what my picture is doing affixed to the mirror of a man I've never met, nor can I account for his interest in a murderer of hapless prophets and the soon-to-be ill-fated, but I imagine that Augustus Breedlove has simply crossed paths with one diviner too many and has decided, like Nestor Dethloff, like me, to assassinate faith before it beguiles another gull, to root out before it's too late the kind of stubborn faith required to believe a little boy might somehow have survived his own murder and be living a barefoot happy boy's life downstream.

☽   ☽   ☽

As we approach the Garden of Eden, Magog, Marjorie, and me, the moonlight on the snow glitters in a way that makes the drifts look like a clean, ankle-high city spruce and lit up for the evening. Marjorie, who reminds me of Mary Alice before the fever, told us the Garden has more to say at night. There is a bracing wind that makes me feel skinned and the branches of drooping trees appear to flap, but these trees have become ambivalent about being trees, relaxing their roots and wasting, and will never be airborne. As we stroll the perimeter of the Garden, sculpted concrete rises up vividly all around us like an aerial carnival that will one day begin suddenly to crumble and brain its audience, a spectacle thumbing its nose at gravity, man, woman, beast, and banknote all heavily looming: an all-seeing eye on a stalk; a dog chasing a fox chasing a chicken chasing a worm; homicidal Cain with a rotten pumpkin, Abel holding a handsome sheep gloatingly by the horns; a ravenous, monopolizing octopus dipping its tentacles into every pocket, greedily wrapped around a bag of money, a soldier's haversack (no victuals, no soldier!), more tentacles squeezing the snow out of the North Pole and twined around the Panama Canal; Labor crucified upon the cross; some storks with baby faces hidden in their feathers; and on and on, a ponderous nation floating above us, colonizing the sky. Snakes and storks spit light from their mouths and the Goddess of Liberty holds a beacon above her head. We duck beneath the archway of the clasped hands of Adam and Eve, who remain heavily on earth, the Garden's grounded emissaries, and we walk under the grape arbor. Eve is a big-boned concrete girl with triangular hips built to birth humanity. Adam throttles a snake underfoot, showing more initiative than I recall hearing he possessed, though I'm in no position to sniff at revision. Snow thickens everything, as though the creatures of the Garden are just growing their winter fur. Marjorie is saying, "Hello," "Hello," "Hello" and humming in between. She opens her mouth and takes snowflakes onto her tongue, "The grub of ghosts," she tells me, "who are more plentiful in the winter." The Garden is her kingdom.

I feel a swarming around me, though I see only snow falling in the light, but the light seems off a shade and makes me think a volcano has somewhere erupted.

In the Garden's backyard, we stand outside the mausoleum looking up at the crucifixion of Labor, a man who hangs between a doctor, a preacher, a lawyer, and a banker. The last two figures, Marjorie tells us, are armless because Mr. Dinsmoor lost his eyesight before he could supply them with limbs, and then the idea of that suited him.

"So this is where humanity began," snorts Magog. Marjorie takes my hand and with the other pushes open the door and flips on a light in the mausoleum, where a shriveled, bearded man lies in a crypt beneath a viewing window, the Garden's creator. A fine shimmer of dust swirls before us, and I can see the dust scheming, considering whether it ought to make the effort to reintegrate into an opinionated being with a nose and a spleen and hands with which to gesture, or, having arrived at the destiny of all things, should leave well enough alone. It reminds me of something Vivica once told me, on one of those days when she donned her ceremonial Vandyke. She said the burial chambers of ancient Egyptians were sometimes booby-trapped, the sarcophagus and floor covered with eight inches of powdered Hematite, which would become airborne and choke a pillager when disturbed and would fill his lungs with a lethal dose of iron if he didn't turn tail and flee the tomb. "You have to give him a dollar," whispers Marjorie. I have only quarters and lay them on the crypt. Marjorie looks at me skeptically.

"Say, do you want to know what I think about things?" asks Marjorie. It's not clear if she's talking to me or the man under glass. She told me on the way here she wasn't sure how things would go without a peanut butter sandwich. The dead have their demands, especially in a garden.

"Mr. Dinsmoor says God likes a good mutton chop, so that's why Abel has a lit-up crown hanging over his head and why Cain has a sour crosspatch look. Moses is a man of few words, too few if you ask him, so he had to fill in some details about the goings-on at the Garden and after. Moses wrote it up and he built it according to Moses's sketchy blueprints. He's hoping you're not one of those people who just sees the surface of things. He says that in Abel's day, angels used to come down and cart off the dead, which is more efficient than planting a body in a boneyard 'cause they just don't grow no matter how much you water them. On the other hand, a worm's got to make a living too. The thing about heathens, he says, is that they're just better looking than believers." Marjorie pauses. "Wallis. No, she's from Kingdom Come. She's here about the man. No, sir. Four quarters *is* a dollar." She whispers, "I think he likes you. He don't like everybody," and she rolls her eyes like *boy-howdy*.

"He wants to tell you that Labor has been crucified by a thousand grafters. Bankers, lawyers, teachers—" Marjorie stops and her face crimps like she's ciphering, and then she says, "*preachers*, and doctors. Chiselers, he says. He says they might not all be grafters, but they are the leaders of all who eat cake by the sweat of the other fellow's face."

"How does he feel about…statuesque dames?" I ask.

"You're planetary, he says, you have your own astronomy. He says you are subject to the pull of no moon. He says you are handsome and he would have been happy to know you." Mr. Mundrawala had said the same and then he disappeared. I attract both the dead and dreamy eidolon's in the making. My orbit is fatal. That, Obie, is what the life of God boils down to.

Marjorie reaches up for my hand and I bend to give it to her. "All right," she says, "all right then." She whispers, "He says if we want more than that, we have to pony up with another dollar. And he's partial to paper money."

There's a knock on the door, and I hear Vivica say, "Psssst, Gog. The Edenites are getting restless."

Outside the mausoleum, I see, standing next to Magog, a person I presume to be the sad-eyed, small-handed, shoeless prophet, and I hear Marjorie gasp. Life is always more surprising than death, I think. The man must have only been napping on top of Mr. Dinsmoor when Marjorie and June Rae found him. The features of the man's face seem on the move and I cannot make them coalesce into a picture that I can decipher. His face is a treasure map, a cage of bluebirds, an ossuary.

He takes my hand and flutters his fingers across it, interpreting my vigor like the blind read a limp animal they stumble across that might yet be alive. "You are tall in spirit as well as flesh," says the man, and his mouth stops undulating long enough for me to see it smile sadly, to see it is the mouth of a lost boy, the mouth of a fallen heart, mouth of a witness, the long silent sacramental mouth of Obie Armstrong. My heart skids to a stop, and I feel Marjorie squeeze my mitt again and again, as though my heart has emigrated from behind my sternum to my hand. She means to keep me alive, manually if necessary. The risk of having a heartbeat is that it will stop. Nobody knows how many beats a heart has inside it. I feel my face fly open like a fist releasing a firefly. "You are not Obie," I say, and for the first time since he disappeared, I want it to be true, want him to have spurned his childhood, got shed of Kingdom Come, to have eloped with Nebraska or Iowa, places once more distant to him than the moon, married Madagascar and its keening lemurs, promised himself to far-off farms full of fainting goats struck stiff by the terror that precedes love, hitched himself to Missouri and its history of making Kansas bleed. I want him to have escaped, the flesh, belief, escaped Kansas, and me.

"What if I'm not?" says the man, and this chill and glistering galaxy we're stumbling around in, piqued, begins to howl and churn. The wind lashes our cheeks and the snow circles us like an animal. The sky fills up with wobbling silver saucers humming like bumble bees, failed terrestrials, deflated moons. And the concrete begins to creak and give as if trying to walk after years of watching silently from the mezzanine, and amidst Cain and Mrs. Cain and storks and eyes and octopi and that skinny so-and-so that is the devil on the lurk and unfinished men on a cross, I see other mouths and eyes whittled solid from snow, hands and knees, a lofted caucus: Emily Lipton, Darren Crenshaw, Elise Dimbleby, Eleanor Lehmkuhl, Eva Dugan, Hazard Planet, Ezekiel the Homeless, Tobin Breedlove, Norma's Libby, a brutally scourged man, Zubenelgenubi beside Helmutt von Brautwurst, dear Frances Lee, Eldon Schnitzler, Hannelore Berlin, Fleance Shoptaw, Ludovik Paddletrap, Maddy Teeter, Irmalinda Kinderbein, an eternally swelling cavalcade, and there I am pulling up the rear, and when I look over to see who holds my hand, I see Vivica's smile floating above me, sincere as the sun, prepared to grace the face of the lone Amazon of Kansas. Disappearing into the noosphere, I open my mouth to let the snow dot my tongue. I am eye to ankle with Marjorie of the Garden and soon to sink beneath the crust of snow, to the world that exists beneath the barren white, a giant made miniature at last, shrinking doll in a diorama, hiding in her chest a heartbeat undetectable by the human ear, a body finally moving in the right direction: a violin, a flashlight, a sneaker, potato, a bullet, lone toenail, a cricket, pearl onion, a lozenge, an eyetooth, a mite, mote of dust, an atom, half atom, a god.

ILLUSTRATION CREDITS

p. 27 "Dance Steps Footsteps Ballroom Instruction," by Michael Brown, © michaeldb, Dreamstime.com.

p. 235 "Fig. 1: The Hare," engraving from English dictionary circa 1754, from the Graphics Fairy: graphicsfairy.blogspot.com.

p. 267 "Shown with his grandchildren, the old hare, already bitten by a dog, hastens to tell his tale before hunting season," nineteenth-century engraving by Jean-Ignace-Isidore Grandville, from Grandville's Animals: Dover Digital Design Source, 2010.

p. 296 Robert Hooke's microscope, Wikimedia Commons: en.wikipedia.org/wiki/File:Hooke-microscope.png, from Scheme I of his 1665 Micrographia, on permanent display in "The Evolution of the Microscope" exhibit at the National Museum of Health and Medicine, in Washington, DC.

p. 303 Drawing of nineteenth-century safety coffin, original source unknown; from ariellavl.wordpress.com/.

p. 313 eighteenth-century anatomical diorama by Frederik Ruysch, from The Zymoglyphic Museum: www.zymoglyphic. org/exhibits/ruysch/ruysch2.jpg.

ACKNOWLEDGEMENTS

Excerpts of the novel have appeared in the following journals: *Cavalier*, the *Collagist*, *Fairy Tale Review*, *Meridian*, *Sonora Review*, *Sou'wester*, *Super Arrow*, *Tammy*, *Third Coast*, the *Tusculum Review*, and in the 2010 *Best American Fantasy* anthology. My thanks to the following editors: Matt Bell, Kate Bernheimer, Kevin Brockmeier, Joe Collins, Amanda Goldblatt, JoAnna Novak, Heather Patterson, Anna Shearer, Minal Shekhawat, Astrid Slagle, Rachel Swearingen, Wayne Thomas, Valerie Vogrin, and Christina Yu.

I would like to thank the following organizations for lending support and solitude during the writing of this book: the Rona Jaffe Foundation, the MacDowell Colony, Château de Lavigny, Blue Mountain Center, Hawthornden Castle, and Hedgebrook. I would also like to thank these people, for their kindness, advice, encouragment, intellect, imagination, and example: Valerie Vogrin, Jaimy Gordon, Marshall Klimasewiski, Kathryn Davis, Wallace Stevens, Connie Lunn, Marilyn Annucci, Rachel Cantor, Ander Monson, Margo Berdeshevsky, Kerri Webster, Kathleen Finneran, Bonnie Jo Campbell, Heather Streckfus-Green, Scott Heim, Mary O'Connell, Wes Smith, Brotherjeb Bolan, Matt Dube, Wayne Zade, Meg Sefton, Danielle Dutton, Evan Williams, my terrific writing program and English Department colleagues at the University of Alabama, all the wonderful people who work in the MFA program at Pacific University, and all my fabulist students. I wish to thank Jerry Dziecichowicz of the Chief Medical Examiner's Office of the State of Maryland for speaking with me about Frances Glessner Lee and allowing me to examine and photograph the Nutshell Studies of Unexplained Death. I owe a special debt of gratitude to Kate Bernheimer, without whose fiction and fairy tale championship the world would be less darkly magical and therefore a good deal less inviting. Janie Painter I thank for a lifetime of sisterly wit, warmth, and unconditional enthusiasm. Tom Mahoney I am grateful to for his wise-foolery and love, without which I would never have made it out of high school, or this book, alive.

FIC   Wells, Kellie,
WELLS   1962-

          Fat girl,
           terrestrial.

                    12/3/12